ISBN 978-1511425315

Second edition.

This work is dedicated to my precious Kathy. She watched this story unfold as I would read a chapter and she would ask, "What happens next?" to which I would answer I don't know, it's not written yet! Her patience in my reading to her, her insights and thoughtful suggestions were the fuel that I needed to complete this work. She has been my angel, and I thank her.

Author contact:
Chris Lamela
chris@chrislamela.com

About the Magic Town trilogy series

Jeff, a forty-something aerospace executive finds himself landing in the middle of mystery in the strip clubs of Atlanta, a year later in Washington DC, and a year after that in Silicon Valley. Each time Jeff finds himself trapped in difficult and dangerous cases, each time he is instrumental in their solution. Every time he finds his life endangered from shooting, poisoning, or being blown up. The question is, can he survive! And then there are the women...

About the author

Chris Lamela has published numerous column-length pieces in humor, business and philosophy. His foray into novels intertwines his personal experiences with a rich cast of characters in captivating story lines. The tension, humor, and romance of this writing reveal a writer with a mature perspective and a playful sense of storytelling. The Magic Town series tells of a hapless man's adventures into a world of mystery, crime and murder, and romance with characters that come alive for the reader, told in a way that makes the reader want to get to the next page.

Magic Town

Friday 4:16PM: Getting to the Underground

"Norman, help me! I'm stuck!" the large woman in the back seat of the hotel shuttle van screaming.

The overhang at the Atlanta Sheraton Hotel entry cast a cool shadow in the November afternoon. Tucking his hands under his arms to keep them warm Jeff was amused at this sudden commotion.

The man standing next to the van was her husband Jeff guessed by the way she treated him. Leaning in to fuss with her seatbelt, she pushed him away angrily. He was short, maybe five seven, thick glasses, salt and pepper mustache looking like a small broom under his nose, the same colored hair circling his head, wisps combed over the bald top, middle-aged, couldn't be more than a hundred twenty-five pounds, reaching in to tussle with her seatbelt again strapped so tightly around her large bulging form, "Stop that!" she barked. Stepping away as she screamed, "What the hell is going on here? Driver!"

The husband stepped back, standing next to Jeff.

Jeff turned toward the driver, smiling at his own reflection in the glass, his five foot-ten frame seeming to tower over the small man next to him, Jeff's dark curly hair framing his face.

Turning to the husband Jeff queried, "Why does she even wear a seatbelt in a shuttle?"

Shaking his head, "She's terrified of others driving."

"Like a phobia?" the man answering with a frowny nod.

The shuttle van driver, an older black man, had already pulled out two enormous heavy suitcases and was busy with four large weighty cardboard boxes.

"Driver!" the large woman screaming again.

Jeff shook his head nodding toward the husband, "Let me see if I can help, she looks pretty frustrated," the husband shrugging, Jeff stepping forward addressing the woman with a jesting smile, "Boy you really seem stuck, let me help," starting to reach into the van.

"Get away from me! I don't need anybody's help!" Jeff pulling back with hands held up defensively, "Driver, dammit, I need help!"

Stepping back next to the husband Jeff shrugging, the man

flashing a thankful grin, "Thank you for trying, but she sometimes gets..."

"Helpless?" Jeff laughing, "hopeless?"

Smiling for the first time the man answering, "Yeah, that pretty much sums her up!"

They both chuckled.

The driver finally finished setting down a fourth large box next to the hotel's front door, glancing back at the van with his frustrated passenger.

"Driver! Help me out of this damned thing! DRIVER!"

The driver finally turned back to the van, leaning into the van, with a simple click she was freed. "What the hell kind of seatbelt is this anyway!" she growled. The driver stepping back she struggling with hands holding each side of the wide door, chubby legs flailing, plump feet twirling mid-air trying to touch ground, finally sliding out lurching forward barely catching her footing, stumbling to a stand. With sweaty face, heaving breath, indignantly brushing off her bright yellow flowered dress pulling down wads of cloth caught up under her enormous breasts with both hands, immediately walking toward the hotel's front door pushing past Jeff and her husband.

The driver turned in polite expectation to the husband starting to reach into his pocket for a tip, his wife turning her head screaming over her shoulder, "Don't you dare tip him!" Reaching for the front door yanking it open, "Don't you ever tip people that don't help you!" plowing through the front door of the Sheraton Hotel. The man held out a couple bills timidly with an apologetic grin, hurrying into the hotel, glancing sideways at the massive pile of luggage and boxes near the door, giving a small wave to Jeff who nodded.

The driver walked in to alert the bellman. Jeff stood patiently, looking at his watch, just after four-fifteen. He was glad his meeting up in Norcross broke up early, everybody in a hurry to finish up their Friday to get home to their families.

The driver finally returning to the van exasperated, standing to catch his breath. Turning to Jeff speaking clearly with a pleasant, deep voice, "So sorry to keep you waiting sir, please," motioning to the back-seat door, Jeff stepping forward climbing in.

Pulling out of the parking lot Jeff reached into his inside sport coat pocket, pulling out a tourist guide the bellman had given him with all of the Atlanta sites. Studying the guide, turning it over reading the insets about the different attractions.

Jeff leaned forward, "I want to go to the Atlanta Underground, the bellman told me to take the van."

"Yes sir, but no not really. Ah can't takes you to the Underground, I can only take you to the airport, from there you will take the train. It's only a ten minute ride, quite convenient, really."

"It says here that they just did a big remodel or something."

"It was a couple years ago, in nineteen ninety-two, yeah, that's about right, a couple years ago when the city made a big deal about cleaning that place up." Talking over his shoulder to Jeff. "It got real run down and they started having all sorts of problems down there."

"Problems?"

"Yeah, you know, vandalism, picking on the tourists. Muggin'. I heard of robberies but never any of our hotel guests."

"Do you ever go there?"

"I haven't been there in a few years because of all the riff-raff, but I guess if you come to Atlanta the tourists all have to go see the Underground. Or the Coke Museum. You never been to the Underground?" The driver pulling into the right lane signaling to exit I-85 nearing the airport turnoff. Studying Jeff intently in the rear-view mirror. "Say, don't I know you?"

Jeff didn't answer, busy studying the paper guide in his hand.

"You look mighty familiar, sir."

Looking up, "I don't think so, I've only been here a few times. I always stay up in Norcross."

"No sir, I have a good memory for faces, I have seen you somewhere."

Smiling, "Do you get to Seattle?"

"No sir, I have never been to Seattle."

"I just have a common looking face, maybe?"

"No sir, I am sure I have seen you somewhere. In the newspaper, I am sure. Yeah, that's it, I saw you in the newspaper. Today."

Smiling at the prospect that he was in the newspaper today,

laughing to himself, didn't answer studying the tour guide, flipping it over to look at the inset about the Atlanta Underground. He read the inset about the Coke Museum showing happy families standing in front of all sorts of Coke exhibits, lots of young smiling faces; wondering about all those young teeth in all those young happy little faces drinking all that Coke and all the happy little cavities to come. Looking to the driver, "What do you know about the Coke Museum?"

The driver looking forward. "The Coke Museum is not a bad place. It's got all sorts of history about the drink, about the company. I went there once with my kids and I came out so sick of Coke I didn't drink it for a month!"

Both laughing together.

"That reminds me of the Jelly Belly factory." The driver looking in the mirror with a questioning face. "Jelly Belly, you know those little jelly beans." The driver half-nodding, his eyes saying that he still wasn't sure what Jeff was talking about. "Jelly beans!" the driver smiling nodding. "I was driving from San Francisco to Sacramento one time, saw the sign so I pulled over. Did the tour watching all the machines making jelly beans." Frowning, "Actually that part made you not so interested in jelly beans. They kept feeding us samples of jelly beans the whole time, though. They tasted great, but by the time I got back to my car I wasn't so sure. I was a little sick to my stomach." Laughing. "So I get to my meeting in Sacramento and the first thing they do is offer me Jelly Belly jelly beans!" Jeff laughing harder than the driver though he appreciated the driver trying to show that his little anecdote was at least a little entertaining.

"So okay, maybe not the Coke Museum," Jeff smiling, "but I heard the Underground's pretty cool."

"It is mainly known for some bars. I have heard the guests say that there are some good restaurants there, too. Nice stores, especially for women."

Studying the guide feeling a little bad about going to see these kinds of places without his two kids, Jeff frowned.

He thought about how he just got off the phone with his mother who was watching his children at his house back in Seattle before he headed down to the shuttle. His mother mentioned that Donna, his wife had called and he asked why he should care.

"Oh honey, really?" his mother asked.

Jeff was confused, "Mom, she left me. She left me with two kids. If it weren't for you I don't know what I would do. You tell me why I should care."

"Honey, she was your wife for all those years."

"Mom, you don't seem to get it how much it hurt me, what she did."

"I know, honey, I know you, and that it must be hard. But we never know what will happen in the future, she might come back."

"Mom, *she's not coming back*. She has a boyfriend, remember?" He bumped the phone handset on his forehead. Then he did it again. "Mom, she left me. She is not coming back."

"Look Jeffy," Jeff shuddering at that name she always called him when he was in trouble of some kind, "I think she still loves you. But no matter what, it is going to take time to figure this all out."

"Mom, look—"

"Honey, I'm not telling you how to run your life. This is between you and her, and I'm sorry if this is…I don't know…meddling. I don't want to meddle. I know it's been almost a year since she left, and I know you need to do what you need to do."

Pausing, taking a deep breath. "Thank you mom."

"Well this might not be the best time to bring this up but…"

"But what mom?"

"She wants to bring…I forgot his name…to meet the kids."

Jeff felt his blood pressure rising. "No mom. I won't allow it. It will just confuse the kids and get her to start playing teams again with them with her trying to make me the bad guy here. And who knows who she'll bring next month. It's not right. This is between her and me. Mom, please tell her not to. I don't know why she is trying to do this while I'm gone." He paused banging the handset on his forehead again, "Well yes I do. Duh, I'm gone." Sighing, "But please mom, tell her we'll talk about it when I get home next week. I'll be home late Monday, so tell her we can meet on Tuesday or

Wednesday if she wants."

"Yes…I understand. I'll talk to her."

"Thanks mom."

"But hey, enough of this, honey get outside the hotel tonight, okay? It's Friday night, promise me you'll get out."

"Yes, I will. Last thing I need is to get stuck in the hotel tonight. I promise I will."

He thanked her again and she said that if he had to stay the weekend in Atlanta he might as well get out and have some fun. As they were talking all he could do is wonder at the word *fun*. What kinds of things could be *fun* for a man by himself in Atlanta, even on a Friday night?

Talking to his daughter she said she was going to a party tomorrow with her other ten year-old girlfriends, then to his son trying to explain that it was getting dark where he in was in Atlanta with his son sounding confused because it was still the middle of the day in Seattle; it's a heady concept for a six year-old. Jeff promised that he would explain when he got back home as he pictured holding a flashlight on the globe they kept on the piano. He adored his children with all their activities, their constantly learning new things, how seldom he got to be the source of that new learning any more, how privileged he was when he had the chance. Yes, he loved his kids. And they adored him.

His mother's last words were to tell him again that it was Friday night and it would be good to go get out of the hotel, "But Jeff, be careful. I've heard some stories about Atlanta, you be careful." Jeff assuring her he would be fine, that he would check in again tomorrow night.

How many times has he gone to really cool places wishing he had his family with him? Damn. Washington DC, New York City, Boston, San Francisco. He got tired of buying trinkets at the airport gift shop, a four-inch tall Washington Monument with a thermometer, a Golden Gate Bridge bottle opener. Being in these places only made him feel lonely. For a second he wished he had a woman in his life, someone who could be here with him. A little sex would be sure make Atlanta feel like a more welcoming place!

Leaning forward to the driver, "What other things are there to do for a guy like me from out of town with a couple nights to get out?"

The driver gave a thoughtful expression, brightening, "Well they's lots of strip clubs!"

Jeff laughing, "Strip clubs?"

"Well, they's two kinds, really. They's the ones they call genlemen's clubs," motioning toward a billboard on the side of the road for a Gentlemen's Club *Where Your Every Wish Is Our Desire.* Jeff turning his head reading it as they passed. "Theys those kinds that I never been to. I think they have nicer women but the drinks are more expensive." Glancing to Jeff in the mirror, "But of course that's just what I hears, you know, I'm a family man myself, this is what I hears from the guests."

"Oh, of course, it's just what you hear, right?" both laughing.

"Then theys the strip clubs. Lots of them around and I fo' sho' ain't been to one of those," shaking his head. "I hears those places is really rowdy and all sorts of men goes there, definitely not the kind of place a family man goes to." Frowning into the mirror shaking his head, "No, no, no, don't be goin' to those kinds of places."

Jeff sat back remembering Denver a couple years ago. The company travel department put him in a hotel that he'd never been in. That night as he was driving up to the hotel getting in late after eleven he saw a place across the street from the hotel called Shotgun Wally's. He was tired from traveling all day, hadn't eaten. The idea of a little country western music, maybe some barbeque might be just what the doctor ordered!

He remembered walking across the snowy street hearing loud music thumping as he neared the building. He pulled open the door at Shotgun Wally's, blasted by loud music THUMP THUMP THUMP THUMP seeing a big sign in the entry for *NUDE JELL-O WRESTING!* He could smell food, his stomach told him to go in.

A big bouncer wearing a large cowboy hat put out his hand yelling, "THREE DOLLARS!" Jeff reaching into his pocket pulling out a five which the bouncer took, leading him to a small booth without offering change. A waitress came up, Jeff pointed to a burger on the menu. Peering through the darkness at his surroundings lit only by colored lights swirling around the large room, only men sitting at the tables. A topless woman was gyrating in the middle of the room holding onto a gold colored pole that went up to the ceiling. She swirled around the pole, every so often walking up to a table where men would eagerly stuff dollar bills into her bikini bottom. She was overbuilt, walking up to Jeff, reaching into his pocket pulling out two dollar bills as she stood swinging her body over his table, large bare breasts swinging across his face, turning away moving on to another table.

Soon the announcement was made that it was time for NUDE JELL-O WRESTLING! as the loud music subsided. There was a small square area, maybe ten feet across that looked like a fighting ring with ropes around it. Watching as men left their booths and tables pulling up chairs around the ring nearly blocking Jeff's view, he could see the bottom of the ring covered in what looked like a few inches of green and red Jell-O. Soon two women clad in bikinis came out, bowing to the crowd, proceeding immediately to climb the ropes into the ring starting a kind of mock wrestling throwing hands full of Jell-O at each other, tearing each other's tops off to the howls of the men, soon the women managing to tear each other's bikini bottoms off, the place going crazy. He could see that the women were both shivering from the cold Jell-O. He had to admit that there was something crazy in all this. But it was certainly *not very erotic*.

The loud music starting up again THUMP THUMP THUMP THUMP another woman coming up to his table, "LAP DANCE?" Her body swaying in front of his vision. Sitting uncertain a big woman wearing an apron pushed in front of her setting a plate of food in front of Jeff. The lap-dancer pouting turning away.

Remembering that after he finished eating another woman came up, sitting down next to him, snuggling to him. Looking at her wondering what he was supposed to do with a topless blond woman with a halo of dark roots framing her head sitting next to him, she leaned over close to his face, "You're from out of town, aren't you? Is your hotel close by? Want some company?"

This was *not* good.

She reached her hand down touching his crotch.

Okay, this was *definitely* not good!

He straightened up pulling away, leaning over to her apologizing how he had been traveling all day, he was tired but thanks anyway. With insulted face she jumped up starting to walk away, turning leaning back to Jeff scowling.

"*LOSER!*"

Friday, 5:08PM: Temptation

Looking back to the driver, "Yeah, I don't think a strip club is a very good idea for me tonight. Yep, pretty sure. So the Underground it is!" thinking, well *like where else is there?*

"Will the Underground be worth my time?"

The driver frowning, "I guess, but any more it's just like one of them big malls all stuffed into a cave, except for like I said, the bars and restaurants."

"Mall, you mean like Mrs. Fields Cookies and all that?"

"I dunno if it's that bad, but it's definitely not the underground hideaway kind of place anymore. Just lots of tourists. Probably lots of businessmen like yourse'f down there, I 'magine."

"Anything I should see while I'm there?"

"Like I said, it's been years since I've been there. I used to take my family when my kids were younger." The shuttle driver making a point to get eye contact with Jeff in the rear-view mirror. "But please do be careful, there's all sorts of crazy people around there, so many of them are doin' nothin' but hanging out all over around down there and up on the streets, too, some just lookin' for trouble. All I know is what I read in the paper and hear from the guests at the hotel. I have heard stories that it can be a little scary sometimes."

"You're making me not want to go."

The driver glancing into the mirror smiling at Jeff, "Nah, nah, nah, it ain't all that bad, I'm pretty sure." The driver looking forward, "You just be careful and you'll be fine."

Jeff looked down to the paper guide in his hand in mild wonder.

"Anyway, here we are." The hotel shuttle van pulling up to the curb in front of the big airport Marta train station. "Just go up the stairs and take the train, you wanna look for the Five Points station, and just ask around to find the Underground, it's real close by."

"How will I get back?"

"Just make it back to the airport on Marta, use the courtesy phone to call the hotel, we will come pick you back up, but the shuttles only run until eleven o'clock, so make sure to get back here before ten-thirty, otherwise you'll have to take a cab back to the hotel."

"Sounds simple."

"The trains run until midnight. If you know you're gonna be later than ten-thirty, get off at the College Station instead so it'll be a cheaper cab ride, that station's closer to the hotel than the airport."

Jeff opened the side door holding out three dollars to the driver turning around to Jeff.

"Hey, thanks for this, mighty generous. One more thing, keep your pockets stuffed with dollar bills to give to the homeless guys who come up to you, it's a hell of a lot easier than hassling with them."

"Give them just a dollar?"

"Damn rights, the tourists ignore them like they are invisible and it pisses them off—if you are kind to them, and I'm talking just a dollah, those bastards'll take a bullet for you. Fo' a lousy dollah!" Jeff frowning. "Anyway, be careful out there and forget about all this and go have an interesting evening. Remember to give us a call before ten-thirty otherwise you'll be on your own with a cab."

Stepping out, Jeff thanking the driver once again studying Jeff's face, "And yo' sure ah don't know you. I swear you do look mighty familiar." Jeff shrugging. "Well, you go have yo'self an interesting evening."

Nodding, Jeff turning toward the tall building in front on him, heading for the stairs to get to the trains thinking to himself, *interesting evening*, yeah let's do that!

Up the stairs there was a small crowd on the platform. A couple towing suitcases had just flown in from somewhere walking from the airport, a few commuters, a few teenagers, twenty somethings all earnestly looking down the tracks for an approaching train.

Walking up to the map board, Jeff figured out that either the yellow or red line would take him where he was going, it was just a few stops up, looked like the station he wanted was a main hub, easy to remember. Putting money into the ticket machine, deciding to get his return ticket while he was at it, smiling at his reflection in the glass wearing tan Docker pants, polo, his favorite brown and tan tweed sport coat. Definitely looked the part of the businessman out to do a little touring. He thought of all the times he went out dressed like this in 'business casual' wondering why he didn't wear jeans and a t-shirt. Too late, the evening lay before him, here he was.

Walking up to the newspaper rack seeing the New York Times and Atlanta Journal Constitution, both with headlines about a big storm expecting snow on Monday, the city getting all mobilized. An article about a missing Congressman with a picture, Jeff leaning forward to look. The picture was fuzzy behind the scratched yellowed plastic of the newspaper rack, couldn't make it out. More about the wacky House Republicans making noise about jobs, how they all hate Bill Clinton. And what kind of mother would name her son Newt? And what is a Gingrich? It sounds like a ginger cookie make by a witch. What else? He didn't really care turning to look at the crowd's growing anticipation of the train pulling up.

Just a few minutes later Jeff stepped off at the big downtown station with bustling crowds going every direction. Soon he was out on the street. After asking around to a couple people he was pointed toward the Underground.

He hadn't gone fifty feet when a grungy looking man intercepted him, "Sir, how are you today?" Jeff pausing. "If I could bother you sir, I could really use a little help here."

Pulling out a dollar handing it to the man, "Here you go, is that enough?" The man's jaw dropping astonished.

"Enough? Sir, you made my day, the best I ever get is a little pocket change, god bless you sir!"

Jeff nodded continuing past the man waving the dollar bill at him thankfully making Jeff shake his head muttering to himself, "Wow, times are pretty tough in Atlanta, huh?"

He handed out two more dollars with the same response as he went along, soon finding himself walking under a big curved overhead sign announcing the Underground. It hardly looked like some secret place of legend where the rum runners of old hid their stash. The whole feel reminding Jeff of driving into Reno with its *Biggest Little City On Earth* sign. Tacky. Maybe that was the effect they wanted. A flash of doubt, but figured he was already here so why not.

Another minute later he was downstairs walking slowly looking at the shops. Yep, lots of familiar names just like the big malls. There was a definite charm to the place, the setting in the caves that made the familiar store signs seem different, out of place.

Stopping, looking at the map board trying to get the lay of the Underground, deciding it was best to start at one end to stroll down the full length, figure out where he wants to eat. Turning to his right starting toward the very end.

Reaching the dead-end making an about-face, turning to walk slowly, looking into windows, coming to an Ann Tallot's store, one of his wife's favorite stores that she was always dragging him into. He meandered through the store's front door taking in that wonderful smell of new clothes. With a whole evening to burn he figured why not, began wandering slowly among the racks.

These places usually had old worn-out-looking women working there, nice people, he always thought, always helpful. He always wondered if they somehow represented the clientele the place was trying to attract, if that was the case why on earth his mid-thirties wife went to these kinds of stores. It seemed that she either went to these places or Macy's with nowhere in between. He noticed that the styles in these stores changed a little according to the location. He couldn't help but notice that the styles here were much more youthful than the stores up in Seattle.

"Sir, may I help you?" Jeff looking around seeing a very attractive young woman looking at him with her best sir-may-I-help-you expression. She had dark hair, not black, more tinged with the slightest tone of red highlight—certainly not the common brown color of his hair—curled just slightly at her shoulders, a face with a wonderful open expression like she was waiting for something to happen, all topped by the perfect tasteful eye makeup.

"Uh, well, no, I was just kind of looking around."

Smiling at him. Okay, she has a nice smile he thought. A *really nice smile*. He felt a quick flush that was so out of place for such an innocent setting.

"You must be looking for something for your wife?"

He felt the flush again, "Uh, nobody really, my mom maybe. I'm not really looking. I just kind of wandered in here really."

"What kinds of things does she like?" Glancing over Jeff's shoulder with a motion making him turn his head, "For your mother, huh? We have a really nice collection of scarves." Stepping around him. "And they are on sale! Does she like scarves? Women always like scarves. They are really nice gifts to bring home."

Following her to a wall tastefully draped with a nice assortment of all kinds of scarves, turning to him, "You're from out of town, aren't you?"

He nodded, "Seattle."

"Seattle! That's great, I have some family up there." Frowning a bit, "Well, family sort of. One anyway." Pausing a quick second with the quickest glance down, looking up again smiling holding out her hand, "My name is Jennifer!"

Jeff took her hand, noticing that she just kind of held onto his hand without really shaking hands, he felt the flush again, "Jeff. Name's Jeff." Thinking his voice sounds nervous for some reason, wondering why pulling his hand back. His smile warming, suddenly feeling more relaxed, "Jeff from Seattle," both laughing for some reason.

He saw her glance at his ring finger seeing the white skin of a missing wedding band, "So Jeff from Seattle, are you married?"

He looked to her uncertain, "Well, yes, technically."

Looking back up at his face. "Well, Jeff from Seattle, I'll let you look around, you just let me know if I can help you with anything. I know you said you weren't really looking, but we are having a good sale, it might be a good time to get your mother something for Christmas," glancing at his ring finger once more, smiling again turning to another customer behind her.

He filtered though the scarves, soon finding one he thought his mother would like. Continuing to walk slowly around the store he had the feeling that people were watching him. Yes, they were definitely looking at him, watching him. Shrugging, glancing around the store, all women. Another store staff approached him, he said he was fine pointing toward Jennifer, that woman over there was helping him, "Oh, Jennifer, yes she's good, she'll help you just fine. You let me know if you have any questions, that's why we're here after all."

He looked over to Jennifer standing at the cash register wondering how old she is, guessing about his wife's age, maybe a year or two younger. Yeah, thirty-three maybe. Boy, nice though. *Very nice*. He had a quick flash in his mind about Jennifer but shook it off. Glancing back at her—in what felt like less than a hundredth of a second he lived a whole lifetime with that attractive young woman. How is it that a man can do such a thing? In that flash they met as they just had, met again, fell in love, of course with his wife now gone, they were married, had children and were growing old together. And the sex was great, really great and often often often until there were times he had to pretend to be asleep, they went on glamorous vacations together, their children became doctors and lawyers and gave them beautiful grandchildren, they a had a totally fulfilling life together as his flash reached them sitting on a park bench under blue skies amid cherry blossoms swirling softly around them, two old people holding hands at the end of their richly gifted lives. All in his head. All in a hundredth of a second. This was a skill he was pretty sure that only a man could have. He smiled to himself recalling that he had that exact same flash when he met his wife. Skill only a man has? *If you can call that a skill!* laughing to himself glancing at her again.

Ambling among the racks he couldn't help but wonder why he had reacted like an embarrassed little kid in front of this nice lady. After all, he meets pretty women all the time. Not at his work for sure, it's mostly men with a few secretaries. That's pretty much all you have in an aerospace company. Dull. Glancing back at her, she was looking at him—he quickly turning back to the rack looking away from her, head down.

When he went up to the register, another clerk was there. He heard a voice, looking over, Jennifer walking up speaking to the woman who was beginning to help him, "I was helping this gentleman." The other woman smiled, stepping back.

"So I see you found something." She held it up admiringly. He was taken by her bright voice that was so inviting, lulling him along with her bright eyes. "Your mother is very lucky to have such a nice son," just as a flash of sadness, barely perceptible swept across her face, "what I wouldn't give to have a man like you give me something like this." Then back to her cheerful look, "But she's going to really like this, I'm sure." He nodded. "Did you get a chance to look at sweaters, we have a forty-percent-off sale."

"No, not really, I think this will probably work fine."

"You travel a lot don't you?"

"Yeah, I guess."

"You know this scarf is nice, but I'll bet it will mean a lot to your mother to bring her something really special." He shrugged.

"Look, do her a favor and at least come look," stepping around the counter signaling him to follow her. Pulling the scarf off the counter following Jennifer detecting an aroma in her wake. It was faintly of fruit, no not fruit really, it was a warm smell with just the slightest scent of a summer day, a sensation that he could almost feel rather than smell. He was suddenly aware that the hairs on the back of his hands felt the soft wisps of air streaming behind her, the sensation of warmness on the skin of his face like he was walking in sunshine on a warm day.

She stopped, turning to him with a glowing smile, "So how tall is she?" Jeff said about her height and build, looking down at herself, back to Jeff with a shy smile. "Well, let's see…" turning, picking through sweaters, showing them on the hangar, a couple she tried on to model for him twirling around in them. What a good little sales person, he thought. He was having a *lot of trouble paying attention to the sweaters*. He could still feel the sensation of warmth on his face from a moment ago, wondering if he looked flushed to her. She said something about not to worry that his mother could return the sweater at one of their stores in Seattle to exchange or get a refund, but that these sweaters were very much in style right now, that they make a definite statement, that she imagined the mother of such a handsome man would appreciate one.

Finally she put one on that Jeff could picture his mother in. She laid it on a rack pulling the scarf from Jeff's hands, laying the scarf over the sweater, "Perfect match, good job!" The compliment made him feel a little foolish that he had nothing to do with the match between the scarf and the sweater. He said he would take it, feeling like he was fumbling the words out, like the words were tumbling over his tongue, playful children teasing each other daring the others to come out first. He felt a flush, the children finally emerging from his mouth making their noisy sounds that mimicked words. At that moment he could only guess if the words made any sense to her.

He didn't even bother to look at the price.

She smiled, "A really excellent choice, you have very good taste." Straightening up the rack, the sweater over her left arm, putting her right arm through Jeff's left arm, gently leading him up to the counter again. This time her fragrance *washing* over him as he felt the flush again.

He suddenly noticed her eyes. They were a bright silver color that seemed to carry the slightest tint of the green blouse she was wearing. He imagined that her eyes could look blue, or even purple if they had such a color near them, color that her eyes magically draw from surfaces around them. Jeff always felt captivated by women's eyes, especially when they were an unusual color. Captivated. Absolutely captivated.

Punching some buttons on the cash register, she took his credit card, starting to pull out a box when he suddenly realized where he was standing. "Uh, I forgot, I am not going back to my hotel right now. I'm here for dinner. I don't want to have something to carry with me. I'll just end up leaving it somewhere."

She laughed, "Well, we've all done that before haven't we?" both laughing together.

"Where are you staying?"

"Airport Sheraton."

"Well, I will tell you what. We get lots of traveling customers here. We have a special service for orders over fifty dollars where we will deliver to your hotel for no charge the next day. Will you be there tomorrow?"

"Through the weekend."

"Well then, excellent!" Looking at him for just a second longer with a widening smile, "Yes, *excellent!*" handing him a piece of paper and pen telling him to write down his hotel information saying that she would have it delivered at noon tomorrow.

He scribbled, she held up the paper, "You forgot to put your name on this, but don't worry, I know it's Jeff. Will you be there at noon?"

Thinking for a second, "Yes, I'm pretty sure. Don't know where else I would be. If I'm not can't you just leave it at the front desk?"

"We can, but we do want to make sure that you get it, especially something so expensive, so we will try to deliver it to your room first. Noon." She pulled out a box from under the counter, unfolding it, pulling out tissue paper to lay the sweater into the box, reaching for the scarf.

"I'll take the scarf," he said lifting it from the counter. "I'll just put it in my coat pocket here if it'll fit." He wasn't really sure why he didn't just lay it in the box on top of the sweater but thought he would look foolish to change his mind now.

Signing the credit card slip, she handed him his receipt. He carefully folded the scarf tucking it into his left inside sport coat pocket, standing back with his arms out to his sides. "See? No lost packages!" both laughing together again.

Reaching her hand across the counter, Jeff took it though she didn't offer it as in a shaking of hands, he found her hand laying in his again, "Well mister Jeff, you go out and have an interesting evening." Cocking her head just slightly, "And remember, tomorrow. Noon. Sharp."

Their eyes were locked together when a woman standing behind him with a grumbling *excuse me can I please pay* interrupted their stares. Only then did he consciously realize that they had been flirting, that she was actually flirting back to him, that she thought he was handsome, how surprised he was that this meant something to him. It was flattering. He felt a tingle that this pretty woman was paying this kind of attention to him. The woman behind him made a frumping growl, he took a step back, the woman pushing past him to get to the counter while their eyes still held the other's, looking over the old woman spreading her items on the counter.

"Uh, thanks, thank you really, you've been really great," nervously backing away. She gave a little wave with her fingers as he turned to the right walking slowly to the door, glancing over his shoulder seeing her eyes following him even as the grouchy woman was crabbing for her attention.

Turning left out the door, Jeff shook his head, starting walking. "Wow, what was *that?*" out loud. He stopped, looking back at the store. She was out of sight, turning around, continuing walking. Looking down at the receipt he wasn't surprised that he had just spent two-hundred twenty dollars. Forty percent off? Tucking the receipt into his pants pocket, realizing he hadn't even paid attention in the store.

His mother was going to kill him.

Somehow he didn't care. She was just a sales clerk, he said to himself, hustling him to buy a very expensive sweater that his mother was going to kill him over. Just some innocent flirting. No big deal. So why did he suddenly feel so good? Pausing for a second, pulling at his coat sleeves, pulling at the front of his coat, walking on.

Continuing along coming to a Victoria's Secret store, starting to go in. Stopped. Seeing three curvaceous young women standing in the store, one looking at him expectantly, he suddenly had second thoughts.

If he got into so much trouble at an Ann Tallot's store with that little clerk, he could only imagine one thing that would happen to him if he walked into that Victoria's Secret.

I will burn in hell!

Friday, 5:56PM: The Mark

With that thought, Jeff deliberately turned left continuing on.

Walking on slowly keeping his eyes peeled for an ATM so that he could fill his pockets with dollar bills laughing to himself, *"Yep, need dollars so I can have people take bullets for me!"*

Meandering along windows looking in, not seeing anything in particular that he had to have, leisurely walking along to the next. There were a few bars, a barbeque restaurant with blues music spilling out its doors, farther down some kind of Ricky Rocket burger place at the far end by the exit.

There was a funny looking place, Jeff guessing it was some kind of a bar, a wall filled with colorful circles with little pour spouts in front of each. Seeing laughing glassy-eyed adults with colorful plastic drink cups in front of them guessing they were some kind of fruity slushy rum and other liquors. *Slurpees for alcoholics, now that's an invention!* laughing to himself imagining a line of kids at the Seven Eleven all eager for the cherry flavored one. Yeah, this could really be good! You could have seasonal treats, "Here, little girl, peppermint schnapps for the Christmas season!" What flavor would you have for Fourth of July he wondered? Would that be Gin or Vodka? No, on such an *American* holiday it couldn't be British Gin or Russian Vodka! "American," he said to himself, "would definitely have to be Jim Beam." He laughed to himself at the thought of a Jim Beam flavored Slurpee. But he didn't like bourbon, shuddering at the thought.

Unlike your usual bar with dim lights, this place was all lit up, every seat at the counter taken by mostly Yuppy looking younger people; bleary eyes saying a good time was being had by all. Smiling watching at the window, "I guess that's the advantage of public transportation, right? You don't want a bunch of alcoholic Slurpee drivers out there!" making a note to come back to have one of those slushy drinks after dinner.

Finally, Jeff came to the Underground's last exit, seeing the evening's darkness coming through the glass doors. Turning around seeing an ATM sign down the way past the Ricky Rocket's thinking he must have missed it, walking back toward the ATM sign.

Walking up to the ATM seeing that it was going to cost him a dollar-fifty to use the machine, "Charging me to get my own money back," out loud frowning. He was a businessman; he knew that businesses had to make a profit. But somehow paying to get your own money had some fundamental flaw in logic. Oh well, it didn't matter, he was almost out of cash. He thought for a minute about how much cash he would need. This was Friday night, he needed money for tonight, then for the weekend, then enough to get him around until his flight on Monday afternoon back to Seattle.

Inserting his ATM card, pausing, "Oh, what the heck," he punched in one-hundred twenty dollars. The money came out, he stuffed it into his right pants pocket, took the receipt, studying it realizing he had entered two-hundred twenty dollars. He pulled the money back out of his pocket counting it. Sure enough, two hundred twenty dollars, stuffing the money and receipt back into his pocket.

Glancing to his right seeing a black man about his height, portly build, standing next to him watching Jeff's hand at his pocket. "Looks like a man who is out and about, ready to have an interesting evening! I mean, you probably have credit cards, so why would you need cash?"

Turning to the man, the man pulling back startled!

The man leaning toward Jeff, "What are you doing here!" Taking a step back. Studying Jeff's face. Jeff feeling uncomfortable, taking a half-step back from the man. The man examining Jeff's face, scanning him up and down. "Wait. You're not him, are you? Who are you?" leaning toward Jeff with an intense glare.

"Name's Jeff, who are you? Why are you talking to me?"

Jeff glancing quickly around nervously wondering at this man, why was he talking to him? Satisfied that there were people around feeling reassured, looking back at the man in front of him.

The man still stood there silently studying Jeff, "Well, I'll be. Jeff, huh?" Jeff nodding timidly. "Well I'll be. It's like his own twin brother…" the man's voice trailing off. The man's face was youthful looking with small pock marks on his cheeks, chicken pox or acne as a kid maybe, sparkling dark eyes, a big wide smile with bright white teeth that contrasted with his dark face, beacons gleaming from shadows.

His voice was low, almost sonorous, robust with just enough of a Southern accent to make it charming. What is it about the Southern accent that can sound so charming coming from one person but come across like finger nails on a chalkboard from someone else? Maybe it's the twang, but this man standing in front of him had a rich southern voice with an open sincere look, no twang, still though…

The man had a stout build, not fat, certainly not Jeff's thinner build. His expression seemed like it could be friendly if it wasn't so intent on Jeff at that moment. He wore a dapper black hat with a small front brim, turned up in the back with a silver hat band. It reminded Jeff of hats he saw in some old Cary Grant movie. Rarely did Jeff ever see a man in anything but a baseball cap, maybe an occasional cowboy hat. This style of hat made the man in front of him seem well turned-out, suited his manner.

The man continued examining Jeff, suddenly starting to reach up to touch Jeff's chin. Jeff stepping back pushing the man's hand away, "Hey, what are you doing? Who are you?"

"Sorry man, didn't mean to scare you or anything, just being sociable." A smile creeping onto his face as though he was satisfied with something. "Pete is my name," holding out his hand, "My friends call me Pick."

Jeff looking around him, uncertain what to do.

"You look worried there, no need there friend Jeff, I'm just out and about myself and am always looking to make a new friend."

Reluctantly Jeff reached out shaking hands meekly.

"Where are you from?"

Jeff still unsure, muttering, "Seattle."

"Seattle! Well, what do you know, you're from a place that's actually rainier than Atlanta!" the man laughing out loud.

"Yeah, it's pretty rainy up there, it rains a lot here?"

"You're obviously not from here or you would know. When did you get into town?"

"Day before yesterday."

"Let me guess, businessman, right?"

"Yeah." Jeff taking another small step back.

"Well we get lots of businessmen down here, all by themselves and want to get out of the hotel, right?" Jeff's uncertain smile. "Yeah, I've met lots of businessmen down here. All kinds. Nice guys, mostly."

"Yeah, I guess." Jeff wondering at the sound of this man's voice. There was a certain lulling quality to it, a mild smoothness that had a way of saying *don't worry everything is fine here*. The words of the shuttle driver and his mother's warnings suddenly ringing in his ears, feeling his expression tightening wondering what to do here.

"So, you getting a chance to get in a little early Christmas shopping for the wife? Lots of nice stores here."

Reaching into his coat pocket Jeff pulling out the scarf, holding it laid out in his hands, "It's for my mother."

Pick leaned forward to look at it, "Nice! From Tallot's! For your mother! What a good son! That had to cost what, thirty dollars?"

"It was on sale, I don't remember, but there was a nice lady there who helped me buy a really nice sweater that was a heck of a lot more than thirty dollars."

Pick nodding, "Yeah, I hear rumors there's an enterprising young lady that works there."

"Yeah, she's a heck of a sales person. Kind of cute, too!"

Pick flashing a knowing smile, "Yeah, well I'm pretty sure you'll see her again." Jeff didn't pay attention to the words eying the man in front of him suspiciously. "But see, that's the Underground for you! Nice stores, very friendly clerks to make sure you spend as much money as possible!" waving his hand around the cave, at the stores in front of them, Pick laughing, Jeff tucking the scarf back into his pocket.

"And there you go, you gentlemen come down here, spend a few dollars on a gift for the wife," smiling, "or your mother, then wander around without a clue about where you are, where to go next and miss all the good things about the place you're wandering." Taking a half-step toward Jeff who didn't back away this time. "Well, if I was you I would want someone who knew the place. And seeing as I am the only one here, I'd be happy to be your someone—kind of a guide if you want."

"A guide?" Jeff thought of the confusing tourist booklet he got at the hotel, how he had tried to make order of it as he was hopelessly trying to plan his evening. While he was in the shuttle he had actually wished he could pay the driver to be his guide but he knew that couldn't be arranged. It would be nice to walk with somebody who knew the ins-and-outs of the place. Maybe this wouldn't be such a bad thing. Still, there was just something about this guy putting him on edge.

Pick throwing up his hands in declaration, "Hey, if this makes you uncomfortable, then I guess, but really," leaning forward, "but I'm a nice guy, lived here all my life." Seeing Jeff's expression slowly turning to a scowl. "And there's no harm in a little company right? I mean, you probably get around a lot, right?"

"Yeah."

"And how many times do you go back to Seattle without ever having a chance to get to know the place you spent so much time in, I mean, how many days are you here?"

Counting days in his head, "Three, uh, five. Wednesday, going home Monday afternoon."

"Exactly, and how many of those nights do you get to tour around?"

"Tonight and tomorrow night, I guess." Flashing the alternative of either touring around or just sitting at the hotel bar or in his room. Besides, what is there to do in his room, watch TV? Not exactly the things you want to go back home to tell your mother about, huh? *Hey mom, guess what I did in Atlanta? I sat in my hotel room and watched TV!* Probably even his mother would be upset.

"Exactly!" Pick smiling, "And when you go back to your hotel won't it be nice to have had dinner and a couple drinks with someone nice—that would be me by the way—get to know the town a little?"

Jeff feeling himself warming to the idea. His mind flashing to what he had already discovered about business travel. His friends and family were constantly asking about where he had been lately,

Toronto, New York, Washington DC, Silicon Valley? He had been traveling like this for a few years. People seemed to think there was some kind of glamour to it all. He often wondered what they pictured. Oh, yeah, glamorous business travel. A hundred thousand miles a year only meant a hundred thousand hours of butt in the airplane seat, a thousand times through airport security, a thousand times checking into hotels, checking out of hotels, meeting a hundred thousand faces that he would never see again, getting up a four-thirty to catch a shuttle, going places where people had families. If he was lucky he might get one early dinner at some restaurant where the food tasted just like the last restaurant only to have people start looking at their watches trying to get home to tuck the kids in to read them bedtime stories then get to climb into bed with their wives or husbands so he could go back to the hotel, maybe have one more drink before passing out in front of David Letterman. And then doing it all over again tomorrow. He frowned about the week when he had very late dinners at four different TGI Fridays in three states because it was the only restaurant open by the time he checked into the hotel. Talk about food tasting the same!

But mostly business travel is lonely. Just plain lonely. In an instant he brightened that there might be someone who wasn't rushing home to tuck in the little ones. Pick could see Jeff's expression start to open, a smile beginning to creep onto his face.

"And if you don't want my company, just walk away. No harm, no foul, I won't try to stop you. Of course it might cause me to question if I have lost my charm," making a motion as though to elbow Jeff, "just kidding about that part." Jeff nodding smiling. "Then how about we go and explore this place? I know just the place to start!"

Hesitating, glancing left, right, back to this man, saying slowly with a cautious smile, "Okay, I guess there's no harm."

"Exactly! No harm, see? Don't you feel better already? You met me and I'm gonna give you an Atlanta tour that you'll remember for a very long time. A *very* long time." Big smile, "Okay?"

Jeff shrugging, "Okay, it's Pick right?" Pick nodding. "Okay, Pick," Jeff smiling, "I'm in, lead on!"

Reaching out pulling at Jeff's arm, "Then come my friend, just follow me. It's time for a little rum."

Smiling Jeff turning to Pick as they started off, "Drink, yeah, I could definitely do with a drink."

Soon Jeff found himself standing at the well-lit bar with the colorful circles of alcoholic Slurpees spinning in front of him. There was only one seat at the bar, Pick insisting Jeff sit there while he stands next to him. "Okay, here's how it goes. They give you a sample of whatever you want. Some of the names are pretty easy to figure out what's in them. But like that one, the Blue Fizz, you might have to ask or just get 'em to give you a sample."

The bartender walked by, Pick calling to him, "Two Blue Fizz samples here!" The bartender giving Pick a knowing smile that was not lost on Jeff. Soon two tiny plastic cups appeared before them. With a small touch of tiny cups in a toast, they were swallowed down. Jeff could taste the bourbon trying not to wince; the cool slushy sweetness definitely softening that nasty bourbon taste on his tongue.

"Bourbon," said Pick, "how do you like it?"

"I'm not much of a bourbon guy, is there some rum drink here?"

"Yes, rum you want?" Pick calling to the bartender, "Pink paradise!" In a few seconds two tiny pink sample cups appeared in their hands.

Jeff tasted it more carefully than before, smiling, throwing the rest into his mouth, "That's nice, okay, I'll have some of that."

"Yeah, well, I'm a tequila man myself!" With that declaration Pick ordered two drinks, one pink the other a bright orange. Jeff noticing again an expression that the bartender gave Pick making him wonder how often Pick comes in here.

Jeff sipped at his pink drink, enjoying the sweet taste of rum. Looking around the room he noticed how the mix of people had changed since he first looked in through the window. The crowd was definitely older now, he thought that maybe the others he saw earlier were office workers, now these were more their managers from the high-rise office buildings a block away out for their end-of-week alcohol relief break.

The bartender walked over stretching across the bar talking into Pick's ear, pointing to a group across the room. Pick turned nodding.

Pick turning to Jeff, "Will you excuse me a minute, there's a man over there I need to speak with." Jeff nodding slurping from his pink drink as Pick got up, walking to the table the bartender had pointed to. Jeff watching, Pick standing with his back toward him, the others at the table leaning anxiously toward Pick. Money appearing moving to Pick's hands, handshakes, walking back toward Jeff.

"Everything okay?"

"Yeah, they just need a little help with something."

Jeff shaking his head finishing off his drink, "How often do you come in here?"

"Oh, I get in here once in a while, not as often as I'd like," taking a deep slurp from his drink finishing it off, Pick signaling to the bartender for another round.

The people next to Jeff got up. Pick came around sitting next to Jeff. Soon new drinks appearing, the bartender holding out the tab, Jeff signaling he'd take it, looking at it, asking to keep it open, handing it back to the bartender with a credit card. Jeff had a second thought, signaling the bartender back, asking him if he could have some change, handing the bartender his wad of cash from the ATM machine.

"How do you want it?"

Jeff pulled back five twenties, "Twenty in ones if you have it, the rest in fives and tens, mostly fives," the bartender turning, "make sure at least twenty in ones!"

Turning to Pick, "That's for the pan handlers, need to be prepared, right?" Jeff wondering at his order for change, but chalked it up to the colorful drinks laughing shrugging it off.

Pick leaning to Jeff, "Whatever, brothuh, but that's easy for the bartender to do, they get their tips all in small bills."

Jeff looking around at the crowd hugging the bar, along the back wall. These were definitely an older crowd than before, imagining that they would be a lot more generous tippers than the younger ones here earlier.

The bartender returned with a much bigger wad of cash than Jeff had imagined. He set about counting it turning away from Pick, suddenly realizing that he had way too many eyes on him so he just stuffed it all into his pocket. He couldn't help noticing the bartender's smile to Pick, wishing he had the nerve to count the money.

Jeff stood up, "Uh, I gotta go to the men's room."

Pick pulling his arm down, "No, no you don't. Not after you just flashed that big wad of cash. You'll get a big smack on the head and that'll be it for your night. Sit down, hold it, we'll get to it on the way out."

Looking suspiciously around him Jeff realizing that Pick was probably right.

Soon they finished their drinks. Pick ordering another round, in a moment they were both working on their next drink. Jeff feeling a genuine buzz sipping slowly trying not to drink so fast that he would get a cold headache, *piggy pains* as his brother called it. The drinks were strong!

He could feel himself warming up to his new-found friend's company. Pick began talking all about the history of the Atlanta Underground, about Atlanta in general. Jeff noticing a few second glances at him, the same he saw in the Tallot's store, as people sat or walked by. He didn't pay much attention.

Pick described, "Atlanta is the black man's paradise!" Jeff nodding. "The mayor is black, the police chief is black, most of the city council are black, this is the kingdom of the black man!"

Jeff reflecting, "How does that work? I see lots of white people around."

"All tourists and white people from the suburbs."

"I do business up in Norcross, is that where you mean?"

"Exactly, the only black faces you see there are waitresses and taxi drivers. Black people don't live up there, god no! But here, the black man rules." Pick went on to talk and talk and talk about Atlanta, how it is the land of opportunity for blacks, how he was in such a good situation.

"What exactly is your situation? Do you work?"

Pick hesitating, "Work? Oh, yeah, I work. I work hard!"

"What do you do?"

Straightening up Pick, proclaiming smile, "I officiate arrangements between certain business parties, taking a commission for those transactions."

Jeff realized he was starting to move beyond the buzz from the alcohol. "Those are a lot of big words there, Pick. What does that all mean? I mean, exactly what is it you do?"

Pick countered, "Well, mister Jeff, you tell me first, what is it *you* do?"

"I work for a company that sends me out to find new contracts. Then I bring them all together to make deals. After that I stay with the deal to make sure that all the contracts are signed, that everyone gets along so they can make money together and my company along with them. Then I go onto the next deal."

Beaming Pick proclaiming, "That's exactly what I do!"

Jeff frowned trying to fill in the gaps that were becoming more than just a bit fuzzy from the rum. Looking at his watch he couldn't believe they'd been at the bar for over two hours.

"Oh, man, I've got to get some food in me. Where's there a good place to eat?"

"I know just the place!" waving to the bartender, "Tab!"

Jeff got the receipt and his credit card back, signing it calculating the tip when Pick leaned over whispering, "Be generous, this guy was pretty good to us, right?"

"Yeah, I was thinking five dollars."

"Five dollars! I'd never be able to show my face back here again!" slapping Jeff on the back with a big laugh, "Ten at least!"

Frowning, Jeff reluctantly scribbling ten dollars on the tab, wondering just how often Pick really came in here.

Before Jeff could put words to his thoughts, Pick stood up, "Okay, where do we get some dinner?" Jeff shrugging. Pick's big smile, "Don't worry, just follow me—I know just the right place!"

Soon they were back walking down the way in the darkened cave, Jeff could feel the effects of the rum, not too bad to worry. There were far fewer people than before. Walking Jeff looking at Pick, "You know, this is nice, like a mini-vacation! I appreciate you taking the time here." Pick responding with that big white-toothed smile.

Passing a newspaper rack Jeff starting to lean to look at it, Pick pulling at his arm, "Hey, no newspapers! You're on your on a mini-vacation here, right? You don't want to be dealin' with the real world on a night like tonight, do you?" Jeff nodding. "I never look at the papers, nothin' but bad news anyway, right? Always bad, bad, bad."

"Yeah, I guess you're right. Never?"

"Nope, one of the very few things I am definitely religious about. Only ever bad news, I get plenty of that already. Any news I wanna know people will tell me."

Twice walking along the darkened corridor with bright store lights on each side Jeff noticed someone's familiar nod to Pick, both times Pick's short flick of fingers brushing them off, Jeff quickly figuring out that Pick was no stranger here, obviously a regular. Jeff wondering what was the game he stumbled into. And more than once seeing those double takes, people passing with quick glances at him, still no idea why people would be looking at him, shrugging it off. But there were definite looks.

Soon Jeff could see the same club he had noticed earlier with the blues music pouring from the door. Pick was pointing toward it saying something when a thought occurred to Jeff. Laughing out loud, Pick turning to him, "Are you okay?" They stopped in front of the restaurant with gaudy neon lights of music notes blinking in different colors.

Jeff laughing again. "Faulkner, you ever read any Faulkner?"

Pick looking puzzled, "What's that? What was the word you just said?"

Turning to Pick with another laugh, "Faulkner, William Faulkner, the author. Ever read any Faulkner?"

"Never heard of it, don't do much reading."

"Yes!" Jeff smiling, "I was just remembering a story, where he meets someone like you. Takes him out, buys his drinks and meals. Faulkner called himself *the Mark*. Am I your Mark?"

Pick's exaggerated pained expression, "Is that what you think this is, that I am taking advantage of you?" laughing in mock hurt.

Jeff laughing again putting his hand on Pick's shoulder, "No, no, I know, you are just a nice guy trying to show me a good time, that's okay, don't worry about it. I'm not upset. Don't worry," chuckling to himself.

Pick frowning, "Really, it's okay?" Jeff nodding chuckling again with his hand on Pick's shoulder.

Jeff thought back to the reading he had done. William Faulkner was a southerner, as he recalled. Had won a Nobel or something if he remembered right. Jeff had read a few of his books way back when he was in college. He read *As I Lay Dying* and some other drama pieces. This situation so reminded him of *New Orleans Sketches*, a collection of short stories filled with all sorts of characters. As he looked at the man standing in front of him one story in that book came to mind, mainly of the character that Faulkner met up with in New Orleans who had taken him for an evening, letting him buy food and drinks the whole time. Faulkner was called *the Mark*. He couldn't remember the ending, but smiled anyway as he was being led along by Pick. Yep, *the Mark*.

Looking at Pick smiling, "Yeah, I'm okay. In fact, I'm having a good time, but I really need do need to get some food in me, and I really need a bathroom!"

"Well, then, you're in luck! This is some of the best barbeque in town."

Jeff turning looking at the restaurant, skeptical. "Best? Here?"

Pick laughing, "Okay, maybe not the best in Atlanta. Atlanta is the barbeque capital of the world you know. Others claim it, maybe, but trust me."

Jeff grinning, "You mean the black man's barbeque capital?"

Pick pulled back with a stern expression that surprised Jeff—just as quickly Pick laughing, "Oh, yeah, right, the black man's capital, right, just like I said. Throw in some barbeque and there you go!"

"Still, the best in Atlanta?"

"Okay, like I said, let's just say it's the best here in the Underground!"

Jeff laughing, "Good enough for me, I'm hungry. Could do with a little barbeque. And a bathroom!" smiling to himself pretty sure that he could have some barbeque tonight without worrying about naked women running all around him like back in Denver. Yes, definitely no strip clubs for him tonight!

Walking into the darkened restaurant, loud blues music streaming from the tiny stage in one corner. A thick haze of cigarette smoke hanging in the room. Jeff coughed a little at first breath. Pick stood scanning the room, Jeff pointing to the men's room, parting company.

Coming back out, Pick pointing to a table. "I'll get us that table in the corner," signaling to a waitress whose expression brightened seeing him, Pick pointing to the empty table in the corner, she gestured back to sit down.

Snaking their way around tables to the corner, sitting down facing the stage. The music so loud that they had to nearly yell to each other, so most of the time was spent signaling each other pointing to the menu, making drinking motions to order alcohol, sitting in silence watching the three musicians on stage. The music wasn't half-bad Jeff thought picking up his drink, realizing it was bourbon, grimacing setting it down again.

Soon the food arrived, the waitress bending over talking to Pick, her mouth to his ear. Jeff figured the music was so loud that's what she had to do, though he did wonder what she had to say to him, what he was saying back to her. He couldn't hear a word but there was a definite exchange of nods that said something important was being communicated.

It probably wasn't about barbeque.

How is it that we can so easily feel like the outsider? Jeff thought about all the communications that are constantly swirling around him, some he doesn't care about—probably most of it—but then there are the things that he wished he was privy to. He thought about in his work, how he was constantly having to piece together little scraps of information, overheard conversations, subtle exchanges of looks mixed with nods, memos that seemed to have some underlying message. He wanted to think that he was good at picking up little undercurrents of dialog. He was continually surprised when things popped out as the formal message was finally transmitted. And that didn't even count his family! He often thought about all the intrigue between his wife's family, her mom and her sisters, though her dad was pretty much a straight-shooter. Then there was *his side* of the family, the way his mother would never tell him what was happening; it was only when he picked up on someone's expression or a slipped word that he could find a handle to grab onto then maybe, just maybe, he could find out what was going on. Even when he did it was seldom the whole story. And here it was happening again with his so-called guide making who-knows-what schemes with the waitress at a place where his guide "*so seldom comes.*"

He gave up watching them, starting to eat immediately when the food was served. Soon Pick joined in, filling his mouth, reaching for this barbeque sauce or that cornbread muffin. Soon the waitress realized Jeff wasn't drinking. She bent back over to Pick, said something Jeff couldn't hear over the music, she took Jeff's drink returning a couple minutes later with a rum drink. Jeff taking a sip nodding, smiling in thanks to the waitress. He had the feeling like he was a passenger on a bus that nobody spoke to—the bus was just driving on, all he could do was sit and watch everything going on around him, flying past. No point in asking questions. They wouldn't tell him anyway.

It didn't bother him until he had the sudden vision that maybe he was just a passenger on the *bus of his own life*. Here he was being led along by this stranger, putting his whole evening into his hands, just hoping that it would all come out in the end. How often was he just led around, how often did he not even know? Chuckling to himself at the funny notion deciding that he'd drunk too much to think about this seriously tonight, making a note to remember the thought. Realizing that he drank too much to put any thought into anything tonight, shrugging to himself taking another swill of his drink.

When his last finger has been sucked free of barbeque sauce, Jeff turned his watch toward the candle seeing that it was already past nine-thirty. Damn, he had less than an hour to get back to the airport to get the shuttle to the hotel.

Pointing at his watch, Pick nodding, motioning to the waitress

coming over to take Jeff's credit card, returning with the tab.
Leaning into the candle light to read it seeing they had spent thirty
five dollars on their dinner and drinks! Expensive! Signing the credit
card slip, starting to calculate the tip, Pick leaning over looking
intently at the slip in the dim candlelight. Though Jeff would usually
give maybe seven dollars, glancing to his right at Pick's expectant
expression, scribbling down fifteen. Pick nodding smiling, signaling
a thumbs-up, Jeff totaling the tab. The waitress came back, picking
up the tab without putting it to the candle light, smiling with a
thumbs-up to Pick completely ignoring Jeff. *She knows I left a big
tip!* watching the pair realizing that he really was being drug around
to these places so that he could leave these exorbitant tips so Pick
could get the credit! Ah, yes, thank you mister Faulkner for *the
Mark.* Oh well, this was his mini-vacation, right? As long as
everyone was having fun, that's all that mattered. And he was having
fun. Good food, great music, his guide that so far was making some
pretty good choices.

Pick was leaning back listening to the music, Jeff pointing to his
watch again. Pick smiling, got up motioning for Jeff to follow him, a
moment later they were back in the quiet of the Underground mall
corridor. There were hardly any people in the Underground now, Jeff
starting to feel just a little uneasy.

Pick turning to Jeff who was looking for something in his inside
coat pocket, seeing Pick looking at him, quickly letting go of his
jacket. "Just trying to see if I had my train ticket." Turning walking
toward the exit, "Look Pick, thank you for everything. I've really got
to get back to the train so I can get to my hotel. They gave me a
deadline to get back in time for the shuttle."

"What? A curfew?" Pick frowning, "Well if that's what you say.
You heading south?"

"Yeah, to the airport."

"Well say, what a coincidence! I'm heading that way, too! Want
some company?"

"What, to my hotel?"

"No, no, my stop is the next one down, I thought you might like a
little company at least part way to the airport," leaning toward Jeff as

they walked, "and maybe a little company from the assault of these panhandlers," one walking up, Jeff reaching into his pocket to pull out a dollar bill handing it to him.

Jeff smiling, "No way, I got a pocket of ones for these guys." Pick laughing shaking his head. Out of nowhere another homeless man materializing in front of them. Pick made to shoo the man away but Jeff was already reaching a dollar toward the man. "Here man, have a good evening," pushing past him.

"Thank you sir! Thank you!" trailing off behind them as they walked on.

"What the hell, are you just giving money away now?"

"Why not, that's what I've been doing all night!"

Pausing with an intense expression, Pick bursting into a good-natured laugh, "Exactly! So what's another dollar, right?" Jeff gave away four more dollars on their short walk to the train station.

The streets were nearly deserted by the time they reached the train station, only one other man on the platform. After another minute they were on board.

"So you're just going to go back to your hotel?"

"Yeah, it's late."

"It's not even ten o'clock. What, you got a date with David Letterman?"

Jeff looking sideways at Pick, annoyed.

"Look, I know a place, it's called Magic Town. It's at the stop I'm getting off at, the next stop, why don't you come spend a few minutes with me there? I think you'll really like it."

Listening to the train's clacking on the rails, soon hearing them slow as the train approached the next stop Jeff looked up seeing the sign for Garnett Station. Looking at the map board seeing that it was just a couple stops from College Station which was the short cab ride to the hotel the shuttle driver told him about, he decided it could be alright.

Jeff smiled, "Magic, huh? That sounds like fun. That could be really cool to see a little magic," thinking about rabbits out of hats and all that. Yeah, a little magic might be just what the doctor ordered! Turning to Pick with a determined smile knowing that he had at least until midnight, he could take a cab from the other station like he was told. "Magic? Okay, you're right, it's early still. Let's do it!"

Rubbing his hands together as the train was stopping Pick stood chuckling to himself, "Yes, sir, magic! You, my friend are going to be amazed. *Amazed!*"

Jeff walked down the isle of the train behind Pick, turning left out the door onto the platform thinking maybe he would do something tonight that he could actually tell his mother about, "Yeah, magic, I could definitely do with a little magic. Yeah, that will be fun!"

Walking along the platform Jeff looked out across the parking lot seeing nothing but dingy industrial warehouses, barely lit, faded signs on their sides barely visible in the light from the Marta station parking lot.

Peering intently across the road, Jeff whistled, "Wow, what is this place?"

"Yeah, well this is not exactly the best part of town, but stay next to me, you'll be fine."

"What kind of place is this for magic?"

Quick glance and wry smile walking as Jeff traipsed beside him, "Don't worry, you'll see. You'll see!" Laughing a gregarious laugh, patting Jeff on the back Pick smiling, "Magic. Yes, let's put a little magic into your interesting evening!"

Jeff laughing again out loud. "Yes! Let's make it an interesting evening!"

Walking along the sidewalk that had been destroyed by years of use, twice Jeff tripping over its jagged surface, looking around wondering where he had managed to find himself. Glancing over his shoulder, all around, peering into the darkness at the darkened tall shoddy buildings, there wasn't a soul to be seen.

Finally, they turned the corner. There in big neon lights was the sign **MAGIC TOWN** with a large neon woman pulling her top up-and-down to expose two enormous neon breasts.

Jeff laughing out loud, "Magic Town! Of course!"

There won't be any rabbits coming out of hats here!

Friday, 10:08 PM: Magic Town

Looking around, there were cars parked everywhere with people milling around or standing in tight groups in the darkness.

In a couple more minutes they were walking through the front door into a short hallway absolutely dark except for an outline of light around a black curtain straight ahead, the floor vibrating to the beat—THUMP THUMP THUMP THUMP—the yelling of what sounded like a thousand men—laughing mixed with yelling mixed with the sounds of glass rattling, hands clapping, slapping on tables. The curtain pulled back, light bursting through on pulses of loud music with the raucous noise. A large black hand appeared on Jeff's left, leaning over yelling in a deep voice, "TEN DOLLAHS, FIVE DOLLAHS EACH!" Jeff could barely hear the man's voice over the racket, the tall man leaning forward speaking directly into Jeff's ear apologetically, "Even fo' you, congressman."

Congressman? Jeff laughing to himself looking up to the face hovering over him, "What did you—"

"Sorry, suh, but dems da rules. But you can have da best table," he motioned to two men standing against the back wall, pointing to a table up front with a flicking motion.

Jeff turning to look at this tall man, probably six-feet-six at least. Reaching into his pocket Jeff accidentally pulled out a twenty that was snatched from his hand followed by a stamp on the back of his hand, Pick pulling him away from the curtain leading them toward a table at the head of an elevated runway that ran from a black-curtained stage against the back wall into the bar area.

The music was blaring. "GOOD JOB! I KNEW HE'D LET YOU SIT UP FRONT!" Jeff stopped next to Pick watching two burley men walk from the back of the room right up to a table in front of the runway yanking the three men sitting at the table by their arms pushing them away, signaling to Pick to come over, a waitress looking over, running up to the table to clear bottles away, giving the table a quick sweep with a dirty towel.

Jeff following behind looking around him, the crowd of men yelling at the stage. It was deafening as Jeff looked up seeing a beautiful black woman come walking through curtains at the back of the stage—topless with her hands on her hips with a come-on expression that Jeff had never quite seen before.

Jeff looked up at this female image before him on the stage, three feet off the floor, as she strutted out on something like one of those Super Model runways running out from the curtained stage, off-center to the room with him and Pick sitting in the larger half, the runway ending twenty feet from the stage.

Jeff was stunned. "*My god, I'm really at a strip joint!*" was all Jeff could think laughing to himself how earlier he had so committed himself that he would definitely *not* want to go to a strip joint.

Looking around him suddenly realizing that *he was the only white man in the entire room!*

Jeff poked Pick's shoulder, "I'm the only white guy in here!" Pick waving his hand dismissively with a big smile, pointing up to the dancer.

He felt like his white face lit up like a big glowing candle even in the pulsing swirling lights on the stage, everyone ignoring him with their faces glued to the woman who was beginning to pull at the straps of her bikini bottom, her large breasts dangling over the table next to them, men walking up stuffing dollar bills into her bikini bottom.

"OFF OFF OFF OFF!" the room started yelling. In answer to the taunting the dancer swished her skilled hand around her bikini snapping up a wad of bills, pulling at the strings on each side, her bikini bottom snapped away, held high in her right hand like some kind of trophy with a wad of money in her left hand, her bikini bottom in her right, the room full of men going absolutely wild! The crowd went crazy with yells that made Jeff's ears saturate with sound, the music went on THUMP THUMP THUMP THUMP with some woman's voice singing words in the music somewhere that could have been Donna Summers, Jeff couldn't hear over the clapping thumping yelling men.

A man's voice roared from the ceiling, "LET'S GIVE A HAND FOR LORETTA AND THROW A FEW MORE DOLLARS UP THERE FOR HER FINE PERFORMANCE!" a rain of dollar bills showering onto the stage, the music suddenly ending with Loretta sweeping up the last of the money scattered around the stage, thanking the room with small bows and waves, disappearing through the stage curtain.

The loud music stopped, "WE'LL GIVE IT FIVE MINUTES AND THEN THROW A LITTLE MORE MAGIC OUT THERE!" Softer music starting up. Jeff actually hearing voices around him.

Looking to the back of the room near a door, Jeff noticed a group of chairs filled by men sitting with no table in front of them, without drinks. Turning back, Pick was motioning to the waitress with a large circling of his finger, some sort of sign that she nodded at, turning away. Putting his arm around Jeff's shoulder, "Well brothah what do you think, huh?" Turning around to the table, Jeff was surprised that all the chairs at the table were suddenly filled, Pick pointing around the table rattling off names which replied with wide smiles directed to Jeff, a couple hands reaching across the table to shake Jeff's hand, Jeff just nodding as Pick continued the introductions, though with all the loud voices and music he couldn't hear a single name.

Soon the waitress walked up with a tray full of Budweisers, distributing them around the table, leaning over to Jeff matter of fact, "Eight dollars." Jeff reaching into his pocket pulling out a ten, she turned, walked away without a word.

"Remember what I said, brothah," Pick patting Jeff's shoulder in a friendly way, "Tip good. Two dollars won't make it, that'll make her slow to serve us, okay?"

Jeff laughing to himself. Ah, yes, *the Mark*.

Looking around the room, the walls were painted dark blue. There were stars painted onto the ceiling, on the back wall there was a cartoon magician ten-feet tall pulling a cartoon rabbit out of a cartoon hat. Jeff laughing out loud poking Pick pointing to the back wall, "So we did see a rabbit coming out of a hat!" Pick nodding, laughing out loud together.

Gazing around the room he noticed a wall filled with bottles on the right-front side of the room tucked into a small space maybe fifteen feet across. There were no chairs at the bar so he assumed it was the service bar for the waitresses. Suddenly he saw a door open

on the left side wall behind the bar. Two large black men came
through the bar, pushing through a swinging half-door from behind
the bar into the room followed by a smaller man, looked Puerto
Rican maybe, shorter than Jeff, wearing a white suit and very wide-
brimmed white fedora. The look reminded him of the *Panama look*
when he was a kid. The three huddled together with the man in white
holding a piece of paper which he read from, pointing generally
across the room at the men sitting on the chairs with no table. One of
the men next to him nodded, taking the paper from Panama Hat,
walking over to the men with no table, leaning to talk to the men
huddling in to listen. When Jeff next looked, the men were gone
leaving the row of chairs empty.

Soon the loud thumping music started up as another black dancer
came out onto the stage, the whole process repeating again. Pick
kept yelling at Jeff to throw money up onto the stage. Jeff
reluctantly, carefully pulled out the wad from his pocket holding it
under the table counting out ten ones. He waited a minute, the music
thumped on. Finally when the stripper was completely naked he
threw five ones, one at a time, onto the stage.

Pick gave Jeff a thumbs-up turning his attention back to the stage.

Jeff laughing to himself that he got all that change at the colorful
circles bar without a clue why he did that. Smiling realizing it must
have been a premonition that he would end up here!

Soon the music faded as another thumpy song came on without
the break they had last time, "NOW FOR A REAL TREAT
GENTLEMEN! MAGIC TOWN GIVES YOU A RARE RARE
TREAT! WELCOME OUR LOVELY SHONNA WHO TONIGHT
IS HER VERY FIRST TIME ON STAGE!"

Jeff was turned away when Pick poked at him pointing to the
stage. Turning around Jeff didn't see a black dancer, instead there
was the most stunning white woman pushing through the curtain at
the back of the room. Blond puffy hair, trim figure, wearing a bikini
bathing suit including the top. She seemed nervous, having trouble
finding the rhythm of the music strutting across the runway in tall
high heels, leaning over shaking her covered breasts over Jeff's
table, looking intently at Jeff. Jeff staring blankly up at her,

fascinated as she leaned over again as though trying to say something to him with her body, with her movements. Keeping her eyes on him as she walked across the stage, scrutinizing him, her expression as though she was trying to say something to him.

The place went wild!

If Jeff thought it was loud before, now his hearing was inundated, his ears stuffed with big wads of sound fuzz being jammed pulsing into his ears. He was trying to watch her feeling a little embarrassed, suddenly becoming even more self-conscious about being the only white man in the room. A hundred-fifty screaming black men, only him and the dancer. Two flames glowing in the room of dark faces.

Pick yelled something.

"WHAT?" yelling back at Pick.

Pick leaned in, "I SAID YOU'RE THE WHITE GUY, GET HER TO TAKE HER CLOTHES OFF!"

"WHY ME?"

"SHE'LL LISTEN TO YOU! ESPECIALLY YOU!" Jeff feeling a dozen hands pushing him up to the runway. Walking around the table to the end of the runway; the dancer strutting up to him leaning over.

"WHAT ARE YOU DOING HERE!" she screamed.

"THEY WANT YOUR CLOTHES OFF!" handing her a ten dollar bill.

"WHAT ARE YOU DOING HERE!"

"THEY SENT ME UP HERE TO TELL YOU TO TAKE YOUR CLOTHES OFF!" Handing her another ten. Turning away from him, in an instant pulling off her top, flinging it toward the curtain at the back of the stage, spinning around with a jerk facing Jeff, her body swaying to the music. Jeff spellbound by her breasts in front of him, medium sized, small even that more jiggled than swung like the last dancers. She took Jeff's two tens sticking them in her bikini bottom being careful that the bills would show.

There was a loud, "BOOOOOOO" from the crowd directed at Jeff as he came back around to the table.

"JESUS, NOW YOU DONE IT!" screamed Pick. Jeff shrugging. "THESE GUYS DON'T WANT TO GIVE 'EM TENS! WHAT

THE HELL ARE YOU DOING UP THERE?"

"YOU TOLD ME TO BE GENEROUS!"

"BUT NOT BIG BILLS FOR THE DANCERS YOU IDIOT!"

Jeff looking helplessly around him, men signaling him with thumbs down, hands cupped over mouths shouting sporadic boos, faces yelling at him but he heard no words over the music and noise. Figuring he had to do something to get these guys back on his side he impulsively reached into his pocket pulling out a handful of five-dollar bills throwing them onto the table. Hands rushing into the pile snatching the money as men stood up reaching to stuff them into Shonna's bikini bottom. Jeff was sure that at least a few of them made it into her bikini though he saw a few disappearing into pockets. Pick gave a big smile with a thumbs-up motioning Jeff to do more.

Jeff stood up with a twenty dollar bill in his hand raised for everyone to see as the room erupted into a chorus of, "OFF OFF OFF OFF!" Jeff walking around to the head of the runway, the music thumping on, men screaming.

Shonna walking over to Jeff, leaning down yelling just loud enough for him to hear, "YOU'RE GOING TO SCREW THIS UP! COME SEE ME AFTER!" Leaning way over grabbing Jeff's twenty with her teeth, standing snatching the money stuffed into her bikini bottom, pulling at the strings on each side of her bikini as it fell away raising the money and bikini bottom over her head like a grand prize. Instantly there was a shower of one dollar bills with a couple fives from Jeff's table raining onto the stage.

Someone yelled out, "SHE'S NOT A BLOND!" the men howling in laughter, Jeff looking at Shonna's dark pubic hairs just above his face, laughing just as loud.

"LET'S GIVE SHONNA A BIG HAND GENTLEMEN—THIS WAS HER FIRST TIME ON STAGE AND YOU NEED TO BE GENEROUS SO WE CAN HAVE HER BACK!" followed by a final sprinkle of ones which were quickly swept up by the exiting Shonna though not quite with the finesse of the other dancers, the music went down, the lights coming back up.

"FIVE MINUTES GENTS, BE RIGHT BACK!"

By now the waitress was returning regularly bringing three more trays of drinks. Jeff making sure to send her away with five extra dollars each time. Feeling a wave of tired coming over him looking down at his watch surprised that it was nearly eleven-thirty.

Jeff felt a firm tap on his shoulder, turning around to see the tall doorman standing over him, "Your presence is wanted in front of the dressing room."

"Dressing room?"

Pick chimed in, "I bet it's the white girl! Man somebody is gonna get lucky tonight!" The men around the table howling with delight that the white guy was going to get the white woman tonight!

Jeff looking around for help from anyone, back at the doorman, "Dressing room?" enthusiastic hands pushing him to his feet again with a big cheer. Getting to his feet walking across the room following the doorman through the black curtain, into the short dark hall toward the entrance, light appearing to the right of the front door as the doorman pushed open a door pointing through it down a stairway. "Go down and wait in front of the dressing room," turning pushing past Jeff back through the black curtain. Jeff peered down the stairs, gingerly making his way down.

At the bottom there was a corridor to the right, two blue plastic chairs in front of a door with a big cardboard gold star taped to a door on the left, a hallway with chipped lime green walls lit by two bare bulbs hanging from the ceiling. It was during a break in the bar, the music was low so it could barely be heard down here.

Stepping down the hall he noticed a tall black man standing in front of a door at the other end, pistol strapped to his right side guarding the door there, Jeff trying to nod to the guard but getting no response from the guard who stood looking stony faced forward.

Moving forward sitting in one of the blue plastic chairs in front of the big gold star, Jeff sitting facing it. Glancing at the man at the other end of the hallway, wondering why he didn't take a load off, just sit in the chair right next to him. Jeff looking at the holstered gun beneath the vacant stare, a tinge of fierce scowl. His eyes staring over Jeff's head not once looking down to him.

Soon the loud music upstairs started up again. Jeff could hear the

THUMP THUMP THUMP THUMP faintly through the ceiling, the men starting up their yelling. He could hear the sound of the announcer's voice, couldn't distinguish the words which was not surprising seeing as he could barely understand them when he was in the bar with the loud music, all the men yelling.

He waited nearly ten minutes before the door with the star finally opened. Shonna the dancer came out dressed in a red oriental design dressing gown without the bright blond wig she wore while dancing. She was even more beautiful up close, her hair was actually a light auburn, no, not really auburn. It reminded him of the dining room set in his aunt's house, the color of light mahogany wood. Her hair was long flowing down over her shoulders, though it was well tended. It flashed in his mind to wonder if her hair was colored, but he remembered he had just seen her naked, that all the evidence pointed to this being her natural hair color.

It didn't matter because the effect was stunning.

Her face was still flushed from her dancing. Jeff felt intimidated. He couldn't tell her height, she was still wearing high heals, her complexion had a bit of an Irish flush that borrowed tone from her hair. She was a beautiful woman. What is it about beautiful women that he always found so intimidating? He guessed that every man must feel that way, especially when the woman is tall. He couldn't really tell how tall she was in those shoes. That didn't matter. He still felt intimidated.

He remembered junior high school, his fascination with Amazon Women. His junior high school hosted a guest teacher who he later came to realize was a feminist before the word had even been invented. Maybe even a lesbian, of course he didn't know anything about that back then either. She taught about Goddess worship of the pagan religions, about the women of Lesbos and the Amazon women. The Amazon women were incredibly fascinating to him. He had spent many a night in his bedroom playing with himself imagining that he had been kidnapped by a tribe of them, a hundred tall buxomly Amazons, where he was required to constantly give them sexual favors. And of course in his adolescent mind's eye he could do so relentlessly until they were all laying fainted upon the ground from utter exhaustion, all from his enormous sexual prowess.

But here was the real thing!

He gulped.

Beautiful.

Scowling.

She stepped straight through the door with the big gold star. Without a word standing in front of him, examining him intently. Pulling the blue plastic chair next to him around sitting backward in it facing him, her exposed thighs sticking out around the chair's back sitting looking straight into Jeff's face. They could hear the thumping music, the faint racket of men yelling through the ceiling.

She studied his face closely, tilting her head, looking at every detail, his dark curly hair, his ears, his hazel eyes, looking carefully at his chin. "My god," her expression got so stern Jeff pulled back, "you're not him, are you?"

"Who?" Jeff felt uneasy as she stared intently at him.

"You're not him." Shaking her head. "Jesus, you could be his goddam perfect twin brother, but you're not him. What are you doing here?" Her expression darkening even more. "Who are you?"

"Name's Jeff, who are you?"

"Why are you here?"

"I don't know. I just kind of followed this guy Pick over here from the Underground. I thought that Magic Town was, you know, where they pull rabbits out of hats."

Glowering at him, standing with a piercing scowl. "You're kidding right? I mean what kind of con-man black guy named Pick brings you to a rabbit hat place on the shitty side of Atlanta?" Looking at him with a disgusted glare, "What? Were you born yesterday?"

"Look, I'm just a business man, a tourist that hooked up with this guy. He brought me here. You know, a mini-vacation. And I think I was having an okay time until you came out on that stage." Looking up to her Jeff returning her intent look. "So what's the deal with you? What kind of nice white chick ends up showing off her ass in a place like this?"

Turning away for a second, back again. "I shouldn't even be talking to you." Turning again, looking at a big chip in the wall in front of her keenly for a few seconds, tilting her head slightly, sitting down again, shifting in the chair as though something just occurred to her. Looking back at Jeff, the corners of her mouth curling into a half-smile as though she was working something over in her head. Jeff staring at her beautiful full mouth with the slightest curl of a smile. Yes, she was pondering something. They sat there for what felt like minutes, total silence except for the dull thumping coming from overhead.

Jeff looking at her face, perfectly shaped, a perfect compliment to her body which was on the thin side with just the right shapeliness. She had fine features, eyelids that hung nearly to the black circle of her retinas that were so focused on him at that moment. Bedroom eyes. He sighed, he was a total sucker for a woman with bedroom eyes. He loved women with eyelids showing; total bedroom eyes.

She had a strong chin though it didn't protrude. Or maybe that was because of the expression she was giving him now. There was no question of her perfectly shaped face that so wonderfully matched her perfectly shaped body. Trying to look beyond her intent expression, he could see a really beautiful woman in front of him inspecting every detail of his face at that very moment. Lines surrounding each side of her smile like they were protecting a sweet secret between them. Sweet parenthesis holding a special secret.

Her face suddenly softening, the corners of her mouth curling into a small smile, "Yes, this is good. This could be very good. Look, I'm sorry, I didn't really mean anything. You know, what I said before." She half-reaching out to him with her left hand but didn't touch him, giving him a little more smile. "I'm a student. Studying business at Brown University. Everyone tells me that the girls can make a lot of money on the stage. Hell, I made nearly a hundred dollars in one dance!"

"Yeah, but fifty probably came from me, maybe more."

Her smile broadening into thankfulness, nodding. "The guys have been trying to get me to do this for months. Okay, maybe I won't get rich, but I'm warning you…you need to know…look, this can be a really dangerous place, these can be really dangerous people. Nice white guys shouldn't be hanging out around here. You shouldn't have come here."

"Well, I'm here." Jeff glancing at his watch. "It's nearly midnight and I probably won't be able to get a train back to my hotel, so what do I do?"

Shonna put her finger to her mouth thoughtfully sighing.

"Your name's Shonna?"

"Yes, with an O and two N's."

"Really, I've never heard it spelled like that."

Jeff suddenly noticing her eyes, at first he could not figure out what was so unusual. Her eyes were a bright gold, almost as though they had started out to become green but just somehow could not manage such an ordinary color. Tiny little flecks of black swam in the golden color of her eyes, sprinkled in surrounding the dark irises that were so intently focused on his eyes at that second. He heard words coming from her but just could not discern those sounds emanating from under those fascinating eyes. The tone of her words kept wanting to express that he was in some kind of trouble, danger even, but those eyes calling to him in another voice, telling him not to see but to gaze, not to hear but to sense. Feeling numb looking into those eyes that spoke to him as plainly as any words he ever heard, but in a language he could not understand. A language he so desperately wanted to understand at that moment.

Slowly starting to hear words again, her eyes finally let loose of their spell allowing sounds to find his ears again. Shonna giving another soft sigh. "I don't know. I suppose you could hang out with us, but I'm warning you this is a really tough bunch. You've got Pick. Chances are he can protect you okay." Sighing. "And I suppose I have no choice."

Cocking his head words were finally processing inside his head, now making sense of those words suddenly frightening him. "Protect me? What are we talking about? I mean, how bad can it be?" Shaking his head trying to make sense of her words, "I mean these are just a bunch of guys having a good time, right?" Now the words of warning from the shuttle driver and his mother rang in his ears. Loudly. He tried to think quickly how he had gone from a little evening out in the Underground to now sitting in this scary hallway with a man wearing a gun on one end, this golden-eyed Amazon in front of him, a room full of guys upstairs that would probably rob and kill him as soon as look at him.

How the hell did this happen?

Feeling a quick rush of panic, deliberately making a voice occur in his head telling him to calm down.

Or flee.

I've been in fixes before, right?

Calm down. Stay calm. Look cool.

Looking at her gown smiling to himself at the black pagoda figures set in the red with little yellow-faced characters with hands together bowing to each other.

Smiling again speaking softly, "Look, you seem like a nice guy who just got to the wrong place. There's no way you're going to get a cab from here and there's no way you can go walking out of the club alone. And I'm sure the trains are stopped anyway."

Jeff didn't even bother to look at his watch, he knew she was right. Waiting, watching her closely, waiting resolution of his mess here.

"You're stuck here. Well, at least you have me and Pick." Looking to him again, slowly, back to examining every feature of his face. "Stand up."

Raising his eyebrows Jeff stood up anyway, turning around as she signaled him with a swirling motion of her fingers.

Putting her finger to her right cheek, "Hmmmm, maybe just a little taller. What are you, about five-ten or so?" He nodded. "Me too," smiling, "it's okay, that's a good height."

"And what about you?" sitting down, "I thought you were a new dancer here and that made me think nobody knows you."

"I told you that I'm a business student, right?" He nodded. "Seems I've got a knack with numbers." Pausing, thinking for a second, "Look, you look like I can trust you. You don't look like the kind of guy who's going to conk me on the head." Considering for a second, "I work part time keeping the books for this place. I spend all my time locked in that room down there," pointing to the guarded door down the hall. "Tonight was just a way to get more people to know who I am. Kind of showing off." Laughing sitting back. "I spend all my time in that room down there or up in the office with the club owner. I wanted to get out, maybe have a little fun. It seemed kind of sexy to get up there to do what I did."

"Well, was it sexy? Was it what you thought?" he smiled wondering.

Pausing for a second with a half-smile. "Yeah, it was sexy. I mean, I've been to the nude beaches south of Savannah so I know what it's like to be naked in front of other people."

Jeff laughing, "Nude beaches in Georgia?"

An indignant smirk, "Hey, we're not all prudes in Georgia. But yes it was sexy, and I have to tell you that having you in the audience really helped!" Tilting his head in question. "I don't know, seeing you out there, I don't know, like being one of my peeps as they say, one of my people gave me a little more courage."

"And I suppose the tens and twenties helped too," he laughed.

A bashful smile. "No, I mean that you have a sense of dignity about you that none of those cats do. You made me feel like I was giving a show, not just stripping my clothes off." Shrugging, "Does that make sense?"

"Yeah, I don't know how, but it does make sense. I suppose I should say that I enjoyed seeing you up there, and well, you know that I was obviously at a strip club and must have come to see naked women." Grinning, "But I really did think Pick was bringing me to a rabbit hat place!" Both laughing, he could tell that she was finally feeling relaxed.

"Plus I wanted to find out about the money the girls get."

"So you're an accountant for this place? Wouldn't you know how much money they get?"

"I'm not *an accountant*. I am *the* accountant for this place. And no, the girls just take their tips."

"But I don't get it." Jeff shaking his head. "This place has to be rolling in dough, why wouldn't they just hire some professional bookkeeper. There must be stacks of cash in that room."

"Stacks, yeah that's sure a word for it." Continuing in an almost casual tone, "Let's just say that a bookkeeper would ask too many questions—they would probably not like the answers."

"Criminal?"

"That's a harsh word. Sometimes it's just not that black and white." Pausing. "So you're obviously some kind of businessman, where are you from, what do you do. Family? Kids?"

Jeff told her the statistics without mentioning his wife's *vacation*. She grew more concerned.

"Well, tell you what. We can't let anything happen to someone with so much responsibility! Jesus, though, I wish you weren't here." Pausing looking at him with a curled lip smile, "You know…" her voice trailing off. She deliberated, studying him more. Jeff could see an emerging look like something was occurring to her, that she was making up her mind about something. "Everything happens for a reason, I guess, and seeing as you are here," a wry smile that she tried not to show, "let's see what we can do with this."

A long silence. There were too many words in the jumble that he was hearing, like a big ball of yarn of loose words, lots of loose ends made of nouns and verbs hanging out, almost too many for him to catalog in his brain at this moment. Loose strings. Jeff starting to fidget.

Giving a quick smile, "Look, I get off in twenty minutes, at twelve-thirty. I've got a car out back. You need to go back up to your friends, buy them another round. Watch for me at twelve-thirty at the curtain, make all your worst excuses and meet me at the front door." Starting to get up looking at him sternly, "But don't go outside! It'll be really dangerous for you. Don't go outside!" disappearing through the door with the big gold star. Jeff guessing it was the dressing room, trying to look around her as she stepped back through just in case he might see other dancers in there. No such luck.

He went back up the stairs. Getting to the table it was the break again, there was only one other man sitting next to Pick. "Hey, my man! You owe the waitress for four more rounds," signaling to her, she turning toward them.

"That'll be thirty two dollars, sugar."

"Sugar?"

A big smile, "Hell yes sugar, you're the best tipper in the room!"

Jeff glancing down at Pick giving a shamed shrug and small sideways smile. Jeff turning back to the waitress, "How many rounds? Never mind, here's sixty dollars and bring us three more here, that should cover it, right?"

Quickly counting the money, "Oh, yes, Sugar, that will *definitely* cover it!" leaning over to Jeff with a quick kiss on the cheek. The whole room roaring up, "Woooooooo!" Jeff sitting down crimson faced.

Glancing over at the chairs that Panama Man had pointed to at the back of the room earlier, there were three different men there now; a door next to them. All this watching and yelling made Jeff thirsty, he drank two bottles of Bud that were stacked on the table in front of him, drinking them straight down, the waitress showing up with three more. Glancing at his watch seeing the stroke of twelve-thirty. Leaning over to Pick, "Hey, man, gotta go. It's late and I gotta get back to my hotel."

"How you gonna do that? No way a cab's coming to this side of town this time of night."

"I got a ride."

Pick giving a big grin, "A ride, huh? Any chance a white woman is your chauffeur?"

"Come on my man, a guy's gotta be discrete, right?"

"Yeah, whatever you say brothuh, but I'll probably catch up to you later anyway."

Jeff wondering at Pick's words he stood up glancing toward the door seeing Shonna standing at the curtain. "Okay, man, gotta go, thanks for everything," waving around the room vaguely at the nods, smiles, hands raised in goodbye.

The man sitting next to Pick looking over to him, Jeff walking away, "Hey, where's he going?"

Pick giving a big smile waving after Jeff.

"The white woman, where else?"

Saturday, 12:48 AM: The House

Pushing his way around tables to the curtained door, starting to push through the curtain, the bouncer stepping in front of him, "Where you goin'? You caint go out there. Yo driver out there?"

Looking up at the black face towering over him, "Out. Back home. I don't have a driver."

"What, did he leave? Dey's no cabs out there, white boy could get himself hurt out there," scowling, "even you!"

"Wait, yes, I do have a driver!" looking up at the face towering over him, "I do have a ride!"

The bouncer pulling back the curtain a bit, glancing through, getting a signal Jeff couldn't see, shrugging, stepping aside, pulling the curtain back, Jeff walking through with a thanks.

The curtain falling back. Jeff standing in the darkness of the short hallway, the music coming up again THUMP THUMP THUMP THUMP, the chorus of men's shouts rising, definitely fewer voices than before. Jeff standing in the dark of the short hall between the front door and black curtain with just the outline of swirling lights around the black curtain behind him, almost total darkness toward the front door with the side door to the right going downstairs closed in the darkness. Remembering Shonna's words not to go outside he could feel trapped if he cared to. Somehow he didn't feel trapped. Just kind of numb. Waiting.

He was surprised at how sober he felt given how much he'd drank tonight. Shonna's words shouted down from the runway came back to him, something about not screwing this up, how she wished he wasn't here. Wonder what that all means? *And who do people keep thinking I am?* And what was that from the bouncer, congressman? Shrugging it off as just something that came out of all the craziness in that god awful loud room with all those drunken men shouting, banging on tables, the alcohol-sloshed high spirits. Smiling to himself, nothing like beer and naked women to get a rise out of a room full of men!

Suddenly two men burst through the front door, Jeff feeling a rush of cool outside air gushing into the stuffy short corridor. The door closing behind them, wordlessly pushing past Jeff to the curtain pulled back, twirling lights flooding into the small corridor. Even though they were both black, Jeff noticed a tattoo, a kind of twisted up snake on a right arm reflecting the light coming from the bar, gone as the curtain fell.

Hearing a voice, Shonna's silhouette in a doorway to the left he hadn't noticed before signaling to him. Stepping left into a dimly lit hallway, Shonna waving him to follow her. They walked about thirty steps, turning left facing a long, dim hallway. Passing a closed door on the left with light around the edges, Jeff hearing faint laughter through the door, thumping music still be heard ever so faintly, so much much quieter. Continuing for what seemed like another fifty steps they turned left again, went another thirty steps, on the right seeing Shonna open a door. Jeff feeling the night's coolness rushing into the stifling corridor.

Stepping through the door emerging into the darkness, the night air feeling so good on his face coming out of the airless smoke-filled building, some kind of back parking lot, a couple flood lights on the building shining down. Looking up, seeing two stars in the sky barely poking through the city lights. There was a group of men on the far side huddled together in the darkness, one glancing over, turning back to the group. Jeff following Shonna winding through the cars until she went around the side of a Mustang, waving him to the passenger side, sidling around the dark blue car opening the door.

Settling into the seat, Jeff automatically reaching for the seatbelt, latching it; Shonna laughing quietly at this fastidious man, didn't say anything, starting the car. Without a word, pulling out of the parking lot, taking a left heading through isles of tall dark warehouses. Soon they were driving through low houses with cars parked everywhere, everything crowded together. Even at this late hour there were people walking around or sitting on front porches or standing huddled in groups in the darkness occasionally turning to look as they passed.

"Did you tell anyone where you're staying?"

Jeff was startled by her voice. Thinking, saying he was sure he hadn't.

"Good, they won't know how to find you."

"Find me?"

Shonna didn't answer, soon the car slowed, turning right into a driveway that was blocked with cars. She slowly navigated around a car in the driveway steering up onto the lawn. Jeff looking out seeing there was no lawn, just a dirt patch in front of the house. Looking at the house, a tiny white building, light coming around drawn curtains, no porch light.

Seeing her look at the light in the window frowning, shaking her head.

"You live here?"

Laughing, "Yeah, if you can call this living. Pretty small, huh?" Jeff nodding with a frown. "You probably live in some big house with lots of sunshine and picket fences. I tell people my house is so small you can see all four sides at once."

Jeff laughing, "That's funny!"

"Yeah, well you gotta have a sense of humor when you live someplace like this. Best part is there is me and two whole families living here. I'm the only one with a room to myself."

"Really? Whole families live in one bedroom?"

"Yeah, our little three-bedroom one-bath paradise. Eleven people." Jeff didn't answer looking around him, for the first time seriously starting to regret how the evening had progressed.

The car engine stopped. Shonna stepping out. "Okay, we're going in, but don't say a word unless I tell you." Jeff nodding, his attention fixed on the house. "Hope you like the couch, but don't get used to it, you'll be up in a few hours."

Jeff getting out of the car following Shonna to the front door, looking down at the old rain-stained couch and ripped stuffed chair to the right of the front door facing the street. She opened the front door to the sound of voices, a small chorus of greetings, signaling Jeff to follow. Walking into the room there was sudden silence, all eyes on him as he stepped uncomfortably into the room dimly lit with a single shaded lamp sitting on an end table with a broken leg, propped against the faded red couch for support, a second lamp hanging above a small table with four people sitting around it, all staring at him.

Shonna shaking her head at them, "I know what you're thinking, but it's not him." Pulling up another mismatched chair, the others opening their circle, Shonna stepping over sitting down, pointing Jeff to the couch which he stepped over to, flopping down, a small cloud of dust puffing up tickling his nose.

All faces still turned toward him, Shonna smiling, "Something, huh? Whoda thought. Fell right into our laps."

Soon the faces turned across the table, a quiet discussion ensuing.

The tiny room could have only be five paces across each way, a filthy stove covered with dirty pots and pans, a small refrigerator covered with children's drawings, school photographs of small black faces peering into the dim room. There was a small hallway at the back of the room on Jeff's right with four doors, three closed, an open bathroom door.

With voices so low Jeff couldn't hear a word, the group huddling talking softly. Every so often one glancing over at Jeff as though he was somehow part of their conversation. Feeling uneasy, listening intently, can't hear a word sitting there, suddenly feeling a wave of tired washing over him. Starting to close his eyes, getting up going into the bathroom, too many beers. The bathroom was disgusting with rust stains in the sink, towels piled on the floor, a toilet looking like it hadn't been cleaned in a hundred years, feeling uneasy even about peeing into it fearing that something might climb up the stream to infect him with god knows what. At least it flushed.

Stepping back out into the living room, sitting back down on the couch leaning his head back. Out like a light.

A loud laugh made Jeff jerk up his head. Looking around for a second trying to remember where he was, Pick's face hovering in front of his eyes, Jeff pulling back, "Pick!" The room bursting into laughter, Jeff's startled expression making them laugh another round. "Wow, Pick! What are you doing here?"

"I told you I'd catch up with you later!" Jeff shaking his head trying to wake up, looking at his watch, glinting in the darkness to see a few minutes after three thinking to himself, "A couple hours sleep."

"Man, Pick. What are you doing here?"

Pick laughing, "The question is, what are *you* doing here?"

"I followed Shonna, or rather…Shonna drove me here."

Pick signaled Jeff to move over, flopping down on the low couch next to Jeff in a puff of dust, Jeff sneezing. "Bless you, brothah." Waiting for Jeff to stop sniffling, "Well, remember I promised you an interesting evening." The words ringing in Jeff's ears; it seems that lots of people promised him an interesting evening. "Why didn't you leave like a nice white boy and go back to your hotel?"

Jeff paused, reaching for a reason. Any reason. There was no reason. "Well, I was having fun and just kind of missed the chance to leave, and then Shonna drove me here." Rubbing his eyes smacking his lips trying to get the taste of stale beer out of his mouth, "I just kind of ended up here."

Pick chuckled smiling, turning to see waving from the table, standing to go over to the group at the table. Jeff flopping back against the couch. He recalled hearing the word "tomorrow" drifting off again.

"Hey, wake up!" Startling Jeff again, looking up at Shonna, the room quiet, empty behind her. Glancing at his watch, after four-thirty.

"What's going on?"

"We need to go pay someone a visit, we've got to go now." Shonna reaching down pulling on Jeff's left arm, "Come on, sleepy man, time to wake up, we gotta go now."

Standing, stretching, yawning following Shonna out the door. A minute later in the blue Mustang again driving through streets crowded with cars, deserted of people, all the houses now dark. Not a soul to be seen.

"Where are we going?"

"To talk a little sense into someone, but first to get some coffee."

Jeff frowning. "What's going on here, why are you taking me along with you? I mean, in a couple hours I could probably find a cab back to my hotel."

Shonna glancing at Jeff driving silently, Jeff seeing her choosing words carefully. "Look, your coming along like you did…we didn't plan it like this, but you came along…" Pausing, paying attention to turning left with only one car on the street passing as she turned. "Let me ask you a question."

Jeff sat silent.

"Have you ever been in trouble, like you got yourself in over your head and you're not sure what to do?"

"I'm kind of there now."

Shonna chuckling, "Okay, fair enough, but you can make it back to your hotel and fly back to wherever and it be all done, right? But let's say you were somebody else and you got *really involved* in something that was *really* over your head and you felt like you were stuck."

Looking toward her driving, "You mean hypothetically."

"Yes, hypothetically."

"Is this something I did or something that happened to me?"

"Let's say it was something you did to start, but then things happened that made it really complicated and started getting all sorts of people involved and some of those people are not very nice." Glancing at him. "Anything like that?"

Looking off to the high rises of downtown Atlanta in the distance lit up, Jeff trying to think what she was saying. "No, my life's not really that complicated."

"Well, sometimes people do get themselves into complicated things. When that happens, sometimes they just need someone to talk a little sense into them."

Puckering his brow in the dark. "Sense?" looking around trying to figure out where they were. "Okay, so someone needs to have some sense talked into them. But why do I have to come along?"

"Because you're the one who is going to be doing the talking."

Saturday, 5:08 AM: Bernice and the Diner

Soon the buildings were getting taller, occasionally Jeff could see the high-rises of downtown Atlanta lit up, getting just a little closer. The car pulled to a curb in a seedy neighborhood with taller buildings, Jeff figuring they were still south of downtown. Without a word, Shonna got out of her car, Jeff doing the same. She pointed across the street to a tiny little coffee shop, the only lighted-up building along the darkened street.

"Why here?" peering around the dismal scene crossing the street.

"It's either here or a Waffle House. And there's way too many eyes in those places."

Shrugging, following her across the street pushing through the door, straight back to the farthest corner booth away from windows. There was one man, looking homeless with his big stuffed plastic bag on the bench seat next to him, a half-empty coffee cup in front of him, head back, snoring. The entire rest of the room was empty, nobody behind the counter.

Shonna sliding into a booth, Jeff sliding into the opposite side along the pink plastic-covered bench seat trying to move over a big rip near the end, stuffing bulging out. Shonna taking a napkin from the dispenser sweeping a dried spaghetti noodle onto the floor.

Jeff looked up at the bright florescent lights, the translucent cover of one hanging down over the cash register, the bare blue-white light bathing the cash register like some religious icon at the Vatican. A row of swivel chairs turned every which way in the same bright pink upholstery lined up in front of the lunch counter. The walls gray, stained by old cigarette smoke, the floors of black linoleum tiles with wiggles of gray lines, tiles missing. The whole room had a dingy worn-out look.

Depressing.

"So, are you in the game?"

Jeff doing a double take, "What?" Leaning forward. "What game?"

"Look, there's no way I know you from Moses, but something tells me we can trust you, and nobody knows who you are." Pausing with a deep sigh. "Look, I can't tell you everything, but we have a situation that needs your help."

"But why me?" No answer.

Looking around Jeff wishing he had a cup of coffee to hold, that soothing hot black liquid that helps the start of a day feel more cohesive. "Can we get some coffee?"

Cupping her hands around her mouth shouting to the kitchen window, "Bernice!" In a few seconds a rotund black woman in a white apron and hair net pushed through the aluminum swinging doors from the kitchen waddling up to the table holding a coffee pot in one hand, two cups in the other. Jeff smiling at her movements which were actually quicker than he thought she could do given her girth.

"Okay, okay, Shonna, coffee for you and the gennleman, ah sees ya." Setting the two cups down with a bang, filling the cups with the pot never getting within two feet of the table, all without spilling a drop, turning without another word pushing back through into the kitchen with her wide stride, the dented silver-painted metal doors swinging behind her.

Carefully sipping the steaming black liquid, looking to Shonna. "Thanks. Better."

"Okay, then?" Jeff nodding, sipping again. "It's gonna be light here soon. We have to do a little stakeout, then we are going to find someone that we need to find, have a little talk with him, and you are going to have to be somebody you are not." Seeing the puzzled expression on Jeff's face.

He suddenly noticed that she has a kind of lisp when she speaks. Not really a lisp, just the slightest touch of her tongue to her teeth. It was so light, barely audible, giving her voice a certain character that he didn't notice before. He had already thought that her voice had no distinct traits, certainly not a voice that you would pick out in a crowd. The lisp, or whatever it was suddenly catching his ear.

"Look, it's simple really." Bending her neck to look up into his face to catch his eye. "Are you listening? Look, there is a certain, let's call him a respectable citizen, who got himself into a certain situation, and now he can't get back out. Without help. The problem is that if his situation got out to the wrong people a lot of other people would probably get hurt." Looking at Jeff she could see he was trying to follow along. "And things could get nasty if it's not done right."

"What kind of nasty?"

"People could get hurt." Her eyes darting sideways as if in very quick thought, back intently into Jeff's eyes, "Killed."

"Now wait a minute, I'm not signing up to get killed!"

"No, no, there's no chance of that. There's only one little thing you have to do, you will be totally covered the whole time."

"Covered? You're not any little bookkeeper are you? Who the hell *are you?*"

"I can't tell you that." Pausing looking intently into Jeff's eyes. "Let's just say that I'm one of the good guys. And this particular gentleman we are talking about is also a good guy, at least we think." Pausing. "Or at least we hope." Shaking her head. "But okay, maybe he made some bad mistakes. But we are surrounded by some *really bad guys.*"

"Bad guys?"

"Yes, I told you that already. Really, really, bad guys. But not the kind of bad guys that go around shooting people."

"If they don't shoot, then what makes them so bad?"

"They shoot alright, but the bullets they use are extortion and blackmail." Leaning over the table looking into his eyes, "And those bullets can hurt worse than the other ones. Those bullets don't take away lives, those bullets *ruin lives.*"

"Extortion. Blackmail." Jeff saying those words almost to himself in a low voice, shaking his head sleepily, looking back to her, "But why me?"

"Because—" turning looking around her, standing up to reach back for a newspaper laying on the table behind her, straightening it out laying it in front of Jeff.

"Look at this picture," pointing to the picture he had seen in the newspaper rack at the train station through the dingy plastic that he couldn't see through. "This is why you!"

Staring at the picture in utter disbelief, "Wait, that's me!"

"No, it's not you, but it could be your goddamned twin brother!
Your hair's a little shorter, curlier maybe, that's all, but men don't
notice things like that. That would take a woman's eye." How true
Jeff thought. How true. A woman's eye. The eye for detail with the
detailed memory that not a man on earth possesses. Not even really
gay ones. He half-laughed at the thought of the thousands of times
that he and his wife would be out and about when she would make
some comment about someone they see when he realized that she
must be wearing glasses of a different color or something because
she could see details that were completely lost on him. Or when she
would get her hair cut or colored, two days later she would have to
say, "You didn't say anything about my hair, you like it?" He would
suddenly realize what a dope he is saying yeah that he had noticed,
that he forgot to say anything knowing damn well that she knew he
didn't notice. Oh, yes, the eye for detail that men just don't have a
single chromosome for.

Jeff suddenly snapping to, staring in amazement at the photo of
himself, of the congressman on the front page of the paper, reading
the caption below about the missing congressman. "So what—"

"So we have this little situation and we haven't been able to
figure it out and along comes a guy who is a spitting image of the
guy causing all these problems. Seemed too good to be true." Giving
Jeff her first genuinely big smile. "And a nice guy, too, who wants to
help us."

He was lulled by her smile, her voice, couldn't help it, "Help,
yeah..." looking into those golden eyes with the little black flecks
among the gold.

He was lulled.

He sat up snapping back to the moment again, "Wait, not so fast!
First, who is us? And what is this help you need? You need to tell
me what's going on!"

She held up her hands to quiet him down. "Look, not so loud. I
can't tell you everything. That's best for you, really, the less you
know..." her voice trailing off.

"The less I know?" Jeff looking intently at Shonna, bending
across the table trying to get eye contact. She looked up as he hissed,

"The less I know, yes?"

Shonna sat intently, pondering the situation, mulling what to say next.

"Okay, here's the deal. You are a spitting image of this congressman, Frank Schedz, and he has a certain habit of wandering off for a few days, sometimes weeks, without anyone knowing where he is. People think it's all harmless, that he has a mistress or something like that. But the fact is that he has gotten mixed up with some very bad people. All those days off from official business have been to get all mixed up in the local corruption here in Atlanta, with congressman trumps mayor and all that at play."

"Frank Schedz. He's the grandson of the donut king, Earl Schedz, right?" She gave him a half-frown. "He probably has tons of money. What's he doing with those very bad people?"

"He's trying to rip them off, and so far he is winning. But things are getting tight. He is about to get himself into a whole lot of serious trouble. Maybe even physical danger. And that's weird because the guys he's playing with don't usually work like that, but he is really pushing the limits. There's a lot of big names involved, mostly in local politics, but this city is known for that kind of stuff and so people don't take it too seriously. But this Frank congressman is getting reckless and careless and other law enforcement are beginning to think that maybe this is bigger than just some of the usual Atlanta hanky panky. For sure it *is* big. It may be *very big*."

"So where do you fit in?"

"Let's just say that I carry a badge, but you don't know what flavor."

Staring intently into her eyes. "So you've been keeping the books in the middle of all this. You infiltrated their organization, right? How did you pull that off?"

"It's amazing what happens when you play the dumb blond," pulling a strand of her hair around with her fingers in front of her face to look at it, "or dishwater slightly redhead." Laughing. "But it doesn't matter. Those stupid idiots actually believe it!"

Sitting back smiling, "So let me see…Magic Town…the guy in the white Panama…missing congressman…the guys there in the corner and suddenly not there, then more guys again…henchmen, waiting for orders to go set a fire to a liquor store that hasn't paid up."

Looking for confirmation from Shonna, she nodded. This made sense from what little he'd seen. Continuing, "… and I'll bet we can throw in a little mayor and sprinkle it with a few city councilmen? And maybe the police for grins?" Jeff sitting back. "Graft!"

"What, do you read detective novels?"

Jeff smiling, "Big fan of Sherlock Holmes. Huge fan. Read everything ever written. Oh, and others, too. You know, Grisham and those guys."

"You may be pretty bright there, Jeffery my man, and you got some of the pieces, but graft is too a small word for this. We are talking corruption that will blow the lid off of the whole of northern Georgia."

"So you've been laying low, watching the books, and what, is Magic Town like in the middle of all this?"

"Let's just say that those stacks of money in that room don't hardly all come from beer, tits and ass."

"Payoffs of some kind. All cash, right?" Leaning back. "So I show up, looking like this guy so you guys start thinking that you can fix this all up somehow. With me?" Shonna nodding. "But where do I fit in?"

"We haven't exactly got it all figured out yet," standing up, "but let me see if I can find out what's cookin'." She walked to a pay phone hanging on the wall. Turning her back to Jeff she inserted a coin, pushing buttons on the phone. He heard her talking clearly, very quietly into the phone, barely able to pick up two words together. She hung up, making another call spending another ten minutes talking in the same quiet voice. That was followed by a third shorter call.

Jeff sat looking through the grimy windows seeing it still dark outside feeling a drowsy wave wash over him. Glancing at his watch, almost six.

Soon Shonna turned walking to the table, turning poking her head over the swinging doors to the kitchen calling Bernice again, returning to the table sitting down. A moment later Bernice came out to fill up each of their cups with her skillful pour from so high over the table, without a word turning back into the kitchen.

Lifting her cup with a determined smile, "Well, I guess you need to take first shift, so time to drink up."

"First shift?"

Shonna told him that they there were two possible places the congressman would be, that they were going to stake out the place that she liked best.

"So he's what, kidnapped?"

Laughing, "I doubt it. More likely that he's laying in some woman's bed with a very bad hangover about now. That man really does love his drink. We're going to go sit to watch a house where I believe he is. We've got to get hold of him before he leaves, then we'll have the little talk I told you about."

"Get hold of him?"

"Damn rights, we can't have two of him walking around!"

Saturday, 6:12 AM: The Stakeout

Reaching into her purse pulling out a five, Shonna tossing it onto the table. They walked through the door, crossing the dark street to the blue Mustang, Jeff walking around to the passenger door. Shonna opened the trunk pulling out a sport bag, walking to the driver's door, climbing in. Opening the bag, pulling out a pair of very long binoculars and a Nikon camera with the longest lens Jeff had ever seen.

"Tools of the trade," she smiled, turning to lay them on the back seat. Putting the key in the ignition, pulling away from the curb.

In only a few minutes the car was pulled over in a neighborhood a lot like the other they had been in earlier, nicer houses without cars parked helter-skelter, up on lawns, now with a few lights on in house windows.

"See that yellow house with the two lights on the porch way up there?" Jeff craning his neck forward trying to see which house she was talking about, nodding that he thought he knew the one. "Well here's the deal, you got a few Z's last night, so I need an hour. I doubt there will be any traffic yet, but here," reaching back, grabbing the binoculars handing them to Jeff, "keep an eye on that house, if anyone comes in or out, wake me. It'll be light before long. Wake me in an hour no matter what."

Jeff took the binoculars, inspecting them. He had never seen such a nice pair before, focus, zoom, very nice. Looking through them, that door with two lights over it looked like he could reach out and touch the doorknob. He instantly heard Shonna's even breathing, very impressed that she had managed to go to sleep so fast. He also knew she had been up all night. Or maybe two.

Watching that door intently for an hour, nothing happening.

Leaning forward looking up through the windshield watching great gray hands in the heavens slowly pulling the crescent moon back up into the lightening sky, daylight timidly touching the horizon with the slightest golden rim. He found himself looking at his watch every two minutes as the hour approached.

Finally, jostling Shonna who woke so fast she startled Jeff, "What, anything?"

Replying that nobody came or went, she turned the key to look at the car's clock, seven twenty.

Taking the binoculars from him, peering through them suddenly sitting up straight muttering to herself, "Good job, Nancy!"

"Nancy?"

"It's Shonna to you!" sly sideways smile. "Okay, Nancy, but it's Shonna and please don't blow it. If these guys think they've been infiltrated there'll be hell." Looking back at her with a wry grin. "I mean it! It's Shonna. I told you these guys can get dangerous. When you meet my team they will all be calling me Shonna. It's too damned easy to make the slip and it's too dangerous to let it happen."

"Nancy. Nice. That suits you." Giving him a glancing smile peering through her binoculars again.

"So what did you just see?"

"Mayor's chief aid just drove up. Yep, congressman's there. Got to be."

"Why don't you just go in and get him."

Grunting, "No thanks, nice way to get shot for sure. Any idea how many guns are in there?" Watching intently, silent.

Turning his head toward the house, could see nothing.

"So how involved are you in this case?"

"This case? It's *my case*."

"Your case?"

"Accidental, really," glancing at him.

"How is it *your case* accidentally?"

"I'm the one who found the first loose thread and just started following it." He listened, leaning toward her.

"I lived in Georgetown while I was in grad school."

"I thought you went to Brown."

"I did for my undergrad, did my masters at George Washington in DC. Lived in Georgetown, bit of a hustle to the university but what a great neighborhood."

"Georgetown? Isn't that a little pricey for a student?"

Smiling, "Yeah, funny how things work out. I took a room. An old woman, you wouldn't believe her name."

Jeff thought, smiling, "No, don't tell me!"

Laughing softly eyes still pressed to binoculars, "Yep, with an O and two N's." Jeff laughing thinking that spelling had to come from somewhere. "It's the Irish spelling of the name. Anyway, I lived there for two years. We became good friends. She was in her eighties, was declining pretty fast toward the end, couldn't leave the house. So I started doing little errands, pretty soon was doing all the errands, grocery shopping, that sort of thing. She had a part-time housekeeper who would come in and cook and do laundry, but I did the rest of the housekeeping, taking care of her. Changing shitty diapers, washing her." Reflecting. "It wasn't bad, really. It was good, it fit perfect with my school schedule. She was really nice to me, always interested in my studies. And she was so grateful for the care I gave her when her nobody else gave a damn."

Adjusting the binoculars keeping them pressed to her eyes. "Anyway, she died. It turns out she had no family, at least that she knew of. I never knew what that really meant, whether they didn't speak to each other or what, but nobody except a couple of old people who lived in the neighborhood ever came to visit. No Christmas cards or anything. Turns out she left me the house in her will."

"Wow, that doesn't happen every day. That was pretty lucky."

"Yeah lucky, a poor little grad student with a big house right in the middle of Georgetown. And a nice bit of money, too. Got to pay off my student loans with money left over. But it wasn't all a completely clean deal."

"Why, what happened?"

"About six months after everything was settled I get a call from a guy saying that he was her grandson who started asking all sorts of questions. Next thing I know I'm getting a letter from some attorney saying he was contesting the will."

"I guess you would have to expect something like that, right?"

"Yeah. At first I wasn't sure and started thinking that maybe he was right, that he should have something from his grandmother. Then the next phone call he started getting really jerky. Really hostile. So I got to thinking where was he on the holidays, where was this guy when I was emptying her bedpans and wiping her butt? The more I thought about it the madder I got." Pulling the binoculars from her face turning to Jeff. "I mean you don't know me very well, but when I think something is mine I go after it and I won't let anyone take anything from me! Nobody!"

"So what did you do?"

"I asked around the agency—"

Jeff held up his hand, "You keep saying agency. What agency?"

Laughing, "Right, I haven't told you have I?"

He shrugged.

"I work for the FBI."

Jeff laughing, "Okay, now this makes more sense." Pausing a second, "So sorry, tell me your story."

Smiling to him putting the binoculars back to her eyes turned toward the house. "So like I was saying, everyone told me that there is one rule in lawsuits: always make sure your attorney is better than theirs. So I got the name of one of those, you know, really high-powered attorneys you read about in the newspapers who was recommended by my boss's boss who told me to call this guy and mention his name. I just kind of held my breath because there was no way I could pay for a three-hundred-dollar an hour guy. So I told him about the situation, next thing I know I am getting copies of letters sent back and forth between him and the grandson's attorney, then nothing." Jeff watching her in anticipation.

"Finally I got my nerve up to call this attorney, ask him what happened, how much I owe him. He came on the line, said the other guy lost his nerve and didn't I read his letters? I said no, not really, so he told me to go look at the letters and I would see that we threatened to counter sue them. They went away. Well, I was really happy and all, but when I asked him how much I owe him he kind of laughed, said not to worry that it wasn't that much work, that he did it as a favor for my boss's boss. Seems his firm gets a lot of business from the agency."

Both laughing together, Jeff grinning, "Boy, so you were one really well-connected student and didn't even know it, huh? Did you ever go back to read the letters?"

Glancing at him eyes back to binoculars, "Yeah, and what made them go away was my attorney's threat to counter sue and to have the grandson charged with elder neglect! I mean how could this guy pop out of the middle of nowhere trying to get his hands on the estate when he never even bothered to send a Christmas card!"

"So that's what they meant when they said to get a better attorney!"

"I guess so, but it sure was good advice, huh?"

"How is it that someone your age was in graduate school? Isn't that the thing people do in their twenties?" Pulling the binoculars away enough to give him a sideways glance. "Not that you're not in your twenties!" Both laughing together as she squeezed the binoculars back to her face.

"Oh, I don't know, I just kept going in and out of school, each time not finding anything that really got my attention until I happened to take a criminal law class and, well, it just lit me up."

Glancing at him, "Isn't that what you did?" He frowned that she somehow knew this little factoid about him.

"So how does this all fit into this case?"

"Well, the congressman happened to have a house in Georgetown. It was on my walk to the university. A couple times I saw him as I was walking by. No big deal, you saw all sorts of government people on that side of town."

Pulling the binoculars down rubbing her eyes, holding them back up. "Anyway, I started to notice more and more, how would I say it," pausing in quick thought, "let's say non-Georgetown types more and more going in and out of his house. A few times I kept seeing the same black man, a big guy who seemed to go through cycles of hanging out at this congressman's house, so I got curious. I took the license plate of the car he was in one time, contacted the limo company, found out he was the mayor of Atlanta."

Jeff nodding, listening intently, "I was doing my internship at Department of Justice which gave me access to just about any kind of data that could help me figure out if anything was going on." Glancing at him, "I don't know. There was just some kind of gut feel that something wasn't right. So I started doing all the usual checks, you know, income, tax returns, bank accounts, property records, things like that, all the stuff I could get really easy." Shaking her head slowly, "It didn't add up." Jeff cocking his head listening. "I mean, how does a guy who makes eighty four thousand a year as mayor live in a three million dollar house, drive three Mercedes, and have a country club membership? This guy was rolling in dough."

"Well, I suppose…" Jeff pondering, though he really had no clue.

"And none of it come through his bank accounts?" Shaking her head just slightly, not to lose her gaze on the house.

"Anyway, I was just finishing school, took a position with the FBI, got too busy to do anything about it at first, I just kind of forgot about it for a year as I was getting my feet wet at the agency. So one day I happened to walk by his house and there's the mayor coming out of the congressman's house again. So I went to my chief, told him about it and what I had discovered before. I was expecting him to say thanks to watch him hand it to another agent, but instead he appointed me as a co-lead agent and hooked me up with an older colleague who decided this was going to be my case, used it more like a way to mentor me." Turning to him with a satisfied smile going back to her binoculars, "Soon my mentor just kind of backed out of the case and there I was, lead agent by default!"

"Wow, that's quite a story. So this is your case."

Glancing at him with a nod. "That was two years ago. I've been on this case since. I figured the congressman has been involved for four years, a year before I discovered it, the year while I let it be, and two years since. Maybe longer."

Watching this woman sitting next to him he couldn't see her captivating eyes. Looking at her he suddenly feeling a wave of deeper understanding of this woman, a warm flow over his body trickling over his head, through is hair like a warm shower onto his shoulders, washing down around his back as he felt a warm flush across his chest, feeling his face turning flush. He was glad she was looking into her binoculars and not at him that moment.

"So you said I am going to be doing some kind of talking sense into somebody."

Glancing sideways to him quickly, back to the binoculars. "Yes, I believe he's in that house, but we need to make sure he's alone. This is going to be a very serious talk."

"What am I supposed to be saying to this person?"

"Well, you're not exactly going to be doing the talking, more like delivering a message."

"What kind of message?"

"That it's time to straighten up and fly right. Look, don't worry about that right now, I'll fill you in when the time comes."

Sitting in quiet, Jeff squinting in the morning light to see the house. "Oh, good," she said softly, "sweet."

"Update?"

"No, false alarm, that's not who I thought." Keeping the binoculars clutched to her face. "So did Pick get you at the ATM next to Ricky Rocket's?"

"Why?"

"Good. He just walked back out of the house."

"Yeah, Rickey Rocket's. How did you know?"

"I swear every lonely white business guy must go to that ATM at least once in his life. You wouldn't believe the people he hauls to Magic Town."

Adjusting the binoculars, "But I wonder what he's doing there?"

Jeff got a hurt expression, "People, as in other guys? As in lots of them all meeting up with Pick at that ATM?"

"Yep."

"That's his routine?"

"Yep. Always the same. Let me guess, you bought him drinks and dinner, then followed him over to Magic Town and you spent how much there? I saw you spreading a lot of money around. He's the best pick pocket in Atlanta. How much money did he get from you?"

Jeff reached into his pocket pulling out twenty-two dollars doing a little arithmetic in his head, "Two hundred and something, maybe two hundred ten dollars."

Adjusting her binoculars again, "Who's that with him? Hmmmm. All that cash plus your credit card, drinks and dinner, tips of course, always really big tips, right?"

Staring at the money in his hand, "God, maybe three hundred dollars! He did it all with a smile! And I smiled the whole time too!" Chuckling to himself. "Well, I'll be damned, I am the best *Mark* in town, huh?"

"Yep. He's the best pick pocket in Atlanta. Not a police report in sight."

"Well, I'll be god damned. Three hundred dollars." Looking up at the car ceiling laughing out loud, "Pick!"

She laughed with the binoculars to her eyes. "Your common street mugger may get what, fifty bucks? A hundred? And a night in jail for all his trouble! Yep, Pick's definitely a star when it comes to his style of pick pocketing white guys standing at that ATM." Frowning with intent voice, "Well there they go, but who was that other guy?"

Jeff laughing again, "Does he work for your agency?"

"Nope, he's a free agent."

"But you pay him?"

"A few thousand. He is an extra set of ears and eyes for us, nothing strategic. But I trust him and he has given us some really good inside information. Plus," glancing away from her binoculars, "he keeps dragging all you businessmen to Magic Town and we end up with people like you!" They both laughed, Jeff suddenly realizing why him being the only white guy in the club didn't create any stir last night. Evidently it meant that Pick had just found another *Mark*. Smiling at this explanation for why all the chairs at his table at the front of the runway filled so quickly!

Shushing him adjusting the zoom on her binoculars. "What the hell are these guys all doing up so early? On a Saturday? There's something really big going on here." Putting down her binoculars, rubbing her eyes picking them up again, looking up and down the street. "Oh, Christ, please no."

"What," Jeff straining to look down the street, "what?"

"There's an unmarked up the block watching." She sighed. "Protection."

"Protecting what?"

"The mayor's assistant left. That must mean the mayor is in there, no other reason to have a watch. Don't worry, they are about to leave."

"Leave?"

"Yep, his honor is just coming out. Oh, god, the chief, too. Hand me the camera." Jeff reaching back handing it to Shonna, she set the binoculars in her lap. In less than a second the camera started clicking and whirring with the auto-winder, a dozen pictures. Silence. More clicking, whirring. "Jesus, what are all those guys doing there? What the hell is going on? What are they all doing here?"

"Who all?"

"The mayor, vice mayor, two, no, three council members, the police chief, two others, look like captains. God almighty, in uniforms even, arrogant pricks, what's wrong with these guys? Is there a party going on in there? Why are they standing at the curb like that? What are they waiting for?"

Watching intently. "Who the hell are *they?*"

"Who?"

Jeff pulled the binoculars from Shonna's lap holding them up to see two really big black men just coming out of the house, signaling to the mayor. "Smile boys," Shonna smirked as the camera clicked and whirred a few times.

"Wait, that tattoo!" Jeff adjusting the binoculars, "I saw him last night at the club!" He heard three clicks and whirs.

"The mayor's turning to get into his car," she said quietly.

She paused, "Finally Perkins! Damn I thought he abandoned us! Here he comes driving up. Where you been big guy? Out of the car." Long pause. "Good boy, Perk, wave to the nice mayor, grin, let them know you are there and you'll play babysitter. Good boy." Pause. "Waiting till they leave." Pause. "Good. Now go into the house, signal us what's going on, then come back out with your hands on your hips and we'll come have our little chat with the congressman."

"Who is Perkins?" Jeff glanced at his watch noting the time.

"The bouncer."

"The bouncer? You mean the big guy from Magic Town last

night? That guy?"

Still peering through the camera smiling, "You bet, he's our eyes and ears there. Doesn't miss a trick, has this like photographic memory for faces. He thought you were the congressman so that's why he put you up front."

"I thought I got up there because of my tip."

"Oh, I'm sure he was glad to keep your money, but no." Jeff remembering some of the things Perkins said to him, asking about his driver, remembering when he first came in and him saying *even for you, sir, even for you Congressman.*

"So this Perkins, is he a cop, too?"

"No, he works for the club. We manage to pay him on the side but he doesn't know anything about me, about Nancy, he thinks I'm just the *stupid blonde* bean counter, even though I am not even blond." Glancing to Jeff. "I mean you saw all the colors of my hairs, right?" Laughing out loud, Jeff laughing nervously. "I am sure he wants to get into my pants." Laughing, "Especially after last night!"

Jeff giving her a sideways glance that she could sense even with the camera to her eye. Yeah, he thought to himself watching her sitting next to him, *I'd like to get into your pants, too!* Leaning back just a bit he could picture her trim body that he'd seen last night at Magic Town, picture that beautiful body laying on some bed. Any bed. He put that image on his hotel bed, her coaxing him with curling fingers. Him standing there admiring her, undressing with her saying things like what a manly man he was, giving a little shriek seeing him naked, Jeff approaching the bed…

"Yeah, Perkins." Jeff snapping out of his daydream turning to her. "He's a good guy and he's so big people are afraid to screw with him. That helps everyone in the club, *especially* me. Really keeps a lid on things. I really go out of my way to help him out when he needs. Got him out of a couple messes."

Jeff could hear Shonna breathing heavily watching through the camera so intently. She was waiting for something to happen. Motioning to him with her right hand, "Open the glove compartment." In the glove compartment there was a police radio with a little red light zooming back and forth across the face.

"Why don't you guys use cellular phones?" He prided his Motorola *clam phone* the little four-inch square wonder that he carried. It was back in his suitcase because his company was getting all upset that his bill was running over nine hundred dollars a month. They were wanting him to refund his personal calls. The roaming charges were running up to two dollars a minute so he just figured out that pays for a lot of calling-card calls for a tenth of that.

Shonna frowning, "Cell phones are too unreliable. Can't take chances. Maybe when they get the network built out, but we can't take chances of no communication." He nodded, she was right. He recalled a long phone conversation he had once while driving around Los Angeles that was done in seven segments as he drove, the line kept cutting out. That one call cost twenty-eight dollars.

"Hand me the microphone," motioning holding out her right hand, taking it holding it to her mouth. Still looking into the camera clicking the side of the microphone, "Tom, you there?" There was an unintelligible crackling with a voice in there somewhere. Jeff couldn't make out a word. "Good, yeah, Perkins will give the signal in a second. Then we can go in to have that talk with our little man, assuming he's not passed out as usual."

Jeff assuming she was talking about the congressman, wasn't sure glancing at his watch again, nearly two minutes has passed since Perkins went in.

Leaning forward, pressing the camera to her eye, "What's taking him so long?" Another full minute passing, her breathing quickening. "Where is he? Where is he? What's taking so long?"

Giving a small sigh of relief, "Good, there he is."

Jeff glancing at the time again, three minutes passed since he went in.

"What's he doing? He's looking back into the door. He went back in again!"

Throwing the camera onto the back seat pulling the binoculars away from Jeff's face still holding the radio microphone. "Tom, here he comes out again, he's just coming out! But what's he doing, where's the signal?"

"He crossed his arms!" Clicking the mic she screamed, "OH,

GOD, CROSSED ARMS! CROSSED ARMS! WE GOT
TROUBLE! TOM! WE GOT TROUBLE! I'M GOING IN NOW!
WAIT FOR MY SIGNAL!"

"I'M GOING IN NOW!"

Saturday, 8:17 AM: What a Mess

Flinging the binoculars onto the back seat clanking against the camera starting the car flooring it a long trail of skid mark and smoke behind the car screaming toward the yellow house driving up over the curb onto the scrabbly lawn in front of the house careening sideways stopping three feet short of the building Shonna leaping from the car Jeff seeing a flash of Shonna running around the car pistol in right hand Jeff wondering where the hell she had a gun this whole time.

Timidly, Jeff opened the car door stepping out stretching. Walking up to the opened house door. Nobody in the small living room, a coffee table strewn with coffee cups. A sport coat across the back of the couch.

Suddenly Shonna screaming, "OH MY GOD! WHAT THE HELL IS THIS! PERKINS WHAT HAPPENED!"

Perkin's low voice, Shonna's firm voice, words not registering.

Creeping slowly toward the bedroom hallway, Perkins appearing in front of him looking down at Jeff startled, dumfounded stumbling back, jaw dropped.

Jeff looking up at him, "Perkins right?"

The bouncer looking at him blankly, motionless.

"*You, you*—" Perkins stuttering trying to catch his breath, struggling to gain composure.

Shonna stepping from the bedrooms, "Perkins, this is a mess and I've got to figure out what to do here." Perkins swinging his head toward her in disbelief, "but there's gonna be police and you shouldn't be here."

"Okay, miss Shonna, but—" motioning to Jeff.

"Perkins, go!"

"Okay if you say so, but it's him!" pointing weakly toward Jeff.

Shonna shoving him hard. "Perkins, snap out of it! Get out of here!"

"So theys nuthin you need from me?"

Reaching up touching his shoulder, "No, I'm sorry you had to see all this, but I really need to call the police, it would be bad for you to be here, don't you think?"

Nodding, turning, Perkins walking out of the house looking over his shoulder at Jeff in wonder, Shonna following him. Jeff watching her standing at the front door hearing Perkins's car start up, pulling away. She stood at the door with her back to Jeff. A few seconds after Perkins drove away he watched Shonna standing at the door crossing her arms stiffly across her chest without a word.

In less than five seconds Jeff heard two cars with high-powered engines screeching to a stop only feet from the front of the house. Four men running in behind Shonna, passing quickly across the living room toward the bedrooms, Shonna snapping to Jeff, "Stay out here, the couch!" sprinting into the bedroom on the right.

Sitting down on the couch, elbows on knees, Jeff's head spinning, tightness in his stomach like cramps. It was full daylight outside. Glancing around him seeing the sport coat hanging over the back of the couch, impulsively reaching around him picking up the coat to inspect it. It reeked of aftershave or cologne; he couldn't place the smell or the brand. Looking at it closely, holding it to the coat he was wearing. An exact match. Looking at the label. *Calvin Klein* Jeff laughing to himself, pulling open his coat seeing *Calvin Klein*, "Jesus, I wonder what brand of underwear he wears!" Laying it over his knees, beginning going through the pockets of the coat.

The right inside pocket had a money clip with a wad of hundreds and twenties. Gingerly pulling two twenties out of the bundle being careful not to touch the gold money clip he saw a Mont Blanc pen. Using the twenties as gloves, Jeff pulled off the cap seeing blue ink on the tip. There was a gold business card case embossed with the Congressional logo, filled with cards, Honorable Frank Schedz, United States House of Representatives. There was one of his business cards loose in the pocket with blue pen writing on the back, what looked like initials and numbers with a percent sign next to each set of initials. The lettering was very neat block printing in blue ink, carefully done like it was the writer's habit.

Using the two twenties over his fingers, he gingerly pulled out a neatly tri-folded set of papers from the other pocket, maybe twenty five pages he guessed. The first page looked like some kind of a summary with a column of dates going back to the first of November, to the right of each date were dollar figures which he guessed averaged about a hundred thousand dollars a day going back one day at a time, twenty days. The summary page had a bottom number of just over two million dollars for the twenty days.

"Wow, that's three million dollars a month!" a low whistle, "nearly forty million dollars a year!" Jeff thought about what that kind of money can buy here in 1994. This is a staggering sum!

Sitting back realizing that this stack of papers was the evidence of all the corruption.

Looking back at the summary page seeing that every other number was circled in blue ink with lines leading to the letters FS in the right border, written in the same neat block printing on the back of the card. "FS is Frank Schedz," softly out loud, "he's taking half! Or maybe he wants half?"

Oh, my god, he was really in it, just like she said! He sat back recalling all the things that Shonna told him, mulling the conversations they had as they watched the house this morning, smiling at his good guessing about this situation.

He felt the rest of the coat thinking there would be nothing because his coats always had the outside pockets sewn shut, feeling a heavy bulge in the right outside pocket, reaching in pulling out a thirty-eight snub-nosed revolver, holding it gingerly with one of the twenties. It was a *Colt Cobra*, a small handful of gun, a thirty-eight, with a tiny short two-inch barrel. He half-smiled because he once owned one but sold it because you can't hit the broad side of a barn with it. He looked into the cylinder, there were bullets in the five positions he could see. Laughing to himself, "I guess a guy can't be too careful!" Putting it back into the coat's side pocket, folding all the papers together putting them, the card case, pen, single card back into the pockets they came from.

Hearing loud talking in one of the bedrooms, he couldn't see into the rooms from where he sat.

Leaning back, closing his eyes starting to drift off.

Then he heard it.

A sigh. Yes, and a woman's voice he hadn't heard before in all the scuffling, all the activity in the back room.

There it is was again!

Very soft, "Help me."

Slowly standing, creeping toward the bedrooms, passing the room with Shonna turned away from the door kneeling over a man laying on the floor. Coming to the second door on the left looking in. Near the back of the room seeing two men laying in pools of blood, a woman laying on her stomach in the middle of the room, blood circling around her chest. He stood looking down at her.

She moved her hand!

Quickly moving to her crouching down, laying his finger on her hand, her fingers grasping his, soft cough. Reaching his arms under her, gently rolling her onto her back. He gasped at her bloody chest with three wounds seeping blood.

Stroking her cheek with his right hand, her eyes opened quickly, emptiness in her expression. Stroking her face again, turning her eyes to him, recognition clearly in her face.

She thinks I'm the congressman!

Without thinking he whispered, "Hey there." She gave the weakest smile. "Who did this? Who did this to you?"

She coughed, he reached to her right hand, she grasped weakly, starting to speak, wincing in pain groaning.

Stroking her face again she tried to speak. Leaning his face to hers, leaning over her turning his ear to her mouth, in the tiniest voice, nearly just a breath, "Black. Snake."

Pulling back. "A black man?" he asked. She blinked her eyes. His mind racing searching for *snake*. Snake, snake, snake, *what's a snake?* "Snake? You mean like a snake tattoo?" Tiniest nod.

Snapping to, realizing that she was bleeding to death as he was doing his little interrogation. Turning his head toward the door calling out, "HEY, A LITTLE HELP IN HERE!" A call back what did he want. "WE GOT US A SURVIVOR IN HERE! NEED SOME HELP!"

A second later a man came up behind Jeff, looking over Jeff's shoulder, turning running back out of the room yelling into his radio.

In another moment Shonna came in, Jeff looking up to her as she spoke softly, "We thought she was—" a quick second thought, "I mean, we didn't know she was still with us." Peering over Jeff's shoulder, "Good job, you did good! Stay here!" Looking up to her confused, "She needs you, stay here, I'll get help."

Looking down at the woman laying before him. Pretty, dark hair with light eyes, maybe mid-thirties he guessed. She had a strong resemblance to his sister, Leila who died a few years ago about the same age as this woman. His sister died of cancer; he remembered the times he went to visit her as her health spiraled down, each time he visited her she was thinner and weaker as he watched her slowly waste away over three months.

And now here was this woman dying before his eyes. His gut wrenching, a flash of resentment that this woman dared look so much like his sister, for her at this moment dying before his eyes.

That flash flying from him, overwhelmed by utter helplessness, like he had felt with his sister so long ago.

The woman looking to the ceiling, another jolt of pain, eyes back to him. She was looking at his chin, seeing confusion in her eyes.

Her eyes closing with one long sigh.

Silence.

Stroking her face once more, tears streaming down his face. Reaching his hand to wipe his face, slowly pulling his other hand away from hers, her fingers now opened. Looking at her blood on his fingers, wiping them on his coat sleeve.

Never in his life had someone died as he held their hand. Never before had he heard someone's last breath.

Sitting crouched in this silence he wondered at the madness he found himself in where this beautiful woman was murdered, dying as he held her hand. How utterly powerless he was to do anything but hold her hand, stroke her face.

Utterly hopeless. Helpless.

Sitting in this bubble of silence his mind flashed, skipping through the many events of his past, but none came anywhere near this heartbreaking scene. This lovely woman, the prime of her life. Gone.

Trying to muster anger at the tragedy before him, he felt deflated.

Numb.

His mind swirling to his children, his mother, how they were safely away from this craziness. How they would never know the despair swarming over him at this moment.

How could he ever feel safe when such insanity happened? How could he believe that those he loved were safe when such a thing, this woman dying, occurring within his touch.

He tuned out all the bustling going on in the house, and now the hustle and noise surrounding him rose again sitting before this limp form.

Soon Jeff heard the rushing of cars outside. Somehow he was expecting lights and sirens. No lights, no sirens. In a minute three men rushed in, one in front, a gurney being pulled and pushed by the others. Turning to the door, seeing them nearly running into the other bedroom. Standing up to look after them, then back facing the scene he had just witnessed. Shonna came into the room without a word.

Without turning to her he sighed, "She left us. She's gone."

"Look, I'm sorry you had to see this. You did good here Jeff. She needed you. But now we need to get you out of here." Tugging at his sleeve. "They'll take care of her, but we need to go. Come on." Without another word turning to the door, numb, looking back once more at the bloody form he had just spoken to laying on the floor, following Shonna. He got to the living room, following her when he had a second thought turning back to scoop up the stinky sport coat. Soon the car was speeding down the road. Jeff looking at his watch, just after eight o'clock.

"Where's your hotel?"

Directing her to the Sheraton near the airport they reached the hotel a few minutes later. Shonna drove around to the back of the building away from the frontage road and freeway, without a word parking, out of the car. Jeff grabbing the smelly coat following her up to a back door. Reaching into his pocket fumbling for his hotel key, turning the lock opening the door. Shonna scanned the parking lot, following Jeff inside.

Turning to Shonna walking along the hotel hallway, "So did

Perkins know you as Shonna back there?"

"That's all he knows me as."

"Why did he think you came there, I mean wouldn't that be confusing to him?"

"He set up the meeting because I told him that I needed to talk to the congressman, he didn't know what the meeting was about. Of course nobody knew that all those people would be there. He probably went in expecting to see the congressman and a couple other people." Shaking her head, "Instead he walks in on murders. Poor guy."

"Murder. Yeah. I saw three. Were there others?"

"Those three, the congressman is still alive."

"Wow," Jeff wondering. All that violence while he was sitting in that car watching the house with Shonna, feeling a cold chill rushing up his spine.

Turning to her, "Did he tell you why he took so long in the house?"

"He said he was trying to render assistance. That would make sense. Maybe he panicked a little." Coming to the elevators, Jeff leaning forward pressing the button. "He's not the brightest bulb in the pack, so I'm sure he was really confused. It was a hell of a scene, pretty nasty. I'm so sorry you had to see it."

After a short elevator ride they walked down the fifth floor hallway toward Jeff's hotel room door. Stepping over a copy of USA Today on the hallway floor, opening the door, Shonna following scooping up the newspaper, next standing in Jeff's room.

It was surreal to be back in his room, all nice and tranquil, bed made neatly, his suitcase sitting on the stand, ironing board out from him pressing his shirt yesterday afternoon before heading down to the shuttle.

He sat on the bed trying to find some center after what he had just witnessed at that house.

Standing over him, her right hand on his shoulder. "Are you okay?" He nodded. "So tell me what happened with the congressman's aid."

Taking a deep breath, telling her without picturing that scene.

"Black? Snake?" Shonna questioned.

Shrugging. "That's what I heard. But I don't know what it means." Jeff pausing thinking. "Can't make a connection."

Sitting in silent ponder. Looking at his coat sleeve Shonna frowning, "You have blood on your coat sleeve, you better go wash it off," reaching around pulling a tissue out of a box, licking it. "And you have blood on your cheek," dabbing at his face, crinkling the tissue tossing it onto the desk. Looking at the congressman's coat, "What do you have there?" reaching out for the coat.

Taking a deep breath, Jeff standing shaking his head rapidly to rattle pictures from this morning out of his brain, starting to hand the coat to her. Pausing, instead laying it out on the bed, pulling the twenties out of his pocket, gingerly using them as gloves to empty the contents of the coat's pockets onto the bed. Giving him a quick smile, "Smart, no fingerprints."

Shonna sat on the bed, reaching into her purse pulling out a little clear plastic packet, ripping it open with her teeth, spilling out white light-fabric gloves onto the bed. Putting them on, beginning studying the papers. Picking up the card with the scribbles on back shaking her head. "Jesus, the total smoking gun. And you sure you didn't get your fingerprints on this stuff?"

"You will find my prints on these two twenties and nothing else." smiling proudly waving them clutched in fingers, "Sherlock Holmes!"

Turning around, studying him, bursting out laughing at Jeff gingerly holding the twenties in his fingers, laughing again even harder, laughing so hard tears appearing in her eyes, rolling down her cheeks. Jeff couldn't help start laughing himself, that contagious effect plus they were so exhausted that it felt like that's all they could do at this moment. This was the medicine he needed to recover from that house.

Finally catching herself. "Oh, yes, yes, yes, Jeffery, you are my Watson, aren't you?"

Smiling, wiping tears from his cheeks. Both feeling better.

Starting to look through the ledger pages glancing at him questioning. Beginning to paw through the ledger sheets, "These are my accounting sheets, the ones that I did in that damned room in the basement of the club. But look at these numbers circled, lines to FS. He really was shaking them down!"

"They were in his coat pocket."

"These are definitely mine, see the little black pen scribble initials on the bottom? They required me to do that as a way to somehow make sure they are authentic, from me." Flipping between the pages making note of the dates on top of each, "They're out of order, that's good, that means they've been handled, that's really good. God, I'll bet these are a harvest of finger prints!"

Pausing looking at the whole stack. "But how did the congressman get these?"

"When you do your accounting, where does your stuff go to?"

"Antonio."

"Antonio? Who's Antonio?"

"The owner of the club."

Shonna stood reaching for the phone on his table, "I need to use the phone, but you need to step out. Go get us some coffee, be back in ten minutes. But first wash the blood off your coat."

Standing, feeling a wave of tired he walked into the bathroom, wetting a wash cloth, rubbing bar soap on it, scrubbing the coat sleeve, finding two more spots until he could hold it up in the mirror satisfied that the evidence from the horror this morning was gone. Hearing her talking softly in the other room, putting the coat back on looking into the mirror seeing another smear of blood on his forehead, rinsing out the wash cloth, wiping his face. Frowning at his red eyes, shaking his head groaning, reaching into his shaving kit, three drops into each eye of what felt like gasoline they burned so badly, drifting out the door into the hallway, back ten minutes later with two coffees and four pastries.

Taking a sip of coffee, two bites of a donut, Jeff slumped into the stuffed chair in the corner.

Shonna was just finishing a call, "Okay, you set up the first for this afternoon downtown, I'll set up the other for tonight. You can arrange all that? Are you sure?" scribbling in her notebook. "No, no escort, I got him. Could use a guard in the hotel hallway here."

Listening to the other end. "You know how dangerous this is, right? If something happens to him we are *so screwed*," glancing over her shoulder to Jeff, listening. "Yeah, a score for sure. Okay, he'll get some sleep, then we'll come see you there."

Hanging up turning to Jeff, "Okay, we figured out what to do with you."

Looking to her questioningly she smiled.

"Welcome to the United States House of Representatives!"

Saturday, 12:04 PM: Wanted Visitor

"What are you talking about?" Jeff confused.

"Time for a nap," smiling. Jeff looking at his watch, it was nearly nine o'clock. "You've got a few hours to look like you slept all night, you need to look sharp. We've got a hell of a day ahead of us, you need some sleep."

Too tired to protest too much, giving it his best, "I need to know what's going on."

"Sleep. I've got to go. I will be back at four. Make sure you've showered and are in your best shape, okay? When I come back I will tell you."

Pulling everything from the bed, carefully arranging them on a side table, pulling off the gloves, Shonna walking to the window looking down to the parking lot. "By the way," glancing over her shoulder, "you won't be having that little talk with that someone like I told you earlier. That talk has been postponed." Glancing at the clock. "Actually, there's a good chance it'll be canceled."

Looking at her, furrowed brow trying to take this all in.

Four rapid knocks at the door. Shonna stepping across the room opening the door, Jeff hearing a man's murmur, Shonna responding.

Starting to close the door turning to him. "Look, lay down, we've got a busy afternoon and evening ahead of us, you need to be rested," glancing at her watch. "I'll be back at four. You heard that knock?" He nodded. "Don't open that door for anybody unless you hear that knock, okay? Don't answer it for nobody without that knock. There is someone standing guard outside your door. You will be safe." She left the door stepping forward surprising Jeff with a hug and a quick kiss on the cheek, turning to the door, gone.

Jeff fell onto the bed, instantly asleep.

He woke with a start, sitting straight up. The clock said eleven fifty. He suddenly got a whiff of himself, rolling over to get out of bed, walking to the shower. His face in the water thinking he heard the room door open, "Shonna? Shonna?" No answer.

Turning off the water, reaching for a towel, drying off, combing his hair, brushing his teeth, walking into the room naked to grab clean clothes so he could climb back into bed until Shonna returned.

Coming out of the bathroom there sat a woman in the big stuffed corner chair. "Oh my god!" turning back to the bathroom grabbing his towel, wrapping it around him. Coming out again standing looking at a pretty face in front of him. She sat there, light blue sweater, short black skirt, black boots, legs crossed. Jeff standing trying to place the face. Watching his confused expression as he stumbled, "The store yesterday. Right? I'm sorry I forgot your name."

"Jennifer." Looking him over smiling. "Jennifer from Ann Tallot's?" pointing to the box laying on the table next to her. "Remember me? I said that I would drop this sweater to you at noon." Pointing to the clock, "See? Noon! Remember, I told you noon. To deliver the sweater? I got the bellman to let me in and some man standing at your door said I could deliver this, showed him the box and my card, he let me in, just like that! Didn't even have to tip the bellman! Who was that man at your door? Why's he out there?"

Without answering he shrugged, standing looking down at himself in front of her, towel over his body, smiling bashfully. "Uh, well, I guess I should, uh,—"

Jennifer jumping up, "No, no, really, you're fine!" With a determined smile, "I mean, why not?" Reaching down to her right side she pulled the skirt zipper down. Her skirt fell to her feet, stepping out of it.

Jeff crinkled his brow looking at this woman in front of him, naked from her sweater to the tops of her boots. Standing in awe looking at her thin curvy shape, dark pubic hairs neatly shaved into crisp "V" shape. His expression must have been inviting though for the life of him he had no idea what was going on. Crossing her arms pulling her sweater off, reaching her hands around her back, in a second her bra falling to the floor.

Jeff stammering, "What are you doing here? What are you doing?"

"Silly, what does it look like I'm doing here?"

"But I'm married." Stammering, "At least technically married!"

"So what, so am I!" frowning a second. "Well, kind of married. Separated. But I'm technically married, too!" Smiling at him stepping forward, yanking at Jeff's towel as he fumbled trying to catch it with her tossing it behind her. Standing looking down his body smiling broader seeing the effect she was having on him. He glanced down seeing what she was smiling at.

"But I'm…I'm…"

"You're what? Busy? You don't look very busy to me."

"Well, no, but I didn't get much sleep last night and, well, I'm pretty tired."

"Then we'll take a nap together!" jumping onto the bed laying on her back, legs slightly spread toward Jeff, her boots pointing toward him in some kind of salute. Her secret place so inviting.

Jeff was numb. Standing, looking down at himself seeing the very commanding effect this was having on him, stepping to the bed with a *what-the-hell* expression, "I'm sorry, but not with your boots on!" Kneeling on the bed he started unlacing her boots, she giggled. "Sorry," smiling, "if we're going to do this I just can't do the Eva Braun look." Smiling watching him carefully unlacing her boots, with a tug pulling them off one at a time. Reaching up to lay next to her on his back.

They lay there in nervous silence for a couple minutes.

"Now what?"

"Let's just lay here until you're ready," she whispered.

They lay like that for a few more minutes. Jeff rolling onto his left side, planting his elbow, head on his hand. "This is quite a delivery service your store has. I really should shop there more often."

She giggled, reaching across kissing him. He lay looking into her bright eyes, a face even more beautiful close up than he remembered in the store, that same soft floral aroma from her skin. Leaning, kissing her with arms around her pulling her closer. He loved her kisses, wide mouth sucking him into her, his mind spinning, touching skin. Lowering his mouth taking her right nipple into his mouth, swirling his tongue around the soft flesh, giving just a little nibble, she making a soft squeak running her fingers through his hair. Drawing a line across her chest with his tongue to her left nipple, swirling his tongue again, a little nip with his teeth, she softly groaning.

"Come here," she said starting to pull him over on top her as her legs parted.

They kissed deep, rolling over laying on top of her he could just feel her soft hairs on his hardness.

Four rapid loud knocks on the door, bursting open banging against the wall.

Shonna storming in.

"WHAT THE HELL IS GOING ON HERE!"

Jeff rolled over sitting up, "Whoa! You tell me, what the hell is going on here!"

Jennifer sitting up, "What the hell is going on here!"

Jeff jumping up standing naked, "Whoa, whoa, whoa! What the hell is going on here? Why are you here!"

Shonna stopped for fully ten seconds looking Jeff up and down with an expression screaming either *Come here and screw me now!* or *Prepare to die!* Turning to someone standing at the door that he hadn't noticed, pointing to Jennifer, "Please take out this trash!"

A man in an overcoat stepping into the room toward Jennifer commanding her bruskly, "Ma'am, please go into the bathroom."

Jennifer looking to Jeff with a terrified pleading voice, "Jeff, what's all this, who are these people?"

Jeff seeing Shonna's determined expression, "I'm sorry Jennifer, these guys are pretty serious, you better do as they say."

Jennifer got up reluctantly, slowly, Jeff feeling enormous regret—so close to getting inside this lithe beautiful body! Now watching that naked body that was laying beneath him just a few seconds ago glide silently into the bathroom as the man stepped to the big chair, leaning over to the floor gathering her clothing and boots holding out his hand so she couldn't close the bathroom door, tossing her clothing and boots into the bathroom telling her to hurry up and get dressed.

Shonna sat down in the big corner chair without a word as the agent stood with arms crossed at the front door closed behind him. Soon Jennifer emerged dressed, her hair tousled.

Jeff stood gathering a towel around him, stepping to Jennifer with a hug, apologizing. Hugging him, a quick peck on the lips, pushing him away with an angry scowl looking over at Shonna as the agent opened the door, starting toward the hall.

"Wait!" everyone turning to Shonna walking to the desk chair that had been pulled out sideways from the desk, "you forgot your purse." Pulling the purse from the chair, reaching into the purse pulling out an eight millimeter video camera. Holding it looking into the lens, turning it toward Jeff who could see the little red recording light on, "Smile there congressman!"

"Congressman!" Jennifer gasped looking to Jeff.

Examining the controls, Shonna flicked a switch to turn the camera off, pushing a button. With a soft whirring sound a door popped open on the camera. Shonna pulled the tape out laying it on the table, putting the camera back into the purse, handing it to the agent. "More garbage." Looking at Jennifer waving her away, "Make sure she finds her way out of here, and do all the ID checks. I'd like to get that from you later. She's not under arrest but I don't want to see her around this hotel anymore." He nodded turning back to the door brusquely dragging Jennifer out by the elbow.

Impulsively Jeff called after Jennifer as the door began to close, "Maybe another time."

Looking over her shoulder walking through the door she screamed, "You'll never see me again, so don't bother!"

Saturday, 12:13 PM: Preparation

Turning back to the room Jeff deciding he wanted to make some form of protest about what just happened, so instead of dressing he pulled off the towel, climbing under the covers naked, propping his head on his elbow looking at Shonna, finally turning to face him.

"Nice job, there congressman. True to form. Do you go around picking up every little store clerk you can get your hands on?"

"You're talking to me like I'm him. What was this all about?"

"Well sorry to break up your little tryst with your little tramp, but you disobeyed instructions. You were not to open that door to anyone except for the code. The four knocks."

"I didn't let her in, the bellman did, so did your guy at the door."

Sarcastically, "Oh, and I can tell how you objected to her being here."

His face dawning a slight smile, "She was very nice to me yesterday. I was very attracted to her. And her—"

"You don't even know who she is!"

"Name's Jennifer, technically married, a relative in Seattle, thirty three years-old."

Shonna pulling a piece of paper from her pocket. "Jennifer Lowe, age twenty eight."

Jeff getting a big dreamy smile, "Twenty eight? Wow."

"Yes, separated from her husband so it seems that she does know how to tell the truth. But then it's easy to be separated when your husband is in prison." Jeff's jaw dropped.

"Yes prison. Any guesses what for?" Shaking his head slowly in shock. "Extortion." Giving him a hard look, down at her paper, "She has worked for Tallot's for three years, it seems she has a good little side business blackmailing married men who happen to come into her store and she does her little free delivery service to their hotel rooms."

"Blackmail, that means she was going to screw me and try to hit me up for money?"

"That wasn't a makeup mirror I pulled out of her purse, Jeff! Of course she was going to blackmail you!"

Jeff lay quiet, a chill running up his spine thinking that he was literally one inch away from having sex with Jennifer. Feeling pent-up laughter to himself, *but I don't really have a wife! Certainly not a wife who would care. It would have been a waste on me!* "What kind of blackmail are we talking about?" Frowning. "How big are we talking about?"

"Oh, she was pretty smart. All we know is that she was shameless about putting the money into her bank account, some of these guys were stupid enough to actually write her checks so we know who some of her victims are."

"You can do that?"

"Yep. She would only hit them up for a few thousand dollars, though, not so much that the guy would think it was just easier to tell his wife. She was pretty smart."

"How much money did she take?"

"Best we can tell it was way over a hundred thousand in the last year. Closer to two hundred thousand."

Jeff's eyes widening, "A hundred thousand? Two hundred thousand? Jesus, that's a hell of a lot of money!"

"Well, do the arithmetic. Twice a week—"

"Jesus! Twice a week?"

"Say at three thousand a pop, that's up to six a week times fifty two."

"How do you know this?"

"Bank records. Like I said, she was shameless!"

Laying back with his hands behind his head in thought, glancing around him imagining that beautiful twenty eight year-old body laying there what felt like just seconds ago.

"How do you know all this? How did you know I even shopped there?"

Laughing, "Like that's hard! You use your credit card all over the place!"

"How did you know about her little blackmail thing?"

"The store franchise owner told us."

"Why doesn't he just fire her?"

"One guess there, congressman, and this should sound familiar."

"What?"

"He's married. You do the math why he doesn't fire her." Giving him a sly grin, "Plus, she sells more expensive sweaters and coats than everyone else combined!"

Quiet. Looking sideways at Shonna watching him. Suddenly Pick's words echoing in his head, how Pick talked about the *enterprising young lady* that worked at Tallot's, the words *I'm sure you'll see her again*, Jeff picturing that young naked body as freshly in his mind as if she was laying next to him right now.

Shaking his head looking back at Shonna wondering what was going on, how did he keep finding himself in all these situations, looking at the clock doing the math, in the last eighteen hours? Not even eighteen hours!

Shonna looking around the room, reaching down taking her shoes off, stepping around the bed near the wall laying next to Jeff on top of the covers, Jeff still naked under the covers. Glancing at the clock, "So seeing as we have to be somewhere in four hours, I suggest we get some sleep."

Rolling over, fidgeting with a watch, saying in a sleepy voice, "What would your wife think if she found out you were naked with two different women in the same hour?"

Shrugging, "I don't think she'd care."

Turning to him, "Jeff, I am a woman, she'd care. She'd care like hell. Now time to sleep with this woman, and I mean *sleep* with this woman," rolling over on her left side facing away from him.

In a second he was out.

The tweet of an alarm. Sitting up, Jeff looking at the clock next to the bed seeing three forty-five, sighing. Shonna was standing at the ironing board with her back to him, he could see his favorite blue shirt on the ironing board in front of her.

Stretching yawning, "Man I was knocked out." Studying Shonna bent over the ironing board. "What are you doing?"

"Hey sleepy head, how you feeling?" her voice sounding cheerful. There was absolutely no indication in her voice that she was upset at what happened earlier with Jennifer. Surprised at this, he sat up watching Shonna, her back to him, holding the iron. Wondering at the events since she barged into the room, preventing him from the first sex he'd had since his wife left him nearly a year ago. He found himself trying to sort out the scene with him standing there naked in front of Shonna with Jennifer laying naked on the bed, the other agent standing there, and what the heck was that expression on Shonna's face? Was it jealousy? Or was she just there doing her job? Scratching his stomach standing up, groggy.

Stretching, looking around the room. "I'm feeling pretty good, I guess. How about you? Just that little bit of sleep felt good. But what are you doing?"

"Getting you ready for show time," glancing at him. "You need a shower, you need to look sharp, put some clothes on. And hurry, we need to leave in a half-hour."

"I need some food."

"No, you need to get a shower and get dressed," pointing to the Khakis laying on the bed, turning to him with the ironed shirt.

Without a word reaching for the shirt as she looked his naked body up and down closely. "You have a nice body." He flushed. "No, I mean it, that was a lucky little blackmailing slut that was about to get you," the tone in her voice that wasn't registering, a softness, like he was somehow being caressed by her voice in a playful way. It occurring to him that in her mind she felt like she had saved him from a mistake, that would explain the gentle tone of her voice, almost nurturing.

He had learned a long time ago that women communicate in two languages, almost like two separate beams of light, one white, the other colored in some kind of mysterious tone that he had never been able to place on a color chart.

Elusive.

Two beams of light communicating from a woman to a man: words that, you know, even a dumb man can understand. That was the beam of white light, a color everyone can see, even a dumb man. Then there's the second beam of light in that mysterious color. Woman-speak. A cryptic combination of tone, expression, tilt of the head, the words that were just said, the words that are about to follow, position of the body along with a hundred other tiny signs, all too subtle for the male consciousness, all conspiring into a stream of language in which the words themselves are nearly meaningless.

He had first begun to learn woman-speak from his mother, though mother-speak is definitely a different dialect, a different color of light. Woman-speak is a woman's way of communicating to a man that on the one hand attempts to give a man at least the *tiniest hope of understanding what is being communicated* while at the same time offered by her in the almost disdainful knowledge that it will not be perceived. Or at best misinterpreted. Now he was having woman-speak directed at him when he had a night and day of *sleep snacks*, was in a house with murdered people, had a woman die in his arms, was a millimeter from having sex with a beautiful blackmailing slut. And now standing naked in front of a woman even more beautiful than his little hussy.

Far more beautiful.

There was a grace about this Shonna that thrilled him. It was rare to meet a woman who so elegantly radiated her sensuous nature. He had to keep snapping himself on his proverbial ass to make himself listen to her words, the white light, as he basked in the other light, that mysteriously colored beam that emanated from her. He wished he could just stand naked in front of her, like he was on her nude beach near Savannah, get some kind of tan all over his body from that tinted beam that radiated from her when she spoke. Bathe in that light that streamed from her even when she was silent.

"You okay?" interrupting his tanning session.

Jeff nodding, looking down realizing he was still naked laying down the shirt on the bed. Stepping to his luggage pulling out clean socks and underwear, mindlessly tossing them onto the bed, walking into the bathroom.

"And make sure to shave!" hearing her voice calling after him. "You need to look sharp!"

Leaning toward the mirror looking at his eyes. Absolutely blood shot. How is it that he feels so comfortable to be naked in front of Shonna? Shrugging looking into the mirror smiling to himself, "I guess she's got to you. Damn."

Reaching for his shaving kit pulling out a little bottle of eye drops, tilting his head back, three drops into each eye, once more pouring gasoline into his eyes. He really needed another shower, soon standing under the shower head, hot water pouring onto his hair and his face. Feeling just a little more alive he scrubbed with the wash cloth against his face and skin extra hard, shaving carefully in the shower like he always does.

Stepping out of the shower, hearing the hotel room door open, some mumbling, the door closing again. "So much mystery," he said to himself smiling hoping they were letting in more naked women.

After a good scouring with his toothbrush with strong minty toothpaste he felt almost human again. He heard the door open and close again.

Realizing he had thrown his clothes onto the bed forgetting to bring them in, he wrapped a towel around himself stepping back into the room. Shonna was seated at the table studying a sheet of paper with a pen in her hand.

Turning to him, "Okay, let's be fair! Let's see what you look like when there isn't a little naked little tramp in your room!" they laughing as he pulled the towel down surprised that he wasn't embarrassed though he was very erect. Laughing again, "Looks about the same!" looking down at his hardness. "Nice," nodding, "very nice. We'll need a look again later." Squinching his forehead thinking about her words, smiling again, "Just doin' my job, just doin' my job!"

Smiling back to her, their eyes meeting her loving look, a quick shy smile turning back to the paper in front of her shooshing him with her left hand, "Now go get dressed! And hurry!"

Scooping up his clothes on the bed going back into the bathroom, dressing. Coming back out Shonna glancing at him telling him to go back in and dry his hair, make sure to use the blow dryer to straighten his hair because his was curlier than the congressman's. In a few minutes he was standing back in the room.

Turning her chair facing him, "Okay, now say something."

"What?" wondering if she wanted an explanation for what happened with Jennifer.

Frowning, "I don't know. Anything. The Gettysburg Address." Short pause. "Or how about *I love my little whore!*"

Jeff didn't quite understand what was going on here, was she yelling at him?

But not yelling?

Why did she continue raging at him for what he had done—or rather hadn't done—with his little naked sales girl?

But not raging?

"Gettysburg Address? Really?" Smiling. "Or slut." She giving a half-apologetic nod, settling herself back into her chair expectantly.

Puffing himself up, in a brave sounding voice, "Four score and seven—"

"No, natural like."

Jeff glancing toward the window seeing the sunny day outside making him feel a little better, stronger. Collecting himself, starting again, "Four score and seven years ago—"

"Wait, let me think. Yeah, I think the timbre is good, that's lucky, but his voice is a little lower, maybe even just a little nasally. Your mouth is the same size as his, I think, but somehow his smile is bigger. Politician's smile, maybe. Practice a bigger smile."

"Nasally? Smile?"

"I can't explain it exactly. Just think about it a bit. Can you try that?"

Looking confused for a second, "How much time did you spend with this guy? I mean speaking of sluts, did you ever sleep with him?"

Disgusted grimace, "He was always hitting on me, constantly. Offered me money, jewelry, even his wife's jewelry! I would rather have sex with…god, I don't know, but not with that sickening little pig!"

Jeff laughing, "You know, you should be careful. If don't start speaking your mind you'll end up with an ulcer!" Both laughing signaling him with a sweep of her hand to continue.

"Okay, okay. Four score…"

She had him practice over and over and over until she finally said that it was close enough. Reaching for the USA Today she scooped up as they were coming in earlier, holding it up toward Jeff. "He has a small mole, right side chin."

"Mole! That's it!"

"What's it?"

"The congressman's assistant. She looked at my chin as though she was looking for something!"

"Well I don't know about that, but I do have to put one on you." Reaching into her purse pulling out a woman's eye-brow pencil. Stepping to him looking at his chin, reaching up grabbing his chin firmly with left hand fingers holding his chin tightly, turning his head putting the pencil to his chin spinning it with her finger tips. Gingerly at first, but she kept spinning the eyebrow pencil, pushing it harder and harder into his skin.

"You're pushing pretty hard, it kind of hurts."

She kept spinning it pushing it harder into his chin, "So how was it with your little floozy?"

Jerking back, "Ouch! I said, that hurts! What are you jealous or something? What the hell's going on! I already told you I didn't let her in." Glowering at her, she glared straight back at him. Looking intently into her golden eyes with those little black flecks expecting to see, he wasn't sure, hatred or something. Instead he saw a look of need, ever so fast, so faint, in a half second disappearing.

"And just so you know, we didn't do anything, you broke in before we could even get started!" Groaning to himself, *so close!* "Your timing was really awful," craning to see his new mole in the mirror on the bedroom wall, looking back at her, "or maybe it was really excellent..." His voice trailing off.

Her face suddenly brightening, her head half-cocked, "Good!"

"Which part?"

Glancing at him reaching for the congressman's coat, handing it to Jeff, "The *really excellent* part!" smiling at him putting the coat on.

Taking a sniff of the jacket, "Jesus, you'd think he could afford better aftershave."

"Cologne," she said, "and it's expensive."

"But why do I have to wear this with all this stinky cologne? My coat is exactly the same."

"You have to wear that because *it is* stinky! *Details!*"

Shrugging reaching into the pocket pulling out the gun, holding it like he was weighing it in his hand, "What about this?"

"You know how to use it, right?"

"I used to own one. Can't hit the broad side of a barn with it. But yes, I know how to use it."

"Good, then keep it. You never know, right?"

Putting it back into the outer coat pocket, Jeff grimaced patting the pocket.

Four quick knocks at the door, a man coming in setting a tray of food on the table, quickly excusing himself leaving.

Shonna stepping back reflectively, motioning for Jeff to turn around which he did. "You've got a cuter ass than him, but it's men we're trying to convince so it won't matter." Turning away from him under her breath, "It was certainly good enough to get that naked little slut in here."

Hearing her, ignoring this, laughing at women being more observant again. She was right, he could probably walk into a room with a Quasimoto hump limping and men wouldn't notice if they were expecting to see the congressman. A woman would notice if his new little mole was moved one millimeter!

Shonna didn't understand the source of his laugh with an indignant frown afraid he was still thinking about his little tryst.

"So what next?" he said sitting on the bed.

Motioning to the tray of food looking at her watch saying they had three minutes to eat, then time for the real rehearsing. Three minutes later the tray was empty except for two bottles of beer standing opened. "What's this for?" he asked.

"It'll make you a little more relaxed." Grinning, "Plus he always smells of alcohol."

"Details, right?"

"It's the details that kill you."

"Unless it's in front of men, right?"

"Men or not, we're not taking any chances, details for everyone. Drink the first one now, the other as we're leaving. Drink up, we need to practice."

Lifting the bottle pouring it down his throat even though it was a Bud, he hadn't realized just how badly he could use a beer. It seemed like he got the buzz almost instantly, unsure if he was just still tired from the long night or his less-than-smooth day already.

"Okay, let me tell you what's going to happen," holding the piece of paper she was studying when he came out of the bathroom. "You are going to do a press conference downtown that has been hastily called because you, the congressman, are announcing that you have been assisting in a major corruption investigation and that next week the FBI will be releasing the names of the suspects which you will be providing to them on Monday afternoon."

"Wow, I've never done a press conference."

Shonna paused, "Hmmmm, we can fix that." Reaching for the phone calling room service to order another beer. "I saw you last night and you can hold your booze, but you have got to be in the groove. If you look too nervous you'll blow it. This Schedz guy is a smooth talker, you have got be him. Maybe we should have let you get laid, maybe you would be more relaxed." Frowning at him, "Even by your *little slut!*"

"I doubt I would be more relaxed after you shoved one of her boots up my ass!" Both laughing, the mood softening even more. Looking at himself in the mirror again, chin turned forward.

She laughed again, "Yeah, we can't have you walking funny can we? Well, maybe it was a good thing the way it worked out." All he could think was *you got that wrong!*

Handing him the paper asking him to read it, casually but with purpose. Reading through it mumbling to himself asking about a correction she made. Reading it through once, she made a couple comments, reading it again three more times out loud.

"Stop! Good job, we don't want to make it look rehearsed. Think you can get through it?"

He shrugged nodding.

"Good, we need to wait one minute, then we'll go. Here," reaching for the second beer, "drink up."

Sitting down on the bed sipping the second beer, his head

swirling with pictures of everything that happened since he climbed into that shuttle van yesterday afternoon. He found his brain doing a kind of fast-forward movie in his head, like little characters walking around in his brain moving quickly, talking in high-pitched voices like an audio tape on fast speed, little mice voices in his head starting with that fat lady trying to claw her way out of the shuttle van, her meek little husband trying to slip the driver a couple bucks, the shuttle driver suggesting strip clubs, Jeff's deciding *he definitely wasn't going to a strip club*, the clothing store, how he leered at little Jennifer, how me must have looked like some dirty old man picking up on a twenty eight year-old for god's sake, Pick and his smooth-talking tour guiding, Magic Town, seeing Shonna naked on the runway, meeting her downstairs, how taken he was with her eyes, the armed guard at the other door, the table with the people looking over at him in the house, Bernice and the filthy little diner, the stakeout, that woman dying in front of him, his being *this close* to sticking his dick into the blackmailing little slut, and now sitting on the bed with a mole on his chin. The way things were going, he was sure there would be much more to come.

He felt exhausted.

He felt exhilarated.

What was coming next?

He had no clue.

Four rapid knocks at the door brought him back.

Shonna scooped up the papers putting them into a neat stack, carrying them to the door. She barely opened the door to hand the papers out without a word, pulling back a Budweiser with the twist-top still on. Jeff seeing the shadow of someone in the hallway.

"Ready?" Shonna opening the door sliding the unopened beer into her coat side pocket. Jeff downing the last of the second beer following her out as they went the same way down the elevator, out the back door where they had come in.

Getting into her car, starting to pull away Jeff looking sternly at Shonna, "Look, you told me you would let me in on what's going on. I feel like I'm being kidnapped."

Frowning, thinking for a second, "Okay, but I am only going to tell you what you need to know, we don't have time."

Leaning to her intently she glanced at him, "You, Mister Holmes here, figured it out pretty good. We got a crooked mayor, some city council, the police, but most of all a very crooked congressman who has muscled his way into their thriving little business that sells, how shall we say, very specialized kinds of insurance policies."

"Protection. Extortion."

"Yes, but not just your little donut shop making sure that their business is adequately protected from accidental things like fire bombs. We're talking big fish, too. Prostitution, unions, drugs. If it has money attached these guys are in it. All of northern Georgia, not just Atlanta. Maybe even farther. We've heard little hints about Miami. Cubans."

"How long has this been going on?"

"Who knows, maybe twenty years."

"Twenty years?"

"It all started small, probably. Just a little extortion among a small circle of friends, but over the years it has grown bigger and bigger." Jeff smiling to himself wondering if Ringo Starr had any idea that his *getting by with a little help from my friends* included extortion and murder. Probably not. *Joe Cocker, though…*

"You saw the numbers on those pages," steering onto I-85 heading north toward downtown. "Remember I told you about my loose thread I discovered all those years ago. By then the congressman was in the deal. It seemed to be going fine for these guys, but the group just kept getting bigger and bigger. We'd have found out about it eventually even if I hadn't found the loose ends way back when. So evidently this congressman learns about this four years ago, figures out that he can get into the game, threatens to call for a congressional investigation or some damn thing. So they cut him in. His cut wasn't big at first, but having his name attached to it attracted more players, big players, kind of like having a big star on a baseball team." Grinning, "So the sorry bastard starts getting greedy, figuring out that he is the big fish, that it has grown so fast because he was the star attraction. When I say he got greedy, I mean *really greedy*."

"Like fifty percent. That's what it looked like on those papers."

"We had no idea he was in it so big, it was a shock. Really." Frowning continuing heading north toward downtown. "I mean a congressman. And probably the biggest criminal corruption case involving a congressman in the history of the whole damned world! We didn't get it at first. He was already wealthy, came from a rich family, didn't live the high life best we could tell." Thinking for a second, frowning. "Greed and arrogance. Pure and simple. He is a total pig."

Driving in silence for a minute Jeff spoke up, "Okay, so what happened back at that house we staked out this morning?"

"Remember what I told you that these guys don't play rough?" Jeff nodding. "Well the game just changed." Jeff's expression turning to worried. "Let's just say that three people are going to die on Monday night in a car accident in the big snow storm."

Jeff sat silently as they came to Peach Tree Boulevard, the main downtown exit. "So who was—or rather who is going to be—killed?"

"Somehow that damned congressman managed to take four bullets; he's been in surgery all day. Greed, arrogance, and bullet proof, too. One tough bastard, that's for sure."

"He was wearing body armor?"

"Nope, he just was lucky. So far, at least because we're not sure he's gonna make it."

"Who were the others?"

"The woman was one of the congressman's staff and the two men haven't been identified."

Jeff thinking about this, the car winding its way through the tall buildings of downtown Atlanta. "How are three strangers going to end up in a car together on Monday night?"

Shonna giving a small laugh, "They won't actually be in a car. If the congressman dies then he will be in the same car with the woman." Glancing at him, "There might have to be two accidents if we can't ID that the other two belonged with them. Very tragic." Leaning forward toward the right rear-view mirror, Jeff leaning back to give her a clear view, she signaled to make a right onto Peach

Tree something-or-other street, avenue or whatever.

"You guys can do that?"

"Yep."

"Why are you doing this now, this press conference, why so quickly after what just happened this morning?"

"We actually know a lot about this operation now, one thing for sure is that it's very well organized."

"So why this?"

"We've got to get them off balance. These guys have been very fat and sassy for too long, we've got to find a way to shake it up."

The Mustang wound around downtown Atlanta between buildings towering over them surrounding them in shadow as they turned right toward a big building, winding up the parking structure to the top. Driving toward the building Jeff looking out his window, up at the blue sky over them, darkness beginning to set in. A nice crisp November evening. Beautiful here, really, he thought.

Even though it was Saturday afternoon the parking lot had many cars, most notably there were those television vans with their dish antennas pointing all sorts of directions with letters like NBC on them. There were people milling around, coming in and out of the building. "Does anyone know what this press conference is all about?"

"Of course, how else are we going to get coverage?"

Four men were standing near the entrance, two holding rifles waiting for them, one motioning toward a parking place. Just then three other men came out of the entrance, trench coats, hands in pockets; Jeff half-grinning to himself thinking that the trench coats were such a nice touch.

"So you have what, some kind of team of analysts that sit around all day to plan strategy and tell you what to do?"

"Hardly. We had a meeting this morning to discuss all this, we decided this was a good way to get things stirred up, of course I had a small *slut interruption* so we had to cut the meeting short," giving an amused glance at Jeff, "but sometimes you just have to go with your gut, my gut is telling me that we've got to stir this up as much as we can as quickly as we can, and this is the best way to do it. If people think their position is threatened they may expose themselves to defend their position. We need to get in front of these clowns and the only way to do it is if they feel like something is closing in on them."

Pulling into the parking space looking to him.

"We need to bat the beehive."

Saturday, 5:02 PM: The Press Conference

A minute later Jeff was in the elevator surrounded by heavily armed men in trench coats who didn't say a single word to either of them. A few seconds later the elevator doors opened.

Jeff could hear the din of a hundred voices talking softly somewhere down the hallway.

Shonna motioned to her escorts to go on ahead, turning to Jeff while pulling out the bottle of Budweiser from her coat pocket, Jeff laughing. "Down you go!" handing him the bottle. "Details!" she said with a grin. He twisted open the bottle, she reached for the cap, he gulped it down tossing the empty into the trash can next to him as he noticed a man standing down the hallway watching them. Shonna glanced down the hallway reaching into the bin, pulling it out putting it back into her coat pocket leaning to him whispering. "You may look like him, but you don't have his fingerprints."

"Details?" Jeff frowning. She nodded.

Walking a few feet she stopped, turning giving one more inspection. "Remember the voice, and relax." Glancing over his shoulder at the room filled with reporters. "Don't worry about the smile, there's not a lot to smile about here." Standing behind him as he turned facing a long corridor. Leaning forward speaking softly into his right ear, "You saw those men that brought you up here. There's nothing to worry about here, they are stationed all over the place. You are completely safe." Glancing nervously toward her, she gave a soft smile. "Relax. Ready?" He nodded. "Have your speech?" Nodding, pulling it out of his pocket wafting with the congressman's smelly cologne. "Okay then, show time!"

Taking his arm leading him through the door into a large room, instantly he was surrounded by his escort. She turned away, another man walked up to Jeff to lead him up to a podium bristling with microphones. He stepped forward to the podium cringing when he saw CNN on one microphone, ABC on another, all the others with some other letters or numbers.

Jeff walked up to the podium looking up to see that they were in a large atrium with a huge sloping glass ceiling above them, the evening's new darkness above. The room echoing with voices. His only thought was wondering what was going to come next. Now here he was walking out in front of the world to impersonate a man he had never met, until this morning had never even heard his name. Some congressman from some place that he knew very little about. Or nothing. He laughed to himself at all the self-importance that congressmen exuded when they were absolutely unimportant to those that didn't know them and only minimally important to the people who did.

Standing for a second in wonder, starting to definitely feel the buzz of that last beer. The room starting to quiet. He looked down to the paper in his hand. Glancing to the right at nobody, he imagined the congressman's aid standing there as if he had been the real congressman, suddenly feeling a surge of courage.

Clearing his throat, the room went silent.

"Thank you all for coming here on such short notice. I look around and see a lot of familiar faces from the media. I know that you would all rather be home with your families on a Saturday, and I thank you for coming. The purpose of this press conference is that there have been urgent developments that I feel I need to talk about today." Clearing his throat again seeing a bottle of drinking water in front of him wishing he could take a sip. The lid was still sealed; he didn't want to fuss with it.

Suddenly realizing he wasn't in the groove. "Look, for the last two years I have been cooperating with federal law enforcement in a wide ranging investigation of official corruption in the greater Atlanta area." Giving a stern glance around the room. "There are some bad sons'a'bitches doing some bad things and we want to get to the bottom of it."

A buzz of voices rose in the room, grins of anticipation, thumbs up rising in the room.

"The focus of this investigation has been a number of city officials including the Atlanta mayor's office, the city council, a number of city agencies, and the Atlanta police department. All sorts of dudes doing bad things."

The buzz foaming into a small roar. Jeff raising his voice,

suddenly becoming more self-conscious about the nasal thing though feeling very confident anyway. "Excuse me!" Raising his hands quelling the voices, leaning into the microphones clearing his throat again, "Excuse me!" The roar subsiding.

"I will be meeting with the FBI on Monday afternoon to provide a long list of names of officials who I and my staff, working with the FBI, have identified as the center of this scandal." Jeff pausing, surprised at the room's perfect silence. "I expect that there will be an announcement as early as week's end by the FBI that they have obtained the names and what their next actions will be."

A mix of voices rose when one spoke out loudly, "Congressman Schedz, what has your involvement been?"

Looking over to Shonna she motioned a slicing across her throat with her finger signaling him to cut it off.

Looking into the crowd as he folded the paper in his hand leaning to speak into the microphones, "Listen guys, I can't answer any questions, but I am sure you will get details in the FBI's briefing next week." Turning stepping from the podium, the room climbing with excited voices. Three escorts intercepting him before he could get four feet from the podium, joined by the other men in trench coats. Jeff looked around for Shonna, nowhere to be seen.

In a minute he was stuffed into the back of a black limousine with the windows blackened, whisked away.

"Where are you taking me?"

The driver looking back over his shoulder. "Back to your hotel. There will be people to meet us there. Sit back, it's just a few minutes."

Looking back seeing that they were being followed by a big black car, another ahead of them. An escort, Jeff thought. *Cool!*

Sitting back in the darkened silence of the space made for eight people his head churned with anxiety at the events of the day, how he had just walked from the podium announcing something he knew nothing about concerning people he had never met. Mayor? Chief of Police?

And all those guns! Shaking his head muttering to himself.

"Jesus, what have I gotten myself into?"

Saturday, 5:34 PM: Back at the Hotel

The limo drove up to the same back door they used last time. Before Jeff could open the car door two men in trench coats appeared, one opening the door, leaning in telling Jeff to have his key ready. He reached into his pocket pulling it out emerging from the car.

One of the men walked up to Jeff speaking in a quiet firm voice, "This situation is very serious, you are to follow only my instructions or Agent White. Do you understand?"

"Agent White?"

The man couldn't help himself breaking character with a small grin, "Okay, Nancy, or—" turning to the man next to him, "what's her alias again?" then answering his own question continuing, "oh, yeah, or *Shonna* as you probably know her."

"I didn't know her last name," Jeff grinning at the man, "not that it matters I guess."

They moved in unison toward the back door of the Sheraton Hotel, a man stepping through it from the inside, holding the door open, they walked through. Soon he was standing at his room door. The agent leaned forward giving it four rapid knocks. The door opened. There stood Shonna with another man behind her.

Shonna leaned forward giving Jeff a light hug, "Hey, that was a good job back there! You looked natural, and your adlibs, they were great. I think we pulled it off! I've already gotten a call saying there's a meeting at the club in," studying her watch, "almost four hours." Thanking the men as they turned away, the other one in the room pushing past them into the hallway. Turning to them, "Thanks guys." Smiling to Jeff, "Well, don't just stand there, come in!"

Walking into the room Jeff noticed some kind of electronic box sitting on the round table, a laptop computer connected to it with a cable. He walked around the table, admiring the laptop thinking this was probably only the third one he'd ever seen, they were so new.

"What's that?" he pointed to the rig on the table.

"Surveillance gear. We've been listening to conversations going on at Magic Town and a couple other places. You would not believe what we stirred up. It's more than we were hoping!"

Jeff walked up leaning over the computer screen. He saw what looked like a floor plan, recognized it as Magic Town including the hallway that Shonna had taken him down last night to the back parking lot. He could hear a low volume of voices coming through the speaker of the computer.

"We've got about a thousand ears on the place right now, ears all over the city, we won't miss a word. Antonio's phone has been going off like a fire alarm!"

She smiled, "We gave that beehive *one hell of a whack!*"

Jeff heard the name Antonio again, trying to remember who it was, but was too distracted to ask. Standing up straight, stretching, pulling off the stinky coat, "God I gotta get that smell away from me. I hate cologne!" Shonna turned her face from the screen lowering the headphone she had cupped to her ear. Sitting watching him.

He yawned, "Man, that really took a lot out of me. You know, I could really use a nap."

She smiled, standing up, "Listen, I have a change of clothes and I could really use a shower, so why don't you stretch out and I'll wake you in a few hours."

Jeff sat on the bed pulling his shoes off slowly. "So what's next?"

"Sleep." She hung a dress on the back of the bathroom door, grabbing a small bag going into the bathroom, pulling the door closed, it didn't latch because of her dress hanging on the top of the door.

Jeff flopped onto the bed thinking that he would just fall asleep like he did this morning. Instead he just lay there trying to keep his eyes closed. Glancing over at the clock which said almost six o'clock. Hearing the shower start, he got up stepping to the bathroom door, banged on it, the door opening an inch. He talked through the opening, "How much time do I have to sleep?" He passed his eye quickly through the opening seeing her naked form behind the marbled glass of the shower door. He sighed.

She replied with the shower's echo to her words, "Until eight, so go lay down!" Jeff glanced at the clock, turning stepping back to the bed laying down again. He closed his eyes listening to the quiet chorus of voices coming from the laptop computer, wondering why he had never seen such neat technology. Before he could give it another thought he was asleep.

Jeff opened his eyes. The room was dark except for a small reading lamp in the corner. He was laying on his left side, Shonna laying next to him asleep. She was turned on her right side with her face only a foot from his. He listened to her soft regular breathing. As she slept he studied her face. Her features were soft, her nose came to a point, sort of, not a sharp point, very shapely, very feminine, he thought, with just the slightest upturn that made her look slightly aloof though not snotty. Her facial features were fine, like one of those two-foot tall dolls you see in the store usually dressed in Victorian-era clothes. He could smell just the lightest fragrance of perfume. Or was that the soap she used?

I wonder what she would do if I kissed her?

He felt an urge to touch her in any way. Just the softest brush with his hand, maybe. Thinking about everything that happened today with his *blackmailing slut*, he doubted that she wanted his advances. Watching her, listening to her regular soft breathing, wondering what she was really like, if they had met some other way, some other time. He tried to do his little tenth-second flash like he felt when he met Jennifer. Somehow it wouldn't come. Her being here now made her too real for that. She had somehow managed to peek around that façade of fantasy.

There was something very different about this woman. He knew he had never met another quite like her. Her mix of determination, feminine beauty, intelligence, street smarts made for a very unusual combination in anybody let alone in such a wholly encapsulated woman. Part of him was intimidated by her; part of him felt like he knew her his whole life. He tried to measure her against all the women he'd known in his life. His mind flew through his catalog of faces, voices, bodies, smiles, eyes. He couldn't think of any woman who compared. Not even close. He tried to go through the little collection of conversations with this woman. They were so varied.

Moments of near lovingness, moments like the one when he was standing there naked when his little whore was laying naked next to him. Yeah, he was pretty sure a kiss wouldn't be welcomed.

Laughing to himself rolling over onto his back, turning to the clock which said seven twenty-two. Sitting up crossed legged on the bed, surprised that he felt so rested, frowning thinking that it can be another all-nighter.

It was more than a half-hour later when Shonna's alarm went off. She rolled over with it in her hands pressing a button to make it stop. Rolling back over to Jeff who was laying down again next to her. Smiling, "Hey there. Did you get some sleep? Sounded like it from the snoring."

"Sorry, didn't mean to wake you. That happens when I'm really tired."

"Don't worry, nothing could keep me awake, I've only had what now, five hours sleep in the last forty hours?" A light stretch, swinging her legs off the bed.

"Okay," she said walking up to the computer, "What have you rascals been up to?" Sitting down in the chair at the table holding the computer's mouse, clicking a couple times, leaning forward staring intently at the screen, text flying by. "Oh, yeah, come to mama," speaking softly.

"What are you reading?"

"Transcriptions of everything that has been said in that building since this morning."

Swinging his legs to the floor, stepping to look over her shoulder. "Wow, look at that," watching the words fly by. "Are there people doing all that typing somewhere?"

"Yep."

"Can you do searches for words?"

"Yep. Watch." Typing in the word *money* in a small box on the screen, suddenly there were lines of text on the screen with the word money highlighted.

"Cool, how about congressman?"

Typing it in, just a couple lines showed. She laughed, "Watch this!" She typed the word *scrooge* into the box, the screen filling with lines showing the word highlighted.

"Why scrooge?"

"That's your tag. Your nickname they call you."

"Scrooge?"

"Must mean you're cheap. Miserly maybe. Greedy, I guess. Maybe they think you are stealing their Christmas!" Turning her head, glancing at him with a smile, "But it could have been worse, right?" She laughed, "Wow, you are taking this seriously, *that's not really you,* you know."

Jeff laughing, "Yeah, it's pretty funny that would hurt my feelings, huh? It's not like I am the congressman."

Turning to him again, "But that ownership is very good, though, that will really help us tonight because it will be all up close this time."

"Where?"

"Magic Town, of course."

"What?" Jeff's horrified expression screamed of the murders this morning, "Why are we going back there? I'm worried this is getting *way too* dangerous!"

Turning her chair toward Jeff squinting at him, giving him a long searching look. "Yeah, you have seen a lot today. And I am so sorry for that. You can just walk out that door and be done with all this and fly back to wherever you came from. But just so you know, you probably wouldn't make it to the airport." Jeff's incredulous expression struck her as she studied his eyes. "Like it or not mister Jeff, you are in this." He rolled his eyes toward the darkened ceiling. "Until those sons'a'bitches are in custody I am afraid that you are in my loving care."

He paused at the word *loving,* thinking maybe he should have kissed her after all.

Suddenly he came to his senses. "Wait! I'm trapped!"

Jeff turned away angry, pacing the room in front of Shonna. Feeling a wave of confusion washing over him. He remembered as a kid being on cliffs along the Pacific Ocean, suddenly surrounded by the shadow of a huge wave over his head barreling down on him, the feeling of utter helplessness, the enormous wall of foaming water smashing him against the rocks, receding quickly with a thousand wet hands pulling at his clothes, foamy wet fingers tugging, clawing at him, dragging him over the precipice, off the cliff's face down into the wet churning swarm twenty feet down—no way to come back up—with only one way the story could end if those hands succeeded in their mission to pull him over. Only his desperate tearing at the cliff's erosion-smoothed face saving him as the foamy beast retreated leaving him hanging face-down looking over the edge into the cold roiling froth below.

Here he was again, utterly overwhelmed as though he was being pulled over another inescapable ledge, the same sense of panic, fear of drowning overtaking Jeff, gasping for breath, "This is not right! *This is not right!* You sucked me into this thing without ever telling me what's going on! You have spoon fed me like your little trained monkey with just enough so that I would do the next trick! *This is bullshit!*"

Pacing back and forth, turning to glare at her, pacing again without looking her direction. Turning to her sharply, "So now what, are you going to put a stick up my ass and run all over Atlanta waving me around! Or like some kind of human red cape in front of the bull?"

Glowering at her, she sat silently watching him. "What!" he snapped.

Replying softly, "I knew this would happen. You would have to be a dope not to know the danger we have put you in. But these are a bunch of really, really bad men. It's your duty to help us."

"Duty? What, are you waving the flag now? Duty? DUTY!"

She stood up quickly, "Keep your voice down! Let me speak!"

Jeff turned sitting firmly on the bed. A minute of silence except for the ongoing soft hum of voices coming from the computer.

"It's just not that simple." She looked to the ceiling thinking. "Sure, along comes this good looking man who happens to look like the frigging twin brother of a man we have been tracking for two years. That man who has defiled his public faith and who has enabled the largest criminal enterprise in Atlanta history." Looking at Jeff with an almost scowling expression. "That man is a pig! And the people he has roped into this are animals, demons, whatever you want. And they have to be stopped."

She stood up starting to pace in the same path Jeff just circled. "There were three people murdered today by these animals. Murdered, Jeff. Gone. One of them a thirty four year-old mother of two." She stopped turning to him. "You saw her die. She died in your arms!" Panting, pausing with short breath, turning to him. "You have two kids, right?"

Bolting up looking at her intently, "Yes, I do! And I intend to go home to them on Monday afternoon! Is there a problem with that?"

She stepped to him reaching, taking his hands. "Look, Jeff. I'm sorry. I know this is a mess, and we didn't mean to get you this involved." Sighing. "It just…kind of…happened."

Pulling away from her, Jeff burying his face in his hands. "I dunno. I just *don't know!*"

He looked at his watch. It was past eight. Turning to Shonna, "Look, enough for now. I have to call to say good night to the kids. Can you give me a few minutes?"

"Sure." Stepping to the door, turning back with a doubtful expression as though she was going to warn him about something, with second thoughts she turned back to the door, looking both ways along the hallway, stepping out closing the door behind her.

Jeff sat for another minute, reaching for the phone. After two rings his son picked up the phone saying hi daddy and was it dark where he was. Jeff smiled feeling better. "Yes, honey, it's dark here. Is it dark there yet?"

His son Scott chuckled into the phone saying brightly, "I saw you on TV today!"

Jeff felt a lurch in his stomach, "TV? You saw daddy on TV?" The room collapsed around him listening to his son prattle on about seeing him on TV when he was changing the channels.

"Uh, honey," his son continuing on, "Scott? Scott!" His son paused, "Can I talk to gramma?"

A second later his mother's voice was laughing talking to his son, "Yes, you can watch Doug and Pork Chop, but it's not on until after dinner." A pause, "So Mister World Traveler, how was your grand night out?"

Jeff hesitated...the words flowing out, "It was fun. The Underground, wish you guys had been here, it's kind of a cool place."

"I tried to call your hotel room, I don't know, must have been around nine, midnight there, but you didn't pick up. You sounded kind of down when you called yesterday, and I wanted to make sure you were okay."

"Yeah, I guess I lost track of time." He felt calm, pretty sure she couldn't tell he was lying. "Lots going on there. Had dinner, listened to a blues band in some barbeque joint at the Underground, missed the train and had to take a cab back to the hotel. It was nice, guess I just lost track of time. Why, is everything okay?"

"Just miss you, the kids sure miss you."

"Mom, you have no idea how much I wish I was home."

"By the way, your son says he saw you on TV today. Must have been around two this afternoon when he was flicking channels looking for cartoons when *he wasn't supposed to be watching TV*," Jeff heard her directing that to Scott, "but anyway that's what he said."

"TV? That's funny." Jeff could feel his heart beating in his chest. "Me on TV? Really? Wow, that would be something."

"Yeah, he came screaming into the kitchen to me to come look but by the time I came out there was nothing but a story about some press conference with some congressman, but there was no picture of him."

"A congressman from here, yeah I read something about him in the hotel newspaper." He suddenly flashed that he may have said too much.

"You read the USA Today? That's funny, I didn't think you read those things they toss onto your hotel door. You said you don't like it because it has no comics, right?" laughing.

"I was looking for the weather to make sure Monday'll be okay flying. There's supposed to be a big snow storm coming."

"Jeffy, is everything okay? You sound...I don't know...kind of tense." Pause. "Jeff, are you all right?"

Sighing, "Yeah, just tired and a little lonely. Look mom, did you talk to Donna?"

"Yes, she called and I told her I didn't think it's a very good idea for her to bring anybody around here."

"What did she say?"

"She didn't sound very happy about it but said she would wait to talk to you next week."

"Thanks mom. Thank you for not mentioning me."

"Yeah, she can be pretty stubborn and I didn't want any confrontation, especially when you're not here."

"Thanks mom."

"Listen, honey, you sound exhausted. Sounds like you've had a busy day."

Jeff smiled to himself that she had no idea, knowing that *was* him on the TV today.

"Honey, why don't you take a nap or something? You need to take better care of yourself. Sounds like you're trying to do too much. Maybe go to bed early."

She paused, he could almost feel a hug from her.

"Honey hold on." She cupped her hand over the phone, "You two stop it! Nicole, leave your brother alone. Scott. Scott! Leave your sister alone!" Uncupping her hand, "Look, I've gotta go. I swear when gramma's on watch they seem to think it's free-for-all time." Cupped hand, "You two!" Uncupped, "Sorry, honey. But hey listen, get some sleep. Give us a call tomorrow night, okay?" Saying their goodbyes hanging up.

The call definitely raised his spirits even with the sense of *the inevitable* washing over him. He sat on the bed looking behind him trying to picture Jennifer laying naked there just a few hours ago, the side of the bed where Shonna lay as he wondered if he should kiss her. "God, I'm a mess," out loud. Shaking his head vacantly thinking of his mother, "She would not understand." Sighing. "Not a minute of this."

He always marveled at how his mother had a way of seeing solutions in situations that totally evaded him. How many times when he would see a situation—or be in a situation—that he couldn't figure out which way was up when she would offer up the simplest perspective, even to complicated situations in his aerospace work, the easiest solution would just appear on her lips. Just four words sometimes, so simple, so succinct. A perfect solution for situations that utterly baffled him. He wondered what she would say to all this nonsense he was involved in here. He knew how he got here, could see the cascading of events, how one event led to the next, how he was about to be dragged to god who knows where, be put in front of god who knows who, in god who knows what situation.

Yes. He knew exactly how he got here.

But then, he didn't have a clue.

And now he was going back to Magic Town.

He stood up starting toward the window when there were four quick knocks at the door, Shonna walking into the room.

"Everything okay at home? Your mother sounded pretty concerned."

"You listened?"

"Yep."

Turning to her with angry face.

"Hey, listen, that's what we do." Walking over to the table, the door closing behind her, sitting in the chair casually. "Okay there, congressman, get the frown off your face and sit down, let me tell you the plan."

As Jeff sat down there was four quick knocks at the door, the door opened, an agent walking in with a tray of food from room service.

Shonna cleared a corner of the table as the man set it down, without a word he turned back out the door, closing the door behind him.

Uncovering the tray, "What say we eat while we talk? We're expected at the club at nine." Jeff suddenly realizing he was famished. Pulling the other chair up they dug in. There were four more opened Budweisers on the tray, after three bites he emptied one as quickly as possible. Motioning to Shonna to take one, she shook her head barely able to say, "On duty," between bites.

After they both began feeling a little less empty, she turned to Jeff, "How about we start with questions first. Then I will fill you in."

Without thinking Jeff asked, "Is it going to be safe tonight?"

"We've never ever fouled an op before." Taking another bite. "Not to say that it can't happen, but we've got tonight under good control," pointing to the layout of Magic Town on the screen. "We've been patiently waiting, but then all the sudden all hell broke loose and we've had to play catch-up."

Jeff swallowed, picking up the second beer with a sip, "And the congressman, how's he doing?"

Frowning, "He died in a tragic car accident day after tomorrow in a big snow storm. Very tragic, very sad."

Jeff felt a short choke, coughed, another swig of beer. "Any idea yet who were the other two?"

"The congressman's body guards."

"I thought you just said that you've never had an op go bad? And what kind of congressman needs body guards?"

"That wasn't our op." Putting her food down looking at Jeff, "And when you're that particular congressman, I guess even body guards don't help." Giving a chew. "Look, we don't know what happened. The only witnesses were the ones who left that house this morning assuming it happened when they were even in the house, the mayor and all, we have no idea who saw what." Picking up her food again, taking a bite continuing talking with food in her mouth. "We'll probably never know. The only thing we've got going is that they think he survived and is alive and healthy and getting ready to blow the whistle on the whole thing." Wiping her hands on a cloth napkin with a soft burp, reaching for a glass of water, smiling, "So how you doing? Feeling a little better about this?"

A reluctant nod.

Glancing at her watch, standing up, "Okay, let's get you back into costume."

Jeff stood reaching for the smelly jacket. "No, you can wear the one you had on last night, your jacket. We'll probably be in a really smoky room so nobody will notice. I think you'll be more comfortable and we want you to be *totally* comfortable."

"Are you sure?"

Nodding, "But wait, you need a polo shirt, I ironed one earlier. It's in the closet."

Jeff stepped over to the closet pulling out a long-sleeved collared polo shirt, thought twice, pulling off his t-shirt walking over to his luggage, pulling out a clean t-shirt. He'd only been in his t-shirt for a little while but he felt like his sweating in the last hours made him smelly. Pulling on the polo.

"What about pants?" pointing down to his pants.

"There is an ironed pair of blue Dockers in the closet."

Walking to the closet pulling them off the hanger, realizing he was just too tired to go into the bathroom, stripping off his pants to put on the new ones.

"Ooooh, black underwear. Sexy!" He looked over as she gave a small whistle. "I've seen you every which way but in your underwear!" Laughing together. He suddenly felt more relaxed. Somehow this beautiful woman seeing him in his underwear seemed to put some form around their relationship that he hadn't felt before. How was it that her seeing him naked, he smiled to himself, didn't have the same effect as her seeing him in his underwear? Maybe it was because her response was actually playful, though he did like it when she complimented his body earlier. Yes, this tiny moment had a tiny effect on him and Shonna. Tiny. But it was there.

Tucking in his shirt, putting on his favorite sport coat, "So how do I look?"

"Let's see your mole," stepping forward inspecting his face. "No, it's smeared. You've really got to be careful not to touch your face, that could be a real problem."

Jeff went into the bathroom to wash his face with soap and a wash cloth. It felt good. A moment later he had his beauty mark again, this time not *pressed* onto his face. Twirling for Shonna she smiled, "Very good, very good!"

Jeff sat on the bed glancing at the clock. Almost eight-thirty. "So what's next, boss?"

"Like I told you, we're heading to Magic Town right now. Should only be Antonio."

"Antonio? You keep saying that name."

"Yep. The white fedora. You called it a Panama."

"Oh, Panama man! Antonio, huh? That's right, you mentioned him earlier. A new name in the cast."

"There are lots of names in this cast, you almost need a program to know who's who in this little drama. Antonio is owner of the club, at least we think, but the main man running it for sure. Seems he likes his little cash cow there and feels his turf is being threatened. My guess is that the bad guys are trying to put the squeeze on him."

"So what does he want to talk about?"

"I think he may be ready to give up some names. Your little press conference this evening is definitely making everyone nervous," grinning glancing over to the box and computer sitting on the table with voices still emanating from the computer's speaker, "and my guess is that he wants to stay ahead of the wave. Yeah, I think he wants to offer up as much as he can without pushing too many buttons with the bad guys. All my accounting work only ever deals with initials. I mean I can guess who they are taking all that money, but that's hardly good evidence for the prosecutor. I think he's ready to give us some names to go with all those initials." Pausing frowning in thought.

"But why give names to the congressman? Doesn't he already know that I'm—he's—already involved in all this?"

"Of course he does, but my sense is that he wants a more formal relationship with the congressman, like they say, mano a mano."

"Why?"

"That's easy, guaranteed immunity. At least that's what we're guessing he's hoping for. No matter how honest he thinks he is, he knows he's not totally clean."

Jeff paused, his hand cupped around his chin being careful not to touch his new mole. "So let's take a step back. The bad guys think the congressman is meeting with the FBI on Monday and is ready to give up names. Right?"

"Yep, that's my guess."

"Antonio wants to do a preemptive thing to stay on the good

guys' side."

"Yep again."

"And getting the congressman killed would be very bad for that. It would make things much worse for him. Much worse."

She smiled, "Keep going, Sherlock."

"That means he either wants to make a deal or he wants to help us take down the bad guys or at least get them out of his hair." Pausing, "Or both."

"Yep exactly, without the congressman, those names are nothing but names, no key witnesses, no protection." Smiling. "Yep, you got it. Good job!"

Still, Jeff felt a sinking feeling pondering the possibilities.

Jeff stood up determined. "And if Antonio has his way, you get the bad guys delivered on a plate, he gets to go on his way, and I get to make it back to Seattle in one piece Monday afternoon." Shonna nodding, half-smiling. "And so here we go into the dragon's mouth."

Jeff frowned, looking at the computer screen. "As long as the other bad guys don't show up then it should be fine, right? And what fool in his right mind would go to Magic Town after everything that happened today?" She nodded looking at him thoughtfully. Jeff was still trying to convince himself, "And who in their right mind would go into the dragon's mouth if things happened the way the bad guys think they did."

Jeff held out his arms as in, *Well?*

"I guess we'll go," Shonna glancing around the room, "but I need a little conference with the guys, so let me step outside for a minute."

Ten minutes later, four knocks, a key rattle. Shonna coming back in. "Well, Mister Congressman, you just got yourself two new body guards that just happen to carry badges."

Jeff shrugging, "I guess we go now?"

Shonna walked over to the table with the congressmen's coat contents spread out, picking up the snub nosed pistol, turning handing it to Jeff. "And you really know how to use this?"

"Remember I told you I used to own one." Taking the gun, "And you still can't hit the broad side of a barn with it."

"You won't be shooting at barns."

Trying to reach into his coat side pocket to put away the gun, "Damn, sewed shut." He tried tucking the gun into the inside breast pocket, it made the coat sag.

Watching this Shonna smiled. Finally, Jeff took off his coat reaching for the congressman's stinky coat, putting it on tucking the little gun into the right outside pocket.

Frowning, patting the bulk in the pocket, "You know, though, this may be a bad omen, he never even pulled it out."

Shonna shook her head. "It's only a bad omen if you don't pull yours out *first*."

Saturday, 9:08 PM: Antonio

Soon Jeff was in the back seat of a black Ford Crown Victoria, a *Crown Vic* as the cops liked to call it, with tinted back windows leaving the hotel parking lot. The agents shook his hand introducing themselves warmly which surprised Jeff because they had hardly said a word to him all day. Ted and Vic. Ted was driving with Shonna next to him, Vic was in the back seat with Jeff.

Before long they arrived at Magic Town, pulling right up to the front door.

"The front door?" Jeff asked with a worried tone.

Ted looked over his shoulder, "No dark back parking lots for you tonight," half-smiling, "congressman."

A young valet attendant ran up to the driver's window, getting out Ted told the attendant, "Antonio says leave it here." The young man backing away without a word.

Jeff could hear the THUMP THUMP THUMP THUMP of the music, the muted sounds of men howling inside.

Yes, it was Saturday night at Magic Town, the front of the building crowded like last night with lots of black men milling around, a long line at the door.

In a moment they pushed past the line, through the front door, the line readily yielding to the men in trench coats. Jeff walking forward to the curtain leading into the bar pushing the black curtain aside as twirling lights cascaded into the short hallway. Perkins the bouncer turned looking down at Jeff with startled surprise—a tug on Jeff's sleeve pulling him away from the curtain, he turned seeing Perkins pull the curtain back to look after him, jaw dropped in stunned disbelief as Shonna tugged Jeff through the side door into the outer hallway he had been in last night going to the back parking lot, Ted and Vic following.

As they stood in the doorway she leaned to Jeff in a firm tone, "Remember it's Shonna. Shonna. This guy is really sharp, he picks up on *everything*. Don't blow it, okay?" He nodded.

They walked around the corner soon turning left into the door that Jeff had seen the light around when they walked past it last night.

The room was softly lit with lamps on tables, stained glass shades, no overhead lights. Antonio standing up walking forward to greet Jeff warmly, "Congressman, you certainly look very good for a man who was shot four times this morning. I heard they killed you!"

Jeff smiling confidently, "The rumors of my death have been greatly exaggerated."

"You know Mark Twain! Wonderful! Come sit down, we have a lot to talk about."

Jeff sat down in a large stuffed chair around a small round table, Antonio facing them sitting in a similar chair, all done in a maroon velvety fabric, a third chair to Jeff's left. As his eyes adjusted to the dark room Jeff saw two men standing against the wall behind Antonio. Jeff turned around seeing Ted and Vic standing against the wall behind him in exactly the same pose with arms down in front of them, hands clasped loosely together.

Shonna came around as Antonio jumped up, stepping forward, "Oh, and my beautiful Shonna, our new rising star!" leaning forward, exchanging a quick peck on the lips, Shonna sitting down with Jeff to her right.

"Let's have a drink!" Antonio turning to a small refrigerator next to him starting to open it, Jeff seeing beer bottles inside. Antonio thinking for a second, closing the refrigerator, turning to the man on his left behind him, "Better yet, call Marla and have her bring us a tray of drinks," looking from Jeff to Shonna, "What will you have?" They spoke over each other with drink names, Antonio put up his hand looking around to the man behind him, "Okay, never mind, just have her bring a full tray, lots of drinks, alright?" The man turning away reaching toward a phone.

Antonio was shorter than average, slim build, light mulatto complexion. He spoke with a slight Cuban accent by Jeff's ear. Jeff guessed that he was maybe his age, around forty, maybe forty-five or even a little older. Antonio wore two-toned shoes, white on top surrounded by a chocolate brown. His hair was jet black, greased back. He sported a pencil-thin mustache, dressed in white chinos and white silk shirt buttoned up to his neck with a shirt collar that came to points five inches from his neck. His face had sharp lines to its shape, chiseled from stone like those Mayan statues with their stern expressions, his forehead protruding over his eyes covering them in shadow in the light of the room. Jeff could see his eyes were black with a sparkly glow as Jeff searched into them trying to read this man.

Antonio seemed amiable enough with a very open expression. *Almost honest* looking with his wide Ricky Ricardo grin, you would almost expect to hear Lucy's voice any second, "Oh *Ricky!*"

Glancing around the room Jeff noticed the door on his left that Antonio had gone through into the bar last night. He was trying to figure out the motif of the décor, noticing Antonio's white Panama hat on a rack by the door. The decorating was deliberate without a doubt. While it looked varied, it was not eclectic. He guessed it was a Caribbean style for the overall design, with touches from different cultures, mostly Latin America from what he could see. All done very tastefully and very carefully. Jeff found himself fascinated by the decorating. Here they were in this sleazy strip club where the only decorations were dollar bills hanging out of the strippers' scant clothing and a cartoon magician dangling a cartoon rabbit on the back wall. Then here was this room with everything in perfect order. This is a fastidious man who pays attention to details and likes order around him. Jeff nodding to himself that this man gave away more than he planned.

Yes, Antonio liked order. This went a long way to explaining why Jeff's little press conference had caused Antonio to call this meeting so urgently. He was definitely interested in keeping order.

Any sense of order.

Listening Jeff could hardly hear the thumping music, barely audible even though it was just through the wall behind Antonio. "How did you make this room so quiet? The bar is just on the other side of that wall, right?"

"Triple wall, insulation inside and between each layer. And that door," pointing the door leading to the bar, "has a special sound-proof design. Pretty good, eh?" Jeff craning trying to hear, nodding impressed. "I would like to say this was all my design, but it was not. It was my idea, though, but I had to pay a sound engineer from one of my other little businesses to come in to design it. The ceiling is insulated, too!" Antonio looking behind him at the wall, glancing at the door, up to the ceiling with a satisfied smile.

"So, congressman, I hear you had a pretty busy morning," laughing with a chortle, "body armor is a man's best friend, eh? I tell you what, that Kevlar is some amazing stuff, one of the great modern inventions. Boy, that was smart to be vested! You just never know what can happen in these poor neighborhoods in south Atlanta. I hear even the dogs wear body armor!" he burst out laughing, Jeff and Shonna chuckling nervously along with him. Jeff noticed one of the men standing behind Antonio smiling. "But tell me, how did you know you were in danger? I mean it seems like you were among friends, no? I wasn't there, of course, but you are the man, right? And why would you go around in body armor unless you thought that there was going to be trouble?"

Shonna gave Jeff an almost imperceptible nod, telling him to step up to the plate. He got up his nerve deciding he needed to start controlling the conversation. "Yeah, well, it doesn't hurt to have insurance right? We don't think, 'Hey, I'm going to be in a car accident tomorrow so I better go get insurance!'"

They all gave a little laugh, Antonio smiling, "Yes, congressman, we all carry useless insurance until something happens and it turns out it wasn't so useless after all, eh?"

Jeff liked the amiable tone of the conversation even though he knew everyone was positioning themselves, he wanted to keep the dialog friendly as long as he could. "So, Antonio, tell me about you, where you from?"

"I was just another little kid coming across from Cuba. Funniest thing, I have this uncle who put big pontoons on a '48 Chevy Fleetline, you know, very sleek with a long hood. The car was so round it could probably float by itself! The car was all decked out. It was my uncle's pride and joy. I was only twelve when we came across but I remember how he used to baby that car. He would go out into the jungle to pick plants that he would use to make wax for the car, I don't know what kind, but man he would baby that car. I remember my aunt used to say that he loved that car more than her.

He made sure to tell everyone in the family what a great sacrifice he was making putting his baby in salt water, telling us that we would all have to help clean his baby when we got to Miami."

"My uncle said he picked that car because it had a—you probably know more about this than I do I'm sure—something he called a good center of gravity so the car wouldn't be too heavy on the front or back. People think we were all sugar cane or cocoa farmers in Cuba back then, but my uncle was a mechanical engineer, we were very proud of him. He was the only family member to ever get a college degree! He worked designing power plants in Cuba, not that it helped, nobody ever had any electricity. But I think that center of gravity stuff was a lot of bullshit—it's the only car the family owned!" He laughed, they smiled with him. "He connected a little outboard motor on the trunk and floated sixteen of my family to Miami. The trunk was so small that I was the only one who could fit, I mean there were babies in the car, but none that they could sit back there to steer the car to Miami."

"So he showed me how to fill the tank from the big gas can in the trunk next to me, how to pull the cord to start the outboard motor, then they stuffed this skinny little twelve year-old kid into the trunk and kept yelling, 'Go more right!' or 'Go more left!' or 'Are you awake back there!' and I kept hitting my head on the trunk lid that was propped up with a board. I wanted to lay down in that little trunk and go to sleep but whenever I started getting sleepy I would hear, 'Hey Antonio, you awake! We're almost there!' But we weren't almost there all night until finally the sky was starting to get light and through the little opening under the trunk lid I could see lights in the distance and knew we were coming to Miami!"

"It was a bit rough out there and I got really wet. But I look back and am proud that I drove my family to Miami from Cuba!" He started laughing again. "We started off right after dark on a Tuesday night. We drove that son-of-a-bitch across the channel right up onto the beach! We all got off and pulled and yanked those pontoons off, then we drove to Little Havana in time for breakfast on Wednesday morning!" Jeff and Shonna laughing at his laughter. Antonio taking out a cigar, "Do you mind?" Jeff motioning it was fine.

Jeff did the math in his head, ninety miles or so in maybe twelve hours, that would be seven miles an hour. He wasn't sure that a '48 Chevy, which must have been big car to hold so many people, could go that fast, maybe with the currents…he must have had a skeptical expression, "Yeah, that's quite a story."

Antonio seeing Jeff's doubt, ignoring it, "Do you smoke cigars congressman? No? Well, this is a Cuban hand-made cigar, a Cohiba Habana, the finest cigar in the world! You'll pay over a hundred dollars for a small box at the Duty Free in Paris, and then you'll be lucky if the U.S. Customs doesn't confiscate them!" Laughing. "I'll bet those customs guys get twenty dollars a smoke when they sell them on the black market, eh?" He lit the cigar, "Nah, probably not, those guys probably don't sell them, they must take them home to smoke them themselves. But what a waste if they just throw them away, huh? Sí, that would be a shame!"

Antonio taking a deep drag letting the smoke filter out his nose creating a gray-blue screen in front of his face. He couldn't leave Jeff's doubt behind. "Yeah, Cuba. Look, I was just a little kid and most of what I remember is what my family told me. Hell, they could've told me that Chevy flew to Miami and I would believe them!" the three of them laughing together.

Antonio taking another long drag, setting his cigar in the ash tray next to him. "So congressman, how's business? I hear you have gotten pretty tangled up with the mayor's gang. Too bad about those others today," making the sign of the Cross on his chest. "They are a really dangerous bunch, but I tell you I was surprised. Yeah, very surprised. That kind of thing hasn't been happening for, I don't know," turning to the men standing behind him, "ten years, maybe?" One of them nodding. "Ten years, then all of the sudden this." Shaking his head sternly, "It's bad, bad business. It's going to start causing a lot of trouble." Picking up his cigar giving it a couple puffs. "Yeah, bad business. Muy malo."

The room was quiet except for the very faint thumping sound coming through the walls. They could hear none of the men's shouting. Jeff imagining the scene going on in the next room with tits flying, men yelling pounding on their tables. He wondered if

Pick had another sucker in there that he picked up at the ATM next to Rickey Rocket's and what a ride that man was in for. God, he was sure the poor bastard would be better off looking like Elvis than a certain congressman that had come to be the bane of Jeff's existence in the last, looking at his watch, twenty nine hours.

Antonio leaned forward, "So, I thought it might be a good thing to ask you here so we could talk about this little situation." Picking up the cigar, puffing, pointing it at Jeff. "The way I see it is that they wanted to kill you because you *know too much* about their business." Chuckling, "And I also hear that you maybe you *wanted too much* of their business!"

Jeff starting to speak when Shonna cut him off, "You know, Antonio, it's not like the congressman has to be so nice," giving Jeff a sideways glance. *A signal* it occurred to Jeff. *He was being too nice!* Damn, they hadn't practiced that! How was he supposed to act? Jeff straining to remember anything he could about this Congressman Frank Schedz, he was just one of what, four hundred and something people in the House of Representatives? He could not remember a thing. His local congresswoman just happened to be a friend he'd met a long time ago. That didn't help here. He couldn't even think of the name of the person in the next congressional district. He was clueless how he was supposed to act.

"You know," Antonio puffing giving a slight smile, "Funny thing. I met you once, congressman, you probably don't remember. It was some kind of dinner party or reception, I don't remember what. Lots of people. But I could hear your voice in the room, very loud as I remember, and so I kind of walked up near you and there was this man, this *pompous ass!* He was going on and on and on and people standing around trying to laugh at his bad jokes. He was a buffoon! You could just tell that if he wasn't a congressman that people wouldn't listen to him because he *was* such a pompous ass. I remember walking away thinking what a prick you are. But look at you, here you sit so polite. You're not a prick, you're a nice guy. It kind of makes me wonder…"

Redirect! Jeff felt a flash of panic, "Look, like you said, I've had a long day. You try getting murdered and see if it doesn't take the prick right out of you for a couple days." Antonio burst out laughing again—this time Jeff and Shonna didn't join in.

Jeff scowling, "So you Cuban son-of-a-bitch, why are we here?"

"See! That's better!" Antonio laughing again. "Much better! You really need to practice that more or people will wonder. We can't have them *wondering*, can we?"

Panic flashed through Jeff...*wonder*? What was there to wonder? *Oh, my god, he's got this all figured out!*

Shonna gave Jeff a quick flash look that said *Buck up!* She snapped, "Okay, okay, let's get down to business Antonio."

Antonio turning to Shonna with a sly smile, "So tell me Shonna, why are *you* here?"

Shonna flicking her hair casually without hesitation, "Well, you know I had my first dance last night, and the congressman is sitting in the front row! He waited for me, wanted to buy me a drink, give him a lift back to his house up in Roswell. His driver," glancing at Jeff, "his driver wasn't feeling well so he left and let the congressman find his way home." Tossing her hair again casually. "I see the congressman on TV today, the next thing I know you're asking Perkins to set up a meeting and he calls me, then the congressman asked me to come along." Shrugging, "I mean I can leave if you want, Antonio," signaling toward Jeff, "he's a big boy. He can take care of himself. He knows his business," making no motion to get up.

"No, no, stay," Antonio waving his hands for her to stay down, "you know me, just giving you a hard time. Plus you know so much about this crazy business we are in!"

Finally the tray of drinks arrive. Antonio was very annoyed apologizing saying that it is Saturday night, the place is packed and that it's hard even for him to get good service. Jeff thinking to himself that all Antonio had to do was flip her a few fives and the service would pick up! Everyone grabbing something from the tray; Jeff lifting a Budweiser, taking a quick sip, setting it down on the little table in front of him.

With a sudden purposeful look, Antonio leaned forward, "Okay, let's get down to it. All hell is about to break loose—it already has as you know congressman—and I need some help." Looking at Shonna, "Give our friend here a rough breakdown of what goes on in your little room downstairs."

Shonna glancing around the room, "Everything? The whole story?"

"We're all friends here, right? Everything. He knows a lot about this, but it's good to hear it."

Shonna described the money operation downstairs, four full-time people counting and sorting cash, three part-timers keeping the club's cash straight at night and on weekends, all of them keeping accounting, making bundles for payments. "The numbers are staggering. We'll clear thirty eight million this year."

Jeff whistled, "Wow, this is all in protection money?" He knew the numbers already from the sheets he'd found in the congressman's coat pocket.

"Protection, drugs, prostitution, extortion," glancing at Antonio, "and the operations from the club and other little side businesses."

"Yes," Antonio leaning back proudly, "we even have a little record company, a recording studio!" Motioning to the wall behind him, "That was one of my sound engineers who designed the wall!"

Antonio leaned back shaking his head. "But it seems like they found out about my little cash operation downstairs and decided that I could manage all their dirty business. They give me, what, Shonna?"

"Seven percent."

"Okay, seven percent which will buy a lot of tacos." Taking a long thoughtful puff of his cigar letting the smoke slowly fill the space in front of him. "But I never liked it. I've got a good little business here, yeah it's a little out of—what do businessmen call it—right, a little out of the mainstream. But it's a good little cash cow, it makes lots of money. And I get most of it." Looking at his cigar thoughtfully, "And it's legal! But the bullshit these guys are involved will hurt a lot of people, it is hurting my reputation as a *legitimate businessman* to be associated with these jerks and now everybody is getting greedy, people are getting hurt."

The room was nearly quiet for what felt like a minute as Shonna and Jeff glanced at each other, Antonio puffing thoughtfully on his cigar. "But more people start showing up, messing with my business, more thugs packing guns, all sorts of people wanting accounting, more people getting cuts, and cash coming from *quien sabe*. Who the hell knows where from!"

There were two solid knocks on the door. The guard on Antonio's right walking around them toward the door as Vic stepped aside turning to the door, his right hand slipping into the front of his overcoat. Ted kept looking forward, his right hand making the same move into his overcoat. The door was opened. Perkins stepped halfway through the doorway with his deep melodic voice, "Everything okay in here, Antonio?"

Antonio waved casually at him, "Fine, fine, thank you for your concern, Perkins. Not to worry, we're all friends here."

Perkins looked intently at the two others sitting in the room, Jeff and Shonna turning around to look at him. Perkins gave them each a long, piercing inspection. Jeff feeling Perkins's intense gaze piercing his forehead striking the back of his skull with its intensity, beating against the back of his brain, wanting to turn away from those severe dark eyes.

Perkins shaking his head slightly with ferocity, "Okay, if you say so." Pulling back, the door closing.

"That Perkins, always looking after me. Good man." Antonio took a long drag from his cigar choking just a bit, "Permiso," spitting into the ash tray on his left. "Where were we? Oh, yeah, but the guys running the gang have gotten really careless and there are some very bad people showing up here, so many guns and god knows what. And it's *way too many people* now. It's too much!" Puffing his cigar, "And they're treating me like their little errand boy, like I'm some taxi dispatcher."

Jeff picked up his beer, taking a thoughtful drink remembering the groups of men at the back wall without drinks in the bar last night, "The henchmen, the ones I saw last night in the chairs at the back of the bar, kept coming and going. Enforcers?"

"You are very observant, my friend. Yes, I hate having them here, I hate talking to them, they're the slime of the earth, would kill their own mothers for a hundred dollars. I don't like them mixing with my good paying customers." Leaning over to spit again, this time for effect to emphasize his disgust, "Perkins would not let such people into the bar! Pigs!"

Jeff was amused at the thought that Perkins would actually block any man with money from coming in to spread his dough all over the place—he had been in there and couldn't really detect much difference between some of the men in there and the thugs sitting in the corner waiting for their next mayhem assignment, nodding at the thought which Antonio took for agreement with his last statement.

Antonio glanced around at the four men standing around them, Shonna could see Antonio suddenly realizing they needed ultra privacy. Jeff picking it up seeing the subtle excited expression on Shonna's face that maybe they were finally going to get down to it.

Antonio made a loose circle around his head with his hand glancing behind him, "We don't need these guys in the room, right? Like I told Perkins, we're all friends here, right? What say we let these nice gentlemen go stand in the hallway?"

Antonio motioned to his men as Shonna turned doing the same. In a moment it was just the three of them in the room. Jeff reaching down with his right hand patting the gun in his pocket, Shonna pulling her purse up so it was straight below her right hand.

Antonio reached around behind him pulling a little satchel around on the floor by his left side. Jeff thinking to himself, "Sure no guards. All friends here. All fully armed. *Now that's friends!*"

With the door now closed, Jeff looking firmly at Antonio, "And so you were saying, let me guess, now you want out."

"It's too much. I don't want their money anymore. Nada. But there's no way out of this business. You don't just turn in your notice like, 'Dear mayor, I don't want your stinky little thugs coming into my bar anymore, signed Antonio'" Laughing bitterly, "At least not without writing your will first!" He snubbed out his cigar with a large circular relish in the ash tray. "Pigs!" spitting into the ash tray in loathing.

"Look congressman, you and I have the same problem. When this thing blows up I will have Feds up my ass and lose everything, and I doubt you'll get any medal of honor. I would make a lousy prisoner, mi familia would be very disappointed in me. I can hear it now, 'You steered us across from Cuba just so you could end up in prison!' Even my mama would call me a *pendejo!*"

Antonio leaning in closer. "I want to, you know, kind of join up with you, see if we can't find a way out of this mess together. After this morning you know these guys are playing for keeps. If we don't find some way to get the Federales to take these guys out, then next time body armor won't help any of us."

"And what you did today! A press conference! That was beautiful! My phone started ringing the minute you said your last word, before your feet even left the room!" Leaning back in laughter turning to an answering machine next to him, "My phone rang all evening. The mayor, police chief, and all I could tell them was I had no idea what was going on, *nada!* I had to turn the ringer off it was driving me crazy!" Looking to the machine seeing the light blinking, "And look even now, at late this hour!"

Jeff looked to see the small answering machine next to Antonio watching the number on the face flip from 21 to 22 messages.

Glancing at Shonna, Jeff could see a look in Antonio's eye like he could see through her, glancing at Jeff. "I believe that what you said this evening congressman is true, that the Feds are already in this, and my good Shonna with her little stunt last night and what happened this morning is about to blow this whole thing wide open, isn't it!" Taking a slow drink keeping his eyes locked on hers. "And you know this if anybody does, I am not right our dear Shonna?" Glancing around the room in mock playfulness, "Should I smile for the camera, dear Shonna?"

Antonio stared intently at Jeff as he realized Antonio was looking at his chin, at his penciled-in mole. Antonio leaned back with a wide wry smile.

"Congressman, your mole is smearing!"

Saturday, 9:43 PM: Collaborator

Jeff felt a sharp panic turning to Shonna who sat staring at his chin horrified.

Suddenly Antonio burst out laughing, laughing so hard tears welled in his eyes, choking twice, steadying himself with hands on arms of his chair, tears rolling down his face. Jeff noticing Shonna reaching her right hand down toward her purse with a wary look toward Antonio.

"Wonderful, wonderful!" Antonio continued laughing, but it was not contagious— neither Shonna or Jeff laughed along watching him, glancing confused at each other. "Nobody is who they say they are! Wonderful!" Sitting up, taking a deep breath, "Well, maybe I am, but some days even I am not so sure of that!" He reached across the table offering his hand to Jeff who took it baffled as Antonio shook his hand vigorously. "I mean, how did you do that?"

"Do what?" Jeff looking confused at this man's behavior.

Antonio winked to Jeff, turning to Shonna. "And you!" She shrugged.

"You know," Antonio announced, "it's not often I get to watch a dead man giving a press conference. I mean I don't know he's dead, of course! But that's what I hear. I heard that he *wasn't* wearing a bullet-proof vest and that he took four shots in the chest straight on. I don't know too many men, even a pompous congressman who can do that!" Frowning at Jeff. "I have no idea who you are, but I am pretty certain you are no dead congressman!" Laughing taking a sip of his drink. "And you, my dear Shonna, I can only guess." Laughing again, "Wait, wait! Don't tell me! I don't want to know!" Taking a sip of his drink to quell his throat from the laughing, "No, no, really, don't tell me, let's keep it a mystery, shall we?"

Shonna leaned forward, "Okay, so you figured this out, you know what's going on. Now you've got to get serious and start staking your claim in this. We are getting ready to take this whole gang down, you've got to decide which side you're on!" Looking at Jeff half-smiling as she licked her thumb leaning to her right to wipe the eyebrow pencil from his chin. He grinned sheepishly as she turned back to Antonio. "I've got the numbers and nothing but initials, you've got the names." Leaning forward to Antonio intently. "Now talk!"

Antonio sat back, glancing back and forth between the faces in front of him holding his finger tips together spread out thoughtfully. "Immunity?"

"We can't make the deal here, you know that," Shonna said sternly, "but maybe I can make sure you get a deal."

"Then why…" Antonio sat back looking at her intently. "Okay. Okay. But remember who your friend is. Shonna, or whoever you are." Sipping his drink thoughtfully, "But my dear Shonna you know I am a good man. You know I don't do bad things," chuckling, "well, not *too many* bad things at least." He stared at her eye-to-eye as though he was extracting a deal from her by his sheer will. "But I will go along because these guys gotta get pulled the hell out of Atlanta and you will need to go deep or there'll be no peace."

Taking a sip from a glass of amber liquid with the ice melted. "No we have to do better than that." Taking another sip, setting the glass down looking intently from face to face, "Yes, we have to do better than that. *We need to take them out all at once!*"

Smiling, almost relaxed, "So Shonna, Shonna, Shonna, you ain't the dumb pretty face we thought you were." Chuckling shaking his head putting up his hands, "No, remember now, I don't wanna know," though she never made a motion to offer any explanation.

The three of them spent the next two hours as Shonna pulled out copies of the papers Jeff found in the stinky jacket. They started discovering who belonged to the initials along with all the details that Antonio could offer up as the pages went around the table. When they had those filled in with names, Antonio turned pulling another large stack of papers from a drawer in the end table next to him, a trove of information about victims of the enterprise passing it to Shonna, she handed them to Jeff, "I've seen these." He looked quizzical. "I made them!"

These records were similar in detail to Shonna's financial records, computer printouts showing the same good organization that was consistent with the entire operation. These pages had a date on top of each page and even a page number, the first page with "Page 1 of 42" neatly printed in the top right corner. The pages were in five columns with the titles "ID" with four digit numbers below it, "Name and Address" along with another column headed "Fee Type" with another "Amount" and the last column headed with "Status." They were not encoded like Shonna's other work so it was easy to see who these victims were.

Jeff was amazed at the scale of the gang's activities. Scanning down the pages. The organization was alphabetized by the victims' names. He saw Fred's Hardware Store was paying a thousand dollars a month for fire, "burg" which he assumed was burglary, that Fred was "current" with his payment.

Scanning down seeing a notation "remind" next to a name. He bent over toward Antonio who explained, "Oh, they get a friendly collections visit." He saw Jeff's grimace, "But just to get payment."

Antonio picked the page from Jeff's hand, scanning it pointing to an entry with "late" next to it. "This one gets a visit from our friends you saw in the back of the bar last night. That's not such a friendly visit."

"See this one," pointing to an entry with the notation "enforce" next to it. "Those visits are usually followed by a visit from the fire department."

Antonio shook his head, "Yes, this is very bad business, very bad. *Que muy malo!*"

Jeff shaking his head as he continued exploring the stack on his lap. "What happens when these guys pay for burglary insurance and somebody else breaks into their place?"

Antonio grinning, "Well, that's where the insurance part really *does pay off!*" He looked at Jeff's puckered brow. "This is not such a big town that we can't find out who did it, remember we have *so many eyes on the street!* So our friends pay him a little not-so-friendly visit to have a little talk about good manners and the expense of dental work these days. They are given the choice of being turned over to the police or paying a small regular restitution fee, maybe a hundred dollars a month." Frowning thinking about his words, "But mostly they are drug addicts so that doesn't work out very well and it is a lot of trouble for such a small amount of money so we generally just get them busted anyway, but sometimes we find new recruits to help us keep our business in order."

"Ah," he spat into the ash tray for emphasis, "what am I saying *our business*—this is not my business, this is *their business* and I don't want any more of it!"

Drinks were brought in again along with some tapas. The three of them sat heads down the whole time going over every detail they could discover in the papers and whatever else Antonio could recall.

Antonio reached back into the drawer pulling out a smaller stack of pages setting them on the table. "These are the money laundering channels." He went on to explain that some of the gang's members had legitimate, "Or maybe *not so legitimate*," businesses that their money went through, "to clean it up a little." They looked through these, maybe eight pages as Antonio explained them. These pages weren't as neatly organized in form as the other pages with lots of scribbled notes in different hands. Shonna explained to Jeff that these were as new to her as to him. This was definitely new information to her.

"It's funny business, money laundering. It's for those that feel they have a duty as an *American citizen* to pay taxes on the money they get from the misery of others, like it will ease their conscience. And then you have others like the mayor who can't be bothered and want to take it all in cash!" He laughed with such extreme bitter tone that it scarcely sounded like laughter.

They had spent another hour since the last drinks were brought in. By the time they were done, backs of pages were covered with notes, the stack of paper much thicker.

Finally, they all looked around to each other ready to say they were done when there was a knock on the door, a new tray of drinks was brought in by one of Antonio's men, taking the other trays away. They each took a drink giving a small gesture of a toast knowing this was all they could put together from what they had at hand.

Most important, they had a roster of the gang's members. Jeff looked over at the handwritten pages laying on the table in Shonna's neat writing, flabbergasted at the list of names, the extent of this whole illegal enterprise. It was almost a who's-who of Atlanta area politics as they told him, though most of the names he didn't recognize.

"So how did I do, am I on the good guys' team?" Antonio looked at Shonna anxiously. "Do I get immunity?"

"The game's not done yet. This is good information but you know I already had most of these printouts." Scanning through the pages on her lap one last time, looking at the notes she had scribbled from what Antonio had told her, "You really helped me fill in some details, though." Stacking all the pages together, "Now we have names, that's good stuff. And we have the money laundering data that will help us unwind the financial side for evidence." She rifled through the stack to make sure the pages were in order. "Let's just say that things are going the right way for you, but only if we pull this off. I promise to go to the prosecutor and tell him what you did here. I'll do what I can."

"Certainly, I understand. Just do what you can." He smiled, "The good news is that we all want the same thing, to take these bastards out. We can't be having no big turf war starting up and that's where this is headed. A lot of people will get hurt, and when it gets really nasty most of us have families that get hurt right along with the rest. The mayor sure knows about that!" Sipping from the glass next to him, ice cubes tinkling as he set the glass down.

Jeff did remember reading something about the mayor's family, it had to be more than ten years ago like Antonio said. The mayor was a city councilman at the time. They called it something like a home invasion robbery. He had never heard the term, that's what got his attention to read the article. Seems like gunmen burst into his son's or daughter's or somebody's house and killed all sorts of people, kids even if he remembered right. He squinched his forehead trying to remember. Yeah, a robbery of some kind. Everyone was baffled because nothing was taken from the house. There were all sorts of investigations as he recalled, a stream of articles for a few days. It was just more murder and mayhem in Atlanta from what he remembered, a lot of people seemed quick to dismiss it. The noise died down quickly, he hadn't heard anything about it since.

And here it was back again.

Antonio turned to Jeff smiling. "You know, I figured you out when you first came into the room."

Jeff took a sip of his newly-opened beer. "Oh?"

"That congressman is one pompous ass, like I said, you're just too nice. He'da taken control of everything. Never seen him do it, but I know the type. I am a good judge of character, I didn't need no smeared mole to tell me that you weren't him." Antonio reached for his glass taking a sip, "And I suppose I don't get to find out who you really are, do I?"

Jeff smiled glancing at Shonna who gave him the *do-not-tell* raised eyebrow, "Let's just say that I'm not him and leave it at that."

Antonio laughed out loud, "Okay, okay, but the resemblance is amazing! You practiced the voice, right? I can tell you practiced that and it's pretty good from what I remember, but I only saw you—I mean him—once." Glancing at Shonna laughing, "See, I know all about this and I still get them mixed up!" Shonna nodding as Antonio turned back to Jeff, "Okay, not bad." Antonio smiling turning to Shonna, "But we've got to get this guy acting like him," turning back to Jeff, "to hell with beer! We should be serving you glasses *of nastiness!*" laughing at his own joke as the two stared in wonderment at how this meeting had turned out.

Jeff glanced at Shonna as she gave a big nod, taking a sip of her Cuba Libre. "Yeah, acting like him.".

Giving Jeff a smirk.

"Details!"

They all stood. Antonio leaning giving Shonna a small hug with an uncertain smile, "You are still my accountant right?"

"Everything's business as usual," shaking her head gathering the pages, tamping the stack on the table to line them up, "at least for now. Nothing can change. We can't give these guys any clues that any of the cash operation has changed. We've already sent up enough flares today. We don't need guys showing up with guns to check bank balances, right?"

"*Padre Dios, no!* We have had enough trouble already haven't we? But yes, this is good!" Antonio turning to Jeff smiling shaking his hand. "And you, congressman," he chuckled, "what can I do? I have to call you Congressman, I don't even know your name!" There was a moment of pause as Antonio hoped Jeff would proffer up a name. Jeff only smiled. "Anyway, it was nice to meet you and I am sure I will see you again."

A few minutes later Jeff was vacantly turned to the car's window as they sailed north up I-85 in the late darkness. The clock on the car's dash said that it was past midnight. The windshield wipers were going in a light rain, peering out to the darkness, lights streaking their reflections on the glossy wet pavement as they drove.

Turning to Shonna, "We're not going to my hotel. Where are we going?"

"The hotel's not safe," glancing over at him. "We're going to your house, or rather near it."

"My house?"

"The congressman's house up in Roswell. We just happen to have a safe house, our operations center, near there."

The car took a couple freeway connector bends, soon driving on city streets in what looked like an upscale area in the darkness.

"What about my stuff?"

"It'll all be here. We just couldn't take any chances. These guys have eyes everywhere, they will be watching all the hotels looking for you. They have totally staked out your—I mean *his* house, so we know they want to find you." She stopped at a light looking intently around the empty streets, turning left. Laughing, "Remember we need to get you back to Seattle in one piece, right?"

Jeff shrugging, "Right, I almost forgot." Frowning looking at her, "What about my business meetings on Monday, what's the deal? They are pretty important meetings for my company. How's that going to work with me being kidnapped and all?"

"You caught the flu, can't make it."

"But that's my job, that's how I feed my family, it's an important meeting."

"They already know and have decided to come to the West Coast week after next to meet you in Seattle." Glancing at him. "Don't worry, it's all arranged."

"How did you do that? You can do that?" Jeff already had the very strong impression that he was dealing with people who had all sorts of resources. Tracking down information about his little store clerk through his credit card so quickly, all those taps and bugs in Magic Town and god knows where else, now they were rearranging his life. He couldn't tell if he felt creeped out by all this or whether it was somehow reassuring that these guys really knew how to handle their business. He decided for that moment that he was going with reassured. Frowning in the darkness, after all, it didn't look like he had a whole lot of choice.

She looked over at him smiling at him in the darkness. She could barely make out the silhouette of this man who sat next to her in the car. "You know, I didn't have very high expectations of you when I met you last night." Turning to her, could barely make out her face in the dim glow of the dashboard light. "I mean I didn't even know you yesterday morning, now I've gotten you involved in this crazy scheme to catch a bunch of bad guys just because you happen to look like the twin brother of this congressman." The car stopped at a light, she looked to him. "But you know, you've really done a good job and I am really impressed." The car starting up again. "I probably shouldn't say this." Jeff turning to her in the dark, "But I've been trying to figure out why I reacted so horribly when I found that girl in your room. I guess I should say I'm sorry." Glancing at him. "But she is a bad girl and maybe I thought I was protecting you." Thinking for a second, "But I don't think that's all there is to it. Why I reacted that way."

Glancing at him, "It's just there's something about you. Something different."

He smiled in the darkness, "There's nothing different about me, you just need to get out more."

Looking at him turning her head back to the road, "That's not true, you are different. But you were the same, just like the others the way you jumped on the first little floozy that got into your room with no panties."

Jeff looking forward, quiet.

"This is the part I probably shouldn't say," she hesitated. "But I wish I had been the woman in your room with no panties."

Jeff swung his head around speechless, feeling a sudden rise between his thighs. In the darkness pondering her words, turning to her speaking softly, "You know, I wish you had been her, too."

Reaching her right hand to him taking his hand giving it a soft squeeze. They drove on in silence. Jeff became aware of what felt like magnetic lines between the two of them as they sat in the car, driving in the darkness through the suburbs of Atlanta. He felt like if he tried hard enough he could maybe see deep blue lines, like static electricity, like the sparks between the two poles that you see in the science museum or tiny little lightening being drawn back and forth between them. He wondered if he should have kissed her when they were napping earlier. He was so certain then that she was still angry about what happened with Jennifer so he didn't dare. Now he wishes he *had* kissed her. He smiled to himself that maybe he'd have gotten laid after all, even after they chased Jennifer out of the room.

Soon they pulled into a long driveway, stopping at a gate. She spoke into box on a pillar, the gate slowly opening, the car driving through, pulling up in front of a stunningly large house. The front was huge, it looked like some kind of over-grown tutor style with two large turret kinds of structures on each end all lit up. Jeff could see that it was very upscale with a brick facade and long entry walkway in some kind of stone. Lights filling the windows on both floors.

"This is a safe house?"

She laughed, "More like an operations center with bedrooms." Shonna opened her car door motioning for Jeff to step out, follow her.

Walking up to the door turning to Jeff holding out her hands, "Let me have the things in your pockets." He started to reach into his coat when she said, "No, let me take them," white gloves appearing on her hands as she reached into his jacket, pulling the remaining contents from the inside pockets of the congressman's stinky jacket; he handed her the gun.

They stood in the dim landscape lighting, darkness preventing Jeff from seeing her amazing eyes clearly though he could see a glint of reflections from the ground lighting around them. Impulsively he reached out to brush a few hairs away from her face. He could see an expectant expression on her face even in this dim light as he leaned forward to kiss her with a light peck on the lips saying softly, "I really wish it had been you in my room today."

They both laughed softly, she leaning forward to kiss him in the same fashion. They both laughed again with a funny embarrassed turning toward the house.

Soon they were standing inside the house in front of a tall man dressed in blue jeans and a Rolling Stones t-shirt as she handed everything to him including her gun and Jeff's gun, slid the contents from the coat pockets into a large plastic ziplock bag, reaching into her purse for the stack of papers they brought from Antonio's, sliding them into another ziplock bag, put her arms up so the man in blue jeans could pat her down. Raising his arms Jeff submitted to the same search.

She stood in front of Jeff grinning, "Just precautions, don't worry about it. The operation manager here is kind of a freak for security." Glancing around the room, "I know it's late but come look at what's going on."

Turning to the room in a loud voice, "Everyone!" Jeff looking around seeing ten or more men, a couple women, casually dressed in various poses over screens or with headphones or standing talking or laboring over papers. Everyone quieted turning toward them, "I would like to introduce the newest member of Congress!" There was a dull murmur of applause as two men walked up to shake Jeff's hand, the others turning back to their work.

She motioned for Jeff to sit down at a small sitting area in a corner of the large room. He sat on the couch looking around, guessing that this was indeed a house; the living room has to be fifty feet along one wall, another thirty on the other sides. There were rows of tables loaded with equipment with hundreds of blinking lights. He watched Shonna bending over looking at computer screens turning back and forth to the men on each side of her as she listened and spoke. This went on for twenty minutes as Jeff watched, starting to feel tiredness pulling at him.

Shonna walked across the room followed by a chubby man in tennis shoes wearing an Atlanta Falcons baseball cap. Shonna sat down next to Jeff as the man reached his hand out introducing himself as Agent Shaw, Jeff could call him Arnie. Arnie sat down.

"So Shonna tells me that you are all clued into what's going on." Jeff turning to Shonna smiling, back to Arnie nodding. "Well let me tell you, you have definitely lit up Atlanta today. We had to bring more people in with all this chatter. It's been a little tough to sort through it, but it's clear these guys are trying real hard to circle their wagons." Grinning with a chuckle, "You getting killed this morning is the biggest news in the Atlanta underground since I don't know when."

Jeff smiled at the word *underground* thinking that's where this all started. Arnie was surprised at the smile, sitting back, "I mean, this is tragic," puzzled by Jeff's smile. "Uh, Jeff is it? Jeff, *it was tragic, you know*." Jeff felt he was being scolded for some reason, after all why wouldn't he take the murders seriously? Seeing that woman die in his arms this morning? This made him snap to attention, his smile disappearing. Arnie went on, "But this is not this particular group of bad guys' usual M.O. Honestly, I've been working this for two years, well, eight months really. I had no idea the stakes were this high." Turning to Shonna who gave a who-knows shrug.

Arnie glanced around the room, looking back at Jeff with a reassuring grin, "All I know is that you coming along like you did, and I have no idea how that happened," making a quick motion of prayers with his hands looking toward the heavens, "but this is our chance to close these sons-a-bitches down so fast it will make their heads spin." He peered at Jeff to see if he was taking this all in. "Say, we're hitting you pretty hard, I bet. Can I get you something, some coffee?"

Jeff turned to Shonna, "Does this mean I have to stay up?" Laughing weakly, "After all, I got murdered this morning and I am dead beat," glancing back and forth to their faces, "*but not dead!*" The three laughing together in a tone ringing with relief about this simple fact.

Shonna raised her hand to Arnie, "Okay, he's right, we both could use some Z's here."

Arnie nodded, "Yeah, this can wait a few hours. The next stage is planned for nine," looking at his watch, "that gives you at least seven hours if you guys want to go upstairs. There won't be much more happening before then." Grinning with a soft laugh, "Even bad guys gotta get sleep some time."

Standing, Shonna pulling at Jeff's sleeve, "Come on, let's get some sleep."

Jeff stood, following her across the room, walking around tables to a long, curved stairway with a dark banister, white balustrades in a long graceful arch heading around the left to the second floor. Soon they were standing in front of a door that Shonna pushed open pointing into, "All your stuff's in there, go get some sleep and I'll wake you. We'll have some food in the morning then get started again."

Jeff was too tired to answer, pushing past her hearing the door close behind him. The room looked almost like a hotel room, he half-smiled to see that his night clothes had been pulled out of his luggage, laying on the bed. "Nice touch," he thought, "just like home." He could barely pull off the stinky jacket, pull his shoes off before he fell onto the bed fully clothed, not even pulling covers over him.

He was out.

Sunday, 7:22 AM: What's Next?

Jeff suddenly shot straight up. It took ten seconds to remember where he was. The sun was pushing daylight around the window shade casting a faint light into the room. Looking to his right Shonna was laying on her side facing him, sound asleep. Laying back down, putting his face in front of hers like he did yesterday afternoon in his hotel room. Laying down it was fully with the intention of kissing her like he had wished he'd done yesterday. Somehow listening to the rhythm of her soft breathing, feeling her breath on his face was all he needed.

His eyes traveled slowly down her body, her clothes rumpled from sleeping in them. Who was this woman? What was he supposed to do with this situation? With her? He felt that all these events were making him crazy, that his judgment was *not to be trusted.*

Laying there he thought about *Gulliver's Travels*, about poor hapless Gulliver who kept landing in strange places where he was this absolute freak. The rules of the kingdoms where he was tiny or where he was enormous were all twisted around. Those rules made perfect sense to the inhabitants of those strange places, but in Gulliver's context those social moors were exaggerated, comical. So here he was, being Gulliver in his own way. Sure, he wasn't tiny or huge, but just like those kingdoms in Gulliver's visits the rules here didn't make sense to him either. They were just as exaggerated and comical in a certain sad and twisted way. Unlike Gulliver's experiences, very little of this was funny. Laughing to himself, *Ah, yes, mister Gulliver, what kingdom have you landed in here!*

Watching Shonna breathing slowly, her expression was so peaceful. Why had she reacted that way yesterday when she walked in on him? What would he have done had it been Shonna who dropped her skirt? He had not a doubt that he would have reacted the same way. Or would he?

His mind flashed quickly to imagining his wife dropping her skirt. But he couldn't recall a single time when she had. Not once. He sighed that his wife Donna was now gone from his life and felt a quick sting of remorse that they couldn't manage to salvage their marriage. In a second the feeling was gone as he admired the beautiful woman laying before him.

Shonna sniffed in her sleep, settling again.

She kept saying how special he was. He knew that Shonna was pretty special herself. Her eyes absolutely sucked him in the minute he looked into them sitting in that skanky corridor in front of the door with the big gold star, the man with the gun standing at the door on the other end of the hall. He has always been a sucker for a woman with pretty eyes. He remembered how his wife's bright blue eyes so stunned him when he first saw her, how it made him fall in love with her almost instantly. And Shonna with those bedroom eyes, her droopy eyelids. He was a sucker for a woman with eyelids he could see as she was talking to him. He found that women, and even men, who had those big fat pones under their eyelashes that their eyelids would disappear into so you just had this eyeball looking out at you without the graceful upper framing of an eyelid just didn't look attractive to him. He often found himself repulsed by people with ugly eyes.

He'd had a woman manager once who had evil eyes that would just stare out at him from under a big bulge of flesh as she talked; he kept getting the creeps when she would look at him, repulsed by that woman's evil eyes. But whenever he met a woman with eyelids like Shonna's he found that he couldn't quit looking at her eyelids, sometimes finding himself talking to her eyelids rather than looking into her eyes. Now this woman, Shonna, or Nancy, it didn't matter what she was called, who had these amazingly colored bedroom eyes was here sleeping in front of him. Watching her sleeping, closed eyes, those closed bedroom eyelids, sighing knowing that those amazing golden eyes with the little black flecks that make her eyes all the more amazing were just waiting to look at him once more.

There was more than just her eyes. Shonna's grace and style were intimidating. Her manner constantly made him question if he was worthy to even fantasize that he could have her as lover. He often wondered if other men had the same feelings around women like her. It wasn't a feeling of inadequacy; it came more from a reverence for beautiful women, that they were somehow of a higher place than mere mortals like him, handsome as he may be. Or not. He remembered the words of a long-time female friend who said that he was a handsome man, "But just not *scary handsome*." It was always odd to him that his friend pursued her *scary handsome* men, yet she only ever had relationships with men that were not even close to handsome. Yet she continually showed she had the sharp eye for a good-looking man when they would be out together, "Look at *him!*" she would whisper. The fact that she called Jeff handsome at all was good enough for him.

No, he decided, he would not have just jumped her bones yesterday even if she waved her skirt over her naked body singing *Glory, Glory, Hallelujah!* He knows that he is a *whole body man* that would need to have his mind and heart in the deal along with his body. He would want it to be passionate, slow, with the intense feelings that he felt growing for her inside of him. It would have to be more than just sex.

He reached his face over giving her the tiniest peck of a kiss on her nose, she snuffled a bit, took a deep breath, continuing breathing softly.

Jeff carefully moved his feet to the floor, standing up, trying not to shake the bed, going into the bathroom.

Coming out of the bathroom she was still asleep. He crept over sitting in the large corner chair, watching her, amazed at the woman laying before him. What was he doing here with this woman? How could he be spinning all these fantasies about Shonna? Shaking his head realizing he had no answer. There was something about this woman who lay sleeping in front of him that called to his heart. He felt tormented. Torn. Not guilty, though. It suddenly flashed into his mind wondering if he *should feel guilty about not feeling guilty?*

He heard a yawn, turning to see Shonna opening her eyes slowly, her eyes circling to gain focus, looking to Jeff sitting there.

"Good morning, sleepy," he said stepping over sitting back on the bed.

"What time is it?"

Glancing at the clock, "A little after seven-thirty."

Stretching, propping herself up on her right elbow, "What time did you get up?"

"Just now," without thinking he reached over to kiss her as she offered up her lips, instantly wondering how he felt so comfortable to do that seeing in her eyes that she wondered the same.

"Now that's the way to wake up!" giving him a shy smile. "How do you feel?"

Shaking his head slightly, "Just a little hung over I think." Swirling his head to loosen his neck, "No not that." Stretching his elbows out, swirling them in three deep circles, "Sleep deficit, that's it, but I feel better."

Standing up, he bent over touching his toes a couple times, "Look, I'm going to get into the shower," as he stood back up. "What's it take to get coffee?"

"Just for me to go down to get it, I'll get us coffee and a donut or something. We need to be at breakfast in," leaning over to the clock, "in an hour and few minutes, we have a meeting at nine."

Without another word, Jeff went into the bathroom without closing the door behind him. The water felt soooooo good standing with his head alternately down, the water pouring over his hair, then facing into the shower stream.

Soon emerging, combing his hair with a towel around him. Shonna was sitting on the bed, leaning back watching him casually. "Better?"

"Oh, much!" smiling turning to toss the comb onto the bathroom counter. Sitting down on the bed facing Shonna. "So what's happening?"

She smiled a big wide smile. Jeff hadn't noticed what nice teeth she has, he'd only seen her genuinely smile once before since he met her. Very nice smile. *Wonderful smile.* He looked at her admiring what a beautiful woman she is. Again. He frowned to himself at the thought of how the hell did he manage to be sitting here looking at this beautiful woman in this house somewhere the hell near Atlanta?

Leaning over picking up a cup of coffee, taking a bite of a donut looking at her, "I know what you told me yesterday about your stats and Georgetown and all, but I don't know anything about *you*," sipping at his coffee. "And I don't mean the company bi-line. Who are *you?*"

She looked at Jeff wondering how to respond. "You know that I am an agent, you know I'm with the FBI." He nodded. "Usually we are not supposed to talk about ourselves, I could get into a little trouble here." Reading his blank expression as expectant. "Okay, just a little. I was a student at Brown University, BA in law enforcement technologies, my masters specializing in financial crimes. I told you all about Georgetown." He nodded, still waiting as she continued, "I'm, hum, forty two, no kids, not married."

"I don't get that, why not?"

"Let's just say that the working lifestyle doesn't promote a stable relationship."

"But do you want—"

"Of course I do, I'd like a relationship, maybe even the picket fences. But I never meet any nice men." Smiling at him, "Like you." He shook his head slowly. "I know it sounds like a cliché, but all the good ones are already taken." Smiling timidly, "You, you're already taken." Jeff shaking his head knowing that he wasn't taken now with his wife that left him, but she didn't know that.

Shaking his head slowly Jeff took another sip of coffee, "But there are lots of me's out there."

Shaking her head sadly, her expression darkening. "No. No there's not. Trust me. I know. I've been out there. There's nothing but a lot of jerks."

Without thinking, Jeff leaned over brushing hair away from her eyes suddenly feeling that same wonder of how he could feel so comfortable doing that as a flush radiated from his navel up through his chest so fast he could almost hear a *whoosh*, then ricochet off his heart heading down between his legs where he felt a *twinge*.

Looking at him with a shy expression, he was sure she was being polite not asking why he suddenly got so flushed.

He smiled. "There are good men out there. We are out there, you just have to look for us."

Silence, suddenly brightening looking at him, "Enough of my pathetic life, what about you?"

"The factoids?"

"Don't need those, I already know." He gave her a dark look. "It's my job!" She sat up, "Okay, let's see if I remember." She looked at Jeff with a small smile. "You are my age, married nine years, married twice before, two children ages six and ten, dropped out of engineering school, finishing later, went back to get your BA in business and your MBA."

Jeff looked startled. "How the hell did you know all this?"

"You gave your drivers license at the hotel when you checked in right? And your credit card, remember?"

"Of course, I suppose it was a piece of cake after that?" She grinned, her right shoulder jerking up just a little in acknowledgement of the accusation.

He stood, walking to the window lifting the shade sitting back down on the bed, looking out the window at the morning sunshine. "Well, what else is there? I play guitar, like to dink on the computer, I adore my kids."

"Sex?"

He flushed, "What, do you know about that, too?"

She laughed turning crimson herself, "No, that was inappropriate, really, it's not like there's any…" Silence.

"Look. There's more. I haven't really told you about any of this. I don't know if I should even tell you."

"Tell me what?" Bending down looking up into his eyes, reaching her hands toward his. "What? You can tell me."

"We are separated. Divorce filed. It's been nearly a year since she left."

She reached her hands covering his. "Oh, Jeff. You didn't tell me any of this. I just assumed…well I assumed…"

"That I was happily married? That all this teasing was from a happily married man?"

"Yes, I guess…how was I to know? I'm so sorry, here I am making light of everything. What woman in her right mind would lose a quality man like you? Jeff, I'm sorry."

Shaking his head, "No, it's okay. You didn't know."

Pulling her hand away slowly. "Look, you don't have to tell me anything. It's alright, really."

"No, you might as well know," pausing with a big sigh. "She decided that she had our daughter so young, that her whole life has been spent as a mother, a wife. She decided to go back to school. At first we lived together then she decided that she needed to go find herself. So we bought a little townhouse near the university and she moved out."

"And you were okay with that?"

He shook his head, "At first I thought maybe she needed a breather. You know, get out a little, maybe get laid. After a couple months she changed so much, her attitude toward me. I could see her shutting me out of her life, she didn't want me to be part of her life. It started looking clear that she wasn't coming back, but it took a couple months to see it. I wasn't okay with it at first. The first couple months after that were very hard on me. Sleeping alone, dealing with my kids, my work, all my travel. At first I was so pissed off at me, at her. At us. Why couldn't two people who supposedly loved each other so much work this out." Sighing sitting in silence. "Then it occurred to me that they just couldn't. It was a turning point for me. But then suddenly I was the single dad, working, doing so much travel for my work. Nearly a year." He sat quiet for a full minute. "And she definitely went off to find herself. She filed the divorce, has a boyfriend. I have refused to allow her to introduce him to my kids." Shaking his head, "I don't know, I guess I am worried that the kids will get confused. Plus I don't want her boyfriends in my life. She can keep them, just away from me."

Laughing out loud, "So there you go, I'm not one of the good ones already taken after all." Looking down, then back to her, "I'm not even sure I'm one of the good ones."

"Jeff," she became quiet, sitting for a minute as she tried to catch his eye, he finally looking to her. "You're a really special man, you need to know that." A small laugh, "I mean how the hell did this happen, how did I meet the nicest guy on the planet—" Laughing softly, "Finally one of the good ones not already taken. A man without a wife, a man who is free to find his future. But I can see your sorrow, and I can't imagine how hard it's been for you, and I wish I could make it up for you somehow. My sweet Jeff," reaching her hand stroking his cheek. "You are such a sensitive man, very few of you out there." Laughing, "And now look at me getting all gushy on you, but I can't help it." Laughing softly pulling her hands away.

"I'm bigger than this, really." Turning away with the smallest pout, lower lip sticking out just enough, betraying her emotion, looking back, "I am *so sorry*. I had no idea. I thought here's this great man—a taken man—and it seemed so safe." Lowering her head in front of his face looking up at him, holding out her hand, "And now you are not safe. You are free to find another woman. Maybe even to find me." Long silence. "Even me.

Taking her hands speaking softly, "We both know what's going on here, don't we?" She nodded. "And now that you know this, anything is possible." Pause. "Yes, anything." Smiling waggling her hands, "So what do we do now?"

Shaking her head slowly, "I don't know. Does this just make us friends? Or is there more here?"

Without thinking he put his hands on each side of her head pulling her face toward him kissing her as her mouth opened for just a second, tongues touching with a flicker of a swirl, pulling her head as quickly away, his grip loosening, his fingers still around her hair.

Pulling his hands away slowly looking down, "Now it's my turn to be sorry." Looking into her bright golden eyes seeing her stunned expression. "Really, I don't know what made me do that. Please, I'm sorry."

Looking at him, studying his face. "Listen, don't you ever do that again!" He felt a jolt of regret at these words.

Putting up his hands apologetically, "Please, I said I was sorry. It was impulsive. It was wrong after all my complaining about her. I'm sorry."

With a glowering expression she said sternly, "Look, I am a professional here, and you listen to me!" Jeff looking at her anxiously. "Don't you ever do that again," her expression opening into a big smile, "without giving me more tongue!"

Jeff's jaw dropped, their faces both opening to grins brimming into a burst of laughter. She leaned across giving him another peck of a kiss. He protested, "You said with more tongue!" Starting to reach across to her, she pushing him away playfully, smiling standing up, "Come on before we get ourselves into trouble here, we have a job to do! But first I need a shower."

She went into the bathroom as he decided he would behave himself, though he was pretty certain that he needed another shower that very moment. Soon she came out again in a robe, grabbing her bag, back into the bathroom to brush her hair. In a few minutes coming out dressed, turning to grab her purse smiling, "Let's go down to eat!"

He stood up stepping behind her when she stopped turning facing him giving him a light hug, "I'm glad I met you," another quick peck to his lips, "really glad." Motioning to his jacket across the chair, "But you might want to bring your stinky coat in case we need to leave in a hurry."

Jeff turned around grabbing the stinky jacket, following her out the door. "So about those factoids, I suppose you know my blood type."

"How could we? You never give blood!" Both laughing feeling truly relaxed together for the very first time.

Jeff felt a little dizzy following her down the stairs into the big room that now had many more people, men and women, busy at work in different clusters or spread out at different desks working on what Jeff could only guess. He noticed papers they had brought from Antonio's in a pile with maybe five people around the table sorting through the stack, discussing them in lowered voices.

"This is all our case?" She looked at him appreciating his use of the term *our case*, glancing around the room.

She nodded, "Mostly, but there's another op ramping up." Jeff knew not to ask, though he was curious.

Leading Jeff through a door into another large room with a long buffet table along one wall, a dozen or so tables with chairs around them, looking a lot like the breakfast buffet back at the hotel. They each took a plate, walking along the buffet loading eggs, potatoes, Jeff bending over to smell the quiche, then seeing the biscuits and gravy. He reached over to scrape his eggs back into the egg tray, grinning childlike to Shonna, scooping an oversized piece of quiche onto his plate, two biscuits covered with gravy, grabbing a glass of orange juice already poured on the end.

Sitting down without a word devouring the food in front of them, except for glancing and smiling at each other occasionally, focusing all their attention on their plates until every speck of food was gone.

He wasn't thinking about his food.

It was the kiss, her kiss back to him. *And their tongues touched!* He felt almost foolish feeling like some high school kid kissing a pretty girl under the bleachers. And he knew he was feeling foolish.

But this all felt so good!

Trying to imagine what came over him, why he did he do that? He had never done that before, further more had never even *thought* of doing that before to another woman. Not with all the women he has worked with, in all the situations he has been in while he was traveling.

He remembered the time in Huntsville when he got in late and the hotel bar was the only place serving food, so he ate dinner at the bar. A woman came up sitting next to him. They chatted, he paid his check by signing with his room number, excusing himself. He wasn't in his room two minutes when there was a knock at the door. When he opened it there was the woman who he had talked with at the bar. She had read his room number off of his bar tab! She asked to come in, he knew that there could only be one ending to that story so he apologized saying no, that he had been traveling all day, that maybe they could have dinner tomorrow night, maybe try again. She seemed satisfied and went away. He felt guilty because he knew he would be in Orlando the next night.

So there had been plenty of opportunities. But why with *this* woman?

Wiping his mouth with a cloth napkin starting to push his chair back. Before he could stand up a sturdy black woman wearing an apron snatched up his plate, set down a coffee cup pouring it full. Shonna shoving her plate across the table to the woman as she poured another cup.

Jeff picked up the cup sipping his coffee thanking the server, setting it down, sitting back. "Man, I didn't know how hungry I was." Smiling, "Or that I needed coffee so bad!" Shonna laughed.

They sat in silence for a couple minutes, both enjoying the sunshine coming through the window; it felt like beach sunshine cast upon their table even though it was November. Someone signaled from the door to Shonna pointing to Jeff giving a come-here signal. Shonna got up with Jeff close behind going back into the big room. The man motioned to a door across the room, "They need you in there."

Jeff followed Shonna into a room with a long table, chairs around it, like a conference room, with computers blinking away on a long table against the wall. This must have been the formal dining room when it was just a house, Jeff thinking as they walked in. The walls were a warm tan color with decorative white crown molding along the tops of the walls, elaborate baseboards in white. Jeff glanced back into the big room seeing that he didn't notice before that it was decorated the same.

There were three men and four women seated around one end of the long table with papers in piles and scattered around the table between them; he saw the stack of seventy pages or so that they had brought back from Antonio's. Arnie, the man Jeff met last night gave him a small wave, Jeff returning a man nod. Shonna sat down in an empty chair between two of the men, immediately every head leaning toward her as conversation started instantly. Jeff pulled up a chair on the far end by himself putting his elbows on the table, head propped on his hands.

Jeff could hear all the words, not really paying attention, though every so often something would be said, heads turning toward him. He pretty much assumed that given all the masquerading he did yesterday as the congressman that they were planning for him to do more today. So far it didn't seem very dangerous. He was actually really enjoying playing cloak and dagger with these guys. This was sooooooo far away from his work in the aerospace industry that he felt almost like he was a different person.

Different person. Maybe that was the ticket for dealing with Shonna! Maybe he had to get it in his mind that when he is here that he is a *different person* from that guy who lives in Seattle.

Yes, a different man.

Entirely.

Somehow.

Maybe he needs to find some way to kind of liberate himself to find new experiences. To be free so he can find out how he's supposed to be with this amazing woman, Shonna or Nancy, what his experience is supposed to be in this situation. How it's supposed to be with her. He just wasn't sure what it would be like to somehow zoom out of his body to become this different person, somehow to return back to the family man that his whole context is about, his whole sense of who he is in the world. He tried but couldn't imagine life different than with his kids. This would definitely take some thinking. There had to be a solution that would make everyone happy!

"Jeff, pull up here a little closer," Shonna motioning to him. "Better yet, come sit over here." Jeff stood walking around the table, people moving their chairs to make room, Jeff grabbing a chair behind them pulling up, sitting down next to Shonna.

Shonna looking around at the others, to him, "You're a pretty smart man. We want you to be part of this." Turning to the others nodding affirmation. "Is that okay?" She paused. "I mean, you know a lot. Can you help here?"

Jeff's expression brightened, "You mean you guys, the pros who know my kids' names, my blood type," glancing at Shonna, "okay, maybe not my blood type, are stuck?"

"No," she gave an indignant frown, "we just figure that you know things and can help."

Pausing looking at the faces all turned toward him in obvious anticipation. "Well, okay. I'm not sure how I can help. Maybe, I guess, I can be your helpful amateur," smiling looking around the table. "So do I get a Meerschaum pipe and rag?" Looking around at the blank faces pretty sure his Sherlock Holmes reference fell flat. Grinning sheepishly, "Sherlock Holmes."

A woman at the table spoke up, "Nancy, we need—"

"It's Shonna!" surprised at the woman, "Linda, really? You know the protocol, you know that will put me in danger." Looking around everyone at the table, "Come on guys, it's Shonna! Work with me here, huh?"

The whole table bubbled with a murmur of, "*Shonna*."

All eyes now focused on Shonna. "Okay now, let's start with what we know, can I get some paper and pencil?" They came sliding across the table to her. Leaning over writing carefully WHAT WE KNOW ABOUT, underlined, below it on separate lines, CROOKED CONGRESSMAN - WANTS MORE ... CROOKED MAYOR ... CITY COUNCIL ... POLICE CHIEF ... POLICE ... ANTONIO ... MAGIC TOWN ... MONEY LAUNDERING, pausing looking around her. "Okay, guys, help me here, only what we know."

Uncertain if he was included in this gathering, Jeff called out, "Well, there's what the congressman's aid said." Shonna nodding adding *black, snake* to her list.

Turning to Jeff asking him to tell everyone what happened yesterday with the congressman's aid. He recounted the story, his sadness about what he witnessed but feeling a little more included in the group.

They all took turns adding more items, ending with fourteen names and items by Jeff's count.

"Now the relationships." She began to draw lines with arrows around the page linking names as various fingers reached down to point, erasures, flicking the eraser crumbs onto the floor, more lines, more arrows, a couple more what-we-knows. After fifteen minutes Shonna sat back as all necks craned to look at their product.

Shonna frowned, "This isn't helping is it?"

Arnie smiling, "But you know what, this tells me we know a lot more than I thought we did. Put stars next to the really big players." A few seconds later that was done.

Jeff shook his head, "I don't see it. We need a plan from this, right?"

A dowdy looking woman, a brunette with dark hair pulled back in a ponytail, a gold hair pin on top of her head leaned forward. Jeff smiling to himself at this woman's closed-in face with those spooky dark eyes, thick eyebrows that looked like someone wiped a paintbrush of dark grease across her forehead, dark fur connecting in a perfect line over her eyes. This drab face said softly, "Hmmmm, maybe if we figured out the order that we want to take them out, but what are the implications of what will happen. I mean, what's the goal here?"

The table arose with chatter between everyone with very little order as to what was being said, hands reaching across the table, eyes looking at pages, voices overrunning voices. Nothing getting accomplished.

Jeff thought about the conversation with Antonio the night before. Almost as if talking to himself repeating Antonio's words, "We've got to take them out all at once!"

Shonna looked at Jeff, around the circle of faces, the chatter continuing, sitting back looking at the ceiling, "All at once, that's right!" glancing at Jeff. "All at once. All at once!" Right hand to her chin. "But how?"

The discussion went on, it was clear to Jeff that nobody was paying attention to them.

It was hopeless.

Sunday, 10:18 AM: A Plan Emerges

The next hour found the table with many a scratching head, fingers to chins, lots of frowns, a few smiles thrown in, more scribbles on paper.

Jeff's mind wandered. For some reason it popped into his head as he remembered a broken electric can opener his grandmother once gave him when he was a kid. The motor worked, you could hear it, the can opening part didn't turn. He took it home, pulled it apart thinking he could fix it. When he opened it up there was a collection of gears, maybe six gears from the motor to the cutter. The largest gear had four teeth missing in a row, the gear trying to drive it had nothing to grab onto. He had counted over six hundred teeth on all those gears, only four missing teeth caused the whole machine to fail. They could have been four teeth missing randomly and it would have still worked, but when all four were missing in a row, failure.

Jeff sat up. "We're doing this all wrong, we're missing a clue. Maybe four!" Looking at Shonna who looked back at him, the room quieted. "Details," he said. She gave a slow knowing nod.

The room suddenly quieted as all eyes turned to Jeff.

He glanced around him nervously. "Look, we've got all the clues, we're just not paying attention." Half-nods around the table. "Any of you even read Sherlock Holmes?" This was answered with stares. "Any of you go to seventh grade?" Groans.

"Look, you guys think I'm wacky here, but Sherlock Holmes was constantly saying, 'You have seen the same clues that I have, I just pay attention to them.' I think we have all the clues, but that we are just not paying attention. Sorry, but you are looking at a man that read all fifteen hundred pages of Sherlock Holmes stories, there is a lot of wisdom in there."

Silent stares.

He looked around the table with an incredulous expression, "Come on guys, you're supposed to be the professionals here, I'm only your amateur at best." Waving his hand at the chart of names, "That chart is speculation." Frowning, "Sorry, but it's speculation." Nods around the table. "Like Shonna said, we need to know what we know. Look, Shonna, we sat for how long yesterday morning watching people go in an out of that house?"

She shrugged.

He pulled across a paper with a drawing of the house with little figures showing where the bodies were, studying it. "You have a list of names you recognized, right? Let's start with that. That's what we know!"

"Wait, we've got better than that!" Arnie stood up, walking out of the room returning a minute later with a stack of photographs in one hand, a small stack of papers in the other. He gave an apologetic grin for not thinking of this sooner as he set them in the middle of the table. The color photographs were from Shonna's camera, each one of a person leaving the house the morning before with the time etched in white numbers by the camera onto the film, on each was a yellow sticky note taped to the upper corner with either a name or a question mark. The photos had been enlarged to show the faces more clearly, the resolution was stunning.

The photographs were laid out on the table in chronological order, duplicates were put onto a stack on the side. Jeff pointed to one that was nothing but a picture of an arm with a snake tattoo. "That's Snake Arm." Shonna looking over to Jeff, "the one you commented on when he came out of the house, remember? I asked them to blow that up. Is that the tattoo you saw Friday night going into the club?"

Jeff leaned over the photo, "Yeah, I think so, it was pretty dark, I just saw it real quick." Staring at it, "But, yeah, I'm pretty sure. It's an unusual tattoo, right?"

"Okay, we'll get to Snake Arm. First we need a timeline. But wait, we need one more thing." All eyes turning toward her. "As we begin this, we need to take some notes, we need to keep a list of questions that come up."

Yvonne the dowdy brunette pulled out a pad of paper and pen, "I'll play recorder, help me when we come across a question, okay?" Lots of nods turning back to Shonna.

"Now let's get the timeline." In less than ten minutes they had created the timeline of the stakeout. Yvonne created a single sheet, lengthwise with a horizontal line drawn through the center, little marks with the time and lines drawn down to show who was exiting using the times on the photographs.

"Okay," Shonna pulling the stack of papers in front of her, pulling one out handing the rest to Yvonne, "Can you put these in the same order as the photos?" Yvonne took the stack, shuffling through them. Jeff leaned over seeing police reports, realizing they were rap sheets, police records with names on top, rows of dates followed by text on each line.

"Snake Arm," Shonna reading, "name is William Smith. Alias," she read, "lots of aliases, but here's Snake." Smiling. "Makes sense. Two armed robberies, three, let's see, four drug convictions. Two stints." Frowning studying the page, looking around at the photographs as though connecting two thoughts, pointing to a photo. "Well, look at this, the judge was Harold Thompson every time." Necks craning to look at the photo. "Well, he did time, so the judge didn't go very easy, did he?"

Someone interjected, "Or maybe he did!" A murmur of agreement.

Yvonne sat flipping through the pages she had organized. "Well, what do you know, the good Judge Thompson is on three of these bad guys' sheets. He was the go-to judge, huh? There's what, thirty criminal judges in Atlanta Superior Court, right?" approving nods around the table. "How is it he is he the judge these guys all went in front of?"

Arnie leaned forward to look at the sheets in Yvonne's hands, "Actually, that's more innocent than it looks. The prosecutors have their favorite judges they keep trying to steer cases to even though the system is supposedly set up to prevent it."

Shonna put down Snake Arm's file. "Okay, let's do this carefully." Pulling the timeline in front of her. "In order."

Shonna motioned to Yvonne who handed over the rap sheets. "Let's see. Our good friend Pick. Name, Peter Michaelson, two robbery arrests, no convictions. Drug arrest, no conviction. Weapons. No conviction. Petty theft, no conviction."

Jeff's eyes widened. "You mean I was hanging out Friday night with a felon?"

Shonna smiling looking at Jeff sideways, "Felon maybe, but not a *convicted* felon." Reading the page, flipping to the next page. "Any guess who the judge was every time? The honorable mister Thompson."

Jeff leaned forward with a concerned expression, "What about Perkins."

Shonna turned to him, "I don't even know his name, so we've got nothing."

"Payroll records?"

"We pay him in cash." Shaking her head regretfully, "I don't even know his last name. How did we do that?"

Not a sound except for an occasional flipping of a photograph or page.

Frowning, almost talking to herself, "How did that happen?" Shaking her head, "But so much of the business is done in cash, I guess it never occurred to me."

Jeff pondering, turning to her, "It just really bugs me the way he looked so surprised to see me last night when I opened the curtain at the bar, the way he busted in on us when we were with Antonio." Turning to Shonna, "You saw his face, that creepy expression. What was that?" Thinking for a second, "And the way he was so surprised to see me at that house yesterday morning. He looked stunned."

"It sounds like you are one surprising guy!" she laughed as the room chuckled.

Her expression lightened as she looked at Jeff in an assuring tone, "Look, I'm a pretty good judge of character, and he's okay," nodding as though to convince Jeff. "I'm pretty sure."

The room was perfectly quiet as everyone studied the photos, fingers to chins. Jeff hearing the din of voices from the operations room, glancing at his watch seeing time slipping away.

Shonna slowly flipping through pages, picking up the notes from the meeting with Antonio last night. Motioning with her left hand to the stack of ledger sheets Jeff had found in the congressman's stinky coat, "Now let's correlate this all together." Standing, moving along the table laying down the twenty sheets with the daily reports.

They went through the timeline again which had the names of the people in the house, everyone was candid with amazement at who had come out, someone jumping up volunteering to make more notes on the ledger sheets as names came up which were attached to initials on the sheets in some semblance to the timeline. The honorable Judge Thompson, a Federal judge, four councilmen, the police chief with three captains, the mayor with two of his aids, a couple unidentified people, Pick, finally Snake Arm and some other man. Of course there was Perkins at the end of the timeline.

Shonna reached over picking up the congressman's business card with the writing on the back. "Hand me a blank paper, someone?" it was passed over to her. The card's writing in blue ink had ten lines of initials, next to each a percentage number. She copied the initials onto the paper, the percentages next to each set of initials, adding them, underlining the bottom number in the column writing the total below it: 100%. "Okay, listen, I will read the initials here, someone tell me the name that corresponds. I think this may tell us what the congressman was up to."

Shonna read a set of initials, a name was called out. She went down the list until it was complete. When that was done she stared at the page setting her fingers lightly on the page, closed eyes, chin up slightly with intense concentration. Jeff watching as though the page was some kind Ouija Board that would move Shonna's fingers around on the page to spell out the true meaning of some mystery laying before her. Jeff remembered as a teenager how he and his friends played with Ouija Boards, it was always the *strange kids* or the ones living with a divorced mother who owned one; they always had all the cool stuff. He recalled how mysterious messages would always materialize before his eyes without fail. He never got over his suspicion that his fellow player was guiding that little cursor to make all those messages appear. Some of those messages were quite lude. He suspected his friend; he just never wanted to rule out that the Ouija gods had a dirty sense of humor.

Shonna gasped, "He was going to cut out everyone but these ten people!" Her eyes flew open dashing around the table furtively, "Quick! Hand me the member roster!" The roster was handed across the table to her.

She looked at the roster anxiously comparing it to her Ouija notes. "He was going to cut out twenty-two members!" Everyone craning to look at her pages.

"Look! This roster list has thirty-two names, right? We know who they are. And here, this card in his writing has only ten names with percentages that equal one hundred percent! The top entry is FS, for Frank Schedz with fifty percent next to it! That *greedy bastard!* Look here! The mayor, police chief, Judge Thompson, these other names are all the big players. Look at the ones being left out: the city council, the other judge, and all these other clingers on. Holy shit! Antonio was right! This was going to lead to nothing but a massive blood bath!" Shaking her head staring at the pages.

"No wonder they murdered him!"

The room erupted into voices that went on for ten minutes until they sounded like a big bowl of *voice soup* being poured into Jeff's ears, warm sloshy aural liquid rolling down his ear canals with vowels bumping against consonants creating a resonant concoction yielding no meaning to his ears.

Jeff sat back to make sense of all he had heard. Yes, what Nancy said about what the congressman was up to may be true, he thought, it may even be interesting.

But this wasn't getting them any closer to a plan.

The voices continued as Jeff found himself tuning out the room.

Shaking his head, they were no closer than when they started. He tried to think about what he knew about crime realizing he didn't know squat. All he knew was what he read in the newspapers. Also in his book reading, he'd read lots and lots of murder mysteries. He tried to think: *The Pelican Brief* by Grisham? No. Agatha Christi, maybe something like *Murder on the Orient Express?* No. Who else, who else? There had to be some detective book somewhere that could help here. Lord knows that's all he'd ever studied about crime—if you could call that studying—compared to Shonna's two degrees in law enforcement he felt almost flaccid in his abilities looking around at the people circling the table.

But he knew they were doing it all wrong!

They were trying to solve the crime when there was not enough information to solve it! Why?

It occurred to him that they could have a thousand pages of numbers and names, was that even evidence at all? It was obvious to him that they just *could not solve the crime...so why were they even trying?*

All they really cared about was how to capture the bad guys, *then* try to solve it later. He knew that it sounded backwards, but that is exactly what they need to do.

Take them all out at once. Antonio's words kept bouncing around in Jeff's head.

The ideas flew, voices continuing. No plan emerging. The voices droned on. Jeff fell deep into thought.

All he could think was did it really matter if they figured out all these *silly little details* when all that mattered was that they found a plan to get all these yay-hoos. And do it like Antonio said, all at once! How would they do that without these guys having to traipse all over Atlanta and northern Georgia, maybe even down to goddam Miami kicking down doors only to give everyone a chance to *lawyer-up* then have to deal with a long drawn-out prosecution probably getting in front of judges who were on the payola anyway? Sitting back smiling that he had at least figured that much out.

Suddenly Jeff sat up, "Take them all out at once!"

The room silenced. All eyes turning to Jeff.

"That's it! Sherlock Holmes!" He heard a muttered *oh brother not Sherlock Holmes again.*

"No, wait, listen! Really!" Turning to Shonna, "Remember last night! Antonio said that we needed to find a way *to take them out all at once!"* She furrowed her brow trying to picture where Jeff was leading.

"So we need to take them out all at once! It's simple!" Jeff went on to explain the genesis of an idea that just flashed into his brain from the great Sir Arthur Conan Doyle. He explained about how in the story *The Scowrers*—he was actually surprised he remembered the name of the story—an undercover agent, "Of course we don't know he's the undercover agent, arranges a meeting of all the bad guys so they can all be arrested at once. How the men had taken over this valley so that all the citizens were terrified to confront them. The hero of the story had infiltrated the gang, acted like he was participating when he was really warning people, witnessed crimes that he was helpless to stop. But he was patient. He was waiting."

Looking around the room at faces in rapt attention. "So the main character arranges for all the bad guys to be in one room so they can all take part in the murder of—" trying to remember the name, "yeah, Birdy. Birdy Edwards. All the bad guys show up armed to the teeth so they can each put a vengeful bullet into this Birdy Edwards guy who is about to take down their vast criminal enterprise." Smiling, "And that enterprise was almost exactly like our bad guys here!" Reflecting, "Amazing how things don't change much," glancing around the nodding room. "Anyway, he gets all the bad guys into a room and he says he will be right back to bring Birdy Edwards into the room so they can all ceremoniously take turns shooting him, but instead he walks back in and says, 'I am Birdy Edwards', before the bad guys can react rifle barrels come crashing through windows and they are all busted at once!" Sitting back with a big grin in an utterly silent room.

"Okay, but how do we do this?" came a voice. The table arose to a cacophony of noise again with all sorts of ideas flying back and forth. Jeff feeling a little hurt that there was no acknowledgement of his great idea that was soon lost in the din of voices where he could hardly tell what was being said. The voices turning into a racket beginning to almost reach a frantic level now that they had a semblance of a plan. They simply could not come to any kind of consensus about how to do this.

Jeff mulled the words that he had read in Sherlock Holmes, what was the strategy that the character Birdy Edwards had used for the successful conclusion of the story?

What was it?

What was it?

"Bait!" The room quieted instantly, Jeff sitting back smiling, every face turning to him again.

"We need bait!"

In just fifteen minutes the plan was made, Arnie motioning toward Jeff, all heads following his fingers. "Shonna, where did you get this guy?"

Everyone sat back almost on queue. The room sighed.

As they got up, Jeff's right hand met every other hand with a warm chorus of thank you's and best of luck. It was agreed that they would put the plan into action, would meet again at five for an update. Jeff smiled hearing "Sherlock Holmes plan" as people filtered out of the room.

Jeff followed Shonna into the big operations room which had even more bodies than before, even more activity. Glancing at his watch saying ten minutes after eleven. Shonna walked into the room, hands up announcing, "Everyone!" All heads turning toward her, hands cupped over phones, eyes away from screens, "We got our plan! Everyone on my core ops team, conference room, five minutes!"

Turning toward Jeff, "This is just logistics stuff, you can sit in if you like, but maybe you want to go outside and get some air." He nodded as Shonna waved to a man standing near the back door, "But you can't go out alone, even into the back yard. And stay near the house!" The man stepping up, she asking him to accompany Jeff into the backyard for a few minutes, he nodded turning toward the back door. Jeff smiled at her, turning to follow the man outside.

Jeff was glad to be outside in the warm morning air, surprised at this pleasant temperature so early for a November day. Walking back and forth for a couple minutes, standing still almost wishing he smoked. Smiling to himself, maybe a meerschaum pipe with rag tobacco would be good right now! He was pretty sure that Sherlock Holmes and Watson, too, would be very proud of what he had done this morning in that meeting. "Yeah, even though I ripped them off!" chortling to himself out loud.

The man outside with him never once tried to make conversation so Jeff just walked back and forth across the long veranda with wide flagstones under his feet. The sun was out, facing the other side of the house; this side of the house in shadow, still warm though.

It occurred to him for the first time that this coming Thursday is

Thanksgiving. Trying to remember what the plans are, spending the next few minutes trying to remember what his mother had told him. Guessing that it would be all the usual people, were they going to host family or are they going? He hoped they were going because he knew that when he got home he was going to want to sleep for a week. No way could he picture himself peeling potatoes, chasing to the store nine times around to bring home three forgotten items with each trip. He was pretty sure that Wednesday would find him with a little slip of paper at the grocery store as he tried to find nutmeg on the spice rack wondering why they couldn't do a better job of putting the spices in alphabetical order, whether this or that brand was his favorite. God, what he wouldn't give to be standing in front of a Spice Islands rack that very second.

Looking out across the large yard lined with tall bushes on every side seeing a ten foot-tall stone wall behind them with a foot-tall decorative metal railing on top with sharp points every ten inches or so. That made sense. There was a wide lawn with a fountain in the middle with the usual stone female spouting water out of her finger tips. Trying to remember, Aphrodite or something.

It felt good to breathe fresh air, finding himself taking deep breaths pacing slowly back and forth, a few times glancing at the man who brought him out here, wishing he would make conversation. There was a small stone bench with ornate scrolling around the edges. He glanced at his watch, eleven thirty.

Looking to the door seeing Shonna just coming out waving him in, the man turning to follow Jeff as he walked back into the house. Shonna turned to thank the man, leading Jeff by the arm to a table on the other side of the room, pointing to a computer screen.

"Do you remember the layout of Magic Town?"

"It's not that complicated, is it?"

"There's something we don't know, you would think as much as I have been inside that building that I *should know*." Pointing to the computer screen at the room they had met Antonio in the night before. "Here's the room we were in last night," her finger tracing the outer hallway, "here's the back door." Jeff nodding. "But there's another door." Pointing to a door, the back exit they had gone out the first night, then to a wall at the end. "The plans from the city don't show it, but there's actually a door there. I realize I've seen that door a hundred times. I'm surprised that I never paid attention." Leaning forward as though a door would suddenly appear on the screen. "Any ideas?" He shrugged. "We decided there's a piece missing from our information, that the door there has to go somewhere. It's not on the city plans so it must have been put there after it was built."

"How do you figure it goes somewhere? It could be a closet."

"We've had a watch on that place for weeks, know everyone coming and going." Jeff leaning toward the screen, turning to look at her. "The problem is that there are more people going in than coming out, and the other way around. People coming in and out of the club that didn't come through the front or back doors."

"So you think—"

"We think there's another exit. It's the only thing that makes sense."

"So what does that mean?"

Turning to him with a smile, "I know how much you like Magic Town."

Stepping back with his hands out, "No, no, no, I'm not going back there."

"Listen, to me." Holding him by his arms, golden eyes looking intently into his, "We made a mistake with all that planning we did this morning. "Remember the list of things we know, names and all?" He nodded. "We forgot someone."

Jeff closed his eyes trying to think of who was on that paper, shrugging. "Missing someone. Are you sure?" She nodded. Jeff trying to figure out who they could have missed, looking at Shonna, "Okay, I give up. Who?"

"*You!*"

Sunday, 12:34 PM: Back Again to Magic Town

Grabbing their coats, walking to the door Shonna was given back her gun. The man at the door handing her the congressman's thirty-eight pistol; turning to Jeff handing it to him without a word. Holding it looking down at the letters *Colt Cobra,* he took it slipping it back into the congressman's stinky jacket right outer pocket.

Pulling back onto the freeway. "I don't get it. Why are we going back to Magic Town. On a Sunday?"

"We've got to get Antonio involved; we don't trust the phones, right? Got to give him the invitation for tomorrow's little Birdy Edwards party." Jeff glancing at her with a wrinkled brow. "You get it right? He has to be there tomorrow or they will suspect he's cooperating."

Jeff nodding looking around them as they drove, listening to her. "We've got to find out about that door. I've got a key to the building. Antonio will be there."

"Why do you think he's there on a Sunday?"

"Remember who his bookkeeper is right?" Jeff nodding. "We always review the books for the month on the last Sunday of the month, but given that this is Thanksgiving weekend coming up we decided to do it today so he can go to Miami next weekend. We don't change any routines or we may throw up flags for the bad guys."

"And you have the key to get in."

"Of course!" looking over her shoulder to change lanes merging onto I-85 south heading toward downtown. "My routine is to go into the counting room to get the books then go to his office. He always has a tray of sandwiches, we spend a couple hours going over everything."

"Is that just the club books or the whole shebang?"

"Everything," frowning. "At least everything I knew about." Shaking her head. "But my god, what Antonio showed us last night? But who knew? But yeah, everything that I was aware of."

Looking at her sideways with a frown, "And you can do all that in a couple hours?"

"Usually, but sometimes we just get to talking about things so it can take longer."

Driving in silence Jeff wondering about what it would be like to work for a place like Magic Town, especially given all the mysteries of the mayor's gang.

Shonna, deep in thought, "You know, it really took a while, but we became friends, Antonio and me."

"Just friends?" feeling a strange jealous twinge imagining that Antonio had made many passes at Shonna. Who wouldn't, after all? He did! He laughed to himself, hell, he made passes at both Shonna *and* Nancy!

Sharp sideways glance, "Friends, you bet! And that's it! His wife is soooo jealous. Talk about someone who would murder me! With all those eyes in the club there's no way; someone as visible as me would definitely come out of that feet first!" Nervous laugh, "But, no, just friends. Friendly."

Soon they were back in the seedy neighborhood, passing the Garnett Marta station, in a minute pulling up in front of Magic Town. The streets were deserted like Jeff hadn't seen it the two nights before when there were cars parked every which way, people just hanging around the street in the dark. In the daylight Jeff could actually read some of the faded warehouse signs that he couldn't see when he was there at night. He was surprised to see feed and grain, tractor parts, other agricultural signs. There were also machine shops, moving and storage, other businesses. The buildings looked in a little better condition in broad daylight, they were probably thirty or forty years-old at least, vacant lots where buildings had been before. Down the street he could see one building nearly caved in, blackened ruins from a fire that destroyed the entire building. The leaning shell was all that remained looking like it would all topple over into a heap any second.

Shonna seeing him looking at the burned-out building down the street. "That's the gang's handy work, can you believe it? Two injured fire fighters didn't make the mayor's office all that happy. Less than a block from the club! These guys have no shame! The owner resisted payment, made noises about going to the police. *That* didn't happen! He was smarter than that, or rather he got smart. He didn't even bother to rebuild, last we heard he and his whole family up and left town."

Turning to Shonna. "My god, it never occurred to me...I don't know...the madness. People have to take their families away? Jesus, there must be hundreds of stories like this. And the way you tell me, this is absolutely unfettered—god, I can't believe I used that word! And you're telling me that the police not only stood by, they were taking money from it?"

Shonna said nothing. She had already been through that gut-twisting realization she read on Jeff's face. She remembered Jeff's Birdy Edwards character's *faux participation* in the crimes shaking her head that she was doing the same, often worrying in her heart of hearts that maybe her involvement wasn't that benign. She always fell back on that she was *just doing her job*.

In another minute Shonna unlocked the club's front door, stepping through, Jeff following behind. "Can I?" motioning toward the black curtain leading into the bar, pushing through the curtain. The lights were up, all the chairs were up on the tables, not a beer bottle in sight. A Latino man was mopping the floors as a Latino woman was pulling chairs from tables to wash them down, clean the tables, putting the chairs back up. The room seemed larger than Jeff remembered with all the lights turned up, missing the noise and music and drunken yelling men and flying tits. The cartoon magician, cartoon rabbit dangling from cartoon hands along the back wall looked out of place in this light.

Shonna stood behind him, pulling his sleeve, "Let's start with the mystery door, huh?" He turned back through the curtain following her toward the front door, turning left into the outer hallway walking past the door of Antonio's office with the door closed, heading down the hallway to turn left along the backside of the building. In a few seconds they were standing at the mystery door with the club's back door to their right.

Shonna turned the knob shaking the door. "Locked." Without a word she reached into her purse pulling out what looked like a tiny shaving kit, pulling out a couple thin metal tools, kneeling down, in a second the door was creaking open. Putting the kit back into her purse, pulling out a small flashlight, finding a wall switch, flicking it up putting the flashlight back into her purse.

A gun in her hand. Jeff shrugging not surprised anymore.

Leaning to him whispering, "It's like you thought, not a closet though, stairs to a basement maybe?" Jeff didn't remember saying that, nodding anyway.

She took the first step.

Stopping.

Listening.

Next step.

Listen.

Coming to the bottom of the stairs.

Jeff figured it was about the same elevation as the downstairs hallway with the dressing room on the other side of the building, but he couldn't tell how separated they were from that hallway. At the bottom the stairs ended. There was a long cement-sided tunnel to the right, a door to the left. Shonna turned to the left door twisting the knob, locked. Turning right facing down the tunnel, stepping slowly into the tunnel, listening carefully she moved forward. Walking along slowly Shonna counting her paces in a whisper, gun pointing ahead. The tunnel walls were unpainted, had been skillfully troweled so they were smooth to the touch, it was well-lit with a bare light bulb hanging from the ceiling about every twenty feet. Eventually they came to the end of the tunnel ending at a staircase leading up to the right.

She whispered, "Okay, sixty five paces, that makes it about a hundred-sixty feet. That's more than half a football field, these guys are serious about this!" Turning pushing past Jeff, he followed her back to Magic Town, up the stairs to the outer hallway. She closed the door behind them. "Okay, I'll get that to our guys to see if they can figure out where that comes up and who owns the building. There will be a lot of people happy to know about this. This explains a lot about all those people going into the club and not coming back out. Or coming out without going in!"

Starting back down the outer hallway, "Come on, I've got to go get the books then go see Antonio. You can come along if you want." Jeff thought about the night before. He left last night kind of liking Antonio even though he figured out that Antonio is probably a *very dangerous* man. Shrugging nodding.

Walking along the outer hallway again, going past Antonio's door on the right, turning right around to the front of the building.

"You can wait in the bar, I'll come get you so we can go see Antonio. Give me five minutes."

Nodding to her she started forward down the stairs toward the dressing room. He turned toward the bar pushing through the black curtain. The janitors were at work, looking like they were almost done. He looked at the cartoon magician and rabbit, laughing that they seemed like so harmless in this light.

Suddenly he heard rapid foot steps echoing behind him coming from the other side of the curtain, turning lifting the curtain seeing Shonna dashing from out of the stairs on the right past the front door, in two steps diving into the outer hallway, "OH, MY GOD! OH, MY GOD!" Her words panting, out of breath as she ran through the two doors.

Jeff stopped, hands out.

Confused.

What to do?

Listening.

Nothing.

Suddenly Shonna's screaming from the outer hallway…

"JEFF! GET IN HERE! NOW!"

Pushing through the curtain jumping left toward the door that Shonna just went into, sprinting down the outer hallway, left, Jeff diving toward the light of the opened door of Antonio's office, left into the room.

Stopping, panting, shocked. Two men lay crumpled on the floor near the back walls, their dark clothes in the dim lights made it hard to see them. In the middle of the room lay Antonio on his back, five holes in his shirt, blood tricking from one, Shonna leaning over him.

"Oh my god Antonio oh my god Antonio oh my—HE'S ALIVE!" Bending over Antonio pulling back his right eye lid bending over to look into the opened eye, "Good, response to light!" Scanning Antonio's chest with five holes in it, "Jesus, burn marks, point blank!" Ripping open his shirt, buttons flying around the room, "Body armor! Oh, smart smart Antonio! Smart! Smart!" Shoving both her arms under Antonio, heaving him over onto his stomach pulling off his shirt and jacket as his arms flopped backward almost following her movements, unsnapping the body armor, rolling him over again onto his back. Grabbing the floppy black vest plate, about two feet across on each side, holding it up to examine it. Jeff could see light through a hole near the bottom of the flat-black fabric as she tossed it across the room. "Close range, but you lucky son-of-a-bitch!" There was a round puncture in his skin, blood trickling out just below Antonio's left lower rib, Jeff seeing a glint of reflected light from the blood of Antonio's wound. Shonna leaned over pushing her fingers into the wound—Antonio didn't flinch—pulling out a bullet, "Nine millimeter, Antonio, you are one lucky son-of-a-bitch!" tucking the bullet into her pants pocket.

Standing behind Shonna the whole time, Jeff stunned watching her rapid motions. Without turning away from Antonio waving Jeff over to her, "Come down here, do you know CPR?" He stooped down next to her.

Jeff bending down picking up Antonio's left wrist trying to feel for a pulse, putting his ear down to Antonio's nose listening, "He's breathing! And a pulse! Yes, he's alive!"

"I just told you that! Now we have to keep him that way!"

Shonna stood, looking around the room, stepping up to each man laying by the back wall, kicking at them without bothering to turn them over. No movements. She knew the answer with a deep sigh.

Looking up to her, "What do you want me to do?"

"If he stops breathing you make sure he starts again, okay?" giving him a *well duh* look, starting for the door, turning around again, "Stay here, don't go anywhere, oh, damn, wait." Kneeling down on her right knee, putting her hand to her forehead mumbling to herself. "Stop Nancy, stop. Stop, think, act. What to do?"

Standing up reaching for the desk phone frantically dialing a number, "Man down, many down Magic Town, no lights, need mop-up, NOW! CODES, CODES!" hanging up.

Turning to Jeff, "Got a mess down there! I've got to go back down! Take out your gun!"

Jeff looked up at her astonished, not grasping her words. "Do it!" Standing he reached into the coat pocket pulling out the snub nose revolver without looking at it. "I know you want to help him, but you can't! Help is coming, now we just have to make sure he stays alive! They screwed up murdering you yesterday, they may be back to make sure they killed Antonio. Are you listening?" Jeff's blank expression. "You need to sit in that chair with that gun cocked—you shoot at anything that doesn't give the four quick knocks first, the code. You've heard it, you know what it sounds like, right? Do you hear? Jeff, are you listening to me?" Jeff's face was blank, staring at her. Taking two steps forward, hauling back **SMACK!** slapping Jeff across the face.

His head jerked to the side with the force of the blow, "Goddam it! I heard you! You don't have to hit me!"

"Then do as I say, sit down, cock the gun, shoot at anything that comes through that door without the knock. They could be back. It's really bad down there, I've got to render assistance if it's not too late!" turning bolting out the door closing it behind her.

"Too late!?" he yelled.

"JUST SHOOT!" her voice fading.

Sunday, 12:48 PM: Unwanted Visitors

Looking around the quiet room, turning the chair he sat in last night to face directly toward the door sitting as he was told, raising the gun pulling back the trigger with his right thumb.

"Good god, *what the hell am I doing here?*" he whispered, head swirling at the things he witnessed this weekend. Never in a million years would he have imagined he would be next to a dying woman yesterday, and now here he was next to a dying man?

Blinking, sweat pouring down his face, into his eyes. Wiping his forehead with his left arm, staring at the door. Feeling his right arm trembling holding the gun so tight his fingers were turning white. *Okay, now. Just like at target practice, remember? You didn't win your ribbons by holding your gun like a girl! Relax!* Letting loose of his grip on the gun, right arm still trembling.

Sitting there for what felt like an hour, a quick glance at his watch saying three minutes.

Looking around the room whenever he dared to take his eyes off the door he saw the drawer that Antonio pulled the extortion records from had been ripped out of the end table, laying on the floor near a corner of the room. Jeff saying softly, "They were looking for records!"

A cough! Jeff nearly pulled the trigger! Looking down, Antonio moving. Still watching the door kneeling down whispering, "Antonio." Wiping sweat from eyes with the back of his left hand. "Antonio!"

Glancing down, Antonio's eyes fluttering, barely opening. Jeff seeing the whites of Antonio's eyes. Whispering, "Antonio, can you hear me!"

Antonio gasped, coughed, struggling to raise his head, trying to focus on Jeff. In a weak voice Jeff could barely hear, "You." Cough. Weakest smile. "You. Body armor," weak chuckle.

"Yes! Antonio, it's me, it's me!" Jeff whispering desperately watching the door intently, just a quick glimpse down. "Who did this?" Glance down. "Antonio, who did this to you?"

A gurgle, a cough. Jeff leaning down as close as he could, his eyes on the door. Weak cough.

Jeff whispering, "Antonio, who?"

"Inside," Antonio coughed, "inside," with a gasp his head flopping to the side, eyes rolling up, closed.

"Oh, Jesus, Antonio!" Jeff imploring in a fierce whisper reaching down, shaking the still figure on the floor, "Antonio!" No answer.

Jeff listened, carefully, carefully, hardly breathing. Looking down seeing Antonio's chest barely rising and falling. Sitting back in the chair, gun pointing to the door.

Glancing at his watch, two more minutes.

What a day!

Wiping sweat from eyes.

Total silence.

But wait!

A sound.

A voice!

A whisper!

No.

Yes!

Yes, a voice, very soft, softest hissing murmur.

Coming from the left, down the outer hallway from the back of the building.

Floor creaked!

Just outside the door!

Craning his neck to listen, sweat pouring down his face, soppy armpits.

The door knob!

Slight jiggle.

Raise the gun.

Whisper, he could barely hear.

So soft.

Man's voice.

Leaning toward the door, hearing the words, a whisper, so faint, "I won't let that happen again."

What again? Jeff thinking, tightening his grip on the gun, panicked.

He's talking to someone, is there more than one?
Jiggle door knob, someone holding it.
Leaning forward watching the knob.
Grip tightening.
The knob beginning to turn.
Knob stopped.
Door beginning to open.
Slowly.
So slowly.
Opening.
Barely perceptible.
Opening.
Standing up both arms stiff pulling the trigger straight at the door, **PAP! PAP! PAP! PAP! PAP!** chips of wood flying around the room from the door that seemed to explode with holes in front of him, the door pulling shut again. W-E-E-E-E-E-E-E! his ears stinging with the sound of a high-pitched siren! Cupping hands to his ears, ringing so loud his sight going gray, hearing a muted scream, loud voices, frantic shuffling outside, yelling something, moans fading down the hall toward the back door. Shaking his head to stop the ringing in his ears, punching his wrists against his ears, it didn't subside; the room filled with acrid gray smoke from the gun shots, Jeff coughed.

In a rush of anger he bounded to the door yanking it open gun forward turning left slipping on the wet floor looking down seeing a pool of blood smeared with footprints steadying himself against the wall running down the hall reaching the end turning left expecting to see the back door open on the right instead seeing the secret tunnel stairs door still swinging hearing echoes of steps on the wooden stairs now shouting voices with words he couldn't understand coming up the stairs echoing projected up from the long tunnel.

He ran to the door peering down the stairs realizing that it was really stupid to go down, stand still, hold breath, listen, can't hold breath with panting, so out of breath. Looking down the stairs, light on, trail of blood down the stairs, disappearing to the right. Looking back to the hallway he'd just come down seeing bloody hand prints along the wall, smeared like someone was trying to lean against the wall while running.

Slowly backing away from the stairs, afraid, backing past the back parking lot door, slowly backward down the hallway, head swinging both directions not sure where danger lay.

Reaching Antonio's room peaking around the corner, Antonio still laying unconscious. Walking into the room turning again quickly facing the door hearing foot steps coming down the hall from the front of the building, raising the gun toward the open door.

"Jeff?"

PAP! bullet lodging into the wall next to the door, ears instantly ringing again W-E-E-E-E-E-E!

"JEFF! STOP! IT'S ME SHONNA! NANCY!"

Jeff replying weakly, "Shonna? Nancy?" flopping into the chair gun still pointing to the door.

Shonna peering around the right side of the doorway holding her gun forward, looking around the room, turning to look at the hall, down to the bloody floor, coming through the door, pushing it wide open with her left hand inspecting the door. "Holy shit! Five shots!" Turning to look at the wall, "How many times did you shoot?" Jeff holding up five fingers. "Jesus! Somebody took three shots!"

Looking down at the blood pool outside the door, her eyes following the bloody trail down the hallway toward the back of the building, raising her eyes to see the bloody hand marks along the wall.

Walking into the room slowly kneeling down in front of him, "Are you okay?" He nodded weakly. "Wow, you really made a mess out there!" Pulling up a chair putting her arm around him, pulling him to her. "I am so sorry, I shouldn't have left you here. But I didn't know what else to do. There's a huge mess downstairs, some kind of botched robbery." Looking around the room, the two bodies laying in the back of the room, down to Antonio sighing. "God, what a mess."

Starting to catch his breath reaching his arm over her shoulder so they were linked together arm over arm. "I *shot somebody*. I actually *shot somebody*."

She leaned over, kissing his cheek. "No you didn't shoot somebody. You shot bad people."

"Bad people?"

"Yeah, it's bad when you shoot somebody, but bad people aren't somebodies."

They heard voices in the hall, Shonna raising her gun at the door yelling, "CODE!"

A man's timid face peeked around the corner, "I'd do four knocks, Shonna, but someone seems to have destroyed the door."

There was a weak laugh all around, the room slowly filling with men all wearing body armor, holding all sorts of armaments, their movements into the room pushing the gun smoke into the hallway.

Soon a gurney appeared, in a second Antonio was gone.

Shonna leaned over, kissed Jeff on the cheek starting to get up. Pulling her back down, "One more minute." Putting his head against her breasts closing his eyes. "Please."

In a few minutes another gurney appeared in the room. Shonna looked around realizing this might be too much for Jeff. Standing, pulling him to a stand. "Hell of a day, huh?" He nodded, finally putting the gun back into the stinky coat pocket. "We gotta let these guys do their work, come on." Jeff stood with vacant face. Exhausted.

"You okay?" He gave a half-nod. "Look, I really hate to do this, but I've got to take some time to get a close look here and downstairs, I need for you to wait for me in the bar, okay?" Without waiting for a response, she pointed to one of the men saying something Jeff couldn't hear, the man stepping forward tugging Jeff by the elbow, without a word following the man out the door, right, down the hall.

Soon he was sitting in a chair in the empty bar. The janitors were gone. He guessed they probably fled the building when they heard the gun shots.

Numb.

The man stood to Jeff's left. Jeff glancing up at him with a gun in his right hand next to Jeff's left shoulder. He was being guarded.

Jeff started to look at his watch, his eyes couldn't focus. It seemed like hours before he saw Shonna's face, kneeling down in front of him, looking up into his face, "You okay? Look, we gotta go."

Jeff sat quietly with head back, eyes closed as the Mustang made the journey back up I-85 toward Roswell. He wanted to sleep somehow—he knew it was hopeless.

"Did Antonio say anything?" Jeff keeping his eyes closed, silent. "Jeff, this is important. Did Antonio say anything?"

Opening his eyes straightening up, a bit wobbly, looking around him bewildered. "I think he thanked me for suggesting body armor."

"I don't remember you suggesting it. No, I guess you did talk about it last night, huh?"

He felt better at the sound of her voice, "You mean by the supposed miraculous survival of my murder yesterday?"

"You know what I mean. Somehow that made him put it on."

They were quiet until the first freeway split. The Sunday afternoon traffic was very light. "Anything else?"

Jeff frowned looking ahead though the windshield. "Yeah, he said *inside*. Twice."

"You're sure? Inside?"

"Yes, I'm sure, that's exactly what he said. That's all he said before he passed out again."

"Jesus," Shonna shaking her head. "I was afraid this might happen when there are so many players and there is so much money. That means we got an insider passing information, or maybe even did the shooting." She sighed.

Shaking her head slowly, "Inside."

Sunday, 3:35 PM: Reluctant Shooter

"Inside," Arnie said slowly, stoking his chin. Everyone around the table staring at him. "Does that mean there's an inside guy, a double cross?" Frowning. "Jesus, like we don't have enough problems."

The same group was sitting around the conference table in the safe house except for one unfamiliar face who spoke out, "What's he doing here?" pointing to Jeff. "Why do we have a civilian here?"

Shonna looked dismissively at the woman who spoke out, "You weren't here this morning. This guy is our hero. You would not believe what this poor bastard has been through." Scowling at the woman. "His face *does* look familiar, doesn't it? You *DO KNOW* who is at the center of all this. You *DID READ* the case data. *WE ASSUME!*" Rubbing her forehead looking up again, "The plan we're working came from him YOU IDIOT! Why don't you just SHUT THE HELL UP AND LISTEN!" Jeff felt the ring in his ears return from Shonna's screaming next to his right ear. She looked to Arnie, "Arnie help me here!"

Nodding to Shonna turning to the woman, around to everyone at the table, back to her, his hands raised toward the room, "Look, everyone's nerves are really raw here. A hell of a lot has happened in the last couple days. I am sure Agent White here didn't mean to yell at you, maybe she did, but seeing all these dead bodies has really put us on edge, the scale of this whole operation, having no clue who the shooter is has made us all…well…a little crazy." Giving the woman a condescending smile, "So if it's okay with you, let's move on." The woman nodding sheepishly with her eyes cast down at her hands folded on the big table in front of her.

The next ten minutes was filled with speculation as the evidence papers and photographs circulated around the table.

Jeff was sipping a Coke from the can, dearly wishing it was alcohol.

Hell, he'd even take bourbon.

He sat listening to the conversation leaning, his head back, eyes closed.

They must be missing something.

They *had to be* missing something.

Something.

Eyes closed, listening to the people sitting in front of him, the discussion turning into squabbling.

Jeff spoke up, "Take them out all at once, we already have a plan to do that." Looking around the faces at the table becoming instantly quiet, "What's so hard about that?" Frowning, "We don't really have any new information since this morning other than more dead people, maybe Antonio who might come to long enough to give us a name."

Shonna looked at him, "We need to circle around to make sure we're not missing anything."

Jeff glanced at his watch surprised to see it was almost two o'clock.

Arnie finally spoke up, "Okay, guys, we're losing daylight. Given what we knew before, who came out of that house that we weren't expecting to see?"

Someone said, "Everyone," a small group chuckle.

"Okay, but given this group, who didn't we expect to see?"

Shonna instantly replied, "Pick."

Jeff watched Yvonne write down the question and answer, she spoke. "It seems like we know a lot more now, except what happened in the house and Antonio's room and the cash room."

Arnie spoke, "Okay, let's figure this out." Looking to Shonna. "Gun powder burns at the house?"

"The congressman and the aid were point blank, covered in gun powder, straight at the entry points, but not the others, they were shot at a distance, don't know how far, no powder though, or very little," came a voice.

Shonna looked quickly at Jeff, "Remember I noticed the powder burns on Antonio's shirt." Flipping two pages back on her notebook, "Easy when he was wearing white. And powder on the counting room guard. No powder on the two in the back of Antonio's office, at least that I could see. None on the women downstairs."

Shonna looked up to the ceiling in thought. "That means that the shooter literally walked up to the main victims and shot them point blank."

Arnie's and Jeff's eyes met looking at each other, eyes widening exclaiming in unison, "They *knew the shooter!*"

"And they trusted him," Shonna completing their sentence.

Arnie pulled the drawing of the house across the table, studying it in front of him. "Wait, let's not get ahead of ourselves. Let's see if we can figure out the order."

Questions arose: Was there only one shooter? Why couldn't they hear shots?

Shonna started, "Wait, the bullet!" Pulling out the blood encrusted bullet from her pocket that she pulled from Antonio, passing it around.

One of the agents held it to the light, "Nine millimeter. That means a gun that can hold at least thirteen shots."

"Or more depending on the make and model," someone interjected.

"This is good," Arnie smiled. "This means all those shots in the house could come from one gun without a reload. Probably at the club, too."

The agent holding the bullet frowned, "Feel the weight, light alloy. This came from a low velocity round."

"What does that mean?" Jeff asked.

"It means they used a silencer. A silencer only works with low velocity bullets. Sub-sonic. It's the bullet breaking the sound barrier that causes the bang." Jeff thinking about this, nodding.

"That's why even at close proximity only one round made it through Antonio's vest otherwise there would be no way his vest could stop a full-charge nine millimeter round at such a close distance. At that close range the bullet just has way too much force. Would punch right through the plate. That makes perfect sense that it stopped four and only one got through."

"Yeah, even then it barely got through, I reached right inside of him and pulled this out with my bare fingers," Shonna explained.

Arnie got up heading for the door, "Let me make a phone call, I'll be right back."

The group was mulling together when Arnie came back. "I just got off the phone and got confirmation that the shooter at the house used the same kind of bullets at the club. Of course, we don't have ballistics yet. Could be only one gun, could be more, we don't know. But silencer, Shonna. That's why you didn't hear any shots yesterday."

"Wait!" Shonna flipping through her little notebook. "I forgot to tell you guys about the counting room when I went through it. First, that door is guarded twenty-four-seven, the guard is not even allowed to take a pee break."

Jeff reflected, "I remember seeing him when I was waiting for you on Friday night. There was a chair there, but he stood the whole time."

"Right, he can sit only when nobody is in the hall."

Shonna flipping through her little notebook going on to say that the guard clearly had powder burns, shot up close. There were three women in the counting room when they heard a commotion at the door, what sounded like someone being pushed against the door outside. One of the women, "Shelly, who is a sweetheart, but a real nervous nelly." A sad expression flashing across her eyes, "She ducked down when the door flew open. But the door wasn't kicked open, someone used a key, but burst into the room frightening the women. Shelly didn't see anything, said she could hear four what sounded like snaps, she said it was like those little confetti toys that you pull the string on and confetti shoots out, you know that little snapping sound. That's what she said."

"That's what we thought, right? A silencer." Arnie looking at Jeff with an expression like a tutor, "Silencers aren't completely silent, they still make a small snapping sound like the girl heard."

"The two other girls were killed." Shonna paused in quiet.

"What happened next?" the question came.

"Shelly said that they had stacks and stacks of money out, that she expected it was a robbery. But instead all she heard was the file cabinets opening, the noise of papers and boxes. There were whispers, men she was pretty sure, more than one, but she's not sure how many, said she couldn't tell the voices." Flipping the page. "We don't know for sure, it looked like no money was taken, but every single page of the collections and payment records were gone. Not a single page left behind." Flipping the notebook closed, "Like they knew exactly what they were looking for." Looking around the table. "They knew too much about where everything was. This *was* an inside job!"

Arnie stroking his chin, "Yes, of course. Inside. Just like Antonio said. They didn't care about the money, they only cared about their asses. Jesus, all those people at Magic Town killed just so they could get the records."

Jeff remembered the drawer that held the records they took last night laying in the corner of Antonio's office.

Arnie picked up the drawing of the house, pulling over the layouts of Magic Town and the house with the bodies drawn in, laying them side-by-side. Leaning forward pointing to the house drawing, "Okay, let's try this starting with the house. The congressman is separated from his aid and body guards. Probably because of guns or the shooter convinces them it's okay to be separated, we can't tell. Maybe the mayor or somebody wanted to talk to him in private. Still, we don't know. The shooter walks into the room with the three, gets the guard on the right," pointing to the page, "the one on the left draws his gun but too late, we found his gun next to him. The shooter is standing in front of the aid, shoots her point blank." Silence from the group watching his fingers on the page. "He goes into the other room, walks right up to the congressman or it could have been reversed. Still, point blank." Glancing down at a list of names with the times from the photos, pointing to the page with the Magic Town layout. "My guess is pretty similar with Antonio. Why change what works?"

Jeff reflected, "Antonio put on body armor. He was going to meet with someone that he knew. Knew but didn't trust. The shooter got close to him, we know, so Antonio knew this person but definitely didn't trust him or he wouldn't be wearing it." Jeff remembering Antonio's words from last night, "I remember last night he said, 'Why would you go around in body armor unless you thought that there was going to be trouble?' He knew the shooter but he thought there could be trouble!"

Arnie nodding in deep thought. "Yeah, I need to amend my script with this important little detail." Looking at Jeff nodding, "That's very perceptive. Good!"

"So Yvonne, can we start a what-we-know column?"

"I'm way ahead of you. I also have entries for what we've guessed."

Jeff smiled, "Guys, this is great." The whole room smiling at him, for the first time he realized they were smiling at him without condescension.

A voice came out, "What about the congressman's staff?"

Shonna gave a noticeable jolt, "They're all good guys, let's focus on what's at hand." Jeff noticed the changed pitch of her voice, turning to look at her, she ignored him.

Shonna looking back at the page. "But who? Who's the shooter?" Shonna looking at Jeff, "That means Snake Arm and his buddy probably couldn't have done it. Nobody would have let them get that close to them. We saw them come out of the house last, but there's no way they were the shooters. They couldn't have been." They heard Yvonne's pen writing.

Jeff half held up his hand, "But what about Pick—"

"Pizza!" came from the other room as everyone instantly stood up filtering toward the dining room where they sat to eat, chatting about everything but the case.

Shonna looked at Yvonne as they sat down again twenty minutes later. "Okay, Yvonne, tell us what we know." Looking around the room continuing, "Then we need to take some votes."

"Votes?" Jeff laughed.

"Surprised?" Yvonne smiling at Jeff. "You don't see that on TV, do you? But that's how we do it sometimes." Seeing Jeff's puzzled look, "It prevents one person from driving the solution, group think is always better." Yvonne went on to read her notes which Jeff was surprised at how detailed and well-ordered they were.

Arnie raised his hand, "Okay people, we need to wrap this up. The way I see it is we need a snitch, a shooter, the daily operations guy, and the strategist who could also be our king pin."

Shonna stood. "Okay. First vote. Insider. Snitch. I nominate Pick." A few hands shot up immediately as people looked around at each other, slowly other hands came up until they were all raised. Jeff raised his hand uncertain about Pick as the snitch, not sure if he had a vote in this anyway. Arnie signaling to him that he should raise his hand if he wanted to vote.

"Noted," said Yvonne scribbling.

"Second, one shooter at each scene, same shooter at both scenes." All hands rising immediately.

"Third," Shonna bending over looking at Yvonne's notes as Yvonne spun the page around toward Shonna, "The victims knew and trusted the shooter." All hands raised.

Arnie leaned over to Jeff quipping, "Any more insights from Sherlock Holmes?"

Jeff turned to him, laughing, "Well there's always his most famous saying, do you know it?" Arnie shrugged. "You've heard it before, I'm sure, *the dog that didn't bark in the night.*"

Someone leaned across the table, "Yeah, I remember that, what story was it?"

Jeff tried to remember, "You know, I don't remember, but it was a clue Holmes got from the fact that for the particular crime scene the dog should have been barking. As I recall, that led Holmes to realize it was someone the dog knew, not a stranger who committed the crime."

"Yeah, well, we've already figured that out right?"

"That wasn't the gist of the Holmes story, though, it was about something that didn't happen, it had nothing to do with knowing the person or not. It was about what *didn't happen.*"

Arnie looking to the ceiling, "Something that didn't happen. Something that we would expect from the crime," turning to Jeff, "like something we should have expected to happen but didn't happen."

Jeff nodded. "Exactly. But in this case what would it be?" staring blankly out the window at the bright sunshine in the back yard. "There's maybe something like that here."

Shonna looking annoyed at Jeff and Arnie's chatter, that they weren't paying attention to her. "Fourth, the shooter is—"

"Wait!" Jeff jumped up. "The dog that that didn't bark in the night!" Everyone's head swinging toward Jeff. "I know you guys are sick of hearing about Sherlock Holmes, but hear me out!" Looking down at Arnie speaking slowly, "Arnie here made me remember that line from the Holmes stories. Let me see if I can remember," pausing looking up in thought. "We've been looking at *what* happened, not at what *didn't* happen!" Blank faces around the table except for Arnie's expectant gaze. Jeff nodding toward Arnie, "He asked me a question and suddenly I realized this!" Jeff giving Arnie a thankful smile. "And then something occurred to me!"

The room was quiet, all eyes on him. "The shots were all torso shots!" Nods around the table. "Wouldn't a professional shoot people in the head? I mean," rummaging among the papers on the table, finding a page scanning it, "what kind of hit man shoots the congressman four times, shoots Antonio five times, three shots into his aid in the house, I mean I don't know about the others," turning to Shonna.

Shonna looked at the ceiling doing a tally in her head. "Yes, all multiple torso shots." Looking up approvingly at Jeff still standing, "You are RIGHT! The person doing the shooting wasn't a real hit man!" Leaning over, cupping her face in her hands for a few seconds, looking up. "These people were killed by someone they knew. The shooter couldn't bring himself to raise the gun to their faces! We already know that he did it point blank. It's almost as though the shooter was apologetic, didn't really want to do it." Looking around the room, to Jeff, "Jeff, this is really good! The shooter wasn't a pro! But I mean…does that make sense?"

Arnie stood up slowly in thought, "Yes, apologetic, I like that," looking at Shonna, "good, that means we're dealing with someone who probably has never killed before otherwise he would know that you don't have to go spraying all those bullets around like that. A pro wouldn't care, it would just be BOOM! One shot to the head and goodbye!"

Jeff frowned thinking about all the bullet spraying he had done just a few hours before, filling that door with so many holes. He had done it reluctantly, in the heat of the moment it just happened. Remembering how hard that first shot was. How difficult it was to pull the trigger the first time. As soon as that first bullet left the gun how easy it was to pull it four more times.

"No, he was more than just apologetic," Jeff said in a low voice, all eyes turning to him. "Reluctant. Like I was when I was shooting through that door today." Feeling a chill running down his arms remembering, pausing trying to find the right words, tears welling, "The first bullet was so hard, I mean so hard, but when I shot that first one the others just kind of kept coming. The first shot felt like it was impossible to do, but the others just came streaming out." Looking around the table at anxious faces, wiping his eyes with the backs of his hands. "That's our shooter. Reluctant."

"Jesus, Jeff, this is good, really good!" Arnie speaking softly stroking his chin. "This really adds up that it was not a professional, obviously, but even better, someone who was just following orders. Reluctantly." Approving nods passed around.

Shonna raised her hand, "This is really good, congressman, but we're losing time. This information makes only makes it even more obvious to me that for the shooter we should nominate Pick."

She stood up as though making a formal announcement, "So fourth, I nominate Pick as the shooter." Jeff looking around at hands slowly raised.

He kept his hand down.

Shaking his head, "Sorry, I can't do Pick as the shooter."

"Why, because you think you know him?" Shonna replying almost angrily.

"I'd like to think I'm a little better judge of character, I mean I know he's a felon and all—an *unconvicted* felon—but I just don't buy it. I mean I saw those people coming out of the house. I know that we said the people needed to know the shooter, but I would rather pick someone like Snake Arm. I mean, I heard what the congressman's aid said, at least I think. But Pick just doesn't strike me as the follows-orders kind of guy in this situation."

Shrugging, "And I know Snake Arm doesn't fit the model of people knowing him so he could get close. And I know the congressman's aid talked about a black man with a snake tattoo. Well, at least I think she did. But I just can't buy it. I mean, does Pick have a snake tattoo? But it doesn't matter. Sorry, but when it comes to Pick, I just can't buy Pick as the shooter."

Yvonne noted one abstention.

Shonna shrugging, "Okay, tactical guy, operations. I nominate Antonio." All hands raised.

Jeff smirked, "That's easy, *he told us!*" Shonna shooting him a disapproving glower.

"Strategist and maybe our main man." Shonna finally continuing looking around the room. "I nominate nobody." She half-grinned, "Or everybody." All hands raised. Yvonne scribbling. "One thing for sure, put this down, this business was probably mostly conducted at Magic Town, but we never saw these characters coming in and out because they were using a tunnel from the warehouse next door!" Turning to Arnie, "By the way Arnie, can you get someone down to city hall first thing tomorrow to tell us who owns that building?" He nodded, Yvonne's pen scratched.

Looking around to everyone Shonna smiling. "And last that our Sherlock Holmes plan still stands for tomorrow as our best strategy." All hands shot up except Jeff's as heads turned to him, feeling a flush, raising his hand with a timid smile.

Shonna looking at her watch. "Okay, almost four-thirty. Next, show time coming up! Do we have all the unit support set up?" Nods from two men at the table. "I don't expect surprises tonight, but with this group god knows." Turning to Arnie, "Are you good to go for one of our little visits tonight? Pretty sure we're going to need you." He was just standing, turned to her with a smiling thumbs-up.

Clapping her hands twice loudly, "Okay, let's go."

Leaving the conference room, Jeff walked into the operations room which had many fewer people. It was beginning to get dark outside. Jeff went up to Shonna asking if he could step outside for some air. She motioned to the agent who had guarded him before, leaning toward Jeff, "You've got ten minutes."

"What happens in ten minutes?"

"We have to turn you into a prick."

Sunday 4:34 PM: Laying the Net

Ten minutes later Jeff found himself standing erect as a man named Joel circled Jeff slowly, inspecting him. "Jesus, he could be the congressman's twin brother, where'd you find this guy?" Jeff had been introduced to this man named Joel something, the *Chief Aid* to the congressman as it had been announced by him to Jeff. He instantly disliked this man's presumptuous and arrogant manner.

Shonna watching this process, "That doesn't matter, anything we need to fix?"

"He's just a little taller, I don't know, maybe a half-inch, but he can't slouch because the congressman never slouches. But other than that, congressman's hair is a little straighter, but everything else is perfect! I can't believe they're not identical twin brothers!"

Joel stood in front of Jeff, "Say something."

Jeff turned to Shonna half-smiling, back to Joel, "The Gettysburg address?"

"Go ahead, say anything," Joel instructing.

Taking a deep breath, Jeff spoke some words. Joel made the same comment about his voice needing to be a little lower, much more gruff, that's almost always how the congressman speaks. They spent the next ten minutes with Jeff practicing the term son-of-a-bitch, the only curse the congressman ever says—though it is his favorite curse that he says in about every other sentence, with that certain roll off the tongue—how to walk in the congressman's aggressive gait, how Jeff probably could not be gruff enough even if he tried so not to worry about going overboard being the biggest prick he could possibly muster. And being proud of it! *Wow, this must have been quite a fun guy to be around* was all Jeff could think.

A woman walked up to Jeff with an eyebrow pencil. He offered his chin up as Shonna smirked, "This one won't rub off!" Jeff frowning still remembering the baffled expression he got from the congressman's aid when she looked at his chin, and of course Antonio saying, 'Congressman, your mole is smearing!'".

Joel turned to Shonna, "So what's this all about? Where is Frank? Why is this guy impersonating the congressman? And what the hell was that press conference?" Turning to Shonna with a scowl, "Shonna, what the hell is going on here, and who is this guy and who is trying to run this show?" Jeff was concerned watching this man change character so quickly from warmly smug to almost whiny. And what was *who is trying to run this show?*

Shonna seeing Jeff's concern, giving him a quick sharp look as in *let me handle this* pulling Joel aside. Jeff could tell that she was saying absolutely as little as possible, what he heard make it clear that she was feeding him all sorts of wrong information. He gingerly took a half side-step toward them, listening in while pretending to look away, it was clear that the information she was feeding him wasn't random, there was a clear strategy to what she was saying. He didn't recall any discussion about this with the team. Was she winging it? Was this discussed in that little meeting while he was out in the backyard?

Soon they walked back to Jeff, in a minute Joel shaking Jeff's hand with a confused face, "Well, good luck, whatever it is you guys are doing."

In a few more minutes they were at the door. Once more Jeff was handed the little *Colt Cobra*—this time he didn't question the wisdom as he slipped it into the stinky coat pocket.

Ten minutes later Jeff found himself sitting in Shonna's car heading toward downtown once more. "Someone asked about him in the meeting and you brushed it off."

Glancing at him, back to the road, "I knew he was going to be coaching you, I didn't want you to be nervous."

"How involved is he?"

"We don't think too much, but he is certainly the telegraph between the gang and the congressman."

"So your bringing him up to Roswell sure blew your cover didn't it?"

"We did that deliberately."

"You *wanted* him to know that you're FBI and the Feds are all around this?"

"Yes."

"When was this decided?"

"It was my decision. We keep talking about wanting to get these guys off kilter. This is an extension of that with a little divide and conquer. If Joel knows that we are circling around this he will start trying to figure a way out of this if he is involved, or at least be willing to give up some names if he's not. He's got to be near the top of this or at least knows who is."

"But if you knew this, why did you nominate Antonio? I thought that you guys all voted on that stuff." Driving on. "So the only reason why I didn't know about this guy was because of the coaching." Jeff watching her as she nodded.

Something in her expression whispering there was more to the story.

"I don't believe you."

She didn't take her eyes off the road, "Actually, we think he is *very* involved. We just don't know how much. Even with all of the congressman's famous absences, there's no way he could have enough time to be involved that much in the gang. And he wasn't really all that bright. There has to be someone else. And Antonio is just too much of an outsider for that group, there is no way that Antonio could be doing much more than just moving money around and sending out the monkeys to raise hell." Glancing quickly at him. "Joel could be a much bigger player, we're just not sure." Pondering silence. "We just don't know. There are also some other players, but I suspect we are going to learn an awful lot in the—" glancing at the car's clock, "in the next twenty hours."

Fifteen minutes later they pulled into the garage at the main Atlanta City Hall, soon they were on an elevator heading to the third floor. "Just remember, don't be calm, be gruff. These city council guys don't know you all that well so think of this as practice."

Soon they were led into a room with the door marked Private City Council Chambers. They walked into a room with two women and eleven men sitting around a long table with the head of the table obviously reserved for them. The two walked into the room, stopped, standing at the door causing many to twist around in their chairs toward the visitors.

Jeff worked hard to keep a determined frown as he spoke. "You all know who I am, what you don't know is why I'm here."

"Well actually," said a short balding black man in the rear of the room, "we have heard certain rumors of why you are here. We all are here because we take those rumors very seriously. And what about that press conference? Are you really going to spill us all to the Feds?"

Jeff ignoring him as he scowled around the table from face to face getting thirteen concerned frowns back.

Jeff spoke firmly practicing the gruff tone, looking at the man who'd just spoken, "I didn't come here to answer your questions you little bald son-of-a-bitch, so shut up!" The man cowering lowering his head as Jeff turned to the whole group, "Listen all you sons-a-bitches, we've had our nice little business here now for four years since I've been involved, and things have always been working fine, a lot of it thanks to a couple of you. Maybe." Tightening his scowl. "But suddenly things have started getting a little crazy." The faces around the table turning more grim. "If we don't act, there's no telling where this will go. I don't need to tell you the downside. For you. For your families! Just ask the mayor. He will tell you in case you have any doubts!" A low grumble arising from suddenly terrified faces.

Jeff turned, walking down one side of the table, people turning around to look at him as he passed. Slowly circling the table with a menacing glare face by face, each turning away with a frightened jerk.

"I am getting crap that the split's not fair, that some of you are getting more than you deserve from this operation." The grumbling became louder, fright turning to anger. "But I'm not so sure."

A voice was heard, "Why are you here, why isn't Joel here telling us this?"

Jeff felt a startle that he turned into a flash of anger, "Son-of-a-bitch! WHO SAID THAT!" Nobody offered up a hand. Jeff thought what the hell is going on?

Improvise! Improvise!

A voice came, "It's because—"

Shonna stepped forward, "You know it's not your place to ask any questions!" Glaring at the room. "You little shits are lucky to even be in this business. We could have pulled this off just fine all these years without you—you know it!" Looking from face to face with stern hatred. "That's why they want to cut you stupid bastards out!"

The room was perfectly quiet except for the roar of seething faces pressed against Shonna, enraged silent expressions swinging to Jeff, back to her.

Jeff stepped forward, "There's a meeting at Magic Town tomorrow. The whole deal is going to be redone. If you're not there then you are cut out!" The angry expressions suddenly turning to astonishment, not a sound heard.

"If you sons-a-bitches want to continue to be part of this, just be there tomorrow!" Without another word he and Shonna walked briskly through the door.

They got into the car. Shonna pulled away screeching her tires in the echoey enclosed parking lot. Jeff finally gasped, "Oh my god, I thought I was going to die in there!"

Shonna looking at him sideways smiling, "But you did good! For a second even *I* thought you were the congressman!" Turning out of the lot, turning left silently pondering. "Why was Joel mentioned? What is his role?" Speaking softly almost to herself. "He must be the go-between, the messenger between these creeps and the congressman. Yeah, that all makes sense. It's what we suspected, right?"

Jeff shrugging looking out the car windows at the near darkness.

Glancing at him, "Good recovery back there. I was surprised too. I expect we'll hear his name again tonight."

Soon they were pulling into the parking lot of the main Atlanta police station, a tall building buzzing with people around it even on a Sunday evening. Pulling into the multi-story parking garage Shonna glanced at a piece of paper she was holding, steering to the second level toward the building. Turning off the engine turning to him, "Hold on to that style you did back there, maybe even a little more gruff, you almost got it. The biggest shows are still coming."

Signaling to him to wait getting out of the car, Jeff noticing her holding a gun with both hands raised in front of her chin. Emerging from the car very slowly, scanning in all directions, closing her door slowly, bumping it with her hip to latch it. Looking down signaling with her gun for Jeff to get out, he did the same routine with his door, bumping it closed. Moving toward a door, Jeff walking forward as Shonna walked backward continuing to scan the parking lot they were leaving, gun in front of her face as they neared the building.

Soon they found themselves exiting an elevator. A policeman was waiting for them, without a word signaling them to follow him down the hall to an office with only one word on the door, "CHIEF."

The door was closed behind them. There sat the man Jeff had seen in one of the photographs from yesterday, behind an enormous desk. Four men were seated on his left in a row, all with badged hats in their laps. Without a word the Chief pointed to two chairs, both walking forward standing behind the chairs.

The room was an enormous office, Jeff guessed it was the size of his living room at home, all in rich wood paneling, shelves of trophies and commendations along both sides, family photos, grown kids maybe, a woman who could be his wife.

The chief wore a closed expression with dark eyes even for a black man. Jeff guessing he had to be more than a hundred-fifty pounds overweight at least, sitting his belly extending over his belt laying in his lap.

"Well, congressman," said the Chief in an almost warm expression. "What brings you out here on a Sunday night?" looking intently at them standing there, "And why are you here and not Joel?"

Jeff scowled, "Why are to asking me anything? Why are you talking to me! I'm the one who came here to do the talking so shut up you son-of-a-bitch!" Jeff could tell the Chief was used to controlling conversations, certainly not used to someone talking like this to him in his own office. The Chief squirmed in his chair ever so slightly—Jeff knew he was in control!

He felt himself swelling with confidence.

After everything he'd been through in the last forty-eight hours

Jeff was in no mood to be screwed with.

They *wanted* a pissed off congressman? They *were going to get* a pissed off congressman!

"I came here only for one reason. Seems word's getting around that you guys aren't doing a very good job in this deal."

The Chief jolted out of his chair to half-standing, his fat belly bobbling, "What the hell are you talking about!"

"SIT THE HELL DOWN!" The Chief scanned the four to his left with a dumfounded expression, back to Jeff, slowly lowering himself back into the chair, hands on arm rests to steady his huge frame, clasped on the handles like he was ready to jump up again as Jeff took a half-step forward pointing to the Chief's face, "And don't you dare raise your voice to me again you son-of-a-bitch!"

Jeff's expression suddenly softens, the slightest smile of sorts, "Look, look, we're all friends here, right?" Nothing. "But it seems like there's been a lot of bodies floating around Atlanta all the sudden." Shrugging. "I mean, whose job is it to worry about that? Mine?" Nodding toward Shonna, "Hers?" Scowling at the Chief. "What the hell is going on, and why the hell can't you stupid cops manage to stop people from running around killing everyone! There have been some very important people who have gotten hurt very badly, killed, and this is really *pissing me off!*"

"We don't know nothing 'bout that!" the Chief scowled.

"Of course you don't! YOU'RE INCOMPETENT!" Jeff paced in a small line back and forth as though in deep thought speaking as he paced, "You are getting paid a lot of money from this deal and all we ask is a little order, but all you do is sit there on big your fat ass while some shooter goes running around killing people!" Suddenly finding himself so worked up that he was nearly spitting the words, "You and your stupid cops are screwing this whole thing up!"

The Chief started to speak, Jeff put up his hand to stop him. In a softer, almost consoling voice he continued, "So you see the problem. Seems like certain of our partners are beginning to question how committed you are to our little business venture."

"What the hell's that supposed to mean?"

"It means that people are talking about wanting to re-do our little understanding, maybe change it up a little." He thought about his little press briefing yesterday, "Maybe give some names up to the Feds, *that* would certainly thin the roster out!"

The Chief jumped up again, "If anybody tries to cut me out there'll be hell to pay! You go talking to the Feds and we'll kill you!"

"You mean like you TRIED TO KILL ME YESTERDAY?" The Chief looking to his captains in vain for support. Their eyes locked forward staring into space. Expressionless.

Jeff catching his breath putting up his hands in a calming fashion, "Look, we understand that things can happen, but next thing you know people misunderstand, start thinking that maybe we don't really need you." His expression changing to deeply questioning, "And then we see you coming out of a house with bodies laying all around inside?"

The Chief gasped as though choking for air, "I had nothing to do with those murders. NOTHING!"

"I said…" leaning toward the Chief, "SHUT UP!" Jeff pacing the room again throwing his arms around in theatrical fury, coming to a slow stop in front of the Chief again, deliberately performing an exaggerated act of calming down. Looking eye-to-eye at the Chief.

"So as I was saying, there are some who think you should not be part of our little club anymore." The Chief choking in anger, Jeff continuing firmly, "Not me, mind you!"

"Who then!"

"I just hear rumblings, and I don't want any trouble," continuing his consoling tone.

The Chief shaking his head, "I knew it, that greedy *bastard mayor!*"

"Look," Jeff continuing, "All I know is that we've got to get this straightened out before it gets even uglier. We have a meeting tomorrow, noon at Magic Town, a meeting that we have been needing for a while, and it has been decided—"

"Decided by who!"

Jeff ignoring him, "Like I said, it has been decided that we need a meeting, tomorrow. Noon. Whoever doesn't show is out. Period. We have too many players and the cuts keep getting thinner and thinner, and given all the bad stuff that's been happening we need to rein this in so it doesn't get even more out of hand."

Turning to Shonna with his gruffest voice, "We're done with these sons-a-bitches! Come on!"

Reaching for the door Jeff heard the clicking of a trigger being pulled back. Calmly turning around seeing the Chief standing with his arms extended holding a gun on Jeff. Jeff was surprised at his own calm, "Now Chief, this is a nasty place for a murder, isn't it?" Glancing at the four captains who had sat with those silly blank expressions without a word the whole time. "And in front of so many witnesses?" Small laugh, "That is of course if they have the balls to be witnesses to my murder." Back to the Chief raising his gun even higher.

"Tomorrow! Noon!"

Jeff taking a few extra seconds to smile condescendingly at the Chief slowly lowering his gun. "Noon. Or you're out."

Retracing their steps, Shonna did the same routine with gun to chin, only this time she guarded all sides walking quickly to the car, Jeff close behind relieved that nobody happened to be in the garage either time when she was doing her *Dick Tracy pose*, but he was very happy that she was doing it.

Jeff closed the car door as Shonna got in beside him, "I think I pissed my pants!"

Shaking her head turning to him astonished, "You were *amazing* in there!"

Looking at her, a moment of silence, bursting out laughing as she turned the key, the engine starting as they laughed again. Pulling out of the parking lot, "Okay, one more stop. This will be the tough one." Jeff flopping his head back with a thump on the head rest. Glancing at him, "But we have a little surprise for them that I think you will like."

Heading to the freeway, turning south for a change explaining that the mayor wanted the meeting at his house. Jeff looking at her worryingly asking if they will be away from people, on their own. She laughed saying that they have suspected him of so many things that his house has been wired for years.

Soon they were passing the Hilton on their left, his Sheraton on the right. He smiled watching the tall building pass, remembering the event with his naked little tart yesterday. That building passing by seemed like a metaphor for this weekend, so much passing so quickly, every moment a distinct distant memory.

Every moment streaming by uncontrollably.

Driving she leaned slightly to the steering wheel looking to her right at Jeff as though she was inspecting him. He returned a puzzled look with a little smile. "You know," she said softly, "I have no idea where you get this amazing courage from. I mean, you are what we call feet off the street, you have no training in this at all. But I swear I saw our asshole congressman in there, maybe even better than the original." Leaning back again. "I just want you to know that I am way beyond impressed. Way beyond. I really admire you for doing this and putting your whole heart into it." Glancing at him with a thankful smile, "What I said about not being impressed when we first met? Cancel that. At this moment there is no limit to my respect for you."

He felt a little embarrassed by this sudden gush of accolades, nodding, "Thank you. I'm not sure who I'm really doing this for, who I'm trying to impress."

He knew it was for her.

Jeff asked her about the mayor's involvement, what she knew about the murder of some of his family ten years ago. She explained what he had read before about Atlanta politics, how they have been notoriously corrupt since the dawn of time as far as she knew. There are city leaders, city bureaucrats and others always getting arrested for all sorts of graft, so it's hard to know when noise is not just noise. She said she didn't know all the inside, had read up on it in preparation for the case, that the murders are unsolved, her guess is that they will never be solved.

"There are just too many people involved in this stuff, sometimes justice is contrary to peoples' interests." Glancing to Jeff, "Monetary interests."

Jeff suddenly curious. "You've been with the FBI now for what, a couple or three years?" She nodded, head forward. "So all these bodies, is this the first time you've ever seen this? I mean your first murdered bodies?"

Taking her eyes off the road to give him a long look. "Once while I was still interning there was a case when I saw one dead man, similar kind of crimes, but not nearly as big as this." Shaking her head slowly, "This is like nothing I have ever seen. They did a lot to try to prepare us in training. But it's impossible to train you for this. Impossible. You just have to go through the experience."

Turning to her in the darkness, the instrument panel light outlining her face. He couldn't help but admire her courage. Her *grace and style* still coming through even with all this pressure. Feeling that rush in his chest again hoping it was too dark for her to see his flushed face yet one more time.

Driving for over a half-hour, long past the airport, Jeff looking up out his window seeing a bright starscape overhead so far away from city lights. Laughing to himself that he could see only two stars when they stepped out in front of the filthy little coffee shop yesterday morning in the dark, now the stars so bright they nearly lit up the landscape even without the moon.

Soon pulling off the freeway, turning right, heading through what looked like a tunnel with tall trees on each side arching over the road, the canopy blocking the stars overhead. Soon taking a left, going a mile or so, turning right into a driveway with imposing pillars and a gate. Rolling down her window hearing a crackle of a voice, "Congressman Frank Schedz and escort." A few seconds later the gate beginning to open with a low hum, driving through.

Jeff guessed the driveway to be two hundred yards long at least, leading to an enormous house, lit up grandly with floodlights. A man greeting them at the door, leading them toward the back into a large room with dark paneling, well lit, five men sitting on couches or large stuffed chairs. One man standing walking up to Jeff, "Good evening, congressman, thank you for coming." Jeff recognizing the mayor from the photos. The other men standing up in turn shaking Jeff's hand, Jeff recognizing two of them from the pictures.

"Sit down, please," the mayor motioning Jeff to a chair.

Jeff immediately going into character, "I didn't come here to chit chat you son-of-a-bitch, I'm pretty sure you've gotten calls already, you know why I'm here."

"Yes," the mayor smiling sitting down, "I've gotten a number of interesting calls, but one call in particular was *very* interesting."

Jeff looking intently at the man, trying to keep his best scowl.

"So tell me, congressman," the mayor looking down at his hand as though admiring his fingernails casually, looking back up to Jeff, "How well does an eyebrow pencil work when making a fake mole?"

Jeff turned to Shonna, startled, her eyes telling him she already anticipated this treachery, before he could look back he heard the click of a gun's trigger pulled back. He sighed, tired of hearing that sound, slowly turning to look at the mayor standing holding a gun on him. "Funny, there congressman, you sure fooled everyone else."

"Let me guess," Jeff shaking his head, "Joel, right?"

The mayor nodding, "He's our eyes and ears. He's our main man. He's our everything, but you already knew that, right?"

"So what are you going to do, shoot us?" Jeff looking around at the men sitting next to the mayor not surprised at their blank expressions. How was it that rooms full of grown, supposedly responsible men can just sit in this kind of situation expressionless? He saw it in the Chief's office, now here it was happening again. At least the city council people looked more engaged for god's sake. All he could think is who the hell are these people?

"Whatever it takes to keep you from going to the Feds tomorrow. But shoot you here? Oh, no, no, no, I like my furniture way too much. And blood is so hard to get out of expensive carpets." Motioning to the outside glass door with his gun, the door pitch-black with darkness behind it, motioning the same to Shonna.

Suddenly Shonna stepped toward the mayor, "Mayor, you really don't want to be doing that right now."

The mayor smiling, "And why is that?"

"Can I use your phone?"

"Why would I let you do that seeing as I am just going to kill you, that could be inconvenient. Seems unnecessary really."

"I just wanted you to talk to the man who is watching us."

The mayor's startled expression making Jeff smile, Shonna moving slowly toward the phone, picking it up pushing buttons. "Arnie? Let me put you on speaker phone." Pushing another button, "Can you hear me?"

In a second the clear sound of a voice on the line, Arnie's familiar voice, "Now Shonna, why would you just go over to the mayor's house all by yourself? Oh, you're not alone, hi there congressman!" The mayor's eyes widening. "By the way, mister mayor, I hate that blue polo you're wearing. My wife gave me one just like it, I gave it to the housekeeper for a rag. So mister mayor, please put down the gun."

The mayor turning his gun to the phone as though he was threatening the caller, "Who are you? You're the Feds!" the mayor yelling glancing from phone to Shonna to Jeff, back to Shonna, back to the phone, gun still pointing to the phone.

"Now mister mayor," Arnie continuing with a chuckle, "shooting the phone is not going to help you here," Arnie making a big out-loud mocking laugh, Shonna smiling.

The mayor slowly lowering his gun looking back at Jeff and Shonna, continuing a confused round of looking between the phone and them standing there. Jeff noticing the four men turning to each other, finally showing expressions—of worry.

Arnie's voice continuing on the speaker phone, "Let's just say we're people who are very interested in getting this whole situation calmed down, there's been way too much shooting lately, we want to find a way to get this operation all resolved."

"You're not with the Feds? How—how—how did you wire my house?" the mayor stammering speaking to the phone.

"Mister mayor," Shonna smiling tersely stepping forward, "we're all friends here, right? But everyone is getting so *jumpy*. The reason why we came here is because we're hearing all sorts of nasty things about how you're screwing up the operation, there are people who want to cut you out." Now the four silent men finally sat up taking frightened notice scanning back and forth between each other, Shonna, the mayor, Jeff, the phone.

"So mister mayor," Shonna stepping forward, "we're going to invite you to a meeting tomorrow at Magic Town. Noon. Just a nice little chat about what's been going on, maybe take another look at how we're running the business."

The mayor scowled at her, at Jeff, "Look congressman, or whoever you are, you and this *bitch* are not reducing my share! Not one penny! I don't care who told you what, I've been holding up my end, so has my staff," nodding to the four sitting next to him each responding with exaggerated expressions of approval.

Shonna pulling Jeff by the sleeve, "Come on, let's get out of here," turning to the mayor. "Here's the deal. Show up tomorrow. Noon…or get cut out…period!"

Without another word she turned to the door walking out, Jeff following her, looking back seeing the mayor's defeated expression, gun dangling by his side. Arnie's voice, "Okay then Mister Mayor, you have a good evening. See you tomorrow."

Jeff looked out the window into the darkness, the Mustang turning onto the freeway, "God, I am sure goddam tired of getting guns pointed at me!" Laughing, "But I sure as hell am glad that nobody's shot at me!" Looking to Shonna, barely able to see her face from the dim light of the dashboard. "At least not yet."

Both laughing out loud.

"So Joel warned him I was fake?" Shonna didn't answer. "Joel."

"Yep."

"You knew it." He remembered again when someone asked about the congressman's aids in the meeting when she jumped in to deflect the question.

Glancing at him, turning looking forward to the road. Knowing what he was thinking. "I told you I didn't want you to be nervous when he was coaching you."

"But you had him coaching me…" his voice trailing off. Driving for another ten minutes, "You did that deliberately to let him into the investigation, you set him up!"

"Yep. I knew there was absolutely no way to fool him with your impersonation, so I decided to let him feel like he's one of the good guys, maybe at the same time make him start doing desperate things as he starts feeling the jaws closing on him and the whole operation. And with Arnie's phone call to the mayor it looks like it's working."

"And we just found out that he's the main man!" he said with a big smile.

"Yep, quite an evening there, mister congressman!"

Sunday, 9:32 PM: "I killed a man!"

An hour later walking into the safe house, Arnie signaling coming up to them, "Guess who showed up at Grady Hospital?" Shonna and Jeff shrugging still walking toward the dining room exhausted. "You'd know him." Shrugs again. "You'd know him by the snake tattoo."

Shonna and Jeff stopped dead turning sharply to Arnie. "Yep, seems they dumped the body there. And check it out, three bullet holes, all thirty-eights." Looking at Jeff with a grinning smile, "Good shootin' there Jesse James!"

Jeff's jaw dropped, looking down at the floor trying to take these words in. "I killed someone?" Arnie shrugged, turning to Shonna. "I killed someone?" She gave a regretful shrug. Jeff felt his knees start to fall out from under him when two strong hands grabbed each arm leading him to a chair. "God, *I killed someone.*"

Arnie walked away, Shonna kneeling in front of Jeff, "Hey, you okay?" Staring vacantly at her. "It's not your fault. Remember, we think he was the shooter." Squeezing his shoulder, massaging it with her finger tips. "He killed so many people. Jeff, he would have killed you too." Pausing trying to get his eyes, blank. Sitting like that, Jeff couldn't remember how long. "Hey, if it's any consolation, you were the one that guessed he was the shooter, right?" Jeff didn't respond.

Standing up pulling at him, "Look, it's been a long day, let's get you into bed. Come on."

Jeff heard his voice without feeling his lips moving, "I really need some food. Screw it, no, I really need a beer. Real bad, maybe two."

"Maybe bourbon."

Shonna led Jeff into the dining room, sitting him down, poking into the kitchen, in a minute appearing with three opened beers, "Here," she said putting one in his hand, "I ordered sandwiches, they'll be out in a minute."

Lifting the bottle to his lips, without drinking putting it back down turning to her, "He was a really bad man, right? I mean I'm not going to be arrested for murder am I?"

Smiling, "Take a drink first, come on, bottoms up, me too." Both raising their bottles giving them a light clink together, tilting them back. Jeff taking a long swallow, a second, a third, slamming the empty bottle onto the table so loud that two people sitting behind them jumped looking around for the noise.

"There now, better, right?" she said in a soothing voice.

Jeff looking at Shonna, questioning, "But that doesn't make sense. They wouldn't have let him get up close to them. It couldn't have been him," squinting his eyes in thought, "could it?"

Reaching out holding his hand, "It doesn't make total sense maybe, but he was coming back to finish off Antonio, right?"

"But I think I heard another voice, what if I shot the wrong guy? There were definitely two people. What if Snake Arm wasn't the real shooter and I happened to shoot him instead of the real shooter. Wouldn't that make sense?"

"No, I don't think so. Look I can't explain it all, but everyone thinks you shot the right guy. The shooter was Snake Arm. You said the congressman's aid told you it was a man with a snake tattoo."

Sitting shaking his head, two arms reaching down between them holding two plates with sandwiches. They both ate slowly without speaking. When they were done Jeff stood up without a word starting to turn to the door, listlessly turning back sitting again. "Wow, what a day. I can't believe this. What a weekend! Nobody will *ever* believe this." Glancing at his watch seeing it was nearly ten o'clock, with a start, "Damn, I've got to call home!" Looking anxiously at Shonna, "What am I going to say?"

She smiled, "Like always, love you, can hardly wait to get home. You know. But take a deep breath first. It's your mother there, right? Careful, women can hear these things, you need to be calm."

"Can I do it up in the room?" She nodded. "In private?" Nodding again.

Standing walking out of the dining room, he found the stairs feeling like he was just floating up the stairway.

A few minutes later he came back down.

"How'd it go, everything okay?"

"I think my mother could tell." A weak smile. "It's kind of hard to be totally cool when you know you just killed someone, Snake Arm or not." Picking up the second beer, seeing the kitchen helper walk by as he motioned for another.

"So tomorrow…" turning to see the kitchen helper walking up handing him his opened beer, nodding thanks. "Tell me about tomorrow."

She sat up, "Well we know more than we did a few hours ago that's for sure. We'll start out with a team meeting, probably at nine, make all the preparations for the Big Show. We will have to do a very careful job in this planning. We've laid the net, now we want to make sure we get all the fish."

"What more do we know?"

"We think we know for sure who was the shooter." Jeff nodding reluctantly. "We know this guy Joel could be the Big Cheese, for sure he's at least the main go-between representing the congressman, but my guess is that he is much more involved than just that." Thinking for a second. "We've seen the faces of the bad guys." Looking to the ceiling counting in her head, "Well most of them anyway, but there may be more we still don't know about. This is one very extensive criminal enterprise." Pausing sipping from her bottle. "Yes, very impressive. We'll find out in the morning about who owns the warehouse, that might give us more information."

"But what about the big meeting?" Sipping his beer. "I mean if the word has gotten out that I'm an imposter where does that leave me?" Pausing looking exhausted. "I mean," yawn, "am I supposed to stand up in front of these guys?"

"That's what we'll figure out at the meeting in the morning."

"And if Joel knows that the Feds are on this, how will that all play out?"

"Oh, don't you worry about mister Joel, he is already working hard to position himself as having been the undercover guy in this all along, that maybe he has just been following the orders of the congressman. After all, the congressman can't defend himself, right?"

"Any way he can really sell that?"

"At trial you mean?" Shrugging sipping her beer, "Who the hell knows. I mean, look at OJ Simpson, right?"

Jeff nodded thinking about that trial last year, concerned. "I mean, what's supposed to happen at this big meeting at noon tomorrow?"

"It all depends. We will know a hell of a lot more at noon tomorrow."

Shaking his head like they were talking in circles.

Finally getting up from the table going upstairs to the room that they had slept in the night before. His luggage was still there, though his luggage was now closed. The room had been straightened up. His pajamas weren't laid out like before.

Jeff didn't say a word as he turned flopping onto the bed saying weakly, "I want to brush my teeth, but I can't."

She laughed softly, "Did anyone ever tell you that you're whiny when you're tired?'

Laying down on the bed next to him, her body touching his, running her forefinger down his nose, "You did really good tonight. I could not believe how much courage you showed when everyone was pulling guns on you."

"On us," he replied sleepily.

"Okay, on us," smiling. "Look it's been a hell of a day in so many ways. I must tell you mister Jeff that you are a hell of a man. And I am so happy to know that you are not one of the good ones already taken."

She wasn't sure Jeff heard her last words.

His breathing said that he was already asleep.

Monday, 2:37 AM: Fallen

Jeff woke with a start.

The room was completely dark except for the faint green glow from the clock. He lay trying to get his bearings, rolling swinging his feet onto the floor going into the bathroom, closing the door. Coming out, bathroom light still on, door half-closed he saw Shonna laying on the bed next to where he had been. The clock read two thirty-seven. Turning back to get a drink of water, he came out again, sitting in the large stuffed chair in the corner, soft light from the bathroom on Shonna. He sat watching her sleeping finding himself wondering about her.

Again.

What would it be like to touch her, to make love to her?

He could only imagine what it must be like to have her in his life. She had a warmth that defied what she did for a living. How could a woman who was so attractive, smart, funny, so sexy end up toting a gun for a living? What was it that brought her to such a job when there were probably a thousand industries she could have gone into that would have at least given her a shot at picket fences? But we all make our own choices, right? Maybe she's not the picket fences kind of woman. She complained that her working lifestyle made relationships difficult, yet she chose the job. So in a way was she choosing not to have a shot at a stable relationship, marriage even, by having this job?

She moved slightly in her sleep, smacking her lips softly as he watched. He closed his eyes, his head swirling with their kisses, her touch, her affection. Inside him he worried that she may be falling in love. Not falling in love *with him*. That's impossible, *she doesn't even know me*. She's falling in love with the *idea* of falling in love. She desperately wants a relationship in her life, along comes this dope who just happens to look like another man, all the sudden she's supposed to fall in love with him?

Leaning his head back closing his eyes with the thought of making love with Shonna.

When he awoke the sun was just coming up best he could tell. He looked just as she rolled over looking toward the clock seeing it was seven twenty two, rolling back with a groan.

"Good morning, sleepy," he said.

"Why are you up, why aren't you in bed with me?" She rolled over leaning up against the headboard. "Uh, sorry, I didn't really mean that."

Oh, yes, you did!

She yawned, "But I did like the sound of that."

That's more like it, as he jumped up, "I need a shower, why don't you go get us some coffee and pastries or something?"

"Okay, okay, you get in the shower. I'll be right back."

Smiling at her, heading into the bathroom. Figuring there was no hurry he really took his time letting the water flow over his hair, onto his face. Finally soaping himself, rinsing off, picking up the shampoo starting to lather his hair.

He heard the door open and close, "Shonna?" hearing her voice, couldn't hear the words over the running water. Leaning into the shower water rinsing his hair he heard the shower door sliding open, feeling two hands on his shoulders. Trying to look back, shampoo in his eyes; finishing rinsing his hair turning around to see Shonna standing naked in the shower with him.

She was holding a bar of soap rubbing it between her hands making suds, "You were taking too long, so I figured I better get in here with you!" Rubbing her hands on Jeff's chest like she was soaping him down. Reaching his hands around her pulling her to him as their mouths met in a deep passionate kiss. He pulled back, "You said more tongue next time, remember?" She smiled pulling him to her as they kissed deeply, passionately. He could feel his hardness against her belly as she pulled him closer, her hands swirling around his body, down his back, clutching his ass. Kissing he felt his head whirling, his chest filling with a glow not coming from the shower's warm water.

Pulling back he looked at her in front of him. She had medium, some men might say small breasts, his very favorite size. He leaned over sucking her right nipple into his mouth swirling it with his tongue sucking softly, her hands pulling his head to her breast. He moved his face to her left breast taking the nipple into his mouth, the shower echoing with the sucking sounds, water pouting onto her chest, flowing down onto his face as she laughed at the sounds of his sucking reverberating in the shower.

He stood up, she reached down cupping his hardness in her hand, they kissed all the more passionately, his hands reaching down to her nether sweetness, parting lips so gently with fingers.

"Oh, Jeff," she said, his head swooning, her hands still holding him as his fingers reached up into her, "Oh, Jeff, Jeff, Jeff. Oh, Jeff," kissing feverishly, mouths interlocked, tongues dancing together.

"Oh, Jeff I love—"

Suddenly she pulled back, "Oh my god, Jeff, oh my god!"

"What?" he asked confused both bolting up straight, hands to sides.

"We did it, oh, Jeff, I did it. Oh goddam you Nancy! Stupid Nancy!" Backing away, her hand reaching for the sliding door, "Oh, Jeff, I am sooooo sorry! What am I doing! I am so sorry!" In an instant sliding open the shower door, jumping from the shower, sliding the shower door closed behind her.

He stood in utter dismay watching her naked shape through the marbled glass. Just a second ago he had this amazing woman touching every inch of his body, her body was a gift to him to suck and caress and touch, water pouring over them, precious seconds from utter ecstasy. He was given the chance to adore her sweet body as he had seen in his sleepy dreams just a few hours ago, laying in the chair watching her sleeping. They were so close to the ecstatic first moment, so close at hand. Why all the sudden did she jump out with such a start? What had he done? His head spinning in confusion at what had just happened!

Reaching down turning the water off, sliding open the glass door stepping out. He could see her in the room standing looking out the window, a towel around her. He dried, barely, sweeping fingers through hair.

Without thinking he nearly ran out of the bathroom naked tossing his towel on the bed. Now she was sitting in the big stuffed chair, a towel wrapped around her in the corner where he'd slept the night before. Accidentally. He had wanted to lay with her as she slept, why did he get up like he did? Was this because he had done that?

Was this all his fault?

Stepping into the room looking down at her, she turned away. "What happened in there?"

She sat silent, hands cupped over her face.

He glanced around looking for something to cover up with but felt precious seconds slipping away, kneeling down in front of her. She wouldn't turn to him. Reaching his hands up turning her head, gently pulling her hands from her face so he could see into her golden eyes, could see her frightened expression, tears streaming down her cheeks.

Her face was between his hands as she looked straight into his eyes, face wet with tears. "I'm so sorry for this," she whispered softly. "I don't know what we're doing, all I know is that I am drawn to you with such...that I would...I wish we could..."

Kissing her gently, "It's okay. Really. We're two people. You know, a man and a woman. Grown ups. These things happen." Smiling at her, she gave just the tiniest shy smile in return, her golden eyes filled with soft tears. "I don't know what's going on here, and I am just as frightened as you are." He paused thinking about his family, his wife who had left him so suddenly. "Even more frightened maybe." She gave the slightest nod, sniffing as the tears slowed. "You're afraid, aren't you? You're afraid that something is going to happen between us, then I'll just get back on the plane and disappear." Looking up into her eyes, feeling a warmth wash over him that made him feel high.

Dizzy with the glow from her teary eyes.

His head spinning.

Terrified.

"What happened Saturday," he smiled, "you know, the slut. All I know is that I could never do such a thing with you." She looked at him confused as he shrugged, "I mean, yes, of course. Of course I could. I mean of course I could...with you..." voice trailing off at his babbling with a timid smile. "But there is something very, very special going on here. When you left the shower I didn't understand, but suddenly I do. It only took only one second for me to understand."

A small frown, "I think."

Sitting on the floor with his back to the chair, his naked body turned away from her, "I don't know what we're doing here. I don't. But I do. I do know what we're doing here. All I know is that I am scared shitless that I am falling in love with you." Shaking his head, "I know that my wife is gone, she made that pretty clear, no going back there. It's just with my kids, your work, the distance. Our different lives, work lifestyles. I think I know what I want here. But I am afraid. This all feels so right, these feelings I have for you."

Turning to her, expression changing to bewildered. "And I see what we are doing here, what is happening to us. And I know that we can't let that happen. We can't." Shaking his head, "Yes she has moved out, she's made it clear with her boyfriend and all that she's never coming back. Still, I am so afraid that you and I will connect and then…then…" Tears welling in his eyes, "Then we would have so much more to figure out. I am afraid, what if we can't work it out? What if we fall in love but the world just won't let us be together?" Pausing, "The world just seems to work like that sometimes. I worry that I could hurt you, and I can't do that."

Turning to her again kneeling, "But when I look into your wonderful eyes, when I see your beautiful face, when I see what an amazing woman you are, I realize that my mouth says I can't," looking away, back again, "but my heart says I must. My heart says I want to fall in love with you." His voice becoming very quiet, barely a whisper, "And it's too late. It's already happened."

Reaching up gently wiping tears from her face, "I look at you and I am terrified to say those words." Kissing her nose, "I am terrified to hear those three silly words from you. Maybe not such silly words. From you. But in the last three days I have needed to hear the words, to say those words."

Cupping his face in her hands, "Please, I want more than anything in the world to hear those words from you, but please don't say them." Smiling kissing him softly on the nose, "But I can't promise that I won't say them first."

"For now, neither of us will say the words, okay? For now." He smiled tenderly.

Smiling kissing him, "For now," with a playful smile, "for this morning, anyway."

Determined, "You know, what I said last night in the car about not knowing who I was doing this for, who I was trying to impress?" She nodded. "I lied." Tilting her head as he smiled tenderly, "This is all for you."

"I know," she smiled shyly, "I know that you are doing all this for me. I've always known that."

Kissing her softly again realizing that he was still naked, standing up, "Seems like you see me a lot like this when there's pretty women around, huh?" She sniffed. Her smile slowly emerging into a soft laugh.

He started to turn when she stood up pulling him by the arm motioning toward the bed. He grabbed his towel pulling it around him, tucking it in front. They both sat down on the bed. She looked at him with a demur expression that he hadn't seen on a woman's face for a very long time. "You are a very, very special man. I wish I was that woman in your bed. Partly. But I don't know what's going on here either." Shaking her head, "But I then I do. I am petrified that I feel like this and you don't. It will kill me."

Kissing her, "But I do." Kissing her again, "You are safe with me. And I believe I am safe with you." Kissing her on the lips as their tongues touched for just a second.

Wiping her cheeks with her hands. "Maybe it's all the stress of the case here. It's what they told us about in training how two people can get a false sense of connection when they are in these situations."

Jeff smiled, she could tell by his smile that maybe it wasn't so here. His gentleness told her that he genuinely felt something for her. That he might be falling in love with her. That somehow frightened her even more. "Maybe there is something here, maybe there isn't," she said resigned.

He reached to the pillows, fluffed them, leaning them against the headboard, both sitting back. He spoke softly, "I don't know. I feel like there are things you should know about me that aren't anything in your long-arm capabilities to know." Glancing at her, reaching holding hands as they sat. "You know that I have been married, now three times. I have been with many women in my life, and I regret many of those relationships. It seems like I have only had three kinds of relationships," thinking for a second, "who knows maybe there are only three kinds for anyone."

Speaking softly to her, "There have been the ones where I just really didn't care. You know, a few one-nighters and other girlfriends that didn't have much value to me. I mean, they were all nice women, some of them beautiful, some of them were only meant to be throw-away relationships that ended the minute I quit calling them." Pausing remembering the two that did try to call *him* again that he never bothered with. A flash of remorse poking at his heart.

She drew lines along his hand with her fingers listening. "It took a long time for me to realize that those were wrong. It's very possible that those women put hopes into me that I totally disregarded. I mean, I'm a nice man and all, right?" She nodding affirmation, smiling.

"The second group were those that I wanted to care about. For whatever reason, though, I couldn't find the connection with them that it needed to turn those relationships into love." Glancing at her, "Do you know what I mean?" She nodded. "Those I don't feel so bad about in some ways, but I came to realize much later that there were a couple of them, maybe more, that really cared for me, maybe even wanted me to be in love with them. I believe that a couple of them were in love with me. It seems odd that I feel less remorse about those than the others that I didn't give a hang about. Maybe because I did try to give them a chance, which I never did with the others, but it just didn't work. You know, the old college try thing." Pausing reflecting. "I have no idea how many women were like this. But I do worry that it was more than I realized."

"It's kind of funny to say," laughing softly, "my second wife was that category. We both *wanted* to love each other, but we didn't. I was a reasonably good catch, I think, so was she, she wanted a ring on her finger. She pressured me to move in with me then pressured me to marry her. I remember her saying that if the relationship wasn't moving to marriage then what was the point? Don't know if she would have left me, maybe it would have been better if she had. She was a beautiful woman and well, I just was tired of looking I guess, fantasized that I could settle down with her," grinning, "but I couldn't."

Shaking his head in silence.

Turning to Shonna, "And then there's the third kind of women I have met. My first marriage was very young but we grew apart. No, we more like flew apart when it became obvious that we had really different life goals. The second was a rebound, we never were in love with each other. We tried to love each other like I said. I honestly don't know, but we were certainly never *in love*. There wasn't that *special sparkle*." Smiling at him knowingly at the words *special sparkle*. "Then there was…" his voice became quiet, nearly whispering, "Yeah, her."

Deep sigh, turning to Shonna.

"Then there is you," smiling as she squeezed his hand. "I wasn't looking for you. I wasn't looking for you because I didn't want to find you. I have been blissfully happy in my little bubble, my picture-perfect life with a good job, smart and beautiful kids, nice house, you know all that picket fence stuff." Squeezing her hand. "I figured I would meet a nice woman where I could pick up again in the love department and life would be perfect. But I haven't found any. I kind of gave up looking."

Lightly waggling their hands together up and down on the bed. "I wasn't looking for you, but you did come along." Pulling up her hand to his lips kissing it. "And now you're here. And I have made up my mind that I am going to be completely open to whatever happens here, be damned at whatever comes from it," leaning over kissing her on the cheek. "I can tell you that if we ever do get the chance to make love that it will be the most amazing experience because I know that you won't do it unless your heart is in it. And just so you know, neither will I. We are both whole-body people. And I know that if more grows from that I will be ready."

She started standing, unsteady, Jeff reaching out to hold her up, she turning to sit on the bed again facing him. "Jeff, I hear what you're saying, thank you for telling me this. Really. But I just don't know," tears appearing in her eyes again. "I don't know what I am *doing here*, I've never done this before. I know you are separated, but you are still a married man!" Wiping her cheek with the back of her hand. "God, a married man! I hear what you've just said, but I just don't know that I want the responsibility. Even if she has gone off. I worry that there's the chance she will change her mind." Turning to him, "And baby you are a very fragile man right now. I am not sure you'd have the strength to turn her away if she wanted to come back. And I can't be the *other woman.* I am so sorry. I mean I know you're sincere, and I believe you, but I'm so scared of this."

Tears appearing in her eyes again, "I just can't believe I've let myself be in this situation. I just don't know what's come over me." Looking at the clock seeing eight twenty. "This is just not like me, I've never done anything like this."

He reached taking her hands, "Baby, she is not coming back. I know you think I'm vulnerable, but you are beginning to make me bullet proof." Laughing softly, "It seems that I am bullet proof these days, doesn't it?" Smiling at his little joke. "But that is all gone now. This is what I want."

Both climbing from the bed she wiped a tear from her cheek looking down at Jeff, smiling he was still in his towel. She reached out pulling the towel off him, tossing it on the floor, looking down admiringly at his arousal, "I can tell you, though," in a soft commanding voice, "that if you don't get clothes on soon I won't be able to guarantee anything!"

"Yeth ma'am!" he said in his best Daffy Duck voice, saluting, she laughed at the two soldiers saluting her, "but is that a threat or a promise?" she laughed again, he hurriedly started dressing.

Turning seeing her composure returning, feeling better. He walked into the bathroom, looking at himself in the mirror laughing out loud that his hair was almost comical from his finger combing earlier, quickly re-combing it, brushing his teeth, a quick shave. He came out as she was picking out clothes from the closet, then going into the bathroom. Jeff finished dressing, sitting in the big chair in the corner. He could hear her pissing with the bathroom door still open, the shower start. He sat wistfully, remembering a girlfriend a very long time ago—one from the first group he had talked about that he never really cared about—who had taken him to her apartment and she pissed with the door open. At the time he took is as a good sign that he was going to get laid, and he did! He smiled at the prospect as he sat back watching the open bathroom door.

He heard the shower water stop, the sound of a hair dryer, moments later she emerged from the bathroom dressed, ready for the day.

Stepping up to him, a quick peck on the lips. "You are really something mister Jeff. I just want you to know that. I hear you, and just so you know I feel exactly the same, if I do let myself go, I will let myself go completely. And whatever comes will be wonderful." Her resolute expression giving him a moment of hope that it might come true, along with a definite rise between his legs. Shaking her head slowly looking up to the ceiling, "And somehow we're going to get through this. Somehow. How I let you affect me is just not like me." Looking to him, "I could be disciplined for this."

He started to say something, putting her fingers to his lips, "Don't worry about that. But everything I said is true. I know everything you said is true. But we have work to do, very important and dangerous work, and we can't—I mean I can't—let anything get in the way. And now, damn you, now I *really can't* let you get hurt!"

Taking a step back holding out her right hand, "Partners?"

He smiled taking her hand, "Yes, partners."

Taking his hand looking deeply into his eyes shaking her head, another small tear finding its way down her cheek. "Sorry," she sniffed, "but it's too late."

He smiled nodding knowing they were both feeling exactly the same thing.

Smiling at him. "I'm sorry," sniffing, "but we are way beyond just partners."

Wiping her eyes with her finger tips, "Well!" snapping to, "if we don't get down there we won't be able to eat before the meeting, come on, let's go!" Pulling him by the elbow, heading to the door, Jeff turning grabbing the stinky coat and a Danish pastry from the plate, taking a bite offering it to her as they turned left walking down the hall toward the stairs.

They ate quietly with long steady gazes into each other's eyes. He was even more captivated by her eyes now that he'd seen tears coming from them. As their eyes met he felt an overwhelming gush of warmth pouring onto his chest, like someone was holding a giant teapot over him, hot water washing across his chest. Feeling like he was becoming that different person, that different man. That he had somehow awoken this morning in an entirely different life, like in a movie. He wanted to reach across the table to her, to draw her to him and never let her go. He struggled with this as his mouth moved up and down, food passing down his throat.

"We can do this, right?" she asked with an expression that wanted *Yes* or *No* or that was *terrified of any answer*. He swallowed hard nodding with his best warm smile.

"Oh, my god," he thought, "*she did it!*" Looking into her golden eyes knowing, "Yes." *And I did it too.*

I've fallen.

Monday, Noon: The Trap

A few minutes later walking into the conference room, everyone was in place plus a couple others Jeff hadn't seen before. After quick introductions and handshakes everyone sat down as they all huddled together. The air was thick with anticipation.

How many meetings does this make?

He'd lost count.

They were always so serious.

Now there was *serious* sewn through the entire room, an intensely orange thread passing through one person stringing to the next, binding them together in a focused purpose unlike the meetings before. They were just three hours from the climax where Jeff's Sherlock Holmes plan will come together, all the names on those papers scattered around the table will suddenly betray their owners in what everyone hoped will be a surprise to end all surprises. Dozens of arrests to cap two years of investigation, a long line of handcuffs leading to the Federal prosecutor's office.

They spent the next ninety minutes going over the developments, deciding for sure that Jeff had taken care of the shooter with his five bullets through that door, congratulating Jeff for his marvelous insight in not voting for Pick yesterday.

Jeff still had nagging doubts that Snake Arm was the shooter. The only thing that added up was that Snake Arm took delivery of the bullets sent express mail through the door of Antonio's office along with the congressman's aid's dying words with her *black* and *snake*. That part made sense, but he just couldn't see how Snake Arm would be allowed to get close enough to shoot them point blank. Everyone else in the room was way past this, taking it for granted that not only did Jeff identify the shooter using his skills of intuition, but that Jeff also dispatched the shooter with his volley of bullets through that door.

One of them said that the warehouse at the top of the stairs they found in the secret passageway is owned by someone with the same last name as the mayor, "Brother, uncle maybe? We don't know, but there's a definite connection there." They pondered what to do now that there was a good chance that Jeff had been exposed. Try as they might there were no good insights other than pondering what move Joel might be up to. They decided that until they knew how deep he was involved that they would keep teasing him that they were buying into his being Mister Undercover. There was a long discussion about Jeff's safety. It was agreed that they just didn't have enough information to know.

Detailed questions were asked about how the night's meetings went, everyone laughing at Shonna and Jeff's recounting of Arnie on the phone at the mayor's house.

Everyone was pleased that the Sherlock Holmes Plan still seemed viable.

Arnie gave a big smile, "Tell you what there mister Jeff, we couldn't have come up with better bait if we tried." Nods all around. "Maybe you need to write a sequel to the Birdy Edwards story!" There was a moment of chuckles and grins around the table, "Or write a book of your own about all this when it's done!" as the room nodded strong affirmation of these words. Jeff smiling to himself, *Wow yes, I could write a book about this, huh?* Shaking his head to himself, *Nah, nobody would ever believe it!*

Finally, about ten-thirty they broke for an early lunch, people either going into the lunch room or split off somewhere else. Again, no discussion about the case whatsoever at the tables.

At eleven o'clock Jeff was following Shonna to the front door. The same woman from last night stepping up to Jeff, efficiently anointing his chin with the mole. Once more Jeff thought about the congressman's aid looking for a mole on his face. He thanked her, turning away.

Arnie stepped up cradling the *Colt* snub nosed pistol laying it into Jeff's hand. Arnie smiling as he handed it to Jeff, "Cleaned and reloaded." Flicking a button on the gun, the cylinder swinging out, holding the gun so Jeff could see the tips of the bullets, "Hollow points." Jeff's questioning look. "It's to make sure that any misses stay in the building. We were lucky that the two slugs that made it to the wall from that office hit nice thick wood and stayed in the wall. I guess the whole building is like that. But the last thing we need is

bullets flying around our little warehouse district down there."
Flicking the cylinder closed with a quick motion of his right hand,
"Plus these will make sure that whoever you do hit gets *really* hit."

Jeff frowned reluctantly taking it, "Hollow points," softly
nodding to Arnie remembering years and years ago when he actually
kept a gun in his house for *personal protection* though now he
couldn't remember exactly what he was protecting himself from.
There was a debate among his gun friends about non-jacketed,
jacketed, hollow point bullets, the guy at the gun store giving him a
lecture about how responsible people always used hollow points
telling Jeff, "You don't want to miss and have the bullet kill your
neighbor, do you?" He was finally convinced that was the right thing
to do. Fortunately he never had to shoot at anyone. After his
daughter was born he had serious second thoughts about having a
gun in the house at all, so he sold all his guns.

"You know, Arnie, thanks, but I've really had enough of guns,"
holding it out to give it back to Arnie. "After what happened
yesterday, I don't know."

Shonna nodding to Jeff, encouraging him. "You never know, you
really should take it." Touching his arm, he felt a zing like she
touched him with a small cattle prod, turning to her with a jerk.
"You've already seen how things can get out of hand so quickly."
She smiled at him gently, "I would feel so much better if you were
carrying this."

"Besides," Arnie smiling at Jeff, "insurance!"

"Yes!" Shonna smiling, "We can never have too much
insurance!" they all had a short laugh, Jeff noticing his laugh had a
definite nervous tone. Putting it into the stinky coat right outside
pocket standing for a second patting the heavy weight at his side
with a sudden flash of regret that he was here at this moment. This
whole adventure had been, how do they say it in the CIA movies?
Oh, yeah, *above his pay grade*.

Thinking about what had happened that morning in the shower,
that long soulful talk he had with Shonna, how he was getting a just
little crazy about her. More than a *just a little crazy*. How he felt the
little shock when she touched him just now. Remembering his

promise to think about being a different person, he had to do a compartmentalize thing, at this moment be a different person. He just wasn't quite sure what person he was supposed to be.

Turning, thanking Arnie smiling at Jeff she made a motion with her hands to push on.

Soon Jeff found himself climbing into the Mustang, a few moments later back on the familiar I-85 passing downtown Atlanta heading for Magic Town.

"Just remember, be calm. If anything happens, drop to your knees and crawl the hell out of there."

"What do you expect to happen?" he frowned.

"Well, you've done a really good job planting seeds. Distrust, confusion. We just need one more element. If we played our cards right, just maybe we'll get it."

Looking at her as she drove, "What? What do we want to get?"

"Chaos."

"Chaos? That's a scary word in this context."

"Yeah, well, I've figured out that Joel's name comes up so much that he must have a more important role than we thought before. Good chance he's running the entire operation. One thing that is so consistent in all this is how well it's organized. I've been thinking about it, ledgers—my ledgers—neatly stacked piles of money with those little initials tags, the little henchmen so well organized. But you know, the victims list gave it away. It was sophisticated, detailed. It takes someone with an education to do that, it could not have been done by Antonio. No way. I've got to give it to whoever is running this show with so many people involved, this gang runs like a well oiled machine. Everything is in order. Everything."

"So you think a little disruption is the best strategy." Looking forward at the road nodding slowly in approval. "Create disorder in this well-oiled machine, yeah, a little chaos so we can get people out of their comfort zone, really smoke them out."

Turning to her with quizzed expression. "But didn't the press conference do that? And the meetings last night? So you want even more chaos? What else can you do to stir this up any more?"

Smiling at him, "Hey, you're the one who came up with Sherlock

Holmes. And you were right. We need to do anything we can, absolutely *everything* we can. We don't just want confusion, we need panic. We've got to get everyone running for cover. If we weren't going to arrest everyone today my guess is that half these guys would be citizens of Brazil by this time next week."

"Yeah, but what more can we possibly do to create chaos?"

"Well for starters, we made a real point to try to make sure Joel didn't find out about the big meeting until," glancing at the clock, "about twelve minutes ago."

"How did you do that? I'd think these guys would be ringing the phone off the hook all night!"

"We blocked his phone. Anyone trying to call him got a fake answering machine, anyone he tried to call he got the same. Everybody was trying to call everybody all night, but wouldn't you know it, nobody was home! We put a watch on his house to make sure he didn't leave. Yep, Joel definitely didn't hear a peep about anything that happened last night."

"I know you can do that so I won't ask."

"I called Joel just before we left. He was shocked about the meeting, sounded really pissed off."

"Oh, god, he's not going to show up shooting is he?"

"No, but knowing him, he sure as hell is going to show up mad!"

"What's that going to do?"

Looking into her right mirror, signaling to change lanes, not answering Jeff.

"So what seed is this going to sew?" he persisted.

"Something this gang hasn't seen in ten years," she smiled confidently. "Chaos."

Jeff confused, "But where in the meetings back there did this get talked about?"

"We didn't talk about this. It occurred to me after the meeting when I realized that nobody got around to notifying Joel about our little party. We know that nobody got through to nobody last night." Big smile, "And *that is good*."

Glancing a smile at Jeff, "That means we are in control!"

Jeff laughed, "So much for all the collaborating and planning, huh?"

Glancing at him, looking forward again, "Those meetings really are to sort things out, to get to the bigger picture, other inputs and ideas. But it's almost always too complex to figure a case out completely like that. Almost never can be done." Laughing again, "Look how much we've gotten wrong, even voting didn't help. You're the only one that got Snake Arm right as the shooter!"

"It was just a lucky guess. I just couldn't see Pick at the trigger man."

"No, it wasn't a lucky guess, it was intuition, you did a good job. You really showed courage when you said you couldn't go along. You keep surprising me at the courage you have, your ability to not be intimidated, especially your quick reflexes when things twist suddenly."

"I've always thought I was brave, but I've never had situations like this to see how brave I can be."

"But your objecting in that meeting made people think things through again. Made me think things through again. It turned out you were not only right about Snake Arm, you killed him, too! And now your Sherlock Holmes Plan. Yes, mister Jeff, I am *mighty impressed!*"

Jeff felt a sudden twist in his gut not feeling any congratulations for having done what he did yesterday. He was still a little angry about being put in that situation. He was just not sure who to be angry about. Maybe it should be Shonna that deserves his anger, after all she was the one that put him in that chair with his gun facing that door. Glancing at her as she was driving, feeling that flush through his chest again realizing he could not be angry at her if he tried.

Looking to him consoling, "I'm sorry, I made too light of Snake Arm. Please," reaching out with her right arm, touching his leg, "I didn't mean to make light of it."

Driving on smiling confidently, "But as for chaos," the car starting to exit from the freeway, "with this bunch, god only knows. I liked your words 'smoke them out' but we need better than that, a little chaos is definitely the way to get this thing to split wide open."

Soon Jeff found himself standing back in the bar at Magic Town. It was all lit up with eight-foot tables arranged in a large U-shape with a break on the left, white table cloths draped over each table with a pitcher of water surrounded by glasses on each. The dancers' runway stood to the right of the arrangement, bar tables and chairs all stacked on the other side of the runway. Jeff turned back to the white-covered tables smiling at this formal setup compared to what he had seen here just three nights ago. Jeff counted the chairs, thirty two, remembering the number of names on the roster they created with Antonio.

Looking inquisitively at the arrangement of the tables, Shonna noticing his expression as she studied around the room, "Nobody will want to sit with someone at their back, that's for sure. I am sure you did an excellent job fomenting distrust last night, so this is deliberately arranged to give everyone a clear view of everyone else, to have nobody at anybody's back. We want people feeling as comfortable as possible, feeling like they have a little control." Looking around the room pointing toward a door. "Do you see the back door over there?" Jeff looking nodding. "That door goes to another set of stairs that lead down to the dressing room. It's usually locked. I unlocked it and the door at the bottom of the stairs. It goes through the counting room. If anything goes haywire, you head for that door down the stairs to the door on the left. Don't use the front door," pointing to the black-draped door they had just come through, "way too much uncertainty."

"Is this the right number of chairs?"

She smiled, "That's our best count from Antonio's roster. I think this is right. Don't worry, there should only be just the one empty chair." Jeff looking to the ceiling trying to think who it might be. Shonna seeing his expression, "Antonio!" Nodding his head, she laughed, "But, hell with our bait we may have standing room only!" both laughing, Jeff unsure if that would happen. The whole gang seemed so damned organized, just like Shonna said in the car. Whoever was leading this had to be very disciplined to lead such a disciplined organization. That was the only way that with so many members that this hasn't blown up before.

Looking to Shonna, "And we're sure these guys are going to show up."

Laughing, "Wherever you find a lot of money you find the evil twins *fear and greed.* You've heard that with the Wall Street types, right? Well in this case the fear part is even heavier, because remember you are meeting the Feds this afternoon right?" He nodded. "So these cats need to know what's going on to figure out how fast they've got to get their asses down to the Bahamas." Laughing, "Oh, yes, fear and greed! And of course they want to be here to make sure they don't get cut out!" Laughing again, "In some ways you have to feel sorry for these bastards because they are *so stupid!*"

Smiling at the thought of the airport suddenly filled with fleeing bad guys as he wandered around the tables slowly, "Did they have the club open last night?"

Grinning, "Money, what do you think?"

"But who ran it, who opened it up and managed it?"

"Probably Perkins, he has all the keys, knows where everything is. He could handle it all by himself." Straightening one of the table cloths, "Perkins is a good man." Smiling turning to the black curtain at the front of the big room, "Speaking of Perkins!"

Jeff turned seeing Perkins pushing through the curtain, so tall that he had to bend his neck as he passed through the door. He gave a silent little wave smiling to Shonna, ignoring Jeff.

Shonna pointed to the table near the door, "That's where I want their guns, there are little tags and a pen to label them so people can get them back." Jeff was curious as she looked to him answering his question without his asking, "We don't want weapons in this meeting. If tempers flair it could get really ugly."

Sitting down at a table, Shonna looking to him shooshing him to a stand. "No, you need to be standing the whole time near that back door." Looking around the room with a satisfied expression. "And remember your speech!"

"What," frowning, "nine words? Yeah I think I can remember." He thought about all the speeches he did in high school, the public speaking class he took in college, the times he'd addressed large groups of business people. He'd always had those little three-by-five cards with little notes, he got pretty good at putting as few words as possible onto them so that he wouldn't feel like he was reading a script. He already practiced his little speech he will be giving when the room fills in a few minutes beginning to wish that even with only nine words that he had one of those little cards handy right now.

She walked up to him leaning over speaking softly, "And if things go wrong, don't go out the front door, go around the outer hallway down through the passageway to the warehouse."

Without thinking Jeff said out loud, "The warehouse?"

Looking over at Perkins who didn't seem to be paying attention to them as he stood stoically at the door just like he did when the bar was filled with screaming men and flying tits. "Shhhhhh!" scolding with her finger to her lips leaning forward to Jeff in a whisper, "Yes! Go around to the front, down the outer hall, then around to the tunnel, the warehouse!"

Voices rising behind the curtain. Soon mostly men started trickling in, a few women in their mix. Perkins greeting them, some reaching into their jackets and pockets removing guns, laying them on the table near the door, leaning over to fill out a tag to stick to their gun. Each person pushing through the curtain looking anxiously around the room. The chairs in the back of the room facing the door filling first, the other chairs soon finding reluctant bodies.

Watching people filing in Jeff noticed some of them handing Perkins money disappearing into his pocket; Jeff didn't give it a second thought because of the way money just seems to flow every which way in this circle. Grinning to himself at how he had given Perkins money that night he first came into this room, how quickly it disappeared. Almost admiring Perkins's motions that were so practiced, so smooth watching bills appear for barely a split second before they disappeared into his pocket. Jeff thought how nice it was that people were tipping him like they were trying to get the best table on a Saturday night.

Glancing at his watch, eleven-fifty. There was very little talking, barely a murmur. He noticed people showing up in groups, the city council people were first with faces he recognized from last night, the police were just coming in. One of the mayor's aids pushing through the curtain with the others following him, the mayor trailing behind. Jeff didn't see a single greeting exchanged between anyone except for Perkins's terse instructions.

Looking around the room slowly filling Jeff thought heck, with this group unarmed this should be a piece of cake!

Soon every chair was full, except for one as they expected for the missing Antonio, the room perfectly quiet. Apprehension and tension filling the room, an enormous ball of fear weighing down every soul, that enormous pulsing sphere pressing against the walls until they bulged out to near bursting with anxiety.

Eye contact between people in the room was rare, everyone sitting in stoic silence, breaths held in anxious hush.

All had come into the room and were waiting patiently.

Jeff was surprised to see only six guns on the table. Figuring that Perkins did his job, that must be it. He couldn't imagine that this group would come to such a meeting unarmed, maybe this whole highly-organized thing made them civil somehow. He was too concerned about the rest of the meeting to give it much thought.

Shonna signaling Jeff. Walking around the tables into the gap they had left between the tables on the left side of the room, Jeff finding himself standing nervously looking around the room remembering needing to get into character. Be calm. Feeling himself pumping up considering what was about to happen, though deep down he was terrified to be looking at this circle of faces watching him so intently.

Glancing at his watch: noon.

Taking a half-step forward.

Clearing his throat, "Thank all you sons-a-bitches for coming here today on such short notice," knowing those weren't his nine words, but thinking at the last minute that he needed an ice breaker.

Ice breaker! Like I could possibly break the ice with this crowd!

Taking another half-step forward, raising his hands like some cheap sidewalk preacher pronouncing, "Gentleman and ladies, this enterprise is—"

"WHAT THE HELL IS GOING ON HERE!" all heads jerking to

the black curtain, Joel bursting into the room, black curtain flying storming in with big deliberate steps. Stopping for many seconds glaring around the room panting, strutting to the opening in the tables as Jeff stepped away toward the back of the room. Joel shouting, "I SAID, WHAT THE HELL IS GOING ON HERE!"

Stunned silence.

Shonna was standing near the curtain as he flew past her. Stepping toward the table in front of her, the people sitting just before her turning around feeling her presence behind them as she put her hands up in a consoling gesture, "Joel, this is a meeting that was called—"

"CALLED! Meeting was called! By who! You?" Flashing a terrible grimace, hateful, utter loathing to Shonna, glancing off Jeff, circling around the room.

"I call the meetings! Everyone knows this is my show! Who called this meeting!"

Without thinking, Jeff said in a soft voice, "I did."

Joel spun around to Jeff, "You did! Who are you, *Mister Nobody!*" Turning looking at the faces behind the tables, looking directly at the mayor. "Do you even know who this man is?"

The room sitting perfectly silent.

Jeff could see Joel struggling—what to do! What to say! Jeff watching Joel's face bubbling even redder, veins in his forehead popping out, arms raised above his head.

Suddenly putting his hands down, it was like a whole different person had suddenly stepped into the room. Jeff watching Joel's expression soften, he suddenly made up his mind to try a different tack! "Why, he's our good congressman, of course!" Pausing waving almost warmly toward Jeff, "But why is he all the sudden calling a general meeting? Without me knowing?" Jeff seeing a plan formulating in Joel's head, watching the transition of expression, gears spinning in Joel's brain calculating his next words, his next action.

As though on queue, the room rose to a din of voices as Jeff looked helplessly at Shonna. She signaled to him to keep going, do it!

Do what?

Jeff edged around the table toward the back door, moving slowly as all eyes were on Joel.

Walking slowly around the inside of the great square of table cloths, Joel going table-to-table looking down at each face, most staring vacantly forward, a few nervously looking up at him or turning to others trying to find any expression of support. Only hopelessly confused silent faces to be found.

Finally composure returned to Joel stepping back to the gap between the tables. "There have been some very bad things that have happened lately." A low hum of voices. "What we do know is that we have this *man* here." The room rising to a dull murmur, Jeff starting to sense that Joel wasn't going to expose him or say that the congressman had been murdered. He could see that Joel was working through this situation in his head, how he could gain *absolute control* of the moment.

What was his strategy?

How could Joel turn this around to his advantage?

Jeff keyed on Joel's dissertation being confused.

Joel wasn't in control!

He didn't know what to do!

He couldn't grab the handles he needed to gain control of this room!

Joel frowning, "The congressman, of course, is right. We need to make some changes." The murmur increasing with angry tone. Jeff realizing that Shonna had somehow managed to plant this seed while she stood aside with Joel at the house in Roswell.

Joel raising his hands for quiet, Jeff impressed at how this guy had succeeded in gaining such control of this meeting then start conducting it like he had called it! It was masterful! My god, Jeff thought, this is clearly the man who is running this whole show! Only someone as skilled as Joel could possibly pull this off! Mulling the meetings in Roswell, how they got to the vote on who was the mastermind when they voted nobody but everybody. Turning to Shonna who was fixed on Joel.

She knew!

She knew all along that it was Joel! Why didn't she tell him?

Joel continuing, now in a more consoling tone, "I know some of you have heard rumors that we are going to cut some of you out."

A voice coming out, "So are they right? Cut us out?"

Voices raising, the muttering louder, Jeff hearing angry voices, people turning to each other shaking their heads. Jeff glancing at the back door. Nobody bothering to turn to look at him.

Joel raising his arms higher, "Cut anyone out? Of course not, once a member always a member, right?" Nods around the room. Jeff suddenly worrying that there wasn't going to be any chaos.

This guy was just too good!

"Then why did you bring us here?" came a voice from the other side of the room.

Putting his hands up as though the explanation was coming, Joel paused a long moment to consider his response, "We do need to make some changes to the distribution." Voices emerging into a roar, louder, Jeff could pick out all sorts of angry words.

The beast was awaking. A dragon opened its eyes.

Raising his hands again, "Please, hear me out!" Joel yelling. The room quieting.

A man at one end jumping up, "You son of a bitch! If you take one dime, one penny out of my share I'll—" whipping out a pistol from his jacket Joel pointing it at the man, "You'll do what, George, shoot me?" The man hesitating, looking around him for support, seeing none, sitting down slowly, angrily.

Shonna standing near the curtained entry stepping forward, "Joel, please put the gun down!" Jeff watching her expression the whole time, could see that she wasn't getting all the chaos she had hoped for. "Gentleman, ladies, you all know me, at least most of you know me, Shonna. I'm the bookkeeper. All I can say is that this business is getting more complicated every day with all the new enterprises. It's becoming a mess." Turning to Jeff, "The congressman has something he would like to say."

Feeling his stomach drop, Jeff's mouth suddenly dry. Looking at Shonna as she signaled him, *good ahead, say it!* Raising his hands, "I have only a few words to say," glancing at Shonna, at Joel, back to the room shouting, "GENTLEMEN AND LADIES THIS ENTERPRISE IS DISSOLVED!"

The room roaring as though the fierce dragon jumped up on its hind legs about to take a lethal swat at whatever was in its reach, everyone jumping to their feet howling. Joel stepping forward a couple steps raising his hands yelling for silence. "QUIET! QUIET! I SAID Q-U-I-E-T!!!" The room falling silent.

Joel scanning Jeff up and down, standing fifteen feet away with utter disdain, "What did this man say? Who cares! He's not the congressman! He's an imposter!" Instantly the room rising again. Well, *that cat's out of the bag!* Jeff suddenly feeling the tightness of fear in his stomach, like someone had just punched him in the gut, landing squarely on his solar plexus, the wind knocked out of him as he panicked looking around the room, but except for a couple glances all faces were turned to Joel. Watching, the noise went on echoing from the ceiling, smashing back into the racket rising from thirty one mouths yelling in confused anger.

Jeff realizing they weren't looking at him!

Everyone was standing, yelling at the tops of their lungs—Joel raising his gun toward the ceiling pulling the trigger **PAP!** ceiling pieces falling into the room. Absolute silence except for the sound of plaster falling to the floor in a small puff of white dust.

Joel looking Jeff up and down. "That's right, the congressman was killed on Saturday, at least I think." Turning to Shonna, "Well, was he?" She didn't answer. The room exchanging baffled glances, eyes bouncing back and forth between Joel and Shonna as though an answer would magically pop out. Jeff could see in Joel's eyes that he was panicked, searching for words.

Joel's cool leaving him!

Chaos was coming!

Chaos!

How could Jeff make sure it came?

Scanning the circle of faces around him, his mouth moving, out of thin air words flowing from Jeff's mouth into the room, "Lots of people were murdered this weekend!" scanning the room intently, all eyes turning to him. "I lost count!" The room shuttering in complete silence. "This whole thing has turned upside down BECAUSE OF THIS MAN!" Pointing accusingly at Joel, "And yes, the congressman is dead. MURDERED! BECAUSE OF THIS MAN!"

Not the faintest response. Perfect silence.

The dragon held its breath. Jeff suddenly seeing the dragon before him, marveled that he had complained he was going into the dragon's mouth.

And now the dragon was before him.

Jeff calling out, "This man is getting people murdered! Nobody is safe!" Voices starting rising in the room, he was getting the response he wanted, "None of you is safe. Not one!" Looking from face to face. "Remember the mayor's family?" The mayor's face turning to Jeff with a jerk of baffled anger, "Do you want those days back again?"

The dragon was breathless…in waiting.

"Well watch your backs because he'll murder you all! One by one, *carefully making sure* that his greed will wipe every single one of you from the face of the earth! And when he's done he'll murder your families too! Your wives, your husbands! YOUR CHILDREN!"

The room rising to its feet again with a perfectly silent slow sizzling intensity, all eyes locking on Joel. Not a sound.

Thirty-one sets of eyes locked on Joel.

As Jeff watched, the flash of fire in those eyes scowled at Joel with evil hatred, Jeff suddenly realizing he was about to be thrust back into the center of this, "Congressman! What a joke! This imposter is infinitely smarter than our famous Mister Frank Schedz. That stupid prick, the only thing that surprised me was when he managed to tie his shoes and get dressed in the morning! But this man is an IMPOSTER!"

Joel panted, "So you all thought that stupid gas bag was smart? I'm the one that keeps this together! You know that! YOU KNOW THAT!" Pointing his gun at the mayor with a side-to-side flicking, the mayor looking anxiously around, "Isn't that right Mister Mayor! It was me!" Pointing his gun at the police chief almost casually, "How does it feel to be such a business bosom buddy with the man who murdered your family, Mister Mayor!" All eyes turning to the police chief glowering at Joel.

Jeff couldn't believe what he was hearing. Chaos! This crazed man admitting in public that he was running this whole show, now he's solving ten year-old murders! "It was me running this show! And now this clown who just happens to look like the congressman—an amazing likeness I might add—" giving an exaggerated curtsey to Jeff, "this man comes along just when all hell is breaking loose!" Waving his gun loosely at Jeff across the room, "You almost screwed this all up there Mister Nobody!"

Looking around the room, "That's right! Mister Nobody!" Looking back at Jeff, at Shonna. "And Shonna, our beautiful Shonna is a Fed!"

"What about the meeting with the Feds this afternoon you bastard! YOU SOLD US OUT!" came an angry voice.

Suddenly the room became the beast, the dragon coming alive, rearing up its fierce smile in a single loud click as the room resonated with the sound of twenty triggers pulled back in unison by anxious thumbs, pistols suddenly appearing out of nowhere with everyone aiming at everyone else, Joel spinning around holding his gun out at everybody and nobody, spinning, the gun flailing in his hand. Three men walking boldly over to the table by the door picking up guns off the table at random with each hand, cocking them turning holding them out pointing blindly at whoever was in front of them. Jeff seeing others suddenly regretting giving Perkins their guns, regretting their thoughtlessly not putting a hundred-dollar bill into the hands of the towering door man, now standing helplessly with their hands out as though they were at the ready to plead for mercy.

The dragon held its breath.

The great square jaw of tables encircling the room became that enormous mouth bristling with teeth made of cold steel pointing inward, snarling at Joel the angry tongue at the mouth, the beast ready to spit its great hot breath at the tiniest movement.

Jeff looking across the room to see Perkins slowly pulling the curtain aside, pushing out of the room.

To Jeff it felt like minutes were passing seeing Shonna take a slow step toward the curtain, watching all eyes following her.

Not a single pistol was aimed her direction.

Not a single gun turned toward her.

Not a single gun dared to take its aim from its mindless target.

Jeff slowly realizing she knew that nobody was willing to take their aim off of whoever was already in front of their gun, willing to risk turning their gun toward her from the insane fear that they would be suddenly defenseless against whatever gun's direction happened to coincide with their place in the room. Inching slowly toward the curtain Shonna watched as Joel screamed, "DON'T YOU ASSHOLES GET IT? Look, we are a team here! She and that congressman, that faker, THEY ARE THE BAD GUYS!"

Not a single gun changing aim.

Jeff watching what Shonna was doing, seeing it was working!

Beginning to mimic her, Jeff slowly making his way toward the back door, his escape only ten feet away.

Exactly the same thing happening.

Eyes following.

Not a single gun changing direction.

Moving so slowly, Jeff feeling like a movie in slow motion. Like those clips you see of a drop of water falling into a pool where you can watch it falling falling falling, touching the surface, rebounding splashes that take seconds to witness. A half-second of motion unfolding into a minute. Now a minute expanding, feeling like an hour.

The great dragon, its huge vicious maw circling the room was breathing in desperate deep pants through thirty two mouths, watching Jeff and Shonna inch to their escapes.

Slowly.

All eyes watching.

Not a single gun moving.

Joel turning his head suddenly to Jeff but making no other movement, his gun steady into its directionless aim. An intense scowl to Jeff. Yet not a single motion toward Jeff.

Jeff continuing to slowly, so slowly inch his way to the back door, but not once did Joel's aim change from the senseless bearing of the gun straight ahead of him.

Jeff finally reaching the back door seeing Shonna waiting at the curtain, her right hand reaching behind the black curtain hanging in the front doorway, ready to push through it.

He saw faintest signal in her eyes that she wanted him to turn his door knob now, she was waiting for him before she pushed through the curtain.

She was not going to leave until he went though that door.

The room was pulsing with its great anxious breath, this enormous dragon barely breathing, panting, slowly, breathe in, holding its collective lungs full, breathe out. This room had transformed into that great beast ready to swallow every person in it, waiting with its slow heavy panting, its bright glistening metal teeth bared pointing inward to the tongue, Joel, standing at its opening, quivering in fear, each tooth bearing tiny letters, *Smith and Wesson, Colt, Browning, Glock*, each tooth itching to spit its fiery venom that would cause the entire beast to lurch up consuming every soul in its reach. Fingers tremoring on triggers as the dragon whispered into each ear with its hot toxic breath, its brutal deep voice.

Be distrustful!

Be wary!

Be ready!

Jeff watching Shonna at the curtain, suddenly seeing that black drape like some kind of magical barrier. That simple piece of dark cloth didn't just separate two rooms, *it was the divider between two worlds*. No, it was *the divider between two universes*. This side was an insane place, a gnarly twisted Gulliver Land that always contained some sort of beast whether is was the volcano of sexual energy of a room full of lusty men or the dragon rearing up before them now with its cruel metal teeth bared. That black drape was the high wall, rails at the zoo keeping a vicious creature from bounding out of its keep devouring every person in its path.

Jeff desperately wanting to be in that other world, with his hand slowly starting turning the knob on that back door, Shonna starting to lean toward the curtain, soon the door in front of Jeff was unlatched. Slowly pulling open the door as she stood waiting, watching her watching him. She was not going to leave the room until he was through the door. Pulling the door outward, it gave a small creak, all eyes darting to Jeff at the door!

Not a single gun changing direction.

"Stop them, you idiots! STOP THEM!" Joel's face turning red as the tendons in his neck strained, his throat pulsing with his heartbeat, "STOP THEM!"

Not a single gun changing direction.

In a second Jeff stepped though the door without pulling the door closed behind him finding he was in a short corridor leading to stairs, he could see only darkness going down. Without thinking, putting his hands on each wall stepping down the stairs as quickly, quietly in the dark as possible. Stumbling when he got to the bottom in the darkness. Looking up, light from the bar framing the doorway above him barely casting the tiniest glow down the stairs. His eyes adjusting to the dark seeing in the faint light two doors next to him, one on the left, one on the right. Realizing that the stairs he had just descended were exactly like the ones they had gone down yesterday to the tunnel, on the exact other side of the door on his right, that the door on his right was the door he had seen facing the tunnel. The enforcers, the thugs who sat at the back of the bar the other night came through the tunnel, this door, then up these stairs to the bar! This was how they got in and out of the bar without mixing with the club's patrons! Remembering his words to Shonna about how the layout of Magic Town's building was so simple. Maybe not so simple. Jiggling the handle, locked!

The door on the left had a faint outline of light, seeing light coming from under the door. Turning to the door, pressing his ear against it, standing listening at it. Hearing soft music, like from a radio, some kind of shuffling noise. Turning the knob opening the door slowly, just slightly to look in.

The door hinges squeaked.

S-H-R-I-E-K! from women in the room. Pushing the door open, seeing it was the counting room that he'd heard so much about with four women sitting in front of stacks of money, all turning to Jeff wide eyed, terrified. Blinking at the room's brightness. One woman jumping up in surprise at Jeff's sudden entry from the back door, her hands held up, ready to defend herself. Not a word.

"It's all right," his hands up in calming, "It's okay, I just need to get through." He'd never been in that room but it was as he imagined. "No mistaking this place," with a wry smile.

The women watching him drop-jawed, petrified with tall piles of cash in front of them. Turning to close the door behind him wondering at this back door, maybe an escape? Now it all makes sense, trying to remember what Shonna had shown him about the club's floor plan. Smiling to himself looking at the four women with rows of stacks of money in front of them, a little yellow sticky label on top of each with two letters, the initials, Jeff realized. *I guess life goes on*, thinking to himself walking through the room noticing a metal secretary's desk with a computer on top thinking this must be Shonna's digs.

Stepping through the room pulling open the second door that he had seen when he was in front of Shonna's dressing room. The guard, a tall black man, jumping up startled with a terrified expression, gun drawn pointing at Jeff.

Jeff raising his hands, "It's okay, really," backing around him. Glancing backward to the door he just came through, "I'm a good guy, just let me get back up to Shonna, okay? I mean bad guys go *into* this door, right?" Nodding at the door standing open, "Not *out of it*, right? Make sense?" The guard looking confused, eyes back and forth between the door and Jeff walking so very slowly down the hall past the door with the big gold star on the right, turning left up the stairs toward the club's front door. Starting to take the first step onto the stairs giving the guard one last nod, the guard looking back absolutely dumfounded with his gun still pointing at Jeff.

Bounding up the stairs, soft steps, soft steps, desperate need to find Shonna. Reaching the top seeing Shonna crouching, holding her gun in her right hand pointing at the curtain leading to the bar, fingers to her lips keeping him silent.

"What now?" Jeff whispering softly.

Pointing to the opened outer hallway door, hanging open on their right, Shonna's motion like a finger to her mouth with her gun signaling him to be quiet pointing with her other hand to her ear wanting to hear what was going on in the bar! Not a single sound coming from the bar. Jeff could hear the dragon's heavy panting through the black curtain. That beast laying in wait only a few feet away. The beast was panting.

PAP! a single shot sounding through the curtain from the bar—**R-O-O-A-A-R!** the dragon spitting its great fiery breath with the deafening chorus of gun fire. Two bullets ripping through the curtain passing in front of Jeff's face smashing through the front door, wood splinters flying onto them, Jeff seeing the curtain fluff from bullets ripping through, tiny dots of sunlight bursting into the little hallway through two small holes suddenly appearing in the front door to his right, another hole appearing to the right of those, more wood splinters flying into the room, another dot of sunlight appearing. Reaching around feeling hair missing off the back of his head, "Oh Jesus!" ducking.

"We gotta go!" Shonna poking him, another hole appearing in the front door, wood chips flying at them, "But not the front door!" Shonna yanking him by the arm dragging him ahead to the outer hallway flying through the door. Turning, slamming the door shut behind them, running down the hall Jeff following past Antonio's office when Shonna stopped, turning back to Antonio's room. Opening the door, stepping in, scanning the room gun held out in both hands.

Jeff standing behind her whispering, "What's wrong?"

Walking around the room looking behind chairs, gun pointed she whispered, "Nothing, just wanted to make sure there are no more surprises," stepping to the door, turning left down the hallway, Jeff following, over her shoulder, "No more surprises for us today!"

Emerging into the hall from Antonio's office, voices coming down the hall from the back of the building.

Standing frozen Shonna craning forward listening, hearing a door slam.

Slowly creeping toward the back of the building. Even with the sound insulation gun shots coming from the bar, single shots, not the roar that erupted only a few seconds before.

They are still shooting!

Occasionally a plunk to their left as a bullet hit the thick wooden walls of the bar, *thank god for old-fashioned construction* crossing Jeff's mind.

Making their way slowly down the outer hallway, Jeff could see dried bloody hand prints on the walls from yesterday when he shot through the door. *Dead man's blood*, Jeff thinking quickly. Soon they went left, coming to the back door to the parking lot.

Shonna leaned forward to the door, Jeff leaning over her shoulder. She pulled the door open slowly peering out. The back parking lot was filled with big black cars, a row of intense faces glaring at the building in wonder at the noises they were hearing, many with guns drawn. Jeff feeling his stomach drop. *These are the bad guys' drivers!*

One man, chauffeur hat on his head turning sharply toward them, his coat flying open Jeff seeing the gun holster strapped to his chest his right hand reaching for the gun, "Hey!" running for the door other men following running after him sunlight glints off guns.

Shonna yanked the door closed, locking it. Shaking her head looking to Jeff intently, "Nope, not going out there!"

A loud THUMP! hit the heavy metal door. THUMP! THUMP! Jeff hearing muffled angry shouts THUMP! THUMP! pounding against the strong metal.

Turning to the left, a few more feet to the door leading to the tunnel. THUMP! THUMP! muffled shouts.

Shonna tried the knob, locked! Taking a step back rearing up BANG! a hard kick the door flying open Shonna diving through the door Jeff on her heels down the stairs, right running down the long cement tunnel passing more dried bloody hand prints smeared on walls Jeff watching the bloody handprints fly past them as they ran.

Sound of pounding on the back door fading.

Coming to the other set of stairs they saw yesterday, Shonna stopping with her hands on her knees bending over, pausing panting. "Wait, catch your breath, I think we're safe!" Listening carefully they tried to contain their breathing, hearing nothing coming from

the club. "Sounds like they're all done. They all killed each other."
Jeff trying to imagine the chaos—*oh my god, chaos!*

They had managed to orchestrate *true chaos!*

Standing just getting their breath hearing faint sounds of police
and ambulance sirens knowing that whatever happened in the bar
was done. Jeff looking at her questioningly, "No, we can't go back,
we don't know what's up there, who's left." Pausing questioning her
own words, "No, too dangerous, we were lucky to get the hell out of
there, we can't go back." Jeff nodding approval. "Let's wait a
minute, I need to think."

She got down on her right knee like he'd seen her do before,
hearing her whisper. "Stop Nancy, stop. Stop, think, act. What to
do?" Her face gaining an almost reverent expression reserved for
people sitting in pews, a tranquil aura arising from her, like she was
meditating.

Jeff feeling minutes passing, getting nervously impatient he
finally pointed to the stairs, she jumped up with a loud whisper,
"Okay, let's go!" Climbing the stairs, "I knew I should have come up
here yesterday, what was I thinking? Now we don't know what to
expect!"

At the top the door was ajar, daylight coming from around the
right side. Creeping up to the door looking through the opening
Shonna whispering, "Some kind of warehouse," listening at the door
looking back at Jeff, creeping up behind her. Pushing open the door,
stepping through, Jeff following. Stepping into the warehouse that
was cavernous with maybe only ten crates piled around near the door
they came out, many of them empty. The front wall had roll-up
doors with barred windows, daylight streaming into the cavernous
building.

Shonna walking slowly, her gun pointing ahead. Hearing a sound,
spinning, "SHOW YOURSELF!"

There was a shuffling sound, a person appearing, the brightness
of the window behind was blinding, squinting to make out the face.

Jeff peering, squinching his eyes, suddenly realizing who it was.
"Jennifer?"

Monday, 12:28 PM: A Bad Meeting

A large arm appeared from behind a crate pushing the girl, she stumbling forward.

Perkins appeared at the end of that arm from behind the crate holding a gun in his right hand.

"Oh, Perkins, it's you, thank god!" Shonna smiling happily looking to the heavens. "Thank god." Lowering her gun, slowly realizing something was wrong watching this tall man turning his gun toward her. "Perkins, what are you doing?" Shonna starting to raise her gun again, Perkins raising his higher, straight-armed, pointing his gun at her with an absolutely blank expression. Lowering her gun again, "What are you doing?"

Jeff standing examining the tall man before him, imagining that there would be some kind of malice in his expression, hatred, something, anything!

Nothing.

Totally vacant face.

Perkins pushed Jennifer hard from behind, she tripped forward, Jeff reaching, catching her as she started falling to her knees. Pulling her back up seeing a gash over her left eye, blood trickling down. "Jennifer, what are you doing here?" Looking past her, "Perkins, what's she doing here? What's going on here?"

Speaking in a calming voice, like she was talking to a child Shonna implored, "Perkins, a lot has happened today. You were in that room, the bar, those people have all murdered each other." Gesturing with calming hands, "You need to put that gun down Perkins so no more people get hurt."

"Sorry there Shonna, but he told me I gotta do this."

Looking at Jennifer, "But why her? Why is she here?"

"He said that she knows too much, been up to the room of the congressman and he might a' told her things."

"Perkins, who is *he?*" No answer. "Is he Joel? Is he the one that is giving you all these orders?"

"Yep." Perkin's small smirk at using Shonna's trademark reply. Raising his gun higher, pointing it at Shonna, signaling Jeff with his gun to get next to her. Pulling Jennifer with him, Jeff stepping sideways toward Shonna. Jennifer peeking around Jeff, looking at Shonna, recognizing Shonna from his room on Saturday.

"Perkins, *what are you doing?*" Shonna looking at him confused. "Why are you doing this?"

Scowling fiercely, "Shonna, or what is it? Who are you?" Finally an expression, making Jeff shiver. "He told me that you was lyin' to us all and that you are some kind of cop."

Shonna standing wordlessly, Jeff seeing her studying Perkins intently just like she had done at the club with Joel.

Calculating.

"This was the best thing that ever happened to me in my life." Perkins's voice a whimper, "I had money for my family. I bought my mother a house. I coulda never done that!" His expression turning to anger, "Then you have to come along and screw it all up!"

"Perkins, I know you made a lot of money from this, but it was all illegal. A lot of people are getting hurt. People are getting killed. Killed Perkins, do you understand that? Those people in the house on Saturday. You saw them Perkins. This has all gotten way out of hand." Pleading, "Look, Perkins, we don't want to hurt you." She leaned over laying her gun down on the floor. "You're innocent in all this. We are your friends." Glancing at Jeff. "This man here, we brought him into this to try to help. To help *you*. Perkins, we are the *good guys.*"

He stood shaking his head, Jeff realizing that she was trying to keep his attention, to draw him nearer to her. "Perkins, listen to me. They're all dead. Joel, the mayor, the chief, everyone." Staring back at her blankly. "We heard it, you saw them all pointing guns at each other, you were there," glancing at Jeff. "They all murdered each other," pointing with her thumb back in the direction of Magic Town, "you were there, I saw you leave just before us!" Her voice pleading again, "Perkins, you need to listen to me!"

Perkins motioned for Jennifer to come over to him. Turning to Jeff her face begging, he could only nod that she should do as Perkins was insisting. Moving slowly toward Perkins, cowering with her hands held up toward him. Signaling for her to come closer, approaching him slowly with her hands up to defend herself.

When she got within arm's reach he reached out, his enormous arm coming down on her, striking her THUMP! on the head with the butt of his pistol, she crumpled to the floor.

Jeff jerked forward, Perkins swung the pistol back at him.

Jeff looking at the form of the woman laying on the floor stunned, "Why did you do that?"

"This don't involve her, I don't know what he was thinking, she don't know nuthin."

Perkins walking toward them. "Now both of you turn around."

Jeff felt panic thinking to himself, *So this is what it feels like when you are about to be murdered.* Turning around as Shonna did the same, hearing Perkins's breathing—hearing his heartbeat in his breath.

Perkins put the gun to the back of Shonna's head, Jeff turning his head to see the metal poking into her hair. Glancing at Jeff, "Well so much for my judge of character, huh?" wincing from the gun pressed into her skull.

Jeff suddenly realizing they had to stall.

Stall.

Stall.

Stall.

"Perkins?" Jeff asked, a half-grunt in response. "How did you guys find out about the girl and me? How did you know?"

"Someone told me she went to yo' hotel room on Saturday, she had a piece of paper with some hotel room on it."

Quickly piecing it together: That means Perkins didn't see his name, he didn't write it on the paper. *Perkins must know that I'm not the congressman! Who does he think I am?* It was hard to think straight but panic kept him going.

"So you guys staked out the hotel?"

"Didn't need to, she told us everythang."

"How did you find out about her, about her knowing me?"

"Somebody told me."

Pick! flashed through Jeff's brain.

"And Joel gave you orders to kill her?"

"Yeah, but she's nuthin. Shy little mouse like that won't talk 'bout nuthin."

Mulling this quickly: *He used his own judgment!*

He didn't follow orders!

There was a chance!

Jeff and Shonna exchanging glances that told him she figured this out too!

Shonna speaking in a very contained voice, "Perkins, you've always liked me, I've always been good to you, haven't I?"

"I knows dat, and dats why it hurts to be doing this."

"Your name, Perkins," Shonna trying to glance around at him, poking the gun into her neck, "why couldn't we find out anything about you?"

"Cause you don't know my name, dat's why."

"What is your name, Perkins?"

"Perkins's my last name, took it from some man my mother lived with so ain't no record of me. Don't even remember my real name."

Glancing to Jeff, "Boy, we sure missed *that detail*," Shonna whispered. "Why are you doing this? Do you really need to do this?"

"They are going to pay me a lot of money."

"How much? I can arrange to pay you more." Waiting. "Perkins, you don't want to kill an FBI agent. Did you know that? I work for the Feds." Her mind swirling.

Buy time.

Buy time.

Buy time.

Wait! Jeff found an opening, he couldn't believe Shonna missed it! "Perkins, you know they all murdered each other up there. There's nobody left to pay you." Jeff detecting uncertainty in the slight movement of the gun at Shonna's neck.

It was working!

Trying to turn her head, the gun wasn't forced quite so hard to make her look straight, "You love your mama, don't you Perkins? You bought her that house, you're her special son. If you do this you will never see her again. When she hears how you killed a Federal agent and an innocent man she will be devastated. She will be ashamed of you. Ashamed!"

Pushing the gun hard again into her neck, "I already done things to make her ashamed of me!"

"What, Perkins! Come on, it can't be that bad!"

"I killed all those people."

Starting to turn her head again to look at him, poking the gun harder into her neck making her wince.

"Perkins, what people?"

"The congressman, his bodyguards, that woman."

"It was *you?*"

Jeff's legs suddenly wobbly, "So much for Snake Arm," whispering to Shonna. *Damn he wished he was right about that one!*

"You were the only shooter in that house Saturday morning?" No response. "And you went back in, why?"

"One of the men was still alive, he called out."

He went back in! Jeff feeling his knees shaking like castanets—surprised he couldn't hear a rapid wooden clacking sound bouncing off the walls.

"Oh, Jesus, *how could I have gotten this so wrong?*" Shonna murmured. She could almost hear Jeff's tension glancing just slightly to him, trying to reassure him.

"And what about Magic Town? Antonio? The money room?"

"That was me. Antonio, his guards."

"But we thought it was Snake, wasn't it Snake?"

"Snake went back with me when he told me he wasn't sure I killed Antonio. He figured out that Antonio was wearing a vest and I didn't want to make the same mistake I made with that man on Saturday."

"So it wasn't your blood in the hallway, it was Snake?"

"Yeah, he was in front of me at the door, took all the shots." Jeff feeling a flash of regret that he didn't shoot that sixth round, maybe it would have hit *this* mark.

Shonna pausing.

Think think think.

Stall stall stall stall.

"Did you kill the girls in the counting room too?"

"She was gonna call the police, I had to. The other one..." he didn't finish.

"Oh, Perkins. Was it you who took all the records?"

"Me and Joel."

"Oh, Perkins, what can we do here? Is there anything we can do so you won't kill us?" Glancing at Jeff as though trying to give him some kind of signal, but he couldn't make sense of it.

"Sorry Shonna, deys nothin' cause I got to do this." Pausing in confused thought, "Even if they don't pay me, you know everything now. You shouldn't asked all those questions so I wouldn't have to do this."

Shonna, matter-of-fact, "Look Perkins, you shot all the others facing them, at least do the same with us." Her voice was relaxed like she was asking any normal favor rather than the favor of not being murdered, "That's only fair right?"

Slowly turning around to face Perkins, now with the gun in her face, Perkins gasping, taking two steps back in surprise, lowering his gun toward her chest. Jeff turning around to face Perkins.

Jeff gulping as he looked at Perkins' neck, just below his right jaw on his neck there was a tattoo. It was maybe three inches high. Something he had never noticed!

A snake!

A snake tattoo!

It was *him* that the congressman's aid identified with her dying breath! And they thought she was talking about Snake Arm!

"Say Perkins, I never noticed your snake tattoo," motioning to the mark on Perkins' neck.

"Yeah, so what of it?" Perkins scowled.

Glancing at Shonna flashing him another *Jesus! And I didn't notice that either!*

Shaking her head, glancing sideways at Jeff in a wry tone, "Say Jeff, how's your *insurance?*"

Looking at her confused thinking why the hell was she asking about his insurance now? Like his kids were going to get his life insurance?

"I said, how's your *insurance?*"

Oh, *insurance!*

Jeff shot a quick eye to Shonna speaking up, "Perkins, wait! Let me talk!" Perkins taking another step back, the gun now pointing at Jeff's chest. Feeling an almost out-of-body sense he took the smallest step toward Perkins who made a slight flick with his gun warning him not to step closer. Standing with his stoic blank expression as though all feeling, all sense had left him, just him holding the gun on two people, just following orders, confused by all this new information.

Shonna speaking softly, Perkins turning the gun back to her, "So Perkins, you really want to do this. To kill the only woman besides your mama that has ever protected you, that has ever helped you?"

Jeff looking to her suddenly remembering what they talked about in that meeting: the reluctant shooter! The reluctant shooter!

Jeff studied Perkins face, the blank expression being replaced with confusion.

The reluctant shooter!

Jeff motioning with his hands to make Perkins turn the gun back on him, "You said they are going to pay you. Maybe they will, maybe they won't. But look, I know you're going to kill us—and believe me I *sure wish* you wouldn't—but I've got to know…I don't know…I have been through a lot here and I just need to know." Glancing at Shonna who was ever so slowly moving to her right away from Jeff. "Look at me, Perkins, here, look at me. I need to know. Perkins look at *me!*" Perkins turning to Jeff facing him squarely. Jeff speaking in a softer voice as he ever so very slowly circled left around Perkins away from Shonna, Perkins turning slowly following Jeff with his gun as Shonna kept easing away from Perkins's vision, now moving a little more quickly.

Looking into Perkins's eyes Jeff could read Perkins's reluctance, witnessing the struggle between his orders and his secret love of Shonna. Jeff knew that Perkins had given himself judgment with Jennifer, the single act that suddenly made all this so confusing. Had he just followed orders with Jennifer this would be so much easier for him.

Jeff was reading a book in Perkins's eyes, pages unfolding, laying before him as though opened in the palms of his hands.

He could read the story in those eyes, the struggle, *the uncertainty*.

Stall stall stall.

Looking down at Perkins's gun, "Silencer, huh? I've never actually seen one. Seen them in movies and all." Jeff stopping his motion when Perkins finally had his back to Shonna. "So that's why we never heard any noise from the house. Nice touch." Jeff surprised at his casual tone, Perkins trying to keep his stoic blank expression. But it was too late—the book had been pulled from the shelf, now laying open between them, watching the swirling of conflict, Perkins desperately grasping to know what to do.

The confusion.

Jeff could see the doubt in Perkins's eyes!

Remembering the blank expressions on the police captains' faces in the Chief's office, the mayor's staff, Jeff wasn't close enough to read their eyes. For them it was like there was no there, there. Perkins was different. His eyes were screaming the terrific churning of emotions, the doubt. Jeff could see that glimmer of confusion on Perkins's face growing to uncertainty.

Yes, *the reluctant shooter!*

That was it! Ask questions to make him more confused, keep Perkins's attention focused on him!

More confused!

More reluctant!

"So tell me, Perkins. Please, I want to know before you kill us. There's no harm in telling us, right?" Nervous laugh, "I mean, who are *we* going to tell after all, right?"

"I don't know what you want," Perkins's expression genuinely confused, puzzled.

"Who ordered all this?"

"Joel."

"Yes. Yes, you told us that already, didn't you. Is Joel going to pay you to kill us?" Perkins nodding still watching Jeff intently. "You know, Joel's dead over there," a quick nod toward Magic Town. "Yeah, I'm pretty sure he was the first one murdered. No doubt. And you know Shonna controls all the money, she's the one that would pay you. She's the one who can pay you still. You know, without her you won't get paid. You'd go to prison with no money."

Perkins whole face suddenly flushing with worry, in his eyes intense doubt.

Glancing around Perkins Jeff saw Shonna now ten feet away. He had a quick flash in his mind how *really good* she is at that move. *Amazing*, he thought. She made a motion like she was reaching into a coat pocket, he gave just the slightest nod.

Perkins turning his head, seeing Shonna so far away he spun on his heals, holding the gun up at eye level at her when she shouted, "Insurance Jeff!"

Yanking the gun from the stinky coat pocket cocking it Jeff jamming it against the back of Perkins's head—Perkins whirling in a wild swing Jeff twisting away as an enormous left fist grazed his chin Jeff falling backward onto the floor his gun spinning away toward Jennifer Perkins stepping over Jeff bending to pick up the gun Jeff seeing a streak of silver light come crashing down on Perkin's back **CLANG!** "UGH!" Perkins collapsing to his hands and knees his gun flying out of his hands sliding across the floor Jeff leaping around Perkins diving for the nine-millimeter gun laying a few feet away grabbing it spinning around seeing Perkins on his knees with the snub nose raised at Jeff!

CLANG! PAP! a bullet whipping past Jeff's ear.

Jeff watched in horror, Perkins on his knees, eyes rolling up, collapsing forward face-down onto the concrete revealing Shonna standing behind him holding an eight foot galvanized pipe.

Shonna smiled, shrugging, "Insurance!"

Shonna threw the pipe down with a resonating rattling clang echoing in the cavernous space, stepping over Perkins to Jeff, both flopping down onto the floor panting, leaning against a crate. "And boy that is one tough son-of-a-bitch!" Both in great relieved laughs.

Shonna pulled Jeff's face to her, a quick kiss on his lips, pulling his face back looking at his chin, "Did he hit you?"

Rubbing his chin, "Grazed me. I don't know how he missed me, it was close, that son-of-a-bitch would have knocked my lights out."

Laughing, "I think he was aiming for the mole!" Both laughing again.

Looking to Jennifer, still in the pile where she dropped, Jeff shaking his head.

"Wow, we did it!" Jeff smiling leaning over to give her a quick kiss on the cheek. "Or should I say, we *lived through it!*" both laughing so loud hearing their laughter echo around them.

Hearing more sirens he said, "Sounds like ambulances?"

"Yeah, I guess someone managed to live through that hell in there, you think?"

"Wow, I guess anything's possible, don't you think?"

"Yep!"

Monday, 12:57 PM: Choice to Make

They managed to tie up Perkins; he came to in a few minutes. He had a mountainous lump starting to show on the top of his head, blood flowing through his curly black hair onto his shirt. Shonna went around to the doors in the warehouse, all chained shut from the outside.

"Well, back through the tunnel!" Shonna signaling Perkins to stand up as she held a gun in each hand. Looking over at Jennifer still laying on the floor. "Can you carry her?" Jeff nodded. "Good, she's what, maybe a hundred fifteen pounds? Can you carry her and hold a gun on our friend here so we can get back to the club?"

"I'll give it a try!" She handed Jeff the *Colt Cobra*. Walking over to Jennifer wrestling her across his left shoulder standing upright. "How about a hundred pounds!" both giggling.

Down the stairs carefully, Shonna walking backward, gun on Perkins following still rubbing the top of his head, bloody hands. Jeff following up with Jennifer over his shoulder, gun in his right hand, back through the tunnel, walking with slow purpose, making their way through the tunnel, up the stairs back to Magic Town.

They soon made their way around the outer hallway toward the front entrance finally seeing daylight from the club's front door standing open. Jeff saw an Atlanta Falcons baseball cap pass by the door, "Hey Arnie! Over here!"

Arnie turned coming down the hallway, laughing at the scene before him, turning to whistle loudly, waving toward the door. Two policemen came into the corridor. After an exchange of words taking Perkins away.

"I've got to set this one down," Jeff nodding to his left shoulder at Jennifer, half out of breath, turning back toward Antonio's office. Walking into the room, bending over laying Jennifer down on the same overstuffed chair that he sat in just yesterday pointing his gun at the door.

Sitting down to get his breath he turned seeing Jennifer's eyes fluttering open looking around her slowly. Seeing Jeff sitting next to her, "Oh, it's you!" rubbing the top of her head seeing blood on her hand. "Oh, ouch, what happened? He hit me!"

"Yeah, you got quite a knock on the head."

"That other woman, she was in the hotel room. She was the one who was yelling at me, made me leave."

"Yep, that's our Shonna!"

"So what's going to happen, what's going to happen to me, can I leave?"

Shaking his head, "No, I don't think they want you to leave. My guess is they will want to have a little talk with you."

He smiled to himself at her frightened expression that he hadn't seen on her confident face before.

"You know," he said, "I could use a beer, how about you?" She grinned nodding.

Reaching for Antonio's little refrigerator opening the door just as Shonna and Arnie came back into the room, Arnie signaling beers for him and Shonna, too.

Shonna motioning to Jennifer, "That's our little blackmailing slut that I told you about there Arnie." He nodded peering at her in the dim lights of Antonio's office. "I think we need to have a little talk with our girl here, Arnie, what do you think?"

Reaching into the refrigerator as they sat down, Jeff pulling out beer bottles, passing them around with a smiling frown, "Okay, yeah, that sounds like fun, but can we just have a moment here first?"

There were nods, bottles to mouths quietly, Jennifer taking a long drink.

Finishing her bottle, Shonna motioning to Jeff for another, he complied. Twisting the top off turning to Jennifer setting her bottle down. "So I hear that you have quite a going business that involves certain married men."

Looking down, Jennifer answering softly, "I guess."

"Do you know who I work for?" Jennifer shook her head. "I work for the FBI. You know about the FBI?" Jennifer nodding. "Well, just so you know, your extorting money from your little five-minute sex blackmailing scheme across state lines like you've been doing is a Federal crime." Leaning toward Jennifer to make her look up, to get eye contact. "Federal crimes always lead to time in Federal prisons, make sense?" Staring at Shonna, Jennifer petrified. "You won't even see your husband. He's in Washington state prison, right?" Turning to Jeff, "Clallam Bay, not that far from Seattle, actually."

Jeff remembered her saying that she had relatives, *sort of* in Washington, how she was *sort of* married, shaking his head how little truths sometimes had such big truths behind them.

Jennifer didn't respond, frightened. Jeff was amazed at this given her confidence as she stood naked in his hotel room only two days ago.

"So Arnie, what should we do here with a little blackmailing slut?"

Jeff couldn't believe what he was watching, it was like sitting in front of the TV! Taking a long drink from his beer in rapt attention, realizing it was empty, grabbing and opening another.

"Well," Arnie replying thoughtfully, "We could handcuff her right now and she'd see light in what," finger to his chin, "maybe ten to twenty years with good behavior."

Taking a drink, "If she was lucky, don't you think? Judges look on this kind of thing very harshly." He was almost talking to Shonna, giving Jennifer a harsh sideways glance. Arnie went on, obviously enjoying this, "Hell, she might have even done it to a couple judges. Word like that gets around among the judges club and we could be talking life!"

Taking a reflective last drink from his bottle. "But," Arnie setting his empty bottle down, signaling bartender-of-the-moment Jeff for another, it appearing in his hand, "we could always convince Jeff's little hussy here that a new voluntary career move is in her future and she could find another way of making ends meet."

Turning to Jennifer, "Whadda ya' say? Prison?"

Jennifer shook her head vigorously with a terrified expression feeling the top of her head.

"Or new career?" Arnie taking a reflective sip of his beer. "You have a choice to make." Staring into her eyes. "New career?"

Jennifer nodding enthusiastically.

"Good, because we will be watching." Looking at Shonna, she

nodded once, turning back to Jennifer. "So here's how it goes. First, your employment at Tallot's is ended and you are to return your former boss's special goods to him, which we assume will include eight millimeter video tapes and other artifacts, in private as you beg for his forgiveness, but you are not to have sex with him." Looking at Jeff who smiled shaking his head in no, no, no, "Unless of course your former boss wants to have sex with you, in which case you are to offer it gratefully with no strings attached." Glancing at Shonna's smiling nod as in *go on!* "No, you *are* to have sex with him. Grateful sex to thank him for this wonderful capitalistic opportunity you have done such a fine job of taking advantage of. After that, you will never again have contact with him. Do you understand me so far?" Jennifer nodding, furrowed brow.

"We know how much money you have, we know that you are a very resourceful woman, and we believe that you will do fine until you find new employment. However, under no circumstance will you even *think about* conducting yourself as you have while you were at Tallot's, is that clear?" She nodded earnestly. "Last, consider yourself under a kind of informal probation, parole really, for let's say," glancing to Jeff, "five years. Will that work?"

Jennifer squeaking her answer, "Yes, thank you, thank you, yes five years, make it ten years!"

"Five years," Arnie continuing. "If you so much as look sideways at a married man," glancing to Jeff smiling, "at least after one more thankful time with your former Tallot's boss, or if we hear so much as a peep about you stiffing people, you will be a very old woman before you ever see daylight again. Agreed?"

"Yes, thank you thank you thank you thank you—"

Arnie put up is left hand, getting up stepping to the door, "Excuse me a minute," walking into the hallway. Signaling down the hall, two men approaching, each pulling out a notebook. Arnie spoke with the two men for about three minutes turned away, pointing back to Jennifer occasionally. One man went back down the hallway toward the front door, the other following Arnie into the room.

Arnie stood in front of Jennifer as she looked up at him. "This is Agent Smythe who is going to accompany you to the hospital to get you checked out, then he is going to drive you to your house. That other agent you just saw will meet you two at your house with a search warrant, and you will do everything in your power to make sure they find all the video tapes, letters, whatever you have regarding your, shall we call them, *dates*. Is that clear? And I mean *everything.* If I find out one thing was not turned over…well we know what will happen, don't we?" She nodded in panic.

Agent Smythe stepping forward, Jennifer standing to follow him out the door. Turning back to Jeff apologetically, "I'm so sorry," but all Jeff could do was see her standing in front of him, imagining her naked, knowing it will never happen again. "I wasn't going to do that with you." Tears filling her eyes, a drop trickling down her cheek, "You are really special. I just wanted you to know that I wasn't going to do that to you." He nodded with a weak smile, she disappeared around the corner, gone.

Jeff looked at Shonna as she rolled her eyes, "*RIGHT!*" the three of them laughing together, Jeff pretty certain that his former little slut could hear their laughter down the hallway.

They spent the next two hours drinking beers, Arnie smoking more than one of Antonio's prized Cohiba Habana cigars, swapping stories from each end. Arnie said that Antonio was finally able to talk this afternoon and ID'd the shooter. "But of course you two already found that out the hard way!" They laughed, Jeff laughing until his eyes watered thinking, *Oh god if only you knew how hard!*

"So how is our good Antonio?" Shonna asked casually.

"Three broken ribs one that damn near pierced his heart. They had him under the knife for three hours." Laughing, "Lucky, lucky, lucky, even with a vest. Damned lucky."

"And what about in the bar here today?" Jeff asked.

"Of the thirty-odd people in the bar, seven were killed, even a couple of their drivers came around and got into the mix! Too bad for them. Yeah seven, probably more as the day goes on, lots of bullets in there. Only one came out without any holes in him," Arnie smiling.

Taking a long puff of his cigar, "You know, the Sherlock Plan said we would arrest them, we had the building totally surrounded, we were just about to come in," puffing, "but those idiots solved the problem for us!" Big chuckle.

"Wow, I would've thought more got killed, all those guns in there." Jeff looking at Shonna, "Do you suppose Perkins deliberately didn't take guns?"

She laughed, "It's amazing what a hundred dollar bill will get you when you would rather not part with your beloved *Smith and Wesson.*" He remembered seeing Perkins shoving money into his pockets when he was supposed to be taking guns, shaking his head in wonder at the rules of enterprise.

Arnie sat back taking a long drag from his cigar smiling, "Yep, only one came out with no holes in him."

Jeff leaned forward, "Let me guess, Joel right?"

Arnie frowned. "No, our boy had many, many holes in him." Smiling, "Guess again."

"It's gotta be one of the big ones. Let's see." Jeff rolling his eyes toward the ceiling, turning back to Arnie. "I know, the mayor."

"Bingo!" All three laughing together. "Of course, his honor is right this moment about to get a tour of his own jail!" they all laughing again.

Jeff took a long drink from his beer, "All I can say is that I hope never to have another gun pointed at me for the rest of my life," met with hallelujahs followed by toasts with three clinking beer bottles.

Shonna holding up her bottle, "And not shot at too, I suppose, you're pretty demanding!" Clinking bottles, laughing again.

She turned to Jeff reaching for his head turning it around, looking at the hair missing from the back of his head smiling, "You know, there are better ways to get hair cuts! I don't have a clue how you're going to explain this." She and Arnie laughing at his hurt expression, Jeff feeling the bald spot realizing that it could not have gotten any closer, laughing with them but more from relief.

The three sat in silence when Jeff mused, "So we got it all wrong." Looking up at the ceiling in thought. "Yeah, I think we had a *perfect score of wrong!*"

All laughing, Arnie smiling, "Fighting crime is imperfect business my friend. But you've got to go out with a hypothesis, otherwise you go out there and just flail around." Taking a sip of his beer. "But I was really impressed with the leadership you showed." Shaking his head thoughtfully, "Too bad all that leadership didn't help us figure out the perps."

"Too bad I was wrong about Snake Arm!" Jeff laughing.

Arnie paused with his bottle in front of his lips, "But none of that matters really, we got the job done!" followed by another round of clinking beer bottles.

Jeff starting to stand up, Arnie signaling him to sit down again. "Listen, we can't let you go home tonight. You need to make calls or whatever, we have made special transportation arrangements for you tomorrow. Call your work and family, tell them you need to stay over, tell them you're on the Delta flight that gets into Seattle tomorrow, we'll give you the flight number and times."

"I *am done*, right?"

"Yeah, we have a lot of loose ends to tie up still." Taking a puff. "Lots of them. The poor unfortunate congressman and his staff members died tragically in a car wreck tonight as planned. They say it's not going to snow tonight after all, but hey, who needs snow to get killed in a car wreck these days? But the last thing we don't need is this congressman guy's twin brother walking around Atlanta airport." Smiling at Jeff. "Plus, you really need an evening to decompress a little. You've had a hell of a weekend." Looking to Shonna for support. "Right?"

Jeff pointed to the phone, "Well, I guess I better make a couple calls, okay? Flu right?" Nodding. "Yeah, it's pretty miserable to travel with the flu. Okay, give me a minute." Shonna and Arnie standing, walking from the room.

After a few minutes Jeff came out into the hallway. Taking him by the arm Shonna smiled, "Come on, congressman, I'm hungry. My treat."

"Where are we going to eat?"

"Well, your stuff is all moved to the Hilton in Norcross. They're tearing down our ops at the house in Roswell, bringing in the rest of a new team, there'll be no peace there."

"Tearing it down?"

"Yep."

Walking down the outer hallway and outside to rounds of congratulations, Jeff shaking many hands. Finally Jeff finding himself back in the Mustang heading north once more.

Driving, contemplating all that happened, turning to Shonna, "So Pick."

Glancing at him, "Pick, yes?"

"He had to tell them about Jennifer. He's the only one who knew. I showed him the Ann Tallot's scarf in the Underground, he must have told them."

"That's probably true. I am pretty sure they didn't see her come and go at the Sheraton. So you're probably right."

"What will you do about that?"

"Oh, probably nothing."

"Nothing? Doesn't that mean that he was involved in the gang?"

"I'm pretty sure he passed the information along to somebody, but who knows how or why. Maybe to Perkins when he was at the club, maybe to Antonio, there's probably no real way to know. What we do know is that his name never came up among all the others. I really doubt he was involved, but he probably knew about it." Looking into her mirror, signaling to change lanes. "There is tons of work to do in the investigation. You wouldn't believe it, the hard part of the investigation is just beginning. What with phone records, bank accounts, property records, lots and lots of places to find information, then we've got to connect all the dots so we can take it to prosecution. We'll keep an eye out for Pick, but given all the big fish we have to fry my guess is that if he did anything minor that he will probably walk. If we can, we would rather use him for information. That would be a hell of a lot more valuable than throwing him in prison."

"And why did you let Jennifer go?"

"The prosecution of those cases is always so messy. The victims can be victimized again with publicity. Then there's ruined marriages and all, too much collateral damage. This was the best solution. I'm pretty sure she'll fly straight at least for a while—we definitely put the fear of god into her!"

Nodding, leaning his head back, looking up to see a couple fluffy clouds being moved across the sky on invisible rails. *Marta in the sky*, smiling to himself, going who knows where. Probably not to a rabbit hat place.

Time to get back to the here and now.

Glancing over to Shonna feeling that warm flush in his chest again. Yes, the here and now making an instant decision that whatever happened here he was just going to give in.

He wouldn't fight it.

He would give in.

Monday, 4:28 PM: Three Missing Words

Soon pulling up in front of the towering Hilton Hotel on Peachtree Industrial Boulevard in Norcross. Jeff laughing at the Peach Tree. During his stay he often wondered if people gave the directions: "Turn off the freeway on Peachtree Boulevard, take a right on Peachtree Avenue, go down past Peachtree Road then turn right on Peachtree Street, go three blocks then take a right into Peachtree Court." Yeah, he was pretty sure.

Walking up to the counter in the Hilton, Shonna standing next to Jeff. This was the only other hotel he had ever stayed in while he was in the Atlanta area. Shonna told him they knew that from his credit card records and chose it so that he had familiarity around him. He discovered that he was put into a suite on the top floor, smiling that he never managed that when he stayed here before. His luggage had already been delivered and brought up. Turning to Shonna with a satisfied smile, going up the elevator to the top floor.

Walking into the room Jeff was blown away by the size and elegance of the room. Walking around, poking his head into the two bedrooms both rigged as master bedrooms, large with their own bathroom. Turning to Shonna, "Wow, nice!" Stepping to the window to look at the expansive view as the sky was turning gray, just a few buildings visible over the trees, "And a nice view!"

Setting her bag down, walking up behind him he felt her arms around his chest as she looked over his shoulder, "Yes, very nice view."

Turning to her, instantly in embrace, mouths together, tongues dancing together swirling, breaths quickening. Feeling her hands around his back, sliding down around his ass as he reached down to cup hers in his hands, both pulling the other to them in torrid embrace.

Pulling back to look at his face, her golden eyes locked to his. "Does this mean that you are not on duty?" querying playfully.

"Oh, don't worry, I'm on duty," smiling, kissing again, "my duty is to finally seduce you!"

Smiling at her, "And how much will they pay you to seduce me?"

Kissing her again pulling back with, "You know, you had me seduced at *My god, you're not him are you?*"

Pulling back trying to remember, she smiled. "That's right, in the hall downstairs at Magic Town."

"Actually, you really had me when I looked into your wonderful eyes. I have been hooked ever since." Shonna laughing with exaggerated blinking, eyes upward with a seductive smile.

"So you were teasing me this whole time, mister married man? But not mister married man?"

Pulling back from her sitting down on the couch next to them, tugging at her arms to sit next to him. "Maybe. Maybe I was teasing you. Who knows, maybe I'm not serious."

Her look suddenly like someone had just pulled her little stopper out, air escaping like one of those toy blow-up toys he played with as a kid. Turning to him with a growing sad expression.

Thinking reflectively, Jeff speaking softly, "This is definitely not being a passenger on my bus, is it? I'm sorry for what I said. I didn't mean it. It's just that this is a little confusing. But I'm definitely not a passenger here." Looking at him quizzically, Jeff looking back to her, "Are you sure this is something you want to do?" She nodded. "Are you sure?"

With determined expression, her face tightening, "I've already told you once that when I think something is mine I go after it and I won't let anyone take anything from me! Nobody!"

Giving her just as determined a smile replying stoutly, "Good, because we're not going through this again. I've made up my mind!" Kissing her nose gently. "I am here for you. I am a different man for you if that is what it takes. I will be that different person. Whatever it takes. To be with you here and now."

Kissing him, "Well, what are we to do with a man who has made up his mind!" Leaning forward with a huge warm hug, pulling back. Glancing over his shoulder at the clock seeing it was nearly four-thirty, "The way I look at it—"

Putting his finger to her lips, "The way *I look at it* is that we have sixteen hours to live a whole lifetime!"

Her face swelling with love grabbing his head pulling him to her kissing him passionately, standing, pulling at him leading him to the first bedroom door they could reach.

Standing at the bed passionately kissing, hands flowing over bodies, breathing in long pants starting to unbutton his shirt.

Pulling back, his hands out to her, "One thing though! I need to call you Nancy. I mean I like Shonna, it's a nice name and all, but I need to be with *you*. I need to call you Nancy. Can I?"

Smiling, "Yes. Yes, I'd like that."

Embracing again, hands flowing over bodies, hot breathing on necks, tongues weaving together. "Oh, Nancy," breathing into her ear. She smiling at her name from his lips.

She suddenly stepping back. "No, no, no mister, not so fast!"

Holding out his hands imploringly, "Oh no. Now what?"

Sitting on the bed with a big sexy smile, "I want you to strip for me! It's been years since I've been with a man and I want the whole treatment!"

"Years?" with a sorry frown.

"Just dance!" she chimed.

Giving a gratuitous smile they both laughed. Pausing, turning his back to her, spinning around humming the only stripper song he could think of from the movie *Gypsy Rose Lee* unbuttoning his shirt, swirling it around his head, pulling off his t-shirt swirling it, doing his best bump-and-grind routine while unsnapping, unzipping his pants pulling them down as she screamed, "Woooo woooo! Take it all off big boy!" laughing, he continuing until he was finally naked in front of her. "Yes, that's what I'm talking about, now it's my turn!"

Jumping up, pushing him onto the bed, laughing together she doing her best routine, finally standing naked in front of him, arms outstretched with a big, "Ta-da!"

Both laughing, tears flowing. Nancy walking up to him with her hips thrust forward in her best sexy voice, "Okay, big boy, it's *play time!*"

Pushing him down onto the bed, falling onto his back, using his elbows scooting up on the bed laying down with his hardness in full show. With a wide sexy smile crawling onto the bed on her hands and knees over him, sitting on his hips, reaching back guiding him into her into her, eyes rolling back, soft sigh.

Holding each other in passionate embrace, her breasts touching his chest with their soft warmness, eyes locked, bodies joined. Two bodies moving in passionate harmony amid quickening breaths with movements showing their pent-up desire, their longing for this moment of joining their bodies.

"Oh, Jeff, oh, Jeff," moaning softly, "Oh, Nancy" she starting panting, moments becoming lifetimes until at last she reared up, Jeff moaning, her breasts flushed pink, her nipples hard as a cold day, finally falling back on him.

Laying amid subsiding breaths she rolled to his side, head on his shoulder. Swirling her finger amid his scant chest hairs, silence telling their story. The quiet revealing the passion they had found.

Turning to her, "In case you were wondering, that was just the start," rolling over, their bodies united again. An instant was all that was needed until impassioned soft voices filled the room again.

"Oh, god Nancy, yes, yes, yes yes yes yes yes…" she reaching down dragging her fingernails deep into the skin on his ass, the intensity of the scratches only amplifying his build as she screamed, "Oh, god Jeff, tell me the words, tell me those words!"

"Oh, Nancy, I love you! I love you! I…yes yes yes yes yes yes…YESSSSSSSS!" as he arched his back up she pushing against him.

She screamed, "Oh honey I love you, Jeff I love you…yessssss…hold it…"

"Nancy, Nancy, Nancy, tell me when I can cum!"

"YESSSSSS! NOW!" pulling him into her, in another minute he collapsing on his elbows kissing her passionately, raising her mouth to him.

They lay, breaths subsiding, their wonder in the aromas of sex, her aura of fragrances, scent of her body swirling together with the smell of sweat in that sweet blend meeting them amid the wonder in each other's eyes.

Finally with a soft gentle groan, rolling over to his right laying next to her, his left hand between her breasts. Soft breathing returning slowly, her right hand on his laying across her chest.

In those moments a million thoughts were traded, silent words exchanged in the electricity moving between their bodies. Feeling energy passing from her breast though his arm, electric current passing from her heart.

To his heart.

Laying, darkness creeping through the window, that quiet thief dragging the last of the day away, the last soft light bidding its goodbye waving weakly from the arms of its shadowy kidnapper, leaving the world in silhouettes until its return.

Snuffing his chin against her neck. "We said the words."

Smiling. "We did." Soft sigh, "*We did.*"

Whispering into her ear softly, "I love you Nancy. My god, I am free to tell you this. How did we do this? How did we find each other? My god, Nancy, I adore you."

Turning her head to him, "I love you Jeff." Kissing him on the forehead, "God it feels so good to say those words to you. It has been so long since I've said those words to a man, and never to a man so deserving. I have worked my whole life to be here this moment, to be here with you."

Laying motionless except for soft breaths, their secret loving communication vibrating between them flowing in that current streaming between their bodies. Between two souls.

"I've wanted to say those words to you since I first saw you come out that door with the big gold star."

Laughing, "You mean when I thought who the hell is *this guy?*"

Looking to her with a comically hurt expression, "*This guy?*"

"I did think you were attractive, but only once I figured out that you weren't that damned congressman."

"You didn't like him did you?"

"No, not at all. He was an asshole."

"But you liked me after that?"

"Can I tell you a secret and you won't laugh?" Nodding, his nose rubbing her neck. "My first thought was to take you home."

Pulling up his head, "Just like that?"

"Just like that. The other stuff didn't really come until after we got to the house. Originally I took you there to get laid, but when we drove up to the house and saw the lights on…I mean…we showed up and there were all those people, so there went *that* plan."

He laughed, "You were going after me *that soon?*" feeling a rise between his legs again thinking that she was attracted to him from the start.

"Yep."

Rolling her over on top of him again, they made long passionate love once more.

Finally, the clock said almost nine o'clock. They had made love three times, spending those hours learning each other's inner hearts.

Sitting up he declared, "I want to be seen in public with you!" jumping off the bed heading to the shower.

No sooner getting shampoo in his hair feeling her hands on his back, turning around, she looking down seeing she had his attention. Slowly lowering herself, kneeling, taking him into her mouth, he looking down at her, she sliding him in and out in and out of her mouth until he kneeled down, "Oh, god that feels so good, so good, but I want to make love again."

Sliding down onto her back until she was laying in the large tub, signaling to him with curling fingers, "I am really dirty down there, you need to clean me!" They made love once again.

They were both very clean when they were done.

Monday 9:38 PM: Scary Night Out

A half-hour later they were in one of those TGI Friday's knockoff places drinking beers together at the bar with plates of food just being served to them by the bartender. Chatting, teasing each other, the bartender an older woman kept looking over at them. Jeff thought for sure, *here goes the congressman thing again.*

Leaning over speaking to a man sitting across the bar from Jeff who had occasionally looked over at Jeff. *Yes, definitely that congressman thing.*

A moment later Jeff looked up. The bartender was standing in front of them. "Excuse me," with a motherly expression, "how long have you two been married?"

Looking to Nancy, Jeff smiled, "Married…married." Shonna giving him a cute grin as he insisted, "I don't know, how long, dear?"

Looking at him, at the barmaid still watching them, "At times it seems like I've only know him for three days," leaning over kissing him on the cheek, "other times it seems like a lifetime." The barmaid beaming with a big joyful smile, all laughing together.

The barmaid looked over Jeff's shoulder, leaning forward as though peering at something behind Jeff and Nancy. Jeff turned to look behind him but didn't see anything.

"There's a man who keeps peeking out from behind that wall, like he's looking over here." Both Jeff and Nancy turning around not seeing anyone, turning back again to the barmaid.

"There he is again!" pointing over Jeff's shoulder with a concerned frown. Turning around again, seeing nothing.

"Hold on, let me go have a look," Jeff standing.

Nancy pulling at his arm as he stood, "No, not after today, let me go."

"I'm sure it's nothing, I'll be right back," leaning giving Nancy a quick peck on the lips. The barmaid's eyes following Jeff, Nancy turning to watch him walk over to where he thought the barmaid pointed.

Coming around the corner, Jeff heard a familiar voice, "Yo, Jeff, here man."

Walking toward the voice, peering into a dark corner the room lights had missed.

"Jesus, Pick! What are you doing here?"

Reaching out, Pick tugged at Jeff's arm, pulling him into the dark corner.

"What are you doing here, how did you find me?"

"Shhhhh, quiet man. I got a call the minute you walked in here. This city has eyes, man." Pick looking around the corner, pulling back.

"What is it, what are you doing here?"

"I heard about what happened at the club today, bad scene man. Everyone blames you and word is that there's a hit out on you. You shouldn't be here. You should have gone home. There's going to be trouble. You need to come with me."

"I can't come with you, I'm here with Nan—I mean Shonna."

"Dude, I know about Nancy. I was doin' informing for her."

"Look, I can't do anything without her." Pulling back from Pick, looking around the corner. There was no sign of her, the barmaid leaning over cleaning glasses, the place where they sat cleared away. The man on the other side of the bar gone.

"What the hell? Where did she go?" Jeff starting to walk toward the bar, Pick pulling him back hard. Jeff spinning around, "What's going on? Where did she go?"

"To the Lady's Room, I dunno. All I can tell you is that we need to get you the hell out of here. Come on." Pulling at Jeff's arm turning to go down the hallway toward the kitchen. Reaching the double swinging doors a waiter pushing through holding a large tray of food, tripping on Pick's feet fumbling forward, the tray bobbling around, deftly shifting his hands, in a half-second the tray balancing on his other hand, turning scowling at the two men. "Sorry man," Pick murmuring pushing though the swinging doors.

The kitchen was a long brightly-lit room with a stainless steel table in the middle, stoves on each side with men busily attending pots, flames flaring up over pans twirling flipping in skilled hands.

Pushing themselves through with hardly a notice from the room of focused intensity until they were on the other side. Through another door they emerged into cool dark air with a single stark lamp on the side of the building.

"Okay, man, this way," Pick panting.

"Stop. Pick." Pick stopped, turning toward Jeff in the stark light. "I'm not going anywhere until you tell me what's going on."

Pick paused looking intently into Jeff's face as though grasping for words. "Oh, what the hell. Okay. You know about today right? At the club?"

"I should know, I was there."

"Well then, you know that the mayor made it out of there, right?"

"Yeah, that's what I heard."

"Well, he figured out that you snuck out of the club like you did, so you must be the one who set the whole thing up. Is that right?"

"I guess. I mean it was a whole bunch of us."

"But it was your idea, right?"

"How could anyone know that?"

"Like I said, this town has eyes. It has ears, too. The point is that the mayor has offered a bunch of money to anyone who makes sure you never leave town. That's why I said you shoulda gone home."

"So you're saying that there's someone who is trying to kill me *tonight?*"

"No, someone's going to try to kill you *right now!*"

"You mean they are in the restaurant?"

"You probably saw him, he was across the bar from you."

"Yeah, I guess, a thin man with graying hair. Him?"

"Yes, he's a very dangerous man. Does special projects for the mayor. Outside of Antonio's thing, kind of a freelance."

"Special projects. You mean kills people."

"Yeah, something like that. Look, we gotta go."

"I need to go back in to find Nancy."

"No, you can't. You have to follow me," Pick insisted turning to push across the small fenced area toward a gate.

"Pick wait!" Pick turning around again. "Look, I don't know. I don't really know you. How do I know I'm safe with you?"

"Oh, man, don't tell me you don't trust me!"

"Well…" Jeff pausing, looking for words. "I mean, you probably told people about my little blackmailer from Tallot's. I mean how else would they have known?"

"I might have said something to Perkins or somebody. Hell, I thought it was funny, we was getting a good laugh out of it."

"And now you're telling me to follow you? That there's some guy in there who wants to kill me?"

Pushing open the gate, Pick said, "Yes, you have nobody else right now who wants to help you, I'm all you got. Now come on! And be quiet!"

Stepping forward away from the light through the gate following Pick, Jeff stopped, peering over Pick's shoulder. He could smell the Pomade in Pick's hair, the silver hat band on Pick's hat the only visible element on the dark man in this light.

Crouching down, Jeff following his queue. "Over there, look." Across the parking lot Jeff could see a man in a black Cadillac in the darkness, his silhouette showing in the faint light shining on the fence behind the car. Just then the man who had been sitting across the bar from Jeff approached the car, leaning over, talking to the driver. They couldn't hear any words. Watching as the man standing motioned over to the restaurant, turning, walking back to the building.

"Oh, Jesus," Jeff whispered, "they're waiting for me! Where the hell is Nancy?"

Suddenly there was a sweep of lights across the parking lot as a car turned into the lot from the street. Jeff looked seeing a police car pulling very slowly, very deliberately into the parking lot. The police car crawled along a row of cars, turning to come back the next isle.

Peering into the darkness as the police car came near the building. Nancy emerged from around the building, walking up to the passenger door of the car. Jeff started to stand up, "Hey—" Pick gave a violent yank of his arm pulling him back down.

Pick hissed, "Man, it's in action, leave it be!"

"But it's Nan—"

"I know it's her, but she's doing her thing! Just sit and watch!

And don't do that again!"

Watching, Nancy got into the police car, the car circling back out of the parking lot, turning right onto the street, disappearing into the traffic.

Jeff felt his heart sink. *What the hell is going on? Why did she leave like that? What am I supposed to do now?*

Waiting in the darkness.

Silence.

A couple came out of the restaurant, making it toward their car, a minute later they were gone. Soon a man who definitely looked like he had at least one too many came out. Standing near the door, pulling out a cigarette, fumbling with his lighter, dropping it, muffled curse, leaning over picking it up, flicking it until his cigarette was lit. Soon a cab pulled into the parking lot, a few seconds later he was gone.

Pick kept looking toward the street, as though intently looking for something.

Watching.

Waiting.

Some kind of signal?

Finally turning to Jeff, "Okay, show time."

"Show time?" Jeff whispering back.

"Do you trust Nancy?"

"Yeah."

"I mean, do you think that she's on top of this?"

"I don't know. It didn't..." Jeff's voice trailing off realizing he didn't know what to think.

"Come on. Stay with me." Giving a quick tap on Jeff's shoulder, "Come on."

"I don't know about this, that guy's gonna wanna kill me, are you sure?"

"Yes! He wants to kill you. Now come on!"

Walking around the building but away from it toward the center of the parking lot under a large lamp.

Glancing over his shoulder, Jeff saw the man from the bar coming out of the restaurant, walking toward them. He could feel his heart racing watching the man closing in on them, reaching into his coat pocket.

Suddenly Pick turned to Jeff, "I said you are a pussy!" shoving Jeff.

"Man, what are you doing?"

"And if you ever say that to me again, I'll hit you again!"

Standing shocked at this, Pick walking up to Jeff with a swing to Jeff's stomach. Jeff doubled over from reflex realizing that Pick had pulled his punch.

"What's the matter, you're not man enough to fight?" Pick yelled.

Glancing over his shoulder, Jeff seeing the man in the gray hair slow his pace, hesitant. Jeff standing up, "Oh, is that the best you can do you stupid bastard!" He took a swing at Pick who ducked, swinging to hit Jeff on the shoulder, again his punch pulled.

"I'LL SHOW YOU!" Jeff screamed as he reared his right arm landing a punch onto Pick's chest a little harder than he meant.

Two men came out of the restaurant, seeing the commotion one running back into the restaurant, "Fight! Fight!"

The gray haired man stepping back, people streaming out of the building, Jeff and Pick continuing their faux battle, definitely getting into it, each showing more skill at the theatrics with every fake swing they hurled. A circle of people surrounded them shouting instructions at the two warriors.

Suddenly a police car, roaring into the parking lot, the Cadillac's tail lights illuminating, brake pressed, the car coming to life jerking forward turning into the path of the police car **CRASH!** the police car crunching into the Cadillac's driver door pushing the Cadillac into two cars parked along side.

Jeff and Pick stopped, turned looking at the carnage, three more police cars roaring into the parking lot, spreading around the parking lot away from the crash, the restaurant patrons scattering running back toward the building.

Looking over to see the man in the gray hair pulling back into the shadows, suddenly reversing direction, walking back again toward the parking lot. Craning to look, peering across the parking lot at the man walking, slowly raising his hands. Smiling as the figure came into the light because sure enough, pushing the man from behind was a familiar form.

Nancy.

One of the police cars drove up to them, two policemen jumping out of the car. After a short exchange of words, one stood in front of the man as the other hand-cuffed him, turning him, pushing him face down onto the hood of the car. The cop reaching around the man, rifling through his coat, pulling out a pistol laying it on the hood of the car, pulling out a second pistol, laying it next to the first one. Even at this distance Jeff could see the silencers on the guns.

Jeff could clearly hear the cop reading the man his rights, something about attempted murder and laying in wait followed by leading him around the car, pushing him head-first into the back seat.

Walking up to the car, Nancy picking up the two guns from the hood of the police car as another policeman walked up, "Ma'am, that's evidence." Reaching into her purse pulling out her badge folio, flipping it open without a word, the officer replying quickly, "Oh, yes, never mind then."

Pick and Jeff stood away watching all this commotion, both craning to look across the parking lot, an ambulance pulling up. Two officers pulling a man with blood streaming from a large gash on his face from the wrecked car. The man standing dazed, an officer standing in front of him talking, the other officer stepping around the man putting on handcuffs.

"Looks like those two are going to spend the night away from their families, huh?" Pick laughing.

Jeff looking over to see Nancy huddled with two police officers, all shaking hands. Turning toward Jeff and Pick with a frown slowly melting into a relieved smile walking up to them.

"Well, mister Pick, you did a good job. This was very tidy. I thank you. You will receive a reward for this, I'll make sure you get credit for the capture on this guy. We have been looking for our man there," motioning to the car with the gray-haired man sitting in the back seat, "for a six years."

Finally finding his voice, Jeff clearing his throat. "Who was he?"

"They call him the Janitor."

"The Janitor?"

Pick interrupting, "Yeah, he is a baaaaad dude! How many do you think he's got Nancy?"

Shaking her head, "No way to know, but he was the mayor's go-to guy. We guess maybe a dozen, but no way to know. We will probably never know." The three of them standing in the dim light, the police car holding the Janitor pulling away. Peering across the parking lot Jeff seeing a paramedic putting a bandage on the other man's face.

"So what's going to happen to these guys?"

Nancy laughing, "Well one thing for sure *won't happen* is for the good old days when one of their leashed judges would let them out the next day. After today there isn't a judge on the planet that want their names anywhere near these guys. My guess is that we really got them this time."

Standing watching the ambulance backing out of the parking lot swerving to let a tow truck come into the lot. Slowly the restaurant patrons filtered inside as the police cars pulled away until there was only the tow truck driver leaning underneath black Cadillac to hook it up.

"Well, Pick, thanks again," Nancy smiling, leaning toward each other with a light hug. "I better get this guy back to his hotel." Turning toward Jeff, Pick giving him a full hug, not one of those wimpy *guy hugs* that he was so used to from men.

"Hey man, at least nobody shot at you, right?"

"Yeah, I sure had my share of that lately. Hey, man, thanks. Really. You probably saved my life."

Pick grinned huge, "No my friend, I *definitely* saved your life!"

All three laughing out loud for many seconds feeling relief pouring into their laughter.

"Okay, guys, I'm outta here." Pick turning, in a second out of sight.

"Come on, let's get you back to the hotel."

Walking back around the restaurant, Jeff seeing Nancy's blue Mustang on the other side of the parking lot where they had left it, passing two more tow trucks pulling into the parking lot as they were turning out into the street.

The car was silent driving through the darkness on the short drive back to the Hilton. Arriving they got out of the car speechless, into the lobby without a word, up the elevator in silence, arriving at the room in perfect quiet.

Walking into the room, Jeff continuing into the bedroom, flopping on his back onto the bed.

Nancy following him, standing looking down at the form before her. Coming around the bed, laying down next to Jeff.

"How you doing?" she whispered.

Jeff lay in silence looking up at the ceiling, no energy to reply.

"Quite a day, huh? I thought we were done with all that. Thank god for Pick."

Turning his head toward her. "So you guys had this, like, all worked out? You had this all orchestrated?"

A small laugh. "You'd think so with how it worked out, huh? But no. I had no idea Pick was there. When you left the bar I suddenly recognized the guy across from us. He was one of the men coming out of the house on Saturday that we didn't recognize. One of our team ID'd him from the photos we took."

"So what did you do?"

Frowning, "I knew there would be only one reason why Pick would be there, that his being there was no social call. When I recognized the Janitor I put one-and-one together, figured out what the heck was going on."

"So your going outside, leaving with the cop?"

"It was to make it look like I was leaving. And it worked. At least I think it did. If the Janitor knew who I was he wouldn't have made his move. So I had to make it look like I was gone."

"How did you know that Pick would take me out back?"

"I've known Pick for a while, I just knew."

"And what about him taking me to the center of the parking lot, like a big sitting duck?"

"I was over under some trees. I was signaling him what to do. I needed him to take you into the open. It was the only chance that we could cuff this guy in the act."

"And what about the fake fight scene?"

Laughing out loud. "That was pure Pick. God that guy is smart. He saw me coming around, but the Janitor came out sooner than I planned so he was trying to buy time. He caused the distraction so the Janitor would be watching you and not see me sneaking around behind him. If you two had just been standing there the Janitor would have walked right up to you and killed you both."

"So other than you signaling him to go to the center of the parking lot everything else was just made up?"

Smiling, "Yeah. I guess it was."

"Man, I have got to pee. Give me a second." He sat up, walking to the bathroom.

"Leave the door open!" Nancy called after him.

When Jeff came back out Nancy was laying under the covers, her clothes scattered on the floor.

"One of us has too many clothes on," she chided.

Jeff felt a sudden euphoric sense of abandon, pulling at his clothes, jumping onto the bed straddling Nancy under the bed covers, leaning to kiss her as she reached up pulling him to her lips. He rolled over, climbing under the covers.

They lay facing each other, his eyelids drooping quickly followed by the sounds of his regular breathing.

In an instant he was asleep.

She lay watching his sleeping face in the soft light of the bedside lamp, wondering at the man that so haplessly fell into her life.

Reaching up turning out the light, kissing his nose whispering, "Good night my sweet prince. It was an amazing day with an amazing man. You are my amazing man. And I love you."

Jeff awoke to the door opening with Nancy walking in holding two cups of coffee and a plate of pastries, Jeff laying naked on top of the covers. "Good morning, sleepy head."

Leaning over to her right, elbows bent holding two hot cups, setting them down on the dresser, bringing him his coffee, setting the plate of pastries on the bed sitting down next to him. Sipping, nibbling in silence.

"You're going home today." He looked to her without a reply. "I want you to know that's okay." Sipping her coffee. "That's where you belong. Actually you belong anywhere that's away from all the danger."

"Look, I want you to—"

Reaching over putting her fingers to his lips. "I want you to belong here," dreamily, "god I want you to belong here. Not here, Georgetown, of course. Somehow, if that could happen this would all make sense. I would even promise to not let you get shot at or stalked by the Janitor." Cocking his head waiting for her next words. "I mean, all this time waiting for the right man. For you. To have you come into my life would be more than I could hope for." Sipping her coffee thoughtfully. "When I was downstairs, you know, away from you," her eyes roaming down his naked length, "I realized that we come from two different worlds. You already have the picket fence. I don't even know what a picket fence looks like." Sipping again, "I mean real life when you're with someone is grocery shopping and laundry, wrestling over what video tape to rent, who has to get up to let the cat out." Pausing for a long time in thought. "I've never had that. I've never even had a real relationship. I don't know how to start one." Her expression growing dark, smiling wryly, "I've never even had a cat!"

Looking to her, "You just start, the rest works itself out."

"But don't you understand? We are here right now in a little bubble. The *Jeff Nancy bubble*. No groceries or laundry or cats that need to be let out." Nodding, Jeff waiting to see where this was leading. "If you were here, or in DC, we would have to learn how to do all that stuff together. And I would worry that we would get so busy doing all that grocery and laundry and cat stuff that we would forget about each other. There wouldn't be all this great sex!"

"Yes. That happens. *It just happens*. Let me tell you, when you throw a couple kids into the mix the sex becomes a rare treat sometimes. But you're right, things do change. It's not really as bad as it sounds, your needs change as the relationship changes. As..." pausing finding the right words, "as the relationship matures, I guess. If we loved each other, if we really cared about each other that would all be okay. It would just happen."

Sipping, sipping again, she paused. "No, it wouldn't be okay. Not after this." Sipping once more, "This has all really given me hope, though. You have no idea what it did to hear those words from you." Smiling, "Besides, you owed them to me."

"Owed them?"

"Yes, you were supposed to deliver nine words at the meeting yesterday, but I counted, you only said six." He smiled at her lovingly knowing where this was going. "There were three words missing!"

"And 'I love you' were the missing words? Was I supposed to say, 'Gentlemen and ladies, this enterprise is disbanded, oh and I love you?"

Laughing hitting him on the arm, "Yeah, that would have really set a different tone, huh? The point is that now your contract is fulfilled! You said nine words!"

"I don't care about the other words, there are only three that matter to us!"

Laughing, "Yep, you got that right!" reaching over taking his cup, sweeping the dish of pastries onto the floor swirling her arms around her slipping from her clothes, rolling over on top of him.

Pulling up with him inside of her, "Please say the words again!"

Reaching up to kiss her as her breasts lay against his chest whispering low and breathy.

"I love you."

Tuesday, 12:14 PM: Parting

By the time they got into her car, it was past noon. They were soon on their way down the familiar freeway heading to the Atlanta airport. Nearing the airport Jeff said, "I thought I wasn't supposed to go the airport."

Glancing at him, "You're not, at least not to the commercial side." Guiding the car up a side road, soon at a gate with a guard who let them pass when she showed her badge. Soon they were pulling up to a hangar, steering to one side, stopping the car. "Have you ever been in a Cessna Citation?"

"No, but I hear they're pretty cool."

"Just you and me." Smiling. "Is that okay?"

"Can't I go alone? Why are you going?"

Opening her car door, swinging out her legs smiling over her shoulder, "Because I want to!"

A few minutes later Jeff was seated back in a cushy dark brown leather seat having received the safety briefing from their flight attendant, a beer poured for him, for Nancy a margarita on the rocks. In a few minutes Jeff watched downtown Atlanta to their right as the plane banked heading west leaving Atlanta behind them.

The conversations were light, Jeff feeling a pulling in his chest, somehow thinking maybe they could go find a back row in the plane and…

He was filled with regret that he should have found a way to stay a few more days.

Somehow.

Instead, he knew that he needed to go home. Feeling his heart tearing. Tearing between this wonderful woman with the golden eyes and his life back in Seattle. Tearing like those little Valentine hearts that he played with as a kid, but that he would never dare to tear from a mortal fear of bad luck.

Watching out the window as they crossed the Mississippi River continuing over long, long stretches of farm land.

Sitting next to him holding his hand, leaning his head back closing his eyes.

"Hey, sleepy head, wake up." Jeff jerking awake. "We're almost there, fifteen minutes maybe."

"Oh my god, I slept the whole way?"

Nodding. "Not the whole way, you almost made it to Idaho. Well, Kansas at least."

"Oh, Nancy, I am so sorry, you came all this way to watch me drool while I sleep?"

Reaching out holding his hand. "I just wanted to be here with you. To see you off."

The captain asked them to prepare to land, in a few minutes the plane was pulling up to a hangar next to a limo waiting on the tarmac.

The plane coming to a stop, Nancy turned to Jeff. "I know I'm not supposed to say this." Taking a deep breath, Jeff waiting in anticipation. "But I'll say it anyway." Reaching for his hands holding them tight. "You are the most special man I have ever met. I'm not just saying that because of this crazy weekend. It's been so long since I felt like this, and it is going to be so hard to watch you step off this plane." Her eyes welling. "But you have given me hope. You have made me feel like this again, maybe really for the first time. It has been so long that I had forgotten what it feels like."

"Nancy, oh my god, I could fall in love with you a hundred times. This is tearing my heart in half, I can't bear to walk away from this, from you." Turning away shaking his head slowly in deep thought, looking back. "But that would be so unfair wouldn't it? To you…yeah, you're right…I just can't do that."

Turning away from her, tears coming to his eyes, before he could help himself, trickling down his face. Pulling his face back toward her, tears down her cheeks. "Jesus," she sighed, "what a couple of babies!" kissing deep and passionate, their hands clutched together between them.

Letting go of his hands, taking a deep breath wiping her cheeks with her fingers, "Well, mister Jeff, you're home. We did the best we could to make sure you got back to your family." Looking out the window blankly, back to him. "This may be the quickest limo ride you'll ever have, but it is going to drive you to gate 36 and you will go up the stairs to the jetway and mix in with the crowd. Your luggage will be in baggage claim, and so now you," her eyes welling with tears again, "are free to..." her voice squeaky, "...free to go." Leaning over into one last long passionate kiss, abruptly standing up. "Now if you don't mind, they've got to put fuel in this thing, I have to be in DC by morning."

He stood, pulling him back down into his seat, "Wait, I forgot something." Reaching into her purse pulling out an envelope, "I'm sorry, but we've gotta do this."

The envelope had a return address of FBI, Washington DC. The envelope was not addressed. Pulling out a two-page stapled document, he read it silently. "This is a non-disclosure agreement."

Nodding, handing him a pen, "Just a formality. But you know you can't tell anybody anything about this. Nobody, not even your mother."

Laughing, "So much for my book, huh?" Looking to the ceiling, *"Like anyone would believe me anyway!"* Both laughing.

Scanning the document, scribbling his signature, dating it, deciding not to ask for his own copy.

Reaching out taking his hands. "It's so weird to be giving you back to your family." Tears coming to her eyes, looking down, "But..."

Looking into her wonderful golden eyes with the tiny black flecks, a tear trickling down her cheek, he reached up to wipe it with his thumb.

"Oh Nancy, you're not going to make this easy, are you?"

Sitting up straight, wiping her eyes with the backs of her hands, swiping her cheek with her fingers. "Yes, you're right, we've been through all this. I'm sorry." Looking deeply into his eyes, "You gave me something nobody can ever take back from me." Looking out the plane's little portal window, back at him. "I've said everything I can. You know how I feel. In my heart I know that you love me, and that's enough for me." Looking deep into his eyes barely whispering, "And you've taught me to love again." A quick big breath.

In a louder voice she declared, "And now it's time to send you back to your life!"

Standing quickly, turning walking half-crouched in the small plane toward the door, turning signaling him to follow. Following her out the door, down the stairs. Jeff seeing the limo fifty feet away, the driver coming around the car opening the back door. Starting to walk toward the limo, he turned around coming back to her taking her hands.

"Will I ever see you again?"

Giving him a quick peck on the lips, turning back to the plane speaking over her shoulder with a big smile.

"Yep!"

Made in the USA
Middletown, DE
20 November 2015